Do Overs

Ruthie Robinson

More Than Skin Series

An imprint of ARTWO Publishers, LLC
Publishing Company

ARTWO Publishers
9727 Cinnabar Trail
Austin TX 78726

Copyright © 2016

ISBN 153337872X

ISBN 9781533378729

Cover design by

FoglihtenNo4 Font by gluk

Acknowledgements

Peace Investigation PLLC
Readers: Jennie Rosenblum

Other Books
by Ruthie Robinson

Reye's Gold

Steady

Light's Out

So Different

When You Fall…

Will Work for Food

Games We Play

My Chicken Story

The Odd Ballerz

PROLOGUE

September, week one, Sunday

They were arguing again. At least once a day it came to this. She squared off in front of him, demanding more. As if he wasn't trying hard enough. A small single-wide trailer was the home he provided for her… for them. Standard-issue beige on the outside; worn, beige, *and* brown colored on the inside, and oh, it was clean. The clean part was all thanks to her, and was so unlike what he'd been raised with.

It wasn't huge, their place, but it *was* a start, and given his beginnings, it was a big fucking deal—a home of his own—however meager.

Come through the front door and you were smack-dab in the middle of the kitchen. A table with three matching chairs pushed under it sat on the right side. Behind the table was a sizable window that looked out into the backyard. It helped with the lighting and gave the room a cozy, homey feeling. Directly across from the table was the sink, stove, and refrigerator, all rolled into one small cooking space.

He'd purchased this place for himself immediately after he finished high school, after his parents were killed in a car crash with a semi-truck, and way before he met her. A sleepless driver, carrying goods for one of the national superstore chains, had fallen asleep while driving and plowed head-on into his parents' auto.

They'd died instantly, leaving him with a sizable settlement to start a life with, a life that he wanted to be different from theirs. He could have gone for more money, many had said, but whatever; he was happy to have what he'd gotten. It was more than he'd had, more than he'd thought to have, no need to be greedy.

Two acres were underneath his trailer home, courtesy of the grandparents on his mother's side. He didn't know them, beyond the occasional Christmas gift he'd received, but whatever to that fact too. He was just grateful that they'd passed the land down to their only disappointment of a daughter, who in turn had passed it on to him.

"You can thank your momma for this," his daddy would say as he surveyed the dump they lived in. Unlike his mother, his dad hadn't come from much; had married up, was the way he'd told it.

"She was to be my savior," his father would say, and never was it said with any hint of gratitude. In fact, it usually accompanied by a hard smack across his mother's face, or whatever body part was in the vicinity of his dad's hand.

"Are you even listening to me?" she said, bringing his attention back to the present and to the woman standing in front of him. The one that he was not currently listening to. Her face was a mask of impatience. "In your head again. Always daydreaming," she added.

"I'm listening," he said.

They were standing between the living room and the kitchen now. The living room, complete with a sofa—the wrap-around kind—and a coffee table, was a much bigger space than the kitchen and was located to the right of it and the front door. Everything else—bedroom and a bath—was to the left of the kitchen. Nothing spectacular, any of it, except it *was* a start… his start.

"I can't do this anymore."

"Don't say that. Can't you see that I'm trying?" he asked, staring at the woman he loved so. Twisted-up-in-a-knot kind of love that left him both happy and scared. Scared that she would leave him. It would kill him if she left.

She was tall like him, with dark brown skin—think dark chocolate melted and you had her skin color. It was another thing he loved about her. Late at night, holding her close, gazing into a pair of the most soulful eyes he'd ever encountered. Those eyes of hers had sucked him in, body and soul, the first time he had seen her. He would move heaven and earth to be with her, and loved her more than anything. He was doing the best he could. Why couldn't she see that?

"It's not enough and you can't give me more and do you want to know why?" she asked, moving closer to him. She didn't stop until she stood squarely in front of his face, with her index finger pointed off to the side of his head, like her hand was a gun. "Because you're a pussy. And I'm tired of living with you," she said,fighting to keep from crying. And yeah, she knew he loved her, but so far that love hadn't translated into anything beyond lame-ass excuses. She was tired of those too, but mostly she was tired of him being ashamed of her, ashamed of them.

He hit her then, arm bent at the elbow, pulled back to his chest, and all forward momentum, until it made contact with her throat.

"Oh," she said quietly. Her eyes and mouth formed perfect round saucers of shock.

"I'm sorry," he said immediately. He hadn't meant to do that. "I'm sorry," he said again as the force of his hit sent her flying backwards. Her arms were flailing about now, her face turning from side to side, searching for something to grab that would break her fall and *fuck,* he thought, there was nothing. Her head connected with the edge of the coffee table first before meeting up with the floor, seconds later.

It was quiet after that. She was quiet after that. Quiet and still. Her eyes were open and staring up at him. Dead eyes, he thought. He'd seen them enough in his line of work to recognize the look. He moved his gaze to the blood that was pouring from her head and tears, from out of nowhere, sprang from his eyes, spilling onto his cheeks, onto his shirt, and then onto her as he bent over to check for a pulse, a long shot hope that her blank stare held some form of life.

Such a fuck-up you are, he said to himself, his dad's words in his head as he placed two fingers to her throat, feeling for a pulse and nothing. *Fuck,* he thought again, and moved his hand to her nose then, feeling for air, for any hint of life. *Fuck,* he thought again, as he sat beside her on the floor, looking at her stomach, his last hope for—and no, nothing there either. It was a flat as it had always been, as flat as she wanted it to be after giving birth. She was gone. He should have known he couldn't even abuse her correctly. He'd killed her when all he wanted was quiet.

It was a reaction more than anything, and a dormant one before today. His father had taught him more than he'd realized, he guessed, and as much as he had resisted before, he was finally following in his footsteps. His father was well versed in the ways of striking people. Not really people, just him and his mother. A slap across the face, not intended to hurt, just a heads-up that he wanted your attention. There was the hands-balled-up-into-a-fist punch to the gut that left you breathless, balled over, and fighting back tears. However, neither of those compared to his father's favorite—his swing of choice—a backhanded strike to the throat, identical to the one he'd just laid on her, the woman he said he loved.

Fuck, fuck, fuck, a string of *fucks* ran on replay in his head. He ran his hand over his face before he reached for her, pulling her into his lap. The tears came in full force then as the import of what he'd done sunk in. He had killed the only person who had ever been there for him. *Fuck,* he thought again, fighting against the way of shame that threatened to overtake him. This was nothing new, more of the same old shame and falling short of someone's ideal he'd grown up with.

He pulled her closer, the tears coming in earnest now, at the loss of this one thing he thought would make his life better. It had been better for a while, he reminded himself, a short span of happiness before she got to know the real him. It didn't take long before she was asking for more, asking him to be different, to be brave. He had never been brave, never would be brave, and wishing and asking wasn't going to make it so.

He sat for a while, holding her until he had no more tears left to shed, until the sounds of a baby crying pulled him back into the present. His baby, her baby, their baby was crying. He carefully laid her on the floor then, away from the puddle of blood, and went to see about his son, their son.

He checked to make sure the front door was locked. Now was not the time for visitors, not that many came to call anyway, but you never knew. He kept his place on lockdown for a reason, since that run-in with his uncle, the mean-ass brother of his mean-ass father. An unexpected encounter that had turned ugly and left him scared to bring her around his family again. Scared enough to install that big chain-link fence around his property, with its unbreakable lock to hold the gates closed.

The baby's cry was growing louder now, interrupting his thoughts and anchoring him to the present, for which he was grateful. He could get lost in his mind sometimes, but less so when he had obligations calling him. His child was hungry or wet, he'd bet, and so he went in search of that big-ass purse, black and shiny, that she'd used as a diaper bag. Said she felt less like one of those typical moms, and more fashionable carrying it.

He picked it up from the foot of the table and started rifling through it. There was a stack of tiny-size diapers, along with baby wipes. He took one of each before moving over to the refrigerator, where the bottles of milk she pumped each morning were kept. He'd watched her. It was another effort he'd made to be a different daddy than the one he'd been saddled with.

He pulled a bottle from the refrigerator, taking note of the three that remained. He opened the top and stuck it into the microwave. Ten seconds it took to warm it to the correct temperature. She'd taught him that, too.

With warm bottle, diaper, and wipes in hand, he moved to the bedroom door. There wasn't anything impressive about this room, besides the bed. A square-shaped room, filled with a bed almost as large as the room itself. It didn't leave much room to maneuver, but they'd somehow managed, even laughed about it at first.

Going for big had been his goal when he'd purchased it. No more sleeping on the couch or the floor or wherever. He'd wanted the biggest bed he could afford, which turned out to be queen-sized, with a tall, dark, rich mahogany headboard. A bed of a rich man, he'd thought at the time.

The baby was lying in the middle of the it, looking like his momma, only with lighter-colored skin, a mix of his white and her dark brown skin. Its face was a mask of twisted and angry, bawling to let you know he wanted whatever he wanted and he wanted it now.

He reached for the blanket she'd placed underneath his boy, using it to pull him to the edge of the bed. He carefully unwrapped the tight bundle of blankets that kept him warm, and began the process of changing his diaper. This he had experience with too. Had changed him mostly at night, when she was tired, that wanting-to-help-be-a-better-father thing again.

When he was done, he placed the soiled diaper into the Diaper Genie she'd asked him to purchase and went to wash his hands. It was another thing she had taught him to do.

He returned to a quiet baby, thankfully, but decided to feed him anyway. He had work in a few, and he wasn't sure how soon he would be able to return. He gently lifted his boy into his arms, cradling his head as he placed the bottle into his mouth. A tiny bow-shaped and quiet mouth now.

"It's just you and me, kid," he said, meeting the wide-eyed stare of his boy, suckling from the bottle. Burping came next, he knew, so when the last of the milk was gone from the bottle, he gently placed his boy on his shoulder as he'd seen her do countless times. He softly, with a cupped hand, hit him on his back.

It wasn't long before he heard it, a soft release of air, and it made him tear up again. He held on tightly to his son for a bit longer after that, taking comfort in his presence, feeling both sad and surprisingly uplifted by the knowledge that he wasn't completely alone in this world. He had her baby, their baby still. He re-wrapped his son in his blanket and pushed him toward the middle of the bed.

He stood for a while, staring at him, considering what to do next, with her and with their baby. The thought of both of them gone made his heart ache, and the first in a series of decisions was made. There would be no getting rid of his child.

But what to do with him, he wondered. He had work in an hour. He couldn't leave him here alone. Or could he? He didn't know the answer to that, but he would figure it out. He would take care of his child, some way, somehow, and his second decision was made.

What to do about her? was the next thing he had to decide. He could call someone. He should call someone. It was an accident, after all. Feeling hopeful for the first time, he closed the door to the bedroom and went in search of his phone.

He found it near the front door where he usually left it, put it there right beside his keys, as any family man would do, coming home from a hard day's work. He had been that family man until a few moments ago. He moved his thoughts to finding someone that could help him.

He stood leaning against the kitchen counter, scrolling quickly through the list of names in his phone and trying not to look at her, lying where he'd left her. No one name stood out. Well, one name, a childhood friend, but he was off in another state with his job. He wouldn't be back for another week.

There was nobody else was the conclusion he'd come to, and just like that, the idea of calling for help fell by the wayside. With the exception of his childhood buddy, he'd been a loner kid, and was now a loner man. He'd have to take care of this himself and nothing new there. Plus, too much time had passed, and how would he explain that?

He checked his watch. He'd better get moving if he wanted to move her before he left for work. But where, he thought, looking around his small space. Out back, in the shed, a small wooded structure, four foot by three foot, where he kept his work tools and his lawnmower. Yeah, he decided, that would suffice, until he had more time for a proper burial. Another decision made. He walked back to the bedroom, pulled a blanket from the closet, along with two belts that he no longer had use for, and spread the blanket out on the floor beside her. He rolled her over and over until he reached the middle of the rug.

There was a lot of blood left on the floor, he noted as he finished wrapping her up in the blanket. Head wounds could be huge sources of blood loss, he also knew from his line of work. He'd take care of that next, after he finished putting her away. He pulled the ends of the blanket together and secured it with one of his belt. He did the same on the other end. He lifted her then, without much strain. She was tall, yes, but slender.

It was a short trip to his shed. His dogs met him at the door, two Doberman Pinschers that he'd raised from pups to be ferocious. He wanted them capable of ripping apart anyone who dared to come onto his land. With his extended family showing up whenever they wanted to at first, he'd needed fierce.

He unlocked the lock on the shed and carefully placed his bundle inside. Locking the door behind him, he walked back to his home, the dogs trailing along behind him.

Once inside, he grabbed his stash of towels—all but one, he still had a shower to take—and wiped up the blood as best he could, in a hurry now; he didn't want to be late for work. He stuffed the bloodied towels into a trash bag, the large industrial-strength kind, and took them over to the shed too.

All that was left was to shower and change into his work clothes. His was a short shift today, filling in for a co-worker who wanted a half day, so he'd better get a move on, he thought, standing with his back to the front door, scanning the room, another quick check before moving to the bedroom again.

His motherless baby was quiet now, laying on the bed, staring into the space above its head, making those little baby cooing sounds that she used to love to listen to.

The bathroom was located at the foot of the bed, toward the

right side of the room if you were in bed facing him. Another small space, with just enough room for a shower, toilet, and sink.

He stepped inside the bathroom, turning the water in the shower to hot, as it took a few seconds to heat up. In the interim, he went to find his uniform. It was in the closet, freshly washed and ironed by her. In so many ways both big and small, he would miss her.

The baby was where he'd left him, still staring into space. He watched him as he undressed, reassuring himself that he wouldn't fall, 'cause he was going to have to leave him here, alone. He had no alternative, nothing that wouldn't give him and what had happened here away, and nothing that wouldn't end up with him losing his kid permanently, and he'd already decided that wasn't happening. It was his son and he would take care of him until they met up with her again. And just like that, he'd come to his final decision. He and his son would see her again.

The idea had been skirting around the edges of his brain since the accident, his name for her death, and the answer to the problem of how to live in the future without her. There would be no future without her. There was just getting through the days until they could see her again. He didn't know when, he'd take each day as it came, taking care of his son, until he felt the time was right.

He stepped into the shower, and his tears fell again in earnest now at his loss, mixed in with his dad's words. He was sure his dad would have called him a pussy for crying. He hated the word *pussy*, had heard it too much in his life to hear it from her, but still he didn't have to hurt her, to become the father that he'd grown up hating. No, there was no cause for what had happened today, which is why his decision to join her felt so right... so redemptive.

He stepped out the shower a different man. The last of his tears had flowed down the drain with the rest of water. There would be no more crying from here on. He dressed, quietly watching his son, growing more and more resolute.

When he was done, using the blanket underneath his boy again, he pulled him closer to the headboard. He should be safe there, no chance he'd fall off the bed? He was much too young to do the rolling around thing that babies did, but just to be safe, he removed the pillows from the head of the bed and placed them on either side of his son. That's better, he thought, or maybe not. Pillows could suffocate.

He looked around the room for something else when he remembered the baby carrier and went to retrieve it. It was in the kitchen, on the floor at the foot of the table, near where the diaper bag had been. Back in the bedroom, he carefully placed his son in it, and placed the carrier on the side of the bed closest to the wall, on an off chance that he'd become wiggly and move it somehow. Highly unlikely, but it didn't hurt to be careful. He stood for a while, watching as the eyelids of his son slowly closed in slumber.

It was back to the kitchen then, stopping by his refrigerator for one can of beer, or two, to try and settle his nerves. He needed something stronger, but beer was all he'd ever allowed himself to drink—another thing to steer clear of to keep from falling in his dad's footsteps. He grabbed his keys and was out the front door and locking it behind him.

It took him a minute to unlock the front gate, drive through to the other side, get out, and re-lock the gate. He turned right onto the road, finally headed to work, mapping out when during his day he could safely return to check on his son. His job allowed him use of a vehicle and time, and he would make use of both until he couldn't. Plus he had the two dogs that would die before they'd let anyone inside his home.

He was on much surer ground now, emotionally at least,

having decided the conclusion to it all. It was a weight lifted, not at what he done—no, he'd never forgive himself for that, but he'd settled on a way to redeem himself, at least one that he could live with.

He blew out a breath, letting go of all those useless thoughts of what a fuck-up he was... or had been. All in the past, water under the bridge. He was moving forward now, until he couldn't.

ONE

Thursday morning

Henri sat in his sister's kitchen early Thursday morning. Three thirty in the morning early. He was due in to the construction site in about an hour. He'd been unable to sleep, so he'd gotten up, showered, and dressed, ready to start his day. It was anything to take his mind off of his troubles.

He'd grabbed his laptop, put on a pot of coffee, and so far all he'd done was stare out of the front window, into darkness, working to settle his mind and to keep a lid on his anger that no amount of talks with himself could dissolve.

Funny how things worked out, he thought, staring into the early morning darkness. This trip couldn't have come at a better time. He'd needed a puzzle to solve, something to think about other than his problems, but mostly he'd needed distance.

He looked around his sister's home, or the kitchen part of it at least. It was nice, and larger than he'd thought was needed for a single woman living alone. Counter and cabinets were against the wall, and an island for cooking stood between him and the cabinets. What wasn't a surprise was the stuff that lay everywhere. He'd forgotten how untidy she could be. In a rush always and throwing whatever wherever was her way. A free spirit was what she'd been called growing up as she'd started doing whatever the hell her mind thought up to do. So very different from his path.

He'd fallen in line early, and mostly did what was expected of him. He had been no different from the others he'd grown up with. Like soldiers, they'd all fallen under the requirements of their families. Outside of his college and graduate school years, he'd grown into an outstanding family man, or so he thought. And just like that his anger was back, anger at his soon-to-be ex, but mostly anger with himself.

He could have, should have left his marriage sooner. He'd had his doubts throughout its entirety, but he'd chosen to ignore them, to push and plug on; too stubborn to quit, because that's what he did, and all for nothing.

He sat back in his chair, blew out a breath, took a sip from his cup of coffee, working to put a lid on his anger again.

"Good morning, big brother," Summer, his sister, said in greeting as she entered the kitchen, robe on, feet bare, hair in a tangle, and eyes barely open. "Couldn't sleep?" she asked as she pulled a coffee cup for the cabinet.

"Nope."

She poured herself a cup, filling it to the brim—black, he noticed, watching her as she turned to face him, her back to the counter as if she needed it to hold her upright. His sister wasn't an early riser.

"Got a lot on your mind, I bet," she said.

"I do," he said, watching her move towards the table.

"Mom called last night. Told me everything. So sorry about that," she said, sliding into the seat across the table from him.

"Yep."

"God, it's early," she said, checking out the time on the oven behind her. "Didn't you get in late last night?

Her brother was dressed. Of course he was: white dress shirt, black expensive slacks, his tie a combination of colors that spectacularly went with the rest of his ensemble. He was handsome, her brother; tall, head full of blond hair and he was sporting a beard and mustache combo these days. That was new, nothing huge but noticeable; gave him a roguish, urbane look, if one could combine those two characteristics. It was a good look for him, at any rate, not that he needed any help in the looks department.

"Yep," he said.

"I don't know how you do it... I'd be sick if it were me and someone had done what Karen did. God, what an awful woman, but this we knew. I'd probably have gotten the hell out of Dodge, too," she said, and wished she'd kept her mouth shut. His expression was all anger now. "I talk too much, you know this, right? I'm sorry and after Mom made me promise not to talk about it at all, and here I am, chatting away. Sorry again."

"I'm a big boy," he said.

"I know, right, you are. Tough and smart, and fuck her, right?" Summer said.

"Yep," Henri said, smiling a little at her comment.

"Parents. They're worried about you, you know. But what's new about that, right? This is a first for you though, huh? It's usually me that everyone worries about. I'm sorry," she said again, reaching for his hand.

He pulled it back, not up for sympathy from anyone just yet.

"Too soon to talk about it."

"Yep," he said.

"Fine. I got you. I'll give you some time, a month, maybe two, and then it's all about the I-told-you-so. Let's be honest, you didn't really love her anyway, not in your heart of hearts. You know this and I know this," she said, meeting his eyes. "But even with that, and as much as I detested Karen, I didn't want this for you."

"It's detest now, is it," he said, offering up another small smile, even allowing her to place her hand over his this time. "Thanks. But she's not the only reason I'm here."

"Uh-oh? That sounds ominous," she said, looking into the cup of coffee that she'd yet to take a sip from. It was too early for coffee, too early for anything but sleep, she thought. "Let me guess, you're here to check in on me too. Dad or you have a problem with my work. You're here to either take over and fix whatever needs fixing or make me fix it, right?" she asked, meeting his eyes.

"You've hired a superintendent to do your job, someone from the outside, that is attempting to steal from us," he said.

"What? How do you know this?" she asked, meeting his gaze. "You just do," she answered for him. "I had my reasons. I needed help and I was starting to have suspicions, too, recently," she said to her brother's look of derision.

"You should have said something then," he said.

"I know, I know, and okay, I should have. I was checking into it. I was getting my ducks in a row. I was prepared to handle it, once I had proof."

"And how long was that going to take?" he asked.

She shrugged her shoulders and yawned.

"I'm going to fire him this morning," Henri said.

"Okay then, that sounds about right. I've been busy is all I can say in my defense. Performed my due diligence a little too late it seems," she said, looking around her kitchen. "But all's well that ends well, right? You're here to take care of it and work it all out."

He didn't say anything to that and it was quiet between them for a few.

"Do you need anything else from me before you leave?" she asked.

"No. I don't think so."

"Good, 'cause I'm going back to bed, now that the cavalry has arrived. I'd say make yourself at home, but I can see that you already have." She looked at his laptop on the table.

"My being here, doing this, is not a mark against you," he said.

"I didn't think it was. I know what I'm doing, just in over my head quicker than I thought... my business and all," she said, meeting his eyes again.

"What business?" he asked.

"I'll tell you later and I'm in no way hurt that you're here to take over, so don't worry," she said, while reaching across the table to run her hand through his hair. She received the same look he'd given her as a kid when she touched him or teased. "Really, you don't know how happy your being here makes me. Away from that Karen first and foremost is a good thing, but for other reasons too. Reasons that I'll explain later, at the office, after I wake up for the second time. Much later." She smiled then yawned again.

She looked down at her untouched coffee. "I won't be needing this anymore." She stood up. "See you at the office, later." She moved to the sink to drop off her coffee cup.

He remained seated, following her figure as she cleared the door. He was glad to be here too, he thought again, finding unexpected comfort in being with his sister. Easy, breezy Summer, the nickname he given to her when they were much younger. It matched up perfectly with her personality. Nothing got her down for long, and she was a breath of fresh air to his beleaguered soul.

He checked his watch. He'd better get moving. He had a superintendent to fire and he was so looking forward to it. This Willis Wilson person would be an unwitting recipient and somewhat appropriate person to vent some of his anger upon. He gathered his laptop and keys, poured the remains of his coffee into the sink, and locked Summer's front door behind him. He was ready to start the day, to move his life in a different direction, and to leave his past behind.

***

Thursday morning

Clarke pulled her jeep into the parking lot in front of the construction office. A nondescript single-wide mobile home, it was the local office for Novak Construction in Austin, Texas, the privately-owned family business of her dear friend—and newly minted business partner—Summer Novak.

Field Superintendent had been Summer's position before she'd gone and hired, without doing the requisite homework, one Willis Wilson. As it turned out, Mr. Wilson had a history, and not a very good one. That's what Clarke's background check had determined, much later than was good. But better late than never, she guessed.

As a private investigator, running background checks was one among the many things she did and the reason she was here today to meet with Summer. Willis Wilson had to go, the sooner the better.

Of course, Summer's little car was nowhere to be found, which wasn't that much of a surprise, Clarke thought, scanning the parking area as she drove closer to the office. Summer had always struggled with getting herself to things on time for as long as Clarke had known her. It was one of the reasons she'd wanted someone to fill in for her. Construction site work tended to commence early.

She didn't see Willis's truck either, amidst the other trucks and cars. Just a truck, but a really nice one. A big, black, and shiny mofo, complete with extended cab and a huge bed in the back. It had one of those self-adhesive signs on the side that read *Novak Construction*.

Someone had been sent here from Dallas, the headquarters, to put an end to Willis's employment and maybe even Summer's. Probably not Summer's. Clarke was sure the inability to be fired had to be one of the many perks of being the CEO's daughter. *If the family couldn't have permanent job security, then who could?* she thought, parking beside the truck. She grabbed her purse and her laptop, and it was up the metal steps of the office, her heels clanging an early announcement of her arrival.

She opened the door and stepped inside, scanning for her friend. Nope, neither Summer nor Willis Wilson were present, just a fine-looking man standing behind the desk, staring at her. He was something to see, dressed professionally in a white shirt, tie and dark slacks that settled quite nicely around lean hips, with very strong-looking hands resting on those hips.

Blond, thick head of hair, cut somewhere in between short and medium length, added with a little bit of blond growth on the bottom of his chin—oh, and a little around the sides of his face, and above his lip. A really nice beard and mustache combination, not too thick, she thought, peering closer at it and him. She hated those lumberjack, long and hairy ones. She preferred his, and him, the sleek and polished, not-too-much-facial-hair type. It was sexy on him. An overall well-packaged male, whoever this was.

"What can I do for you?" Henri said, interrupting her perusal. His mouth had tightened a little there at the end, and his words sounded a little terse to her ears. He was staring into her eyes—and okay, those were nice too: a pretty blue, and intense, without a hint of welcome. Nope, his face remained one big mask of annoyance.

She smiled anyway, letting it roll off her back. Being sent to clean up Willis's mess would put anyone in a sour mood, she bet.

"I'm here for a meeting with Summer Novak," she said, extending her hand. He shook it quickly and released it just as quickly.

"Summer is my sister," he said.

"Oh, she didn't tell me you'd be here. Henri, right? Is she not coming? I didn't check my phone. I must have missed her text," Clarke said, trying not to stare as he was even more gorgeous up close. He smelled great too. The clean scent of his cologne floated softly over her nostrils. Was he married? she wondered, ruffling through her brain, trying to remember if Summer had ever mentioned his marital state. She thought maybe...

"I wouldn't know," he said, bringing Clarke's gaze to his again.

"Oh, okay, it'll only take me a second to check," she said, opening her purse to search.

"What business do you have with my sister?" he asked, watching her ruffle through her purse.

"I'm a private investigator, hired to run background checks on her most recent employee," she said.

"Is that so," he said, and that sounded like sarcasm. And had his eye color changed? His gaze seemed icy now, and she was back trying to remember if Summer had said anything more about him, anything that might explain his sour mood.

His phone rang, and he pulled it from his back pant pocket, keeping his gaze on her like she needed to be watched, like if he didn't, she might steal something. What the hell was up with him? He turned his attention to the phone still ringing in his hand. He stood staring at it for a second as if deciding whether or not to answer it.

"What!" he said into it. Rather rudely, Clarke thought, watching him put it against his ear. He walked past her then, and out the door, allowing it to slam behind him. *Talk about rude.*

What the hell, she thought again, continuing to search for her cell, first to check for any incoming texts—there were none—and secondly to call Summer.

She put the phone to her ear, listening to it ring and ring, and roll over to voice mail. "What's up with your brother? You didn't tell me he was coming, did you? Call me?" she said, disconnecting in a hurry in case he returned. She posed the same question in a text in case Summer had her phone's volume turned off.

Okay, now what? she thought, looking around the office, debating where to sit, 'cause there was no way she was leaving, not until she and Fine Rude Boy talked.

One of the first tasks Summer had assigned herself was to change the look of the office from what she called "Dull Man's Dominion" to modern and funky, which meant the addition of red, blue, and neon green colors splashed on the tops of oddly-shaped furniture.

Boring with a hint of color was the way Clarke viewed her friend's foray into office remodeling. It would take more than color to turn this place into something other than a rectangular box of an office, she mused, looking around the space again. The entry put you in the middle of the office. Two beanbaggy chairs, one red and one blue, the kind that belonged in a sixties movie, sat in front of a desk to the right.

Clarke usually avoided sitting in them when at all possible, preferring to sit at the conference table with a red bean-shaped top located to the left of the door. She hadn't known of Summer's penchant for bean-shaped furniture until now, but whatever. The table seated six comfortably, and unlike the bags that sat in front of the desk, these actually had legs underneath them.

Nothing much on the walls to the left beyond the standard-issue whiteboards, filled with papers, plans, and permits on all but one.

Maybe she should move to the table and not give Fine Rude Boy any say in the matter. Or she could wait and see what the he wanted to do. She checked her phone again, sent a second text, and waited for either Summer to respond or him to return, whichever came first.

***

"What?" Henri said, shouting into the phone again, as his first inquiry had gone unanswered. It was his soon-to-be ex-wife on the other end, adding to his already foul mood. It wasn't the first time she'd called since the hospital, just the first time he'd answered.

"Henri?" she said, tentative.

"Who else would it be?" he said tersely.

It was quiet for a few minutes.

"I'm sorry," she said, starting to cry. "I didn't mean for this to happen." That should have been comforting, an appeasement of sorts. Instead it made him angrier, made him feel like an even bigger fool.

"But it did," he said.

"Can we talk about it?"

"What's there to talk about?"

"What we mean to each other."

"What we meant to each other before this, you mean?" he said. Then it was more silence, with her crying into the phone. He sighed. "What choice did I have? What choice did you leave me?"

"We always have a choice. We can work this out."

"No."

"You and I back then were... you know how we were. It hasn't always been easy for us, you know that," she said, sounding tired.

"You're right. It has been tough, but even with that, I didn't cheat. So there will be no talking, or trying to find a way to work through this, at least not for me. Cheating means you were only concerned with you. Why would I want that back?"

"It means we have problems too."

"No excuses, whatever you think of, to try and justify what you did. I don't care. I just want out."

"What am I supposed to do now? I don't have a job. I quit working 'cause you wanted a wife that stayed home," she said, crying still.

"You should have thought about that before... and you wanted to stop working too, it wasn't just me. And why am I doing this, arguing with you," he said.

"I don't want to argue either. I hurt you. I can see that. Give me a chance. Give us a chance. We can work this out. I know you love me as I love you."

"I've hanging up now. I'm filing for divorce. My attorney is submitting the paperwork this morning. I suggest you find yourself a lawyer, or prepare to represent yourself, whatever. And Karen?" he said, wanting to make sure he had her attention.

"Yes?" she said.

"Don't call me again," he said, listening as she continued to cry.

"It's not all my fault and you know it. So don't blame your crap on me. You played a part in this, too."

"Okay, let's say I did..." He started into his defense, then thought better of it, and said instead, "You know what, it doesn't matter. Just don't call me again." He disconnected.

He took a deep breath and stared off in the distance, trying to corral his emotions, willing himself calm. He had no idea how long he'd stood there, staring out over the parking lot, but eventually he became aware of the cars parked in the lot in front of him, one auto in particular—a black jeep—and he remembered there was some-one waiting inside the office.

The inept private investigator his sister had hired to run back-ground checks, the one Willis Wilson had gotten past. She was a perfect target for some of his leftover anger, he mused. He slid his phone into his pocket and headed back inside.

***

Clarke turned at the sound of the door slamming against its frame fifteen minutes later. *He* was back, and angrier than when he left, Clarke thought. His stride, the way he held himself: all signs of some serious anger. Oh, and he allowed the door to slam again, without looking back, like he meant to do it. He met her eyes, and yes, this was one seriously angry dude. She'd lived with her own anger long enough to recognize it when she saw it.

"Summer and I usually work at the table if you want to continue," she said, pointing in the direction of the table and chairs. "Summer thought these were cute, which, as I'm sure you know, is hugely important to her." She chuckled, hoping to lighten the mood.

"Here's good for me," he said, pointing to the chairs in front of the desk, moving around to take a seat in the nice standard chair sitting behind it.

Okay, this would be work, this talking to him 'cause *that*

sounded a whole lot like snarky, she thought. "Of course, 'cause you're the one that's important here," she said, pleased when his gaze snapped around to collide with hers.

She was no pushover, Henri thought, which was good. He wouldn't feel one ounce of remorse afterward. He sat back in his chair and watched as she took a seat in that red ridiculous excuse for a chair in front of the desk. How had Summer thought them a good idea?

He watched her open her purse and remove her laptop. She placed it on her thighs, or it was more she tried to place it on her thighs. It slid down into her lap. He watched her place it on her knees again, the top of them, and watched as it slipped back into her lap. It was those high-heeled boots on her feet, that were the source of her problem; good for showing off the shapeliness of her legs. And yeah, he'd noticed, as he'd noticed how pretty she was. She wore her hair short, loosely curling around and framing a very pretty brown heart-shaped face and if he wasn't so angry, he'd have taken pity on her. Instead, he sat back and watched as the laptop slid down into her lap for the second time.

She looked up then, hoping he would see her dilemma and offer to move to the table. He did not, just continued to sit there behind his desk, staring at her like she was some sort of alien being.

"I'm not sure how much Summer has told you about me," she said.

"Nothing," he said.

"Okay then. She asked me to run a background check for someone she'd hired recently," she said, meeting his eyes, trying to come off as professional in this crazy-assed chair. It was good for fun, but hard to look anything other than silly sitting in it.

"I had to fire the superintendent this morning. Was he an

example of the kind of background checks you run?" he asked, and there was no doubting his sarcasm this time.

"Excuse me?" she said, meeting his eyes, totally caught off-guard by the question and the attitude behind it.

"The way I see it, you or your company owes us for all that Willis Wilson has stolen. All of the damage he's done so far," he said.

"You're kidding me, right?" she said, her eyes locked with his still, her temper on the rise.

"Does it sound like I'm kidding?" he asked.

She smiled. Not a complete smile, just a thinning of her mouth into a straight line. She closed her laptop and slid it back into her purse.

"You know what? I'm going to give you a pass today, 'cause I don't know you, and you don't know me and I can see that something has you upset. I'm going to ignore your anger and your *snarky* attitude, 'cause your sister is a good friend of mine and she would not want me to be ugly to the big brother she thinks so highly of. You can thank me later for that little bit of grace I'm extending to you." She stood up.

"*And,*" she said, pausing to give that word time to sink in, "any work I've done for your sister was done as a favor. While I could use the work, I'm done putting up with asshole men in my life. I'll come back when your sister returns."

"I'm her replacement, come to make sure the fuck-ups end," he said. He was nowhere near ready to give in yet, and was irritated that she wasn't taking the bait. He was so spoiling for a fight.

Clarke just stared at him, not sure what to do with what he'd just said. She looked away and then it was back to face him again. "Did you just call me a fuck-up?" she asked, taking a step closer to the desk, then moving around it until she stood beside him, her temper having pushed her. She was not at all sure what she would do now that she was here, but she was refusing to back down.

The old Clarke had been such an even-tempered person, but that Clarke had gotten the short end of the marriage stick, and left in her place was the more aggressive, contesting-all-evil Clarke, who stood staring down at him now.

He stood up then. God, what she wouldn't give to be even an inch taller, she thought. She came to the top of his chest, and that was with her heels. Hard to be intimidating to anyone but little kids and babies.

The door opened, and they both turned to look.

"Hey, what's going on?" Summer asked, entering the office, her smile slipping a little as she moved her gaze between the two of them. "Clarke, so sorry. I got your text too late. You've met my brother Henri, I see. He arrived last night, a surprise. He was up at three thirty this morning, ready for work. Who does that? And you know I'm not an early riser. Anyway, it put me off schedule, and I forgot about anything other than getting back to sleep after that. Plus, you know me, scatterbrain on a good day." And what the hell had she walked into, she wondered.

Lots of anger radiated off the both of them, a lit match was all that was needed and this place would go up in flames at the heat between them, she thought. Luckily she'd arrived, apparently just in the nick of time, too. Not that she was worried. Henri wouldn't hurt her friend, or at least the old Henri wouldn't have. Who knew what this new, hurt, angry Henri would do. Clarke was the same: not as newly divorced, but the same angry-at-the-world or at those carrying the male chromosome.

"Clarke and I have known each other since high school," Summer said, looking at her brother as she reached them and tried to squeeze herself between the two of them It was enough, as both of them took a step backward.

Summer was the same height, was the same tall, had the same blond coloring, the same pretty as her brother, Clarke noted.

"Clarke moved here after her divorce, same as you," Summer said, winking at him now, continuing with the cheerful.

"I fired the superintendent, whom I assumed she checked out," he said, pointing to Clarke now. "If that's an example of her work, then we are better off without her."

"Don't worry. I'm leaving," Clarke said, staring at him. Henri shot her a quick glance, a dismissive one, which only fueled her anger. It was a good thing she was leaving or else she'd do something stupid, like punch him in the mouth.

"Wilson stopped in on a day that was going to hell in a hand basket for me. I was running late as I always do. He helped me get through it so I hired him on the spot. Not my best decision, but I needed help. This is not Clarke's fault. I asked her to check him out, but only after the fact. We were meeting today to discuss her findings. Unfortunately I overslept, 'cause again I was up at three thirty in the morning with someone," Summer said, pointing at Henri.

She turned to face Clarke again. "It's not your fault, Clarke. You were a bit unlucky in running into my brother this morning, that's all. His attorney is filing his divorce papers with the court this morning, serving his soon-to-be ex-wife too, that's what our mother told me, and the reason he's so angry. He and my future ex-sister-in-law were expecting a baby. The whole family's been expecting this baby, excited for months—the first grandchild and all—and anyways, he walks into the hospital thinking he's going to get a new son, and he does, but this one's a dark brown color, and neither he nor my soon-to-be ex-sister-in-law are brown. Both Caucasians, so you can imagine his surprise."

"Not another word from you, Summer," Henri said.

His mouth was a thin line now, Clarke thought, watching him. She was surprised that any words had gotten past his teeth, so tightly locked together. *Were those sparks shooting from his eyes?* she wondered, watching them focus on his sister now.

"It's okay," Summer said, waving him away. "So maybe we can cut him a little slack. You've been there, not like that, but through another version of cheating. It's all the same hurt, does the same damage, whatever the circumstances," she said, gazing into her friend's eyes.

Turning back to Henri, Summer said, "Why don't we all have a seat and talk this out, like adults?" She was playing the role of peacekeeper until she looked down at Clarke's boots. "Where did you get those? Oh gosh. They're beautiful!" she squealed, clapping her hands together.

"What?" Clarke asked, nonplussed.

"You always find the most perfect shoes. It makes me crazy. I have so much trouble finding them and you... Oh gosh, I adore those. Don't you, Henri? Aren't they perfect?" she said, looking at her brother now. "Even you have to admit how cute those boots are. Come on, everyone, let's have a seat." She put her arm through Clarke's and moved her back around to the other side of the desk.

"Henri wanted out of town, you can understand why, right, the baby and all that divorce business? But he found out about Willis Wilson too, before we did. I don't know how, but he's pretty smart, so I'm not at all surprised," Summer said, in full-out chatty mode now. "He's also here to check on me, not that it's sneaky or anything. Think you could forgive his rudeness this morning? He's not usually this way. Actually, he's a very nice guy." She looked over her shoulder at her brother again as she tried to lead Clarke over to the conference table.

"He owes me an apology. Divorce or not," Clarke said, unmovable from her spot, back in front of the desk now. "He either gives me one or I am out."

"Out works for me," Henri said, staring back at her, not sure why he wanted to provoke this one, but he did.

"Just going to stick with playing the dick, huh?" Clarke said, staring back at him. "Fine then." She meant it.

"Hey, how about we grab some lunch instead? I don't want you to leave angry," Summer said, moving toward her friend again.

"It's not you that I have a problem with," Clarke said, turning to face her. "I'm not in the best of moods now anyway, you can see that." Her voice softened as she met her friend's gaze. "I have a full schedule today, too."

"Sure, later, but please accept my apology on behalf of my brother. He's wrong, he just doesn't know it yet," Summer said.

"Thanks," Clarke said, refusing to look in Henri's direction again. She turned on her heel and marched over to the door.

Angry, not so much anymore, Henri thought, feeling it dissolve with every loud footfall from Clarke, moving her short and shapely body out of his view. Yeah, he'd noticed it, in spite of his anger. Very pretty, he thought again. The slam of the door was the period in her exit. She was gone. He blew out a breath and turned to face his sister.

TWO

"Who are you and where is my brother?" Summer said, meeting his gaze now. "Not this mean man… person, but my real one, the nice guy you used to be." She stared into his eyes like she was seriously searching for something. "Is this how it's going to… how *you're* going to be while you here?"

"We all grow up sometime, so I guess you'll just have to get used to the new me."

"I don't like this you."

"I do," he said.

Like that was to be end of the discussion, Summer thought. And no, it was not the end of anything.

"Clarke's nice, really, and you *will* have to apologize. You should not have taken your anger with your wife out on her. That's what that was about, wasn't it?" she said. He looked away.

"She's not my wife."

"Your future ex-wife then."

"I'm not taking my anger out on anyone. I just don't like incompetence, especially when it costs us," he said, staring at her, his anger reduced to visible irritation.

"It's not her fault. I hired him first and had her run the background check second. You owe her an apology."

He blew out a breath, which meant he agreed but wasn't ready to say so yet.

She wasn't going to push. She didn't mind giving him a little space. He had been through a bunch in a short span of time. "So Willis is gone?" she asked.

"Yes, he is," he said, sitting back in his chair. And yes, he owed Clarke an apology. He sighed and rubbed his hand over his face.

"That's good," she said, sitting in the blue beanbag chair in front of his desk. Maybe it was because of her height advantage, but she didn't have the same problem sitting in it as her friend Ms. Kensington had had.

"Clarke's more than a private investigator, you should know, and that's another reason you'll need to apologize, and the sooner the better too. She's also my partner in a residential business venture."

"What residential business venture?" he asked.

"I'm moving into houses, flipping them. I know you've seen all the TV shows, where everyone's flipping this house or that. That's what I want to do, have always wanted to do, what I asked Dad to allow at first, but he wasn't hearing it. I only accepted this job because Dad wanted me to, as a pre-requisite to starting on my own, to prove that I was serious this time," she said, smiling at his expression. Disbelief. His eyebrow was lifted in that way of his that said he wasn't buying it.

"That's what you'd like to do now," he said.

"Yes. It is what I'd like to do now, and I know what you're thinking."

"What am I thinking?"

"The restaurant, the bake shop, the coffee shop... I was serious those times too. I was young, and it's not me anymore, but thanks for bringing up my many failings."

"You brought it up," he said.

His voice had lost the last bit of its edge, she thought.

"Anyway, I should have believed in myself and gone for it, instead of working here, trying to earn his support."

"You have always had Dad's support."

"You know what I mean."

"You wanted to impress him, to prove something to him," he said.

"Yep, I did. You probably wouldn't understand. He was always impressed with you."

"Not always," he said, and sighed. "I'm not that different from you. Without as many failings maybe, but the same need to be what he would approve of."

"Your marriage?"

"In some ways," he said, and that was all he was going to say on that subject. Summer had just told some stranger his story in one fell swoop, so yes, he was going to keep the rest to himself.

"Wow. I knew your leaving Karen was impactful, but wow, this I didn't expect."

He didn't reply beyond the lift of his eyebrows again.

"Anyway, that's why I hired a superintendent to fill in for me. So I could work on getting my business started. I have my own money that I've saved, and the money left to us from Grandfather Novak. I still have most of that. And I have Clarke, who believes in me, enough to put her money behind me, and I'm not disappointing her or me. She's grounded in a way that I'm learning to be.

"I'm searching for homes for us to flip," she said, still meeting his eyes. "Give me time, that's all I'm asking for." She faced him, as if reading his mind. "You'll see I'm different."

He was quiet, looking at her still.

"You being here is a gift for the both of us. I know it probably doesn't seem like one now, but it is. No more of that terrible wife for you, no more of that terrible superintendent job for me, *and* you can help me… us, too."

"Help you how?" he asked, a little bit impressed by this new Summer and somewhat different Summer, standing up to him, stating her case like an adult. And was that strength he heard in her voice, staring back at him? *When had that happened*, he wondered.

"You could help check out the houses with Clarke and me. I've started searching already, as a matter of fact. I'm close to having three picked out for us already. Clarke knows next to nothing about residential construction, less than I do. She mostly just wants out of being a private investigator at some point, so if we can get our business off the ground, maybe it could be sooner. You can help me… us.

"You have experience, since Dad put you to work when you were a kid, and all your knowledge of constructing things. That's why you will have to apologize. I can't have the two people I love most in the world at odds with each other. Nope, can't have that. You'll be super busy this way, no time at all to think about the woman whose name I will no longer speak."

"Commercial construction is very different from residential," he said. He'd forgotten how many words Summer could put into a sentence. Talking had never been her problem.

"I know," she said.

"Maybe," he said.

"What's this 'maybe'? It's a huge plate you'll have. You'll be helping Dad until the new superintendent comes, unless you're going to stick around and do it long term."

"No. My days of being superintendent are behind me. I'm only filling in until I can find a replacement. Two weeks at least, three tops."

"That's fine then. You can help me until you can't. I won't pay you, of course, as you now owe me a favor."

"For?"

"Hello. I just told you. Aren't you listening? The favor of providing you with a distraction, distractions."

"Maybe," he said, and smiled. It wasn't a huge smile, not like the Henri smiles of old, before Karen had arrived on the scene, when he'd been free and unencumbered.

"So, one last thing and then I'm out of here. This is Clarke's telephone number. Feel free to give her a call anytime," she said, reaching for a sticky note from what was now his desk to write Clarke's name and number on it.

"Maybe," he said.

"Again with the maybe?" she said, standing up and looking around his desk.

"What are you looking for?"

"Your phone, so you won't miss it."

He handed it to her and she placed the sticky with Clarke's information on top of it.

"I will apologize, you have my word. You don't have to worry."

"I know. I know," she said, smiling. "I'm really glad you're here." She smiled more.

"We'll see," he said, smiling back, and this one was a lot closer to his old smile.

It was a start, Summer thought, at the door now. She waved and then she was gone.

***

Summer made her way to her car, thinking about her brother and what him being here meant to her, and all the good that was coming their way. She could feel it; things were finally working out for her, and whether Henri knew it or not, they were working out for him too. She'd watched him, sitting alone this morning, staring out the window, a large mass of angry and wounded male.

He was her favorite and only brother, the golden child for whom things had not turned out so golden, and she hated to see him like this. He was a nice guy, the kind the right woman would have appreciated, except he hadn't found the right one. He'd gotten mixed up with a different kind, and was here licking his wounds while he tried to recover.

No matter, she was happy he was here. He needed to be here, for all the reasons she'd told him, but for others as well. A break in his nice-guy life, a getaway from Dallas and her parents. Nice as they were, the little circle of parents and their friends had this predetermined path picked out for their children to follow, her included. It was enough to suffocate the sturdiest, which he was.

He was nice-looking, her brother. Okay, more than a little. She'd recognized it early, along with all the things women did to get close to him, not all of it positive. Karen the ex was a perfect example of that. He had always been into women. He and his pal Stephen—who was married now, which meant anyone could be tamed—had never suffered from lack of female attention growing up. Ever.

And both of them were sort of rule-following men, who had found the women they loved and settled down to the married life, although she'd bet good money that her brother's love for Karen had skidded to a halt at the start.

He needed a replacement, a good one this time, and she had just the person in mind. They had already met, this morning to be exact. The good that was coming for Henri had arrived. Clarke and

Henri, a clash of two strong-willed people she loved, that had more than a little potential. Clarke had stood up to him, an excellent start for any woman dealing with a strong man. Yes, the two of them locked in combat early had been a thing of beauty to witness, lots of chemistry working between them, and neither one of them had a clue. No worries, lucky for them, she was here to the rescue. It wasn't too soon either, for either of them, in her opinion.

Now how to go about it was the tricky question, it being so soon for Henri. Not so soon for Clarke, but she wasn't over hers either. It would take some skill on her part, but she felt uniquely qualified, up to the task of getting the two of them together.

Yes sir, Clarke as a member of her family as well as a business partner would be an awesome addition. She'd be proud to call her sister. She was skipping the in-law part. She'd always wanted a sister.

***

As soon as the door closed behind Summer, Henri pulled out the scrap of paper with Clarke's name written out in his sister's script. No way around apologizing, as according to his sister, he would be seeing her often.

His future proximity to Clarke was not the only reason he was calling to apologize. He'd been wrong and rude, and she hadn't deserved his ire. He could see that, now that he had blown through the heat of his anger.

He dialed her number, listening as it rang, once, twice, upward to four times, before it rolled over to her voice mail.

"Hello, Ms. Kensington. This is Henri Novak, Summer's brother, the one you unfortunately ran into this morning. I owe you an apology. I'd like to make that apology in person if I could, and

I'd also like to discuss the continued use of your private investigative services as I move forward to find a replacement superintendent.

"So if you would, please give me a call or stop by the office at your earliest convenience. I'm here as early as five in the a.m., until about six in the evening. I look forward to speaking with you again," he said and disconnected. He turned his attention to work, the reason he was here, pushing everything but that into the deal-with-it-later category.

***

Clarke sat outside the Fergusons' home, watching as their four-teen-year-old girl child allowed another equally fourteen-year-old child, male, into her parents' home. Of course her parents were at work, with no knowledge of her exploits. They had suspicions, which is why she was sitting here now, watching.

This wasn't the first time for Baby Girl. It was the fourth time, actually, in a three-week time span, and it was growing progressively worse. Baby Girl was skipping school too—not the entire day, too smart for that, just a class here or there, and never enough that it couldn't be explained away. The bad part, the dangerous part was that Baby Girl was starting into drugs, depending on whom she was with. Not this kid—he was sex—but the desire to fit in, at least as far as Clarke could tell, was the biggest of Baby Girl's struggles.

Clarke checked her watch. It was a little before lunch. Baby Girl had been here at this particular time before and if she stayed true to form—or Baby Boy stayed true to form—ten minutes and they would be out and on their way back to school, just in time for lunch.

Her cell rang, and she checked the number. She didn't recognize it so she let it roll to her voice mail. She returned calls usually after assignments, and this wouldn't be over until she retrieved the disk from the camera she'd installed in Baby Girl's room at the request of her parents. They wanted information but didn't have the heart to actually see it themselves. So they'd hired her, willing to take her word on it after she reviewed the footage. She only shared enough to give them a general idea of what occurred. Actually she already had the general idea, didn't need a camera, but the parents thought she and the boy might be listening to music or some other such nonsense.

True to form, ten minutes passed and Baby Girl was locking the front door, holding Baby Boy's hand. One small, quick kiss and they were walking down the street, headed back to school. She'd wait for a bit, just to make sure the lovebirds had ample enough time to make it to school, and then it was in to retrieve the disk.

Might as well listen to her messages as she waited. Her mother was the first caller. "Baby, your Aunt Glenn called me today. I gave her your number. So answer any calls from numbers you don't recognize. It's probably her. She wants you to go out and talk to your Aunt Veda as soon as you can. Her daughter's missing."

Again, Clarke thought. She'd call her mother back this evening, and the other... *maybe* later on in the week, she decided, not really worried about Aunt Veda's baby. An eighteen-year-old woman, with a newborn baby of her own, was way too old to be babied in her opinion. Plus, Amber sort of came and went as she pleased, usually after some argument with her mother. Amber and Aunt Veda had been arguing since forever, and were hard to take seriously now. Clarke moved on to the next message.

"Hello, Ms. Kensington, this is Henri Novak, Summer's brother, the one you unfortunately ran into this morning. I owe you an apology. I'd like to make that apology in person if I could and I'd also like to discuss the continued use of your private investigative services as I move forward to find a replacement superintendent." Clarke hit the button to delete the rest of his message, not in the least bit interested in whatever he had to say. She certainly had no desire to work for him. *Asshole,* she thought uncharitably.

The next call was from Summer, apologizing for her brother again. She'd only had to deal with Summer. She was only the business partner to Summer. Actually, she thought of herself as mostly an investor, as much as Summer disagreed. What she knew of construction wouldn't fill up one of her mom's sewing thimbles. Her participation was nothing other than her desire for options, something other than being a private investigator, which could be tough on family life. Summer's business was for later, something she could turn to actively when investigating folk was no longer viable.

She checked her schedule. She had two hours to review the tape, grab some lunch, and then it was on to a meeting with the Fergusons to discuss her findings.

***

Henri was here to meet an old friend of his, Stephen Stuart, who he'd grown up with, from grade school through college, with loads of stories—scandalous and not—between them. They had remained friends, not in touch as much as they used to be, but aware of the major things that went on in each other's lives.

Keeping in touch was not an easy thing, as Stephen had made Austin his home. After one hell of a choppy start, he had married the love of his life, Reye. Henri had texted Stephen last night, telling him of his arrival, and Stephen had suggested they meet for lunch.

He entered the small eatery they'd agreed to, located east of downtown. An old house converted to a sandwich shop, it offered both outside and inside dining. He passed the outside patio, scanning it for Stephen. Not out here, he thought, and moved inside to the hostess desk, the gateway to seating.

It was pleasant enough, Henri thought, looking around the two dining rooms that were inside the old home.

He spotted Stephen at a table near the back of the room on the right.

"I see my friend," he said to the hostess, leaving as soon as the words left his mouth, or maybe even before. He was not in the mood for talking or smiling.

"Dude," Stephen said, chuckling, falling back in years to their primary form of communication when they had scoped out women, lived together, generally navigated their way to adulthood. He stood when Henri reached the table, to exchange the man-hug thing with his buddy.

"What the hell are you doing here? How's the baby? I'd thought you'd be knee-deep in diapers by now, one of those tired parents of newborns," Stephen said, chuckling.

"I filed for divorce this morning," Henri said, meeting Stephen's gaze, smiling as best he could, given the circumstances. He took a seat across the table from his friend.

"What?" Stephen said, falling into his chair. "What happened?"

"Where to start?" Henri said.

"Is there a baby?"

"Yep. She arrived into the world two days ago. Six pounds, seven ounces, and not mine."

"Oh," Stephen said. He clearly hadn't expected that answer.

"Yep. I felt the same way. Shocked—and angry still, if I think about it too long. I showed up to the hospital to make a very unpleasant discovery. Did not see that coming. Had no idea."

"I'm sorry, dude," Stephen said.

Henri shrugged, brushed it aside with a wave of his hand, and proceeded to tell Stephen his sad story in detail.

The hostess from the receptionist desk appeared beside them then, wearing an apron around her waist and a sunny smile on her face, interrupting his tale. Maybe it was good thing, this interruption, as Henri could feel himself growing angry again.

"Hey, Stephen."

"Hi, Shelly," Stephen said.

"So you've brought me another customer. Thank you again," she said, smiling brightly at Henri. "Stephen is one of my biggest fans, always bringing people over, spreading the word. Any more referrals and I'll have to start paying him for advertising." She nodded her head in Stephen's direction. "I'm Shelly, by the way, the owner, receptionist, and today your waitress."

Henri smiled, albeit disinterested or distracted. Either one was possible, Shelly thought, watching him. She'd seen both men enter separately, admiring the handsomeness that was the two of them. They were both a little older than her twenty-three years, but she was a mature twenty-three, had grown up fast as the owner of this, her first restaurant by age twenty-one. She preferred older men anyway. Stephen was married, she knew that from the start, as she had flirted at first. She always flirted, but he didn't flirt back, so apparently he was happily married, she had concluded.

"What can I get you two to drink? Or more if you're ready to order."

"Water for me," Stephen said, smiling back at her, darting his eyes over to Henri, whose head was bent, scanning the menu.

"Water for me too," he said, meeting her gaze, his smile disinterested.

"I'd be happy to make a suggestion if you'd like," she said, smiling again.

"I can read a menu," Henri said before he could stop himself. "I'm sorry." He met Shelly's eyes. "It's been a tough few days." He pulled together his best smile, which didn't quite reach his eyes, Shelly thought, but was enough to cover the hurt his words may have caused.

"No worries. I'll give you a few minutes more," she said.

"Thanks," Henri said.

"I didn't realize things were that bad. Shelly didn't mean anything. She flirts with everyone," Stephen said, sitting back in his chair.

"Shelly is?" Henri asked.

"The waitress, the one that was just here. It doesn't matter. I thought things were better between the two of you," he said, moving back to their conversation about Henri's marriage.

"I did too," Henri said, sitting back in his chair. He sighed. "As dumb as it sounds, I thought the baby would make things better, or at least that it would make the disappointment I felt with my marriage more tolerable. Dumb, huh?"

"Who knows, it could have," Stephen said, watching the anger—mostly hurt, he thought—in Henri's expression. "It's probably too early to hear this, let alone say it, but we've always been honest with each other, so I mean what I'm about to say with the best possible intentions. Maybe it's for the best. You didn't love her the way—"

"The way you love Reye," Henri said, finishing his friend's sentence.

"That wasn't what I was going to say, but okay, that works too. You didn't love her, not in the way you wanted."

"Not everybody has what you have, the happily ever after," Henri said.

"Right," Stephen said, shifting his gaze to Shelly, who had returned and stood smiling beside them now, apparently not one to hold a grudge.

"Are we ready now?" she asked.

"We are," Henri said, and smiled. It wasn't one of his finest from the old days, the one that worked so effectively on women, but it wasn't the growl from earlier either, Stephen thought.

"I'll take the lunch special," Henri said.

"The same for me, Shelly," Stephen said.

Henri looked up again, watching Shelly walk away from the table. Pretty and young, and that probably meant talking and energy, none of which he was interested in at the moment.

Two days separated from his wife, not long enough to consider moving on to someone else. He hadn't considered women, other than his wife, in years.

"So what's the plan? Rest and relaxation, hanging out with your sister?" Stephen asked, deciding a change of topic was a good idea.

"I'm here on business actually. Would have been down here sooner, had it not been for the baby," Henri said.

"Novak Construction is serious about expanding into Austin then?"

"We are. Summer was hired to be the acting superintendent on the construction site. As it turns out, she hired some dude without the necessary background checks to do the job. He's been stealing and basically not doing any work."

"I had no idea. She told me she was into something residential, I think? She's grown up a bit, or so I thought. Still hyper... scatterbrained, but less so it seems. You know what I mean, a little more serious, and who thought that was possible. She used to dog our heels something fierce growing up," Stephen said.

"I know, saving money to invest, it's a surprise to me, too and I have to agree with you. She does seem different. More serious, I think," Henri said.

"Having a business partner helps. Clarke is pretty sharp and grounded," Stephen said.

"You know Clarke?" Henri asked.

"I do," Stephen said, watching his buddy closely now. Something about the way he'd looked when he'd asked that question. It was a curious thing, Stephen thought. "Summer asked me to help out a friend, over a month ago now, I think. The friend was Clarke. She's a private investigator, new to Austin. Summer wanted me to introduce her to people that might need an investigator. So I made a few calls, first to check her references, you know. I have a reputation too, but anyways, it was all good from her clients, really from everyone. Didn't hear one negative thing about her. They loved working with her, hated to see her go. Said she's particularly good at family stuff. So you met her?"

"I did, although it wasn't a good meeting. More collision than meeting. She had the misfortune of being the first person I talked to after my phone call with Karen this morning, the first time I'd spoken to her since I left Dallas, since seeing the baby that wasn't mine. It was all on me... my fault. I was angry and spoiling for a fight, tried to take it out on her, and she wasn't having it."

"You *had* an eventful morning," Stephen said, chuckling.

"I *had* an eventful week," Henri said, filling in the details of his argument with Clarke, along with Summer's intervention, including his sister sharing the specifics of his divorce story. "Told her all of it. You know my sister." He chuckled. "I can even see the humor in it now."

"Summer," Stephen said, shaking his head and chuckling too.

"I do owe Clarke an apology, which I will give," Henri said, growing serious. "I'm already on it actually. I called and left a message on her phone this morning. I even offered to give her some work and it's good to know she's good, since I've made the offer."

"It wouldn't be all that difficult to bring her around if you put your mind to it, not for the Henri I know. You and your charm could make it all nice when you wanted. She is divorced, same as you will be soon, and also like you, hers was a bad one. A cheating husband was what I learned from one of her more chatty references."

"I know. Summer told me that too, after Clarke stormed out of the office."

"So maybe you two could commiserate together while you're in town. She's easy on the eyes," he said, smiling.

"She is at that, I wasn't that angry. I did notice that. She's shorter than I like them to be, but everything else was really nice," Henri said, smiling. He was quiet for a few after. Considering, Stephen guessed.

"I should say no to the commiserating with somebody idea, right? It's way too soon for that, isn't it? Except I've been without for a while now," Henri said.

"Things were that bad?"

"Yeah, they were. I had serious thoughts of bailing before Karen conceived and why we were trying makes no sense to me now, but we were. Once the news of the baby came... I was going to stay."

"Sorry, man."

"Me too. So Clarke, huh," Henri said, smiling, wanting to focus on something other than his depressing problems.

"Clarke."

"Think she might be interested?" Henri asked.

"I don't know. All I see is her professional side. I don't know if she's seeing anyone. Summer would have a better idea."

"I won't be asking her," he said, chuckling. "She would never let it rest. Hell, who knows what Summer would do if she knew I was interested." He chuckled, and then he was quiet again. "Now that I think about it, I'm not as opposed to it as I thought I would be. It could only be sex, though. I can't imagine being up for much else. It's way *too* soon for that."

"Sex is good," Stephen said, smiling.

Henri laughed, feeling better than he had felt in a while. He'd felt alone in this before now. "Well, whomever this imaginary sex I'm having is with, they would have to agree… promise, really, not to talk to me before, during or after, especially after. Not one word. So if you think your Ms. Kensington would be interested in that, height challenged or not, then maybe I would be too."

"I could call her, put in a good word for you, help you get back into her good graces, maybe even set something up."

"Maybe. Give me a day or two to think about it. Maybe she's not the best candidate with her so close to Summer and all. I'll let you know," Henri said.

"Okay. I'll wait to hear from you. So you're going to be here working, hiring a new superintendent and living with your sister?" Stephen asked, changing the subject. And yes, he understood the anger that Henri felt, and the hurt that was behind the anger. He'd done the mindless screwing thing once upon a time in his life too, so he got it.

"Doesn't sound all that spectacular when you say it, but yep, that's me for at least the next two to three weeks," he said.

Shelly was back, delivering their food. Henri remembered to smile this time. He found himself watching her move away again. She was an attractive woman, yet he was still unmoved. Too much work and he wasn't up for it, not yet. He couldn't imagine having to make small talk and do all the other things women required. He'd rather be drawn and quartered, he decided, turning his attention to his food. "Smells good."

"It is good," Stephen said, biting into his.

"So enough about me. How's Reye?" Henri said. He'd been the best man at Stephen and Reye's wedding, just as Stephen had been his.

"Reye is fine, pregnant, starting into her fourth month. It's been all morning sickness up until now," Stephen said, smiling.

"It's not nice that you're smiling, you know this," Henri said, willing himself to be happy for his friend.

"I know, but I am. Reye's good, working to sell her business or shut it down. We're headed to Dallas after the baby comes, before if we can swing it. We haven't decided if we want to rent out our home, her old home, or put it up for sale. But to answer your question, we're all good, and who would have thought that?"

"Not you, at least not at first, while I liked her from the start," Henri said.

"I know. I remember, you're one of the few that thought it would work, including me," Stephen said.

"Yep. So much work it took to get you and Reye together, but it turned out be the one that lasted, while mine was easy and not good at all."

"Right," Stephen said, and it was quiet between them for a bit, while they made short work of their lunch. The conversation turned to other things after that, like work and old friends, both from college and back home. Another hour passed, and they were winding down, preparing to leave, and Stephen was handing his card to Shelly, to take care of the bill.

"Basketball this Saturday morning. You've been drafted," he said, while they waited for Shelly to return with his credit card. "We play over at the old rec, on campus. A few friends and I play in a league, so plan on joining us while you're in town. You can meet me there nine, Saturday."

"I guess I can do that," Henri said, smiling and standing up. He had missed his friend, and although they'd stayed in touch, they both had gotten lost in their lives too.

"I will. No complaining if I'm too good," Stephen said, smiling.

"I'm sure your game hasn't changed that much," Henri said, chuckling.

"We'll see Saturday."

"Saturday." Henri smiled, glad to have the distraction of basketball, and of course Stephen's friendship.

THREE

Thursday evening

Henri pulled up to a small house, part home and part office, that belonged to Clarke Kensington. He was bringing the apology to her. It was a spur-of-the-moment decision to stop by, and it also wasn't. Stephen's words about commiserating with her were in his head. Really, honestly, sex with her was in his head.

Who knew if she would even be home, but he'd stopped by anyway. She hadn't returned his call, nor had she stopped by his office as he'd asked. So either she was busy or a carrier of grudges. He'd see, and then he'd see some more. He smiled, glad to be here, glad to have a distraction from his anger.

He scanned the houses on either side of hers. An insurance agency was on the left, and what looked like someone's home was on the right. He was familiar with this part of town: inner city, used to be strictly residential but no longer. It was now a combination of both businesses and homes, or as was the case with Ms. Kensington's house, both. A quaint home was this, painted a light blue and trimmed in white. A yellow awning completed the fairy-tale look of it.

He parked in front on the small paved lot that had probably been grass at one time. She was home. Her jeep was parked beside his truck now.

A very nice woman, according to his buddy Stephen. He

could also trust Summer too, another good judge of people. Neither of them had approved of his first wife and maybe he should have listened. He walked over to the front door where a small sign with the word *Open* printed across it gave him permission to enter.

He stepped into one large living space, a combination of office and home, maybe. A large desk sat to the left with two chairs placed in front of it, the office part. A mid-sized couch sat back against the opposite wall. Another door, directly across from the one he'd entered, stood partially open. It was quiet inside. The door's chime had stopped ringing.

He heard the sound of feet moving toward him. They were her feet, in boots to be exact, ankle-high ones, black and shiny and more than a little bit sexy. He moved his gaze up to take in the rest of her. Pants that outlined and hugged her legs, hips, and ass, and some kind of shirt that floated softly around her waist. She was as he'd thought this morning: pretty, short, and sexy. He did like the look of her and okay, maybe his friend was onto something. He was going to be here three weeks, and if she was interested, then so was he.

"Oh, it's you," she said, stopping in the doorway.

She didn't seem angry that he could detect, more like curious. "It is, and I owe you an apology," he said.

"Yes, you do," she said, leaning into the door's frame, crossing her arms at her chest and her legs at her ankles. He was the same handsome as he'd been this morning, she thought.

"I'm sorry," he said.

"For?"

"For earlier."

"That's not bad as apologies go, just not good enough for me," she said, and smiled.

"Is that so?" he said. And yeah, he was in, intrigued by the attitude.

"It is," she said.

"What would you like for me to say then?" he asked.

"Something more than the basic 'I'm sorry,'" she said, and smiled again. He smiled too. He seemed approachable when he smiled, very different from the angry man she had encountered that morning.

"Okay, let's try this: I'm sorry. I was angry and I shouldn't have taken it out on you."

She tilted her head to the right, as if seriously weighing his answer. "It's better. Not what I would call great, but it is better," she said, and smiled again.

Her hands had found their way to her hips. Very nice slim hips, swathed tightly in jeans, that had really made an impression, he thought, admiring her again. Nice lips. He liked the way her hair framed her face. Her skin was a shade darker than Reye's, not so much brown as caramel. A soft creamy caramel. He hadn't dated any African American women before, not that he didn't find them attractive. He wasn't sure why, timing perhaps. It didn't matter. That would change soon if she were agreeable. With the exception of her height, there wasn't much he didn't like about her physically. Small, round ass, lean legs, small breasts, all of which fit nicely in his wheelhouse.

"If you want, I could help you out," she offered.

"Sure," he said, grinning now. And wasn't she a nice surprise, he thought.

"Okay then. Repeat after me," she said. "Are you ready?"

"As I'll ever be," he said.

"I'm so very sorry, Ms. Kensington, for my behavior this

morning," she said, and waited for him to repeat that line before she continued.

"I'm so very sorry, Ms. Kensington, for my behavior this morning. I was angry when you arrived, as I'd just fired the acting superintendent, who didn't take it well."

"Very good. I like the part you added on at the end. Nice sincerity touch too," she said, chuckling now, and then sighed. "Still not enough, though."

"No?"

"No. Maybe I can help you again," she asked, smiling.

"Okay," he said. She was very pretty, he thought, smiling along with her. And Stephen was right, she would be a really good distraction.

"You caught me at the end of a really bad week. I'm going through a divorce, and I was angry," she said.

"You caught me at the end of a really bad week. I'm going through a divorce—I'm at the start of it really—and my wife called just as you arrived. Between her call and the earlier firing, it has not been a good week for me," he said, sighing at the end and dropping his shoulders.

Going for dejected, she thought.

"Nice touch adding the sigh and the shoulders," she said, pushing away from the wall. She moved toward him then, one slow step at a time. "And...?"

"And I took—or tried to take—that anger out on you, for which I'm very, very, very sorry," he said, chuckling at the end.

"Much better. Thank you, and I accept your apology." She came to a stop in front of him, wishing for the second time today that she could be taller and not have to look up. It was hard to be a badass when you had to look up. "You're not the only one that's been in a divorce. My ex-husband did the same to me. Not the baby, but the cheating, so I've been where you are and I know how angry it can make you. I'm sorry you have to go through that."

Serious now, he thought as he met her gaze.

"Thank you," he said, serious now too. "So will you stop by the office tomorrow?"

"For?"

"I could use someone to run background checks for me. I have to hire someone to replace Summer, and I need the candidates looked into, checked out. Summer's told me that you're new to Austin, starting over, so I thought you might like the business. And you come highly recommended."

"Oh, I do, do I?" she said.

"You do. I *have* heard nothing but good things about your work from my sister, and from a friend of mine, a longtime friend, Stephen Stuart," he said.

"He's a nice guy, Stephen is. He's sent gobs of business my way and your sister has been helpful enough for five people, so you don't have to. I do appreciate the offer though," she said, staring up at him still.

"I'd like to help you if I can."

"Feelings of guilt? I understand. But it's not necessary," she said.

"I don't do things out of guilt. I really would like to help you if I can. Not because of our run-in this morning, but because you could have made this difficult and you didn't. Plus, you're in business with my sister, and we Novaks help each other and our friends. Summer would want us to get along."

It was quiet between them. A stare-off, he guessed, was what they were doing. Strong and no pushover, he surmised, as he'd thought this morning, and just like that his mind shifted back to Stephen and his words again. Yes, her, he could do. The nothing-serious rule would have to apply, but… "Stop by the office tomorrow?" he asked.

"I'll stop by Monday," she said, staring back at him, wondering at the look in his eyes, there at the end. If she didn't know better, she'd have thought sexual admiration… maybe even desire. "Anything else?" she asked.

"Nope," he said.

"We're good then?" she said, moving over to the front door. She turned back and found his eyes on her ass.

"It's impolite to stare," she said, the words tumbling out before she could stop them.

"Was that what I was doing?" he asked, chuckling. "Later, Ms. Kensington."

"Later then, Mr. Novak."

She stood by the door, watching him walk to his truck. She waved, then closed and locked the door. She was done for the day. And wasn't that interesting, she thought, walking back down the hall. She'd been putting dishes in the dishwasher when he'd arrived.

She'd surprised herself, 'cause she'd had every intention of being tough and hard-assed when she encountered him again, but after she walked into her office and found him standing there, looking good enough to do whatever he wanted to do, the same as he'd looked this morning, she'd changed her mind quite suddenly.

Plus, Summer was her friend, a very dear friend, now a business partner, and she could forgive her brother his anger for her. She'd been there too, that space where it's nothing but anger. She really did understand that, and he looked contrite, and interested, and *maybe…* she thought.

***

Henri made the right turn onto the street, leaving Clarke's home behind. If that could have gone any better, he thought, and yeah, if she was up for it, then so was he. He wasn't going to tell Stephen; he'd could do this on his own. His skills might be rusty, but they were still available if and when he needed them. He liked her physically, yes, but also the way she'd stood her ground, this morning and a few minutes ago.

He laughed at the apology she'd extracted from him. Did that combative, contentious spirit of hers carry into other areas of her life? One area in particular was really all he cared about. He sure hoped so.

***

Stephen found Reye, his wife, sitting on the couch, mindlessly rubbing her stomach, a habit she'd started recently. He smiled. He would be a father soon. One huge change. And they were planning a move to Dallas, which would be another one.

"Hey," he said from the front door, smiling at his wife. He didn't think he would ever grow tired of seeing her.

She smiled at her husband, leaning into the door, looking rumpled and sexy at the end of long day. She did so love this man.

"How was your day?" she asked, muting the TV's sound.

"Good. I had lunch with Henri," he said.

"Henri Novak? That Henri's in town? I thought his baby was due soon?"

"It was, except it's not his baby. He's filed for divorce."

"What?"

"That's the reason for the divorce. The baby's not his," Stephen said, and recounted the tale as told to him by Henri.

"That sucks," she said.

"Yep."

"That's too bad. And he's such a nice guy."

"He's not so nice anymore. Or maybe he will be after he gets past his anger."

"That might take a while, I bet. It would if it were me, if I loved her."

"Like you love me."

"Yes, however, you I'd kill, along with the mother of the child. I'd keep the baby for myself, I think," she said, smiling.

"This is going to sound terrible, but I'm glad, really. I never thought Karen was the one for him. Didn't expect it to last this long, and now he's free to try again. Doesn't have any ties to her, which is a good thing. Did I say that already?"

"Yes, you did. How long will he be here?" she asked.

"Don't know, two weeks or three. He's here on Novak Construction business. He's going to help his sister too, Summer, with her business."

"Summer's the one that wanted you to help her friend, the private eye."

"Investigator, and you've been watching too many TV shows. But that's her, Henri's baby sister, his only sister actually."

"What business?"

"Flipping houses," he said.

"He knows all about that."

"I was thinking about Clarke for him."

"Clarke? It's way too early to be thinking about him and anybody. Isn't it?"

"I hear you. Clarke's the private investigator. She and Henri got into an argument this morning, and I thought I saw something in his eye, just a flicker of interest, when he was telling me about her."

"And you're thinking what?"

"Maybe they'd be good together... for each other."

"Too soon? When did he file for divorce?" she said.

"This morning," he said, chuckling 'cause yes, it sounded crazy when he thought long about it.

"That's crazy."

"How about a hook-up then? They could, you know. It's not too early for sex. It's never too early for that," he said, chuckling again.

She laughed. "You know how crazy that sounds, right? Crazy, then. He filed for divorce this morning, and you paired him off at lunch."

"What's wrong with sex as a start? It worked for us."

"It worked for you."

"It worked for us," he said, smiling.

"Not easily it didn't," she said.

"But in the end... and that's all that counts," he said.

"Spoken like a dude, but yeah, in the end, I guess. You came to your senses," she said, smiling too.

"I know it sounds crazy, but... we'll see. Clarke seems like a nice woman, from all that I've heard. She was on the bad end of her marriage too, is coming out of a divorce, and like with Henri, her husband cheated on her. I heard that's the reason she's here, starting over in Austin. What would it hurt to see? I don't have to tell you the ways in which Henri's been there for me, always thought you were great for me, and I don't know, maybe he and... you never know."

She walked over to him and slid her arms around his waist.

"It's sweet, Stephen the matchmaker," she said, smiling. "It did turn out well for you." She put her lips to his.

"There are worse things. I want for him what I have," he said against her lips.

"He'd be a lucky man if he could," she said, smiling.

"Exactly," he said, putting his lips to hers again.

***

Friday evening

Clarke entered the glass door of Stuart, Weston, Drexler, and Jones in the early evening for another meet and greet with Stephen and more of his attorney friends. She had changed into something more professional: a black dress cinched at the waist, jewelry that worked with it, and some really nice black sandals she'd picked up a month ago. *You is smart, you is kind, you is important*, she thought, chuckling at the line from that movie *The Help*.

The first part of her day she'd spent tailing one Raymond Wilson, father to one Sirena Wilson, another of her Aunt Glenn's referrals. Sirena wanted her to check out her father, who she'd thought was long lost, but who had been living up in Waco for the last ten years, and not so long lost after all. She'd left there for a meeting, the second one with the Fergusons and their lovely daughter, discussing the final details of what was to be done with Baby Girl next Tuesday. Up to Oregon to one of those camps for kids was where Baby Girl was headed, and she would be at the Fergusons' home bright and early Tuesday morning to do the pick-up and delivering.

"Clarke Kensington to see Stephen Stuart," she said to the receptionist.

"I'll let him know you're here. You're welcome to have a seat. Can I get you anything to drink?" she asked.

"No, I'm fine, thanks," Clarke said, and took a seat on the

coach closest to her. She checked her watch. It was closing in on five fifty-five which was the time she had agreed to meet Stephen here. Then it was a short trip downstairs to the Basement to meet the other attorneys he'd rounded up for this meet and greet. He had already gone above and beyond as far as she was concerned.

Clarke's business was growing, and she had her friends and family to thank for it. She was proud of all she'd accomplished so far, was glad she'd taken pains with her reputation. Her decision to strive for excellence had paid huge dividends in the referrals and recommendations she'd received from old clients. Starting over wasn't easy, but it was going better than she'd expected. Her calendar was starting to fill up with cases, but she was not overwhelmed. She was done with the days of nothing but work.

"Hey, Clarke. Are you ready?" Stephen asked, coming to a stop in front of her. He was tall, dark-haired, handsome, and married. The ring on his finger she'd noticed right off. Mrs. Stuart was a lucky woman, she thought, not for the first time. Dressed in a suit and tie, the standard dress for most lawyers, he was a pull if ever there was one.

"I am. Thanks for meeting me, and setting all this up. You've done far more than I expected."

"No worries," he said, moving towards the door, allowing her to exit the office first. "So, I heard you ran into one of my good friends, Henri Novak," he said as they were moving toward the elevators.

"Summer's brother, and yes, I did."

"Summer," he said, and chuckled. "Used to bug the hell out of us growing up. Henri's a really good friend of mine. We grew up together in Dallas, down the street from each other, went to the same schools, even ended up at the university for college, fraternity, and graduate school. He went to the b-school while I went the law school route." He pushed the Down button. "He's a nice guy, just in a tough spot, at the beginning of a divorce."

"I know, I heard."

"I heard you and he didn't hit it off so well."

"That's true, but he has apologized. Stopped by my office yesterday evening, even asked me to continue working with him. Easy stuff, background checks, so really it's all good," she said.

"It's hard going through a divorce, as you well know," he said.

The elevator arrived, empty. He allowed her to enter first.

"I heard that too. Summer sort of let that slip. But as I said, it's good. I'm good."

"Great," Stephen said.

They stepped out of the elevator on the basement floor and made the short walk over to the bar. She liked it here, came often for the drinks and the band, but mostly for the solitude that could be only found among strangers.

She'd met a client here, an executive who was interested in what his wife was up to, was how she'd come to know of it. She'd stayed after the meeting, enjoyed the music and the ambience, and returned when she found herself downtown at the end of the day.

It was a man's space, small, intimate, and expensive. It could hold twenty to thirty people on a good day. Six-inch varied-colored wood planks covered the lower portion of the bar, and the same wood, but vertical, covered the walls. Smooth dark silver metal was the bar's surface as well as the surface for the round tables that were scattered about the rest of the bar's space. Benches, tall-backed and covered with plush chocolate-colored leather, served as seating.

The attorneys from Scott and White had arrived early too and were seated around one of the larger tables. She and Stephen made their way over. The other attorney invited from Stephen's firm was Rainey Hendrickson, who had yet to arrive. He handled the divorce cases, was a top divorce attorney in the state, spoken of by other attorneys almost reverently. She was the most eager to meet him.

She turned on her smile and got down to the business of getting to know them.

***

A productive hour all around, Clarke thought at the end of it. The time had passed effortlessly, spent talking, discussing her work and her reputation with the firms in Dallas. She felt good with the results, particularly when Rainey asked her to call his office tomorrow. He wanted her to get on his calendar.

The group began to break up. Everyone was going home.

"That ended faster than I thought," Stephen said, watching Rainey, the last of the attorneys, clear the door. He looked down at his watch. *Hell*, he thought, bummed that they had wrapped up so quickly. He'd invited Henri to join them, told him to be here by seven thirty, and it was barely seven. He hadn't told Henri Clarke would be here, or vice versa. He'd wanted to see their reactions to each other.

"It was productive. Thanks again for setting it up," Clarke said, watching him check his watch again.

"You're welcome again," he said, working on a way to get her to stay.

"Well, if that's it, I'll see you later. I'm going to stick around and listen to the band. I try to catch them when I can," she said.

"So you're into blues?" Stephen asked.

"I am," she said.

"Mind if I join you? I'm meeting my wife for dinner later. I'd thought I'd finish here with just enough time to get to the restaurant, but we've finished early. I could go back up and work, but not when I can listen to good music, right?" he asked.

"Sure. I was going to find a spot at the bar. Will that work?" she asked.

"Sure," he said, checking his watch once more. *Yes!* he thought, at how things worked out. And yes, he was going to take it as a sign that he was on the right path. He took the seat beside her, one that gave him a clear view of the entry.

"You're into the blues too?" she asked, settling on her bar stool.

"I'm pretty open to all kinds of music." He caught the bartender's gaze. "Let me," he said when the bartender stood before them.

"How's business?" he asked after they'd placed their drink orders. "Is it growing fast enough for you?" He kept moving his gaze between her and the door, listening enough to make comments as she talked about the trials associated with setting up one's shop in a new city, while monitoring the door for his friend. The bartender returned with their drinks.

He knew the exact time Henri arrived. He'd been watching Clarke as he talked, didn't want to miss out on her reaction to seeing his friend. He wanted confirmation that she was an interested party too. She reacted all right, nothing huge, a widening of her eyes. And interest, lots of interest, in the gaze pointed in the direction of the door. She caught herself, quickly turning her attention to the drink that sat in front of her. Stephen smiled inwardly and turned to the door for confirmation. Yep, it was as he thought it would be.

FOUR

Henri stood in the entry of the Basement, looking across the room at Stephen, whom he had expected to see, and Clarke, whom he had not. She was seated beside his friend with her head bent, listening to him talk, and she was lovely.

Pretty brown eyes that had flashed in anger yesterday, and later annoyance, had been softly staring at the bartender as his buddy talked, and then they'd softly met his gaze after he'd stepped into the doorway. There was interest in them for him, and desire, lots of it, he thought, as he held her gaze for a second, feeling other parts of his body respond to the look in her eyes.

It didn't take much really. Images of her had floated in and out of his mind since he'd left her home yesterday. Alone in bed, he had nothing but time to picture what she'd look like if she joined him there, the things they could do together.

Would she be agreeable? he thought. Maybe. If the look in her eyes tonight and yesterday meant what he thought it meant, then probably. It had been a while since he had approached a woman in this way, but not so long that he couldn't part a woman from her reluctance if he wanted to.

So hell yes to the two of them, commiserating over their divorces, her strength a match for his anger. As long as it didn't come with strings attached, or meeting Mom, or hell, even talking, he was up for it.

"Open seating," the maître d' said, interrupting his thoughts.

"Thanks," he said.

Clarke looked over in Henri's direction again, curiosity getting the better of her. It was hard not to, especially after she'd met his gaze a few minutes ago. That was interest she'd seen in his eyes, a desire for her. Not her the person, she thought, more for her the female form. That's what she thought she read in that serious blue gaze of his, the same one she'd caught staring at her ass yesterday. She was good with that too. She wasn't interested in him the person either. Him the male form she could work with.

He was moving towards them now, dressed in a dark suit, nice tie paired with a white shirt. Smooth stride. In charge and confident was the way he carried himself, the same as yesterday. *The same as always*, she suspected.

He slid onto the bar seat to the right of Stephen, making him the buffer between them.

"Hey," he said, first to Stephen and then looked past his buddy to her. "Hello."

"Hi," she said.

"Nice place. Thanks for the invite," Henri said, talking to Stephen this time.

"It is, and the band is even better, right, Clarke?" Stephen asked, leaning back in his chair so that the two of them could see each other.

"It is," Clarke said.

"You're here for the band too?" Henri asked.

"I am," she said.

Someone's cell beeped. Notification of an incoming text. Not hers and not Henri's, as he was flagging down the bartender. It was Stephen, looking down at his phone. "It's probably Reye," he said, standing up and moving away from them.

It was quiet as Henri ordered his drink, while she sipped on hers.

"A change of plans," Stephen said, returning a few minutes later, moving his gaze between the two of them. "Reye's not meeting me for dinner after all. She's not feeling up to it. You know how it is, first baby and all. I've got to get home instead." He met Henri's gaze.

"Right," Henri said, not even going to say the words "set up," which he was willing to bet this was.

"Clarke, would you stay and keep my boy here company? I feel bad, leaving him here after I invited him. It shouldn't be too hard on you, since you like the blues and all," Stephen said.

"I'm going to be here, and he can join me if he likes," she said, shooting a quick glance at Henri, whose gaze was on his buddy. She had no idea of the silent communication that passed between them. This was a set-up, she thought. Was Henri a part of it? 'Cause that would mean he wanted to see her again. Good to know that he was interested in her as she was in him.

"Okay then. I'm out. I'll tell Reye that you hope she feels better," Stephen said, smiling as he moved away. He had been watching Henri along with Clarke and made note of the interest he'd seen in Henri's gaze. Both of them were on the same page, he thought. A perfect match, even if it would be a while before the two of them realized it.

So what if it was only a primitive desire to mate? Was that so bad? He didn't think so. It was how he and Reye had started, and they were happily married now. No place he'd rather be than with her, bringing their first child into the world.

He looked back from the door and found their gazes on him. He waved before disappearing from view, hoping it would work out the way he thought it could.

"So was that a yes, you don't mind if I stay, or you do?"

"I don't mind either way," she said.

"That's a yes then?"

"It's a yes," she said, chuckling.

"Mind if I sit closer?" he asked, pointing to Stephen's now-vacant seat.

"Nope, not at all," she said, watching as he removed then folded his jacket, placing it neatly over the back of the barstool. He smelled as good as he looked was her next thought, as she leaned a little closer to take in his scent again. Yep, something spicy and sharp, and did she say he was fine? He was that, and expensively clothed, she thought, examining the quality material of his suit and shirt.

She took a sip from her drink, scotch neat, and continued to watch him from underneath lowered lashes. He was seated now, looking confident and calm in his skin. He must have been really difficult to live with for someone to take a pass on that body of his, she thought. Lean and muscular, nice ass, filling in the slacks, and nothing remotely hanging over the top.

"You good here?" Henri asked, pointing to her drink.

"I'm fine, thanks."

"So you come here often?" he asked.

"Not often, but when I do manage to get out, it's usually here. It's nice, and I like the music and quiet and being left alone. I like that I can have all three in the same place. You know?"

"I do," he said, checking out the room. Not so full of people that it felt crowded. Nice, good design and use of space, he thought, taking in the colors, the silver surface of the bar. Wood underneath, wood everywhere except for the dark carpet and the furniture. "It's nice here," he said.

"I like it," she said.

"How are they?" he asked, nodding his head in the direction of the stage. The bartender was back, placing Henri's drink in front of him.

"Good. The lead guitar is the best of the three, I think... the one with the most potential. Or maybe he's just my favorite," she said, smiling.

He took a sip from the dark liquid in the glass. Nice lips, Clarke thought, watching him admiringly.

"Did Stephen tell you I would be here tonight?" he asked, turning to face her again.

"No."

"He didn't tell me you'd be here either. It seems we've been set up."

"It's what I suspected too," she said.

"Do you have a problem with it?"

"I wouldn't have allowed you to sit if I did."

"I like that you're honest," he said, chuckling.

"I like that about me too," she said.

He laughed. *What a good idea this was*, he thought again, pulling him from his anger. "He and I go way back. He thinks he's looking out for me."

"Really? In what way?" she asked.

"You don't want to know," he said, and it was nothing but feeling her out.

Someone had dimmed the lights in preparation for the trio's play, he guessed, as three men were making their way over to the stage.

"I might. Try me," she said, and he turned his gaze to her once again. Okay, he was one compelling dude, or maybe it had just been awhile.

"He mentioned you as someone I should consider romantically *and* seriously," he said.

"It's kind of soon for that, don't you think? You've been separated for what? A minute?"

"Exactly," he said. She was lovely, he thought again, differently tonight, but the same sexy. She was the picture of elegance and he liked elegance, very appealing in a soft-looking black dress that played very well with her slim frame. The scent she wore, soft and slightly floral, fit in with the simplicity of her attire. "That's what I told him. I also told him I wasn't interested in serious or a relationship," he said, watching for her reaction.

"Really," she said.

"It's nothing against you specifically. It's that the thought of anything serious feels too constraining, confining… like a noose around my neck, and nothing I'm interested in."

"What are you interested in then?"

"Nothing that requires a commitment. It would have to be a no-strings, casual type of thing," he said, meeting her eyes.

She chuckled. "Which is a nice way of saying you're only about the sex, right? That's what you mean by no-strings, casual type of thing?"

"It is. Really, all I want is release, to get lost in…" he said, softly, staring into her eyes.

She couldn't move her eyes from his, intrigued by the way he'd said the word *release*. It had gotten the attention of her body. Or maybe it was his lips, the shape of them, made moist by his drink. Whatever it was, she found herself saying, "Well, believe it or not, I understand the desire for that. The need for the physical without the commitment, and believe it or not, we are in the same space."

"Are we?" he said, staring into her eyes, trying to gauge her. "Is that an invitation?"

"Do you want it to be?"

"I would," he said.

"Okay, it's an invitation. Any ideas as to when you'd like to take me up on my invite?" She smiled softly.

"When would you like?"

"Tonight works."

"I could do tonight," he said, chuckling at the speed in which they'd reached a conclusion.

The house lights were blinking, and the trio was taking the stage, putting a stop to their conversation for now. It was quiet as they sipped their drinks, watching as the band settled in, and pondering each other's words.

The lead guitar player ran his hands across the strings of his guitar now, and all talking ceased as the trio started into the first song. Clarke allowed herself one last glance in Henri's direction before she turned her attention to the stage.

They were good, Henri thought. He took a sip of his drink and looked over at Clarke, staring at the musicians, and he felt his body ease, a bit more pleased at the direction this night had taken. He was attracted to her, intrigued by her confidence and competent manner, but mostly he was interested in breaking up the very long dry spell that was his sex life. Since before the baby, when he and Karen were trying so hard to conceive, to a cold hard stop after she had. She hadn't wanted to while she carried the baby, and how had he agreed to that? He could feel the anger start to creep up. He blew out a breath and closed his eyes.

He let go again and lost himself into the soulful sounds coming from the stage, sounds of the guitar soothing over his anger and pain. And what was it about music that could touch the parts of you that needed it the most? It was the music he'd grown up listening to with his dad, an old-school blues lover, and he'd have to agree with Clarke, the lead guitar player was really good.

It was perfect, this sitting beside a woman in silence. When was the last time he'd done that? He glanced over at Clarke, who appeared to have been similarly lost in the sounds.

The next thirty minutes passed with each of them lost in their own thoughts and worlds for a while, watching the people, some dancing, a few clapping, but most doing nothing but taking in the music, soothing nerves frayed by life and living.

The lights came up sooner than he expected. Too soon, Henri thought, and the band was wrapping up their first set.

"The lead guitar player is very good," he said.

"Yep, told you," she said, and smiled, relaxed as well, brought on by the same things as Henri: good music, good company, and good drink, and pondering what came next too. She was glad he wasn't one of those men that talked too much, spent time telling you what they knew about blues and whatever, and less time listening. The quiet between them had been nice.

"So," he said, turning in his chair to face her.

"So," she said.

"This will only work if we want the same thing. Are you sure you don't want more than what I'm offering?" he asked.

"You make it sound like it will be more than once."

"If we work, why not? I'm going to be here for a while. Would you have a problem with more than once?"

"Nope. I use to enjoy sex until… Anyway," she said, letting the last of whatever she was going to say drop, fighting back her own anger, rising up just that quick, anger at not being enough for her husband. She blew out a breath, letting her anger fall away. "I'm fine with more than once, if tonight works. Good sex is all we desire. No sharing of what happened to us and to our marriages, no bringing up the past, no confiding, none of that."

"Fine with me. We don't even have to talk beyond hello and goodbye," he said, laughing.

He was a very handsome, approachable man when he laughed.

"And why are you divorcing?" she asked, staring into his eyes, captivated by this Henri and his hard-won smile, wondering who in their right mind would let him go. The words tumbled out before she could stop them, before she could remember that it wasn't just the smile and charm that made marriages work. It was the wrong thing to say. She realized it as soon as she said it, watching as his face did an abrupt change and he was back to serious. "I'm sorry. Forget I asked that. Don't know why I did, just... I don't know... just got lost in the moment, I guess—and after I made that speech about keeping the past in the past."

"It's okay," he said, but his smile was dimmer now.

"What about work? Will it interfere with my working with Novak Construction?" she asked.

"Not unless you allow it to," he said.

"I won't, and I don't plan to talk about it with your sister either," she said, a little more forcefully than she'd intended.

"Good. Neither do I."

"Where? Not at my place," she said, ready to get on with it.

"I don't have a place beside Summer's, and that's a no."

"How about a hotel then? We could either split the tab or take turns covering the cost, if we decide to do this more than once."

"Either way, or I could pick up the tab. I can afford it."

"Nope, it's either equal partners or no partners at all."

"Fine, we'll take turns covering the cost then," he said.

"One more thing," she said, waiting for his gaze to meet up with hers again.

"What?"

"I'm only into vanilla sex: no anal, no butt plugs, no ropes, ties, or strap-ons. I'm only into missionary—okay, not only that, but only things one can do without aids," she said, her voice lowered, but her eyes remained fixed on his. "You okay with that?"

"I am," he said, fighting back his smile. She was cute.

"Okay then," she said, chuckling at how crazy that had sounded. It didn't matter. She needed all the sexual cards on the table. A hard-earned lesson from her marriage. She pulled her phone from her purse and selected the app that would take her to nearby hotels.

"Two blocks over is a Hilton."

"We can walk."

"Let me make a reservation first," she said.

He sat and finished his drink as she made short work of booking them a room. "Where did that come from?" he asked, watching her fingers move over her phone.

"Where did what come from?"

"Vanilla sex and all the list of things you named that you don't do?"

"Left over from my ex, I guess. He used to like a lot of things that I didn't care for but did anyway, for him, of course. All that stuff about keeping the hubby happy at home, and I tried. He'd liked it, asked for it on the regular, so I tried to like it too. Loads of regret over all that twisting and turning myself into something he'd find appealing, and for what? But that's water under the bridge, and we're not bringing up our past, remember?"

"I do," he said, and nothing more.

And really, what else could he say to that? Clarke thought.

"Ready when you are," she said moments later, sliding her card toward the bartender.

Henri intercepted it before it reached the bartender and slid it back to her. He placed his on the bar and slid it over instead.

"Thanks. You don't have to," she said.

He shrugged and waited. They stood after he'd placed his card back into his wallet. He slid his arms into his suit jacket, shrugged it on and followed her over to the exit. They were on their way.

* * *

There was a back exit from the Basement, a set of stairs that led up to the street level. A door led to the flight of stairs, which Henri held open for her, following her out.

It was a quiet trip over, nothing beyond the sounds of her stiletto heels hitting the pavement and then the floor of the Hilton. He stood behind her as she checked them in, didn't bother correcting the attendant who assumed that they were married.

"How many keys?" the attendant asked.

"One," Clarke said, followed by "Thank you," as she accepted the key. They were moving toward the elevators that the attendant had so graciously pointed out to them. A few seconds more had them inside the elevator, riding up to the ninth floor.

"910," she said, handing him the key, which he smoothly slid into the front pocket of his slacks as they exited the elevators. The trip to the door was the same quiet as the trip over. She stepped aside, allowing him to unlock and open the door, before she entered first. Quiet were the two of them still as they entered, turning to face each other. She dropped her purse on the couch and started to undress.

She met his eyes, all challenge in her gaze. She was as he

expected, hoped she'd be. Not a word still, as she removed one foot from her shoe and then the other.

He reached for his tie, loosened it and pulled it away from his neck, and began to unbutton his shirt. His eyes never left hers as he stripped, and she did the same: first the dress, then two pieces of very pretty underwear, and then she was nude. He liked her figure, curvy and slim like he'd spent last night imagining, a nice handful of everything. Not a hint of fear did she show, which was way sexy. He loved women who knew their own minds.

She turned and walked over to the bed, and his gaze locked on her ass, small and round and—he couldn't wait, watching it move from side to side, as she drew close to the bed.

He stood and watched, removing his shirt, slacks, socks, and shoes. He continued to watch after she'd turned to face him while taking a seat on the edge of the bed. She scooted up to the middle. She lay back then, not completely flat, resting on her elbows instead. She crossed her legs at the ankles and looked him squarely in his eye.

He so wanted to smile, but didn't. He finished undressing while she watched him this time. He heard her soft intake of air and saw her eyes widen after he lost his underwear. Yeah, he used to get that all the time in the old days, before he married.

He moved toward her then, his eyes locked on hers still. His erection had done all the growing it was going to do. It was full, long as it could be, hard enough to hammer whatever, tight from months of going without and from following her body over to the bed.

"I should warn you that it's been a while for me," he said, standing at the foot of the bed, looking down at her.

"I hope so. Me too," she said. He reached for her ankles then, and pulled her to him, didn't stop until her hips were aligned with the edge of the bed. He placed her legs around his hips and looked down at her, a full scan of her body.

He leaned over her, settling his lips on hers, and slid his tongue into her mouth to meet hers. They played awhile, hands roaming over body parts while their tongues pushed and pulled at each other. One of his hands went to the back of her head to hold her as he deepened the kiss. He loved that she didn't back down, while the other hand went back to her breast, which was the right size and shape. He tugged at the nipple, and she moaned.

He was pulling away then, reaching for a condom from the many he'd tossed on the bed before he'd gotten lost in the warmth of her mouth. She watched, of course, back to resting on her elbows, as if she didn't have a care in the world.

"You sure?" he asked, when he was done.

"Are you sure?" she said, breathing faster now, and then she moaned, 'cause his finger had found her core, and he played for a while there too, wanting her wet, watching her eyelids drop in pleasure at the things his hand could do. He leaned over again, took her right breast into his mouth, bit a little hard around the nipple and felt her response in his hands. He moved over to do the same to her other one and received the same reward. She liked this, her hands cradling his head now to her breast.

"I want," she said.

"What?" he asked, moving his mouth up to hers, a hair's breadth from hers.

"You... this... now..." she said, and met his eyes while he replaced his hand with his erection, and it was one smooth thrust later and it was he that moaned this time.

"So good," he said at the feel of her legs wrapped so tightly around his hips, and at the way she so snugly held him within her body. "So good," he said again before sliding his tongue into her mouth, seeking the wet warmth that held his erection so softly below. He moaned at the pleasure. How he'd missed this.

She lifted her hips from the bed, encouraging him, meeting him thrust for hard thrust. She was just as eager and as needy as he. He pulled out and thrust in again, hard and then harder again, all smooth thrusts inside her warmth. Two bodies, moaning, panting, and writhing over the bed, lost in the moment, but pushing and driving each other toward climax.

"So good," she whispered this time against his mouth, as she slid her arms around his back to pull him closer, watched his chest touch hers. So many things she had missed or gone without, like the feel of a man's mouth, moving over hers. He had a great mouth too: sexy, plush enough, and he could kiss. Actually he could fuck *and* kiss, and the pleasure of having him do both at the same time was more than she expected.

"Harder," she whispered against his mouth. He moaned; his response, she guessed. He pulled his hips back and thrust in again, and then again, moving her up the bed toward the headboard, and all she could do was groan at the way he made her feel. And it was seconds later and she was coming. Dang that was fast, and it had been a long time for her too. He stopped for a second, allowing her time to come down from her high.

He started again, not much later, a relentless push inside her, hips pumping up a storm, and it wasn't long before she was coming again. He could feel the walls of her tightening around him, and he moaned at the pleasure of this. She met his eyes then, blue eyes staring into her eyes, with his hair damp from his exertions. And damn he was fine, she thought again, and she had no idea what his thoughts were. He was a million miles away, it seemed.

She moved her hand to stroke his face, a gesture of affection, no idea why she did that. He pulled his head away, before placing it instead into the crook of her neck. One of his hands was on her breast, tugging and pulling softly, and he was back to thrusting hard into her. Who knew what the hell was driving him, but whatever it was worked for her too.

She gave up and just held on after that, until he came, pushing hard into her body one last time, groaning as his climax rushed through him, and then it was quiet again.

He lay on her, inside her for a few seconds, luxuriating in the feel of her softness surrounding him. He was nowhere near ready to leave. He fell over onto his side eventually, one sated male, and looking forward to something for the first time in a very long time. Nothing but no strings, no anal, no butt plugs, just simple vanilla sex or some version of it. He smiled.

***

Stephen found Reye asleep on the couch when he arrived home. Curled up into a ball, as was her way these days; tired, dragging, eating and sleeping for two. He smiled at the picture she made. He sat beside her, not wanting to wake her. He did anyway.

"So, how did your plan work?" she asked, meeting his eyes.

"Good, a nice start, I think. I left them there, so who knows, but they are at least interested in each other. I could see that."

"Did they think it was a set-up?" she said, sitting up.

He sat down beside her, reached for her, and pulled her into his lap. "Probably… who cares," he said, and smiled.

"I hope it works," she said.

"Me too," he said.

***

He was pushing his hips upwards this next time. Pushing into the warmth of her again, she sitting above him with her legs straddling his hips. Riding him was really what she was doing. She was strong, he thought appreciatively. Her legs were, at any rate; they allowed her to lift and lower her hips in time to the upward and downward thrusts of his.

In and out, a steady thrust upward was this. Sometimes a hurried rush to who-knew-where minutes or seconds later would give over to slow, like now, when her hips did that slow grind over his.

She leaned forward, put her lips to his to kiss him again. She liked to kiss, he'd learned, and he did too. Long slow kisses, where they'd lose themselves for a while, and the lovemaking would slow to almost a crawl. She loved that he liked to touch, loved his hands on her breasts, squeezing them. She kept placing them there whenever they moved away, and that was fine with him. He loved the feel of them, loved to squeeze and pull; a way to release some of the pleasure coursing through his body.

Clarke ran her hands over him, and it was another thing he liked about her. She was a connoisseur of touching too, over any part of his body, as she was doing then, running her hands over his chest while her mouth touched his. He slid his erection into her warmth again and then again. It was too much, and it wasn't enough, all at the same time. And how had he grown accustomed to not having this in his life? The connection, the physical one that he thought he'd never be without?

This was such a good idea, the two of them, he thought, turning her over onto her back, impatient now. Five minutes turned into ten, and then fifteen, and he was coming and coming in hard... again. He moaned once, hips pumping into her, as his release rushed through him. He hoped he hadn't left her behind. He'd made sure the first couple of times, but this last one, he'd gotten lost and forgotten everything but the feel of this.

"Did you...?" he asked, looking down at her when he could think. She smiled, covered in the same amount of sweat as he.

"I did. That was amazing," she said.

"You don't even know how good that felt," he said, rolling over onto his back. He closed his eyes then, feeling more relaxed than he'd felt since he didn't know when. He would love nothing more than to lie there until morning.

But he wouldn't. He made his way to the bathroom, disposed of his condom, and moved to the sink. He turned on the water, washed his hands, and splashed some water on his face. He stared at his reflection, at the truth of what he'd been through, and the absence of so much in his life. This was only one small part of what he'd lost.

He sighed, banked whatever he felt, and started back to the bedroom. She was in the process of dressing, standing in her underwear, pulling on her dress now.

Good, he thought. They were on the same page.

"What?" she asked, holding her shoes in her hand.

"Nothing," he said, reaching for his underwear.

"You were worried?"

"A little... maybe. It's harder on women to do this, usually. They agree at first, but afterward..."

"Well, I'm good, so don't worry," she said, taller now as she slipped on one of her shoes, standing on one leg, meeting his gaze.

"Good," he said, smiling that small smile of his.

"Do you need me to walk you to your car?" she asked, sliding the other shoe onto her foot.

He laughed. "No, but where are you parked?"

"On the street, across from the Basement."

"If you don't mind, or if you aren't in a hurry, we could walk over together. But if not, I'm fine with that too," he said.

"I didn't want you to think you had to. That I needed hand holding."

"I can see that you don't," he said, chuckling. And yeah, he'd been surprised by her equanimity.

"Fine, I'll wait for you then," she said, watching him cover up a body she wanted to spend more time getting to know. They had been good together tonight and if he wanted to, she wouldn't mind doing it again, not that she would say so.

It wasn't long before they were leaving, the same quiet between them on the way down the elevators, then over to her car.

"I had a really good time tonight," she said, standing beside her car door.

"Me too," he said.

"Until next time then," she said.

"We'll text when either one of us want to again?" he asked.

"That works for me," she said, and slid behind her wheel of her jeep.

He turned away from her then, heading back toward the parking garage.

She pulled away from the curb, headed home, pleased with the way things had turned out, determined to enjoy the use of his body for as long as she could, for as long as he was here and willing.

FIVE

Saturday morning

Henri entered the Hancock Center gym early, here to play basketball with Stephen and to sign up for membership. It was busy, just as he remembered from his undergraduate and graduate years. He needed a gym for the time he'd be in town and this one would do just as well as the next. No, he didn't need the tour, he told the young woman at the front desk. He didn't need anything else, either. He was good. He had found the one to take care of those needs, someone more his age, and yes, he wanted more nights with Ms. Kensington.

The basketball courts were located upstairs. A quick sprint up and a walk down the hall and he found them. Three courts, side by side, all with games in play, while others like him stood waiting and watching along the side or from the bleachers. All waiting for who-goes-next. He spotted Stephen standing near the back door.

"You're early," Henri said, sliding up beside him.

"I'm scouting. I'm surprised to see you. Things didn't work out, I guess," Stephen said.

"I needed a membership so I came early to sign up for that. Things worked out fine."

"So you enjoyed your time at the Basement?"

"I did. It was better than I expected."

"Going back again?"

"I think so."

"That's good," Stephen said, watching the play on the court closest to them. The blue team was clearly in control of the game. "So did Clarke enjoy the Basement as well?"

Henri laughed. "I believe so… yes."

"So it worked out between you two… Everything worked out the way you wanted?"

"When did you turn into such an old lady, worrying about the kids?" Henri said, looking around the basketball court. "Set-up, right? Last night. That was you? Intentionally?"

"If it turned out well, then yes," Stephen said, chuckling.

Henri laughed, shaking his head. "Yes, for the last time. It's just sex though, for the both of us, so don't go planning or thinking it's more."

"I like Clarke," Stephen said.

"I like her too. Love that she doesn't talk, doesn't want anything from me," Henri added, before turning his gaze to Joe, who was approaching them now. "Hey," Henri said, smiling, catching Joe in a man hug.

"What are you doing here? I thought you were in Dallas," Joe said, smiling. He had nothing but fond memories of Henri. He and Henri had never had any problems. It had been all him and Stephen that hadn't got along, and even that had changed.

"Here on business, helping my dad and my sister with something," he said, not into sharing his personal life with anyone beyond a few. And he could tell from Joe's clear gaze, staring back at him, that he knew nothing of his troubles. "How's life treating you?"

"Good. Married, baby on the way."

"That's good, man," Henri said, smiling. He'd locked down his feelings, so none of what he felt at being surrounded by yet another happily married man with a baby on the way showed through. "How's your nephew? Is he with you still?"

"No, his mother, my sister, and her husband have him now. He's good, growing up fast."

A few other men walked up, and Stephen introduced them. Sam was African American, and Stephen's brother-in-law. "I don't know if you remember him, but he was the captain of the team that Reye played soccer for. I can't remember their name," Stephen said.

"I do," Henri said, fist bumping Sam's. "The Graduates."

"Good memory. How are you? Still playing soccer?" Sam asked.

"I wish."

"I know, loses its importance, given one's time constraints of work and all," Sam said.

"Yep," Henri said, moving his gaze to the last man, whom he didn't know but who turned out to be Walter, a friend and fellow attorney of Stephen's, who was also African American and tall.

The scoreboard gave off its sound, indicating the end of the game, and they were up next. They had five minutes to warm up, and then play would began.

Stephen stood behind, watching Henri fall in with everyone. He smiled again internally as he warmed up, looking over the other team as they prepared to play. If things could work out for him and Reye, they certainly could for Henri. Maybe there was a light at the end of his friend's tunnel. It was too soon, he knew, and so much could go south between now and then. If Clarke and Henri could get beyond their pasts, then maybe his friend could be happy with a woman who was more his equal, one that might love him. For some reason, Stephen was sure that woman could be Clarke.

The scoreboard gave its loud honk again, and he and Henri

and his other teammates walked out to the middle of the court. It was time to play ball.

***

Saturday morning

Summer pulled into Clarke's drive, on the lookout for signs of foul play. Something had to be up. How else to explain her friend's absence from their weekly Saturday morning sit-down, catch up-and-plan-next-week over tacos and coffee?

Clarke was either dead or sick. She had never not shown up. Hell, she was very seldom, if ever, late. Summer ruled out sickness as being the cause of her friend's absence. Clarke would have sent her a text or called. It had to be something serious, so she'd driven over here immediately.

They helped… looked out for each other, well before they joined forces in their new house-flipping business. High school had been their official start, but they kept in touch off and on over the years. Six weeks ago Clarke had moved to Austin and had called Summer to ask for help meeting people, making contacts. Of course Summer would help. She had called and harassed just about everyone she could think of who might need an investigator.

Clarke had returned the favor by encouraging her at first, then providing financial backing, which really went a long way in saying *I believe in you*. Summer adored Clarke, considered her more of a sister than friend. She parked beside Clarke's jeep, eyes peeled for blood or anything that might provide an explanation to her friend's disappearance on her way to the front door.

She knocked first, then placed her ear to the front door, listening for anything remotely like life. Nothing was going on inside that she could hear. The sign on the door was turned to its *Closed* side, another thing that was unusual.

Summer unlocked the door, using the key Clarke had given her. The front room was empty. It was dark inside, and quiet, but nothing beyond that. No sounds of music or the TV. She made her way down the hall, quietly, until she stood outside of Clarke's bedroom door.

"Clarke?" Summer said, quietly, tentatively, opening the bedroom door. It was dark in here too, though not dark enough that she couldn't see the bundle of something in the middle of the bed covered up by a comforter.

"Clarke!" she shouted into the room, and that worked. Clarke shot up like a top, stumbling out of the bed, looking wild with hair in a tuff on her head.

"Summer? What?" she said, looking around before facing her. "What time is it? Did I oversleep?" She moved to the nightstand to retrieve her phone.

"Must have," Summer said smiling, happy to see her friend in a state of unkemptness, one that she didn't see often enough.

"Oh, crap, I missed our breakfast meeting?"

"Yep," Summer said, all smiles and good cheer.

"What are you smiling about?" Clarke said, moving to turn on the light.

"I don't get to see you this way often. Seeing you unprepared to tackle whatever. It's nice to know you're human."

"I am, very much so. I was out late, and clearly tired… slept like the dead," Clarke said, stretching her arms above her head.

"Work. I know. You have to take it easy sometimes. My brother could give you a few tips on that. Away from his wife, and he was late getting home last night. Not that I blame him. I'm happy for him actually. He could use some mindless screwing with a nameless, faceless woman for a while, you know? Just like in the old days," Summer said.

"Right," Clarke said, doing an excellent job of keeping her expression neutral.

"He apologized to you, didn't he?"

"He did," Clarke said, moving towards her bathroom door.

"That's good at least. You know, he's pretty good, I hear."

"Who's pretty good?"

"My brother," Summer said.

"Pretty good at what?"

"In the bedroom, you know. I've heard stories."

"Really," Clarke said, hoping she sounded uninterested, but yes, she could vouch for the good part.

"Yes, and you know, if you're looking for a... you know, someone to kick it with, he's here, and I could mention you... put in a good word or two," Summer said.

"Oh, that's okay, I'm good here on my own," Clarke said, fighting back her laughter.

"Really, like who?" Summer asked.

"Nobody."

"That's what I thought. You have to get back up on that horse at some point."

"Oh, really?"

"Yes, really. Just think about it, and if you change your mind, all you have to do is say the word."

"Thanks, I think," Clarke said.

"Good. Now, I'll leave you to get dressed while I put on some coffee and grab those tacos I brought along just in case you weren't dead," Summer said, smiling.

"Thanks," Clarke said, standing in the doorway, watching Summer leave. Easy, breezy Summer. She thought of her friend's nickname, shaking her head at the queerness of it all. She was nameless and faceless. She'd never been called that before. She chuckled again, closing the door to her bathroom. She had a day to start.

***

It was late Saturday night before Henri saw his sister again. She found him with his feet up on her coffee table, beer in hand, several empty ones on the table next to his feet, a pizza box not far from his beer bottles, and the television turned to some game.

"Making yourself at home, I see."

"Per your request," he said, smiling back at her.

"How was your day?"

"Good," he said, watching her as she kicked off her shoes and dropped her purse on the table by the door. She had Clarke's penchant for the same high-heeled footwear, which was surprising given his sister's height. Good to know she was comfortable in her tall skin.

"Any more beer left?" she asked.

"Yes, and bring me another one when you come back," he said, and just like that, she was the little sister again, doing her brother's bidding. "Thanks," he said, taking the beer bottle from her hand as she stepped over his legs, which were still propped up on the table in front of him, and took a seat beside him on the couch. It was silent as they watched the game.

"I saw Clarke today," she said.

"I imagine you see her often. You two are business partners, after all," he said. It went back to being quiet.

"I'm a Spurs fan," she said. They were one of the teams moving around on the screen.

"That's good to know."

"So… are you going out tonight?"

"I don't know. I might. Why?"

"I could go with you if you want me to, if you want company."

"I'm okay, but thanks for the offer," he said, chuckling.

"Just looking out for you," she said.

"I know. I appreciate it."

"I know of someone else that might be willing to go out with you," she said.

"Oh, yeah? Who?"

"Clarke."

"Really," he said, going for noncommittal.

"I know you two got off to a bad start, but she's not seeing anyone."

"It's too soon for me," he said.

"But not for nameless and faceless?"

"For who? What?" he said.

"You, out last night, didn't come home until two."

"Okay, Mom, let me just stop you here. Do I need to find a place of my own? It's only three weeks, but I can if I need to," he said.

"No, not at all. I don't mind, I'm not judging. What I wanted to say, or was working up to say, was that Clarke is not that different from you: recently divorced, likes sex… in need of sex. Instead of nameless-faceless, you could…"

"Does she know you're doing this pimping-her-out thing?" he asked, chuckling.

"Of course not, and I'm not pimping her out. She's just alone, and so are you, both out of bad marriages. I just thought she and you could… And I've heard about you. And why not her? I mean, she deserves some good… and since you're here and while you're here, I just thought… But if that's not something you're interested in, and I can see by your expression that it's not," she said, her words tapering off to silence.

"So, while I think your intentions are good, sort of, this thing you're doing here, this wanting to help your friend and I connect, it's not necessary. I'm fine on my own, as I'm sure she is *and* it's way too soon for anything besides nameless and faceless for me. Okay? So, no more of whatever this is that you're doing," he said.

"Okay then. No more help from me," she said.

"Thanks."

"You're welcome. However, let me say one last thing on this subject. Clarke is a really nice woman, and I was just trying to help you both, that's all," she said.

"I'm sure she appreciates your concern, as do I, but no."

"Okay, then," she said, setting her beer on the table. "My work here is done, and since I hate sports, and I'm tired from looking at houses, I'll leave you to the man set-up you have here."

"I thought you liked the Spurs."

"Not really. I was only making small talk. Good night."

"Good night," he said, chuckling, thinking through his and Summer's conversation, smiling, 'cause she had not changed one bit. Pushing her friends on him, not for the first time, and it was probably something he should be prepared for as he started into being a single man again.

Clarke Kensington. He mouthed her name, and his thoughts moved back to last night. They had been some kind of hot together. Just right, like they'd been at it a while. Simpatico, at least as far as sex was concerned. He'd enjoyed his time with her, was pleased that it had not been demanding in any way. It had left him surprisingly in a much better mood.

He wondered at first about her list of what she didn't do, not that it bothered him. He didn't do them either. There was nothing like good old-fashioned sex for those who hadn't had it in a while.

His phone rang, interrupting his thoughts. It was Karen. So much for thinking she'd honor his request and not call him. He sat back in his chair, placed his phone on the table, and sighed, letting whatever she wanted roll over to voice mail. Another beer would be nice, or something equally relaxing, to take his mind off his wife. The thought of her and, just like that, he was reaching for his phone again and pulling up Clarke's contact information, mentally constructing his text.

What to say that didn't sound like the booty call this was? He looked at his screen for a second, searching for how to put this, decided on a simple question mark, and he'd see how she'd respond.

***

Finding the answers you need was part of the mission statement for Secure Investigations, the official name for Clarke's private investigative company. Most people thought PI work was all about ferreting out the dirt, which it was, but it was also about providing peace of mind for her clients.

That's what tonight was about. She was here at the request of the ex-fiancé of one Sarah Greentree. Sarah was currently the lead singer of the band performing on stage tonight and Clarke was here to document her activities.

Two years ago, Sarah had been in love with and engaged to be married to a kid who had backed out of the wedding at the last minute. The kid was Clarke's client, and he left behind a very distraught and mentally fragile Sarah. It had taken her the better part of a year spent in a psychiatric hospital to pull it all back in.

There was more to it, like stalking and attempts to take her life, but all that notwithstanding, she was on stage today, a survivor.

She had re-enrolled in college and from all accounts was back on track, headed in a good direction again, able to put that dark episode in her life behind her.

Sarah hadn't been the only person affected by her nervous breakdown. The young man—the ex-fiancé—had suffered as well. He'd moved to another state and was engaged again but before he moved on, he wanted closure and peace of mind from knowing that Sarah had survived. He didn't want to talk to her or have her back in his life. He only wanted assurances that she'd moved on with her life.

After tonight, Clarke would be able to give him those assurances. Tonight was the final proof, to go along with the other information she'd accumulated, the culmination of a month's worth of work. She had scheduled a meeting with him next week to hand over her findings.

Her phone gave off its familiar beep, indicating an incoming text. It was from Henri. Okay, she was a little surprised. He'd contacted her sooner than she'd expected. She was not sure what she had expected, but the following night hadn't been it. Not that she minded. She looked at the question mark again. A man of few words, Henri was, in all things it seemed. Her response was a question mark of her own.

The Wesleyn was the next text she received. She recognized the place, although she hadn't been there before. A small boutique hotel, it was; an expensive one, located in the middle of town. She knew its reputation. It was more than she could afford, but it was his turn to pay, so who really cared.

Okay was her response. He'd leave a key for her at the desk. She smiled again, at what had been added to her calendar this evening. She'd spent way too much time thinking about last night than was probably good. But wow. And it was nice to not have to worry about all the other stuff that her ex used to want.

It was a welcome change from not having to force herself to relax, or fake excitement about someone sticking something into a body part that had been doing just fine on its own all these years. It was for some, she got that, as were so many other things that were sex these days. Slapping, choking, whipping; no meant yes, and it was cool for someone to ignore your wishes, and of course it wasn't considered rape like it used to be in the old days. But whatever, she just wasn't interested in any of it.

Thankfully, with Henri it had been only one tool that fit into one place and that was nice. Just good plain sex, something she could do easily.

He was good for her, good for her bruised ego, a push-back against all the negativity she'd heard about her sexual abilities over the course of her marriage, which was the reason for her ex's proliferation of toys; at least that's what he told her was his reason.

Henri seemed to like the things she did, and while she wasn't what one would call hugely creative, his eyes had widened at some of her moves, and admiration was always a good thing to receive.

She checked her watch, and yeah, she could do tonight, wanted to do tonight. One final text of a thumbs-up emoji of agreement from her, and they were good to go. She sat back in her chair, checked her watch, and yeah, she was excited.

She looked back at the stage, at a now-dancing Sarah, and she smiled, pleased at this young woman's resilience. Maybe there was hope for her. Maybe. For now, she was content to take comfort in the lean, hard body of one Henri Novak and the perfect way to end this day.

***

Eleven was when she was done. She handed her keys off to the valet. Room 612 was the number to her room, where she'd find her husband, the receptionist said, after giving her the quick head-to-toe once-over.

Swank, Clarke thought of the furnishings, observing the place as she made her way over to the elevators and took them up to the sixth floor, debating with herself the entire ride up. Should she let him know she was here or just surprise him? Settling on surprise, she slid her key into the lock and opened the door.

He was seated on the couch, casual in jeans and a t-shirt, legs propped on the table in front of him, relaxing with a drink of some type in his hand. She could feast on this one for a year or two and not get her fill.

The TV was on, turned to ESPN. He was a sports guy. Which was probably good to know if they were long-term. Since they weren't, who cared?

He looked up, didn't smile, which was cool; she wasn't in a smiling mood either. He sat and watched her, taking that not-talking agreement seriously. They hadn't talked much the first time, and as far as she was concerned, it wasn't necessary this time either. She scanned the room, not surprised that it matched up to the rest of this designer place.

She stopped in front of him, unbuttoned her jeans, and slid them down her legs, which took a little bit of pushing, as her preferences ran to snug-fitting clothing. He watched with nothing but his eyes, and the heat of them gave her all the information she needed. He so liked what he saw, and how nice to be prized. She pulled her shirt over her head, unhooked her bra, lost her under-wear, and walked her nude self over to him.

So very different was this sexual relationship than that with her husband, she thought again. Bold with Henri, and she'd never been bold before. That was another thing she lost with the divorce. No more quiet, simpering flower for the new Clarke.

He didn't move, just continued to watch her as she reached for the button of his jeans. Her face was near his. She could hear his breathing as she unzipped his jeans, pulling the sides open. She shot a glance at his face, waiting to see what impact this had on him. His eyes were closed and his mouth was slightly parted. She ran her hand over him then, and smiled at how nice he felt underneath her hand, how smooth and hard he was. She leaned in and kissed him, feeling in control, moving her mouth softly over his. Nothing hurried in that, just two people slowly meeting each other's needs.

She pulled away, not sure when, and watched as he set aside the glass of whatever he'd been drinking and muted the TV. Nothing but the sound of their breathing could be heard now.

She pulled his erection free, settling the condom he left out on the table over it. She met his eyes then, smiled at the heat in them, before she straddled his legs and slowly impaled herself on his body. She met his eyes again. He was staring intently at her, and he was so with her, feeling the same good as she.

She started moving then, up and down, slowly to the tip of him, and then down. His breathing had changed, and he was kissing her neck and then moving down to her breast, taking one into his mouth, as she moved up and down his erection.

His hands were on the seat beside him now, she noticed, content to let her do the work for the both of them, which was fine. Just as long as he stayed in this one spot, the spot that made her body one puddle of goo, she was good, sliding up and then down him again.

They stayed like that for a while, with her in control, setting the pace, moving them steadily toward climax. He was with her; she could feel it in the coiled muscle underneath her hand, the one that was holding back until she was ready, and she moaned at how good he felt. It would be soon, she thought, moving up and down, with his hands by his side still, not so relaxed as before, but gripping the sofa now. She found his mouth again, and she could taste his urgency there too, in the forceful movements of his tongue, pushing hers around.

Up and down, and she was moving faster, her feet on the couch on either side of his legs, using her legs to lift and lower herself, faster and faster still, closing in on her climax, her arms tightly wrapped around his neck, her faced burrowed into it as well, as she came down hard onto his lap and let go, her climax running through her. He wasn't far behind. His hands were at her waist then, holding her still, and he laid his head on her chest and closed his eyes. It was a bit before their breathing returned to normal.

Eventually he leaned back, looking at the back of her head, still tucked into his shoulder. She looked up then, met his eyes, and gave him a smile which he returned. A small one, but whatever, she thought. He turned her face to his and kissed her softly this time.

He sat back into the sofa after that and held her for a few, content again. How long they remained that way, he wasn't sure, but eventually he stood, wrapped her legs around him, and walked them over to the bed, where he laid her down. It wasn't until then that his erection slipped from her body.

He walked over to the restroom. A few minutes later, she heard the toilet flush, and he was back. She watched this time, as he'd done earlier to her, watched as he lost his tennis shoes, then his jeans and shirt, and finally his underwear. He sat at the edge of the bed and pulled her over to straddle his legs again, and it was different this time. He was in charge and the pace he set was anything but soft. It was all hard thrusts into her. His hands were on her shoulders as he pushed her down to take him in, and then pushed her down again. He fell back on the bed and pulled her forward, his hands at her hips moving her up and down his erection. His eyes were closed, and she wanted them open, to see the heat that was visible, especially when he was just about to…

"So good," she whispered against his mouth, before she took his bottom lip in between her teeth and bit down. He moaned, and what a sweet sound that was.

His eyes opened and he smiled, not a pleasant one, before he flipped her over onto her back and then she just held on. It was all she could do—that and moan, as he thrust into her again, and he didn't stop until he was coming, later, bringing her along with him again.

SIX

Sunday afternoon

Clarke had spent the better part of her morning sleeping off another night of activities. The best kind, she thought; two like-minded people going at it like it would be the last time they could. It was a first for her, sex as recreation and not just something to be endured.

It was up and at 'em by eleven. She'd showered, gotten dressed, and it was a what-to-do-with-the-rest-of-her-day decision to make. She had a meeting in Waco that evening, but until then she was free. She didn't get many free days, so yes to the couch, parked in front of the TV, catching up on the shows she'd recorded.

The doorbell rang, interrupting her plan. It was Summer, Clarke thought. On a Sunday it usually wasn't anyone else. *Surprise.* It was her parents, Sandra and Dwayne Kensington, standing on her door's threshold. Yes, she'd held on to her maiden name during her marriage, and good, 'cause she didn't have to change it afterward.

"Good morning, daughter," Sandra said, smiling back at her. "Since you refuse to come to Dallas anymore, even though it's where your parents reside, and you are their only daughter too, we'd thought we'd bring Sunday dinner to you." Of course, her father stood behind her mother, hands laden with containers of food, delicious from the smells silently steaming from whatever her mom had prepared. What could she do but smile and let them inside?

***

Clarke sat across the table from her dad in her kitchen later on that afternoon, watching him start into his second slice of her mom's famous German chocolate cake. He loved that cake, slightly more than he loved his wife, he'd say sometimes when he wanted to tease. They were done eating the main course. It hadn't taken too long to heat everything up and plow through her mother's pork chops and gravy, rice, and peas. Clarke was stuffed, and unlike her dad, the thought of trying to eat one more thing made her want to weep.

Her mother stood at the sink, repacking things into the containers she brought with her. "You look good. A little on the skinny side," she said, eyeing her from her position beside the kitchen sink. Immaculate in dress and grooming, five feet on a good day, slim and curvy was her mother and it all had passed on to her daughter. She wore her sixty-seven years well, Clarke thought, admiring her mother as she moved about her kitchen, in her heels of course. That was the other thing Clarke had inherited: her mother's sense of fashion, and particularly her penchant for tall-heeled shoes. Or maybe it had nothing to do with fashion, and all to do with being born short.

"Have you checked into Amber's disappearance? Aunt Veda called me again," Sandra asked, glancing at her daughter over her shoulder.

"No, not yet," Clarke said. Aunt Veda was Amber's mother.

"You know they are depending on you."

"I know."

"Have you talked to Aunt Glenn at least?"

"First thing tomorrow morning." Aunt Glenn was Veda's and her mother's aunt, and Clarke's great-aunt.

"They need help, baby. I know that child has run away... left before, but Aunt Veda thinks this time is different."

"I'll check into it tomorrow," Clarke said, and she meant it. Yes, she'd had been putting it off, thinking Amber would show up eventually, and she still might, but she'd check into it anyway.

"Do you know how many African American women go missing every year?" Sandra asked.

"I do," Clarke said, trying not to roll her eyes.

"Then you know how important it is that we use all the resources at our disposal. We have to look out for ourselves. Finding our lost children and women is not at the top of anybody's list. I know Veda and Aunt Glenn would appreciate whatever help you give."

"Tomorrow, I promise," Clarke said.

"Well, I'll put my money on you every time. You'll find her if she is to be found," her mother said, patting Clarke on the shoulder. "How's the rest of your work, your life?"

"Good."

"I wish we could see you more," Sandra said, moving on to the next topic.

"I know."

"You sure you want to continue to live here? You had such a good business in Dallas, and so many friends there. You could come back, live at the house with us. You know we wouldn't mind. And speaking of your business, how are things?"

"Good. I've been busy. It's not easy to start over."

"All the more reason to come home," Sandra said.

"I can't. I like it here, plus Summer and I have that new business we've started."

"How is that, by the way, your and Summer's business?" Sandra asked, wearing her I'm-not-sure-about-all-of-this expression. Clarke had grown up with it.

"Good. We're—rather, she is looking for our first house to tackle."

"If you're sure. She seems mighty flighty to me."

"She's fine, as am I," Clarke said. And she was not going to get angry or irritated by her mother's comments, she told herself.

"I guess she has all that Novak money to fall back on. She's probably been doing that all her life, I imagine, falling back on her family's money."

"I wouldn't know. I like her, Mom. We'll be fine."

"If you're sure."

"I am."

"So, have you met any nice men?" Sandra asked. On to the next subject.

"It's too soon and, again, I've been too busy with work and all to look," Clarke said. And no, she didn't think her mother would consider what she and Henri had agreed to a good thing. Too old-school was her mom, who was of the "sex was designed for marriage" opinion. But it was her life, Clarke thought. Sex with whomever she wanted was nobody's business but hers. The new Clarke had grown up alot after her marriage. The new Clarke made decisions for herself and lived with the consequences.

"You could make time," Sandra said, interrupting her thoughts.

"That's true, but I don't want to," Clarke said.

"Leave the girl alone," her father said, taking a sip of his coffee, finally done with the cake. Not a crumb or smear of icing to be found on his plate. Talk about licking the platter clean. "Yes, leave the girl alone. I'd rather her be alone than to bring home another one like the first one she had," he said.

"Thanks, Daddy," Clarke said, smiling.

"Don't mention it, baby," he said, giving her a fist bump followed by a fluttering of their fingers. He'd come up with that handshake all by himself. Hell no, was he not hip. "Did I tell you I saw that no-good piece of you-know-what that you were married to last week? Had the nerve to stop me for driving too fast."

"Did he?"

"No, *he* didn't. The rookie he was riding with stopped me for speeding. You know I don't speed. He sat in the passenger seat and watched. If I were twenty years younger, I'd have pulled his ass from his car and given him the ass kicking he so deserved. I'd handcuff myself afterward, so he and his whipped ass could take me to jail."

"You be careful, Daddy."

"I will. I got this new pamphlet from the NAACP. Baby, give her one," Dwayne said, pointing to his wife.

"It's in my purse," she said, leaving the room and returning with something blue and white. She slid it across the table to Clarke.

"We carry them with us, to hand out at church to the kids. Tells them what to do if they're stopped by the police," he said, looking at her mother. "It's a nice pamphlet, lots of information, but I don't know if kids nowadays read anything that's not on their phones. Every time I see a young person, they're all hunched over the phone." He chuckled. "You take your time, the right man will find his way to you," he said, his gaze on her mother.

"You think so?" Clarke asked.

"I know so, and we can do without one if we have to. As much as I hate to say it, that may be your life."

"Dwayne," Sandra said, cautioning him.

"Just listen, 'cause this is important," he said, putting his hand up. "I love you, baby, you know that and I know you want to be married. I know it, I understand, but, baby, it's all for nothing if you get your hands on the wrong one. You can see that now, can't you? Life's too short to be saddled with nonsense. You see that now, too?"

"Yes, sir, I can," Clarke said.

"I'd rather see you alone than with something like what you had the first time around. You understand me?"

"Yes, Daddy, I do," she said, meeting her father's eyes. He was giving her his I-mean-business look. She'd grown up with that too.

"I think you should open your heart to them all. I didn't always think that," he added, after seeing her eyes go big. "Life is changing, and we have to change with it. You understand?"

"Yes, Daddy, I think I do," she said and smiled, moving her eyes to her mother, who was shaking her head.

"Alright, baby, we'd better go," her father said, standing. "Leave you with some time. Who knows, you might have a gentlemen caller you want to invite over. Feed him some of your mother's leftovers. If that doesn't bring him around, nothing will." He was standing beside her mother now, with his arm around her waist.

"Call when you get home, don't forget, or else I'll worry," Clarke said, repeating what she heard from them forever. She followed them to the front door, stood watching as they settled into their car and pulled away. She had to be somewhere, and she better get going if she was going to make it on time.

***

Later on that evening

Clarke stood outside the gas station, filling up her car. Another thirty minutes and she would be at the outskirts of Austin, Texas, baby, home from a follow-up trip to *We. Ain't. Coming. Out*, a.k.a. Waco, Texas. She'd driven up to meet with a fellow private investigator whom she'd hired early this week to provide surveillance on one Rayford a.k.a. Raymond Wilson.

Private investigators were known for partnering with others to fill in the gaps, spaces that she couldn't get to. Shaun was her go-to person in Waco, and so far, it looked like Rayford was a con man with a gambling addiction.

Her phone rang. It was Summer, she noted before answering.

"Okay, good news," Summer said, diving into the conversation feet first, which was her usual way.

"Hey," Clarke said.

"Haha, hey, sorry, but I'm so excited. I found our first house, or rather it found me," she said, and squealed into the phone. "So exciting. Such good news! I ran into Silvia Owens. You don't know her, but anyway, her aunt passed two months ago, leaving her with an incredible property. Property she wants to sell. Tomorrow we're meeting at seven to see the house. Are you free?"

"I think so. I'll have to check to be sure. Who's we?"

"Me, you, oh, and before I forget, I need to call your uncle Hamp, our first contractor. I just love your uncle. He's included in the we, along with my brother, if he agrees, and before you go getting irritated, Henri has loads of experience. We might as well use him while he's here."

That was her plan, Clarke thought, smiling to herself.

"You're okay with him, right? He apologized to you, right?" Summer asked.

"Yes, again, he did," Clarke said.

"I keep forgetting. He's really a nice guy. You two have so much in common. I hate that you're both coming out of bad divorces... marriages. Timing sucks, huh?"

"I guess," Clarke said.

"Anyway, see you tomorrow, at seven. I'll text you the address. Let me know if you can't, if something comes up, but please try."

"I will," Clarke said.

"Got to go call the others. Where are you, anyway?"

"Coming back from Waco."

"Yuck. Okay, see you later," Summer said, and disconnected.

Clarke set the gas thing back into its pump and slid behind the wheel of her jeep. It didn't take a whole lot apparently, just the mention of Henri's name, and her mind went back almost immediately to last night, and the night before. *And why not again?* she thought.

She could use a little something to work out some of her excess energy. Did she need an excuse, beyond the fact that she wanted to? *No* was her answer. She reached for her phone, her decision made. A question mark was her text, the same as he'd sent her.

What part of town r u in? was his response, and quick too. She wasn't the only one in need apparently.

North of Austin, returning from Waco, thirty minutes out.

Meet me at the Hamilton on Sixth, I'm heading over now.

It's my hotel turn.

Next time. Check front desk for key.

Fine, she thought. If he didn't mind paying, she didn't mind that he paid, 'cause according to her mother, the Novaks had plenty of money and he could well afford it, divorce or not. She smiled, 'cause he seemed to like doing this as much as she, which was good to know.

She pulled onto her not-so-favorite Interstate 35. It was one of many major highways that ran between Austin and Waco. Really it started way down south, in Laredo, Texas, and meandered its way up through six states, ending in Minnesota. The stretch between Austin and Waco seemed to be in a perpetual state of repair, which was the reason for its slow movement today.

She sped up, in a little bit of a hurry to be somewhere.

***

Another day, another evening in front of the TV, Summer thought, entering the living room to find her brother seated on the couch again. T-shirt and shorts, and smelly from some pick-up soccer game he'd found going on at the park down the street from her home. She'd been working in the kitchen, on her computer, poring over houses, making phone calls and such.

Gatorade this time, instead of beer, sat on the table, but the same feet were on the table in front of her couch, and instead of basketball, he was watching a soccer game.

"You smell," she said, taking the seat beside him. He lifted an arm and smelled it. "Yep," he said, chuckling at doing something he'd done growing up.

"Gross," she said, feeling like the ten she used to be when he'd do that just to annoy her.

"Not going out tonight?" she asked.

"We're not going to do this every evening, are we?" he asked.

"Whoever it is tires you out. You weren't up when I left this morning and you usually are. You sure this nameless, faceless person is good for you?"

"Sorry, Mom. I'm not having this conversation with you again," he said.

It was quiet after that. Summer looked over at him later, found him staring at the TV. This was going to be harder than she thought, this getting him together with Clarke.

"We could go to a movie after you take a shower. I could invite a friend to go with us."

"Let me guess. Clarke is the friend you have in mind."

"You want her to go too?" Summer asked, smiling with a hopeful expression on her face.

"No, I'm good here," he said, chuckling. "Quit worrying about me. I can take care of myself."

"If you change your mind about Clarke, all you have to do is tell me. It's a standing offer."

"Good to know," he said.

"I've found our first house. Can you join us tomorrow for a walk-through?"

"Us?"

"Me, Clarke, and Clarke's uncle Hamp—he's going to be the contractor—and you."

"What time?"

"In the evening, seven."

"I can't promise anything," he said, standing up.

"If you want to continue living here, you will," she said, smiling the smile of hers that promised retribution. "Where are you going?" He was moving toward the front door.

"Out, Mom," he said.

"But you smell," she said.

"See you later." He grabbed his keys from the table near the door. No need to tell her that he kept a gym bag in the car and the place he was headed to had a shower.

"Good night," she said.

"Good night," he said, disappearing through the door.

She heard his truck start up. Her plans to get him with Clarke weren't progressing at all. There was always tomorrow, she thought, nowhere near ready to throw in the towel.

***

Clarke picked up the key from the front desk of the Hotel Hamilton —another hotel she'd never stepped foot in before, mostly because it was also out of her price range. Not out of her taste level, just the price range. Mr. Novak appreciated the finer things, just as he'd said. She headed up to room 720.

The room was empty when she entered, nothing except a bag —his, she guessed—on the floor near the bed. She sat her bag beside it. The shower was running. If she could hear it, he was in it, and since she could use a shower too, she stripped quickly. Naked, she walked into the bathroom, taking in the style of the hotel room, adding it to her "tasteful elegance" assessment of the hotel lobby.

Nice-sized shower, with seating, surrounded by clear glass. His back was turned to her and he was leaning into back wall, moving the small washcloth over his body, apparently still unaware of her arrival. Which was cool. She could take a moment to look. Gorgeous any day of the week was he; lean muscle visible from the top of his shoulders down to his calves, which were attached to some very nice feet.

Must be time to rinse, as he'd dropped the washcloth and was leaning into the back wall again, letting the water rain down. His head was bent forward, so the water mostly landed on his shoulders.

He reached for the soap. No, it wasn't soap, some kind of oil, she guessed, but really it was hard to see through the steam. The dispenser for whatever he was filling his hand with was off to his right side, on the wall. He took a handful of something golden before turning to face her as if he'd known she had been standing there all this time. He moved toward her, over to the side of the shower enclosure away from the water, the side closest to where she stood, staring at him. He was hard to look away from, with his gaze staring so hotly into hers, and his hair wet and falling into his eyes with so much heat in them. It was hell to look away, but she did, 'cause his hand with the oil, and yes, it was that, was moving down his chest, continuing on downward, past his stomach, and then down to his penis.

She could see it now, lying limp against his thigh. Not that it stayed that way for long, not after he'd captured it in his hand. He slid his hand up to the tip of it, and then down. He did it again and then again, and all she could do was stare, a little spellbound by him, the strong lean lines of him, his legs opened slightly, his upper body leaning into the glass wall in front of him. The other hand was splayed against the upper wall; for support, she guessed.

She didn't watch that part of him for too long, too drawn to what his other hand was up to, watching his erection grow and his face change, a reflection of the pleasure he must be feeling. He closed his eyes then, and damn he was fine, and damn this was a good idea, this spending time with him in this way. And up and down his hand moved and she couldn't look away. He opened his eyes again. Piercing was the gaze that latched onto hers as he continued to watch her watch him.

Henri smiled internally at Clarke, nude and very nice, standing there watching him with so much want in her eyes. Not that it mattered; not that she could see him watching her, as her gaze was fixed on another part of his anatomy.

He moved his hand up his erection and then down once more, and she was moving toward the shower now like her body had a mind of its own, her eyes still glued to his hand. He held the shower door open for her and she entered, finally meeting those pretty eyes of his, half-open, and his breath caught at the pleasure that came from the last stroke of his hand, upward.

"I was wondering if you were ever going to join me," he said.

"That was for me?" she asked.

"Yep," he said, pulling her toward him, settling her into the space between his body and the wall, before he lifted her. Her legs went immediately around his waist. "You want?" he asked, moving until her back hit the wall, using his hands to spread her legs wide, and then sliding his erection up to rest at the entrance to her body.

"I want," she said, meeting his heat-filled eyes. She moaned as he entered her then, smoothly and slowly, and thanks to his earlier performance, she was so ready. "Oh, I brought you a present," she said, having the presence of mind to remember this one thing that they needed to do before they started. She opened her hand. A condom sat in the center of her palm, one of the many she'd found lying on the bed.

He smiled that small smile of his and leaned away from her— his upper body did anyway—allowing her just enough space to place the condom over his erection. When she was done, he pulled his hips back and thrust up into her, less patient than before. He was so ready, all of that watching her watch him earlier, with so much desire and need in her eyes, had grown his erection as far as was possible.

Yes, he thought, pulling his hips back and pushing back into her, watching his erection enter her, then disappear again and then again. He looked up then, wanting to see her expression. She was some kind of sexy with her hair wet, falling into her eyes, mouth parted so the little sounds she made as he pushed into her could escape as they did just now, 'cause he had pushed in again, hard, and then harder. Using one hand, he pushed her hair clear, 'cause he wanted to see the pleasure at what he did reflected on her face. He watched her, her face changing as he pushed into her again and then again, so very much in the moment with him, her gaze a balm to his spirit that he hadn't realized he needed.

He took her lips then in a scorching kiss, pushed his tongue through to mate with hers, as his hips continued to drive in and out, and in and out again, and it was a while before he felt the first stirring of her climax, the faint quiver of her body around his erection, that he knew now was a sign that it would be soon for her.

He increased the speed of his thrusts then, using his forearms on the wall to hold her in place as he pumped and pumped into her. And yes, he was coming too, quicker than he wanted or had expected to. And damn, it was up and up and up and then he was groaning into her mouth, as he hadn't released his grip on that part of her yet, putting all the pleasure he felt into his kiss, as his climax rolled through his body.

He could stay here forever was his first coherent thought when he could think again. It felt so good to be here that he didn't immediately move, just continued to hold her in front of him with her legs wrapped around his waist, held against the wall by the strength of his body. He pushed her hair away from her face again to kiss her once more, slowly this time, and it was a minute or two before he pulled away.

"Thank you for meeting me on such short notice," she whispered against his mouth.

"You're most welcome," he said softly, chuckling softly, before he took her lips in another kiss, another slow one, thoughtful-like. "More?" he asked.

"Yes, please," she said, leaning into kiss him again.

SEVEN

Monday morning

Clarke stepped into the hallway of the restaurant owned by her great-aunt Glenn, better known as Mrs. Drake of Drake's Cafeteria fame. She'd arrived just in time for breakfast. Mrs. Drake's wasn't famous in any huge way; more it was a place for lovers of soul food. In the morning it was grits and red-eye gravy, biscuits, ham, and pancakes, all you can eat for the low price of $5.99.

Clarke wasn't much of a breakfast eater, but could be if called upon, as she would probably be this morning. No way around it, not for her aunt, a product of a generation where feeding you was a form of demonstrating one's love.

Clarke stuck her head into her aunt's office while simultaneously knocking on the door. Her aunt was seated at her desk, perched over her computer, with her eyeglasses suspended on the end of her nose.

"Well, look who's here. Come on in, baby," she said, waving Clarke inside. "Let me look at you." She sat back in her chair, running her eyes over her great-niece. She made that harrumphing sound at the end of her perusal. "Are you getting enough to eat? You're getting mighty tiny. Come on out here, and let me get you a plate. You need some meat on those bones. My sister would turn over in her grave if she knew I let her grandbaby starve.

"You're not still pining over that man, are you?" she added, as she stood and reached for her walker.

"No, ma'am, just busy working," Clarke said, stepping aside, not ever going to ask if her aunt required assistance. She'd learned the last two times she'd been here it was better to get out of the way and follow her aunt wherever she had determined she needed to go.

"Of course you are. Men—and I'm sorry for all you went through with your ex. Don't worry, baby, he wasn't for you. Something special is just around the corner, you mark my words. A healthy man who can give you some healthy babies."

Clarke smiled. She doubted that. Not the current man; he wasn't interested in settling down either, too angry and hurt to be of much use to anyone, not that she would tell him that. Their relationship was not about the talking. He was the same as she had been... was, hurt and angry.

It took a good five minutes for them to get from the back office to the front of the cafeteria. Nothing fancy, just a small restaurant that held about ten tables and a few booths near the front window, all decked out in colored tablecloths. "Go on, baby, get yourself a plate and tell me what has you so tied up that you don't have time to eat a decent meal."

Clarke could argue, but again, to what end? She was raised by that generation that respected elders, so no way would she do anything to hurt her Aunt Glenn's feelings.

One bowl of grits and ham later, she and her aunt were seated at the table in the corner of the cafeteria. Her aunt had taken the seat with her back to the wall, *the better to see the goings-on* was what she'd said.

"So how's the digging-into-other-people's-business coming along?"

"Good," Clarke said, chuckling.

"Is the pay good, too?"

"Good enough," she said, after she was done chewing her first spoonful of grits.

"Good, aren't they?" Aunt Glenn asked, smiling and pointing to Clarke's plate.

"Yes, ma'am, they are."

"You stop by anytime you're hungry. Your mother tells me you're into building houses, too. Got your Uncle Hamp working with you, I heard. He was one of the best before he and gambling became good friends."

"Yes, ma'am, but it's more being a silent partner, to a friend that wants to flip houses. Hamp is helping us, as we—or at least I —know next to nothing about houses."

"Is that so?" Aunt Glenn said, eyeing Clarke like she could see through to her soul. "Like on those TV shows?"

"Yes, ma'am."

"You going have someone following you around with a camera?"

"No, ma'am, we're not."

"You tired of the private eye business?"

"Not really, or yes and no. I'm good at it, but…"

"Hard on a marriage and having babies and all."

"It can be," Clarke said, before taking another spoonful of grits.

"Well, whatever makes you happy makes me happy," Aunt Glenn said.

"Thanks," Clarke said.

"How did things go with Sirena? Are you able to help her?"

"Yes, ma'am. Working on it now."

"Good. So now, about your cousin Veda's baby girl, Amber, and her baby that's missing. Did your mother tell you this?"

"Yes, ma'am."

"Well, we thought she was just angry. You know how mothers and daughters can be to each other sometimes. She and Veda have argued before, so this isn't the first time she's walked off, but usually she's back by now, and Veda's worried, as I would be," Aunt Glenn said, shaking her head like the whole weight of the world rested on her shoulders and she was tired.

"Just had the baby about three weeks ago. I drove over the hospital to see it. A cute little thing, with a head full of straight hair. It's too straight, if you ask me, and that baby is too bright to be his. Have you seen that boy D'Angelo?"

"No, not yet."

"Well, I have, and he don't look like the baby to me."

"He doesn't?" Clarke asked, cutting into her ham.

"No, he doesn't. Wish I knew what to do. Veda is beside herself with worry, calls me every day."

"Has she gone to the police?"

"Yes, but what's another black woman missing to them?" Aunt Glenn said. You couldn't tell it by looking at her aunt, but there was a lot of fight-the-power still left in her bones. "I told Veda you'd be happy to help her. Told her you would stop by her house soon, as in today. Can you get by there?"

"Yes, ma'am," she said, but her aunt was looking past her now, toward the register, where a homeless man stood arguing with the cashier.

"Lord, Lord, but these are trying times," Aunt Glenn said, reaching for her walker. She pulled herself to her feet, eyes trained at the cashier and the homeless man. "You stay here, baby. I don't want you getting hurt." Clarke did as she was told. She watched her aunt, feeling confident that Aunt Glenn was formidable enough to take on anyone, as she had done so many times before. A few minutes later her aunt was headed back towards her.

"It will be a cold day in you-know-what when I can't handle my business," Aunt Glenn said, and that was that. "I'll tell Veda that you'll be stopping by today?"

"I have one stop to make and then I'm on my way out there," Clarke said.

"Good. Thank you, baby. Now, you keep me informed, you hear?" Aunt Glenn said, stopping in her trek to the back to point a bony finger at Clarke.

"Yes, ma'am, I will, and thank you for sending me Sirena," Clarke said.

"Another child with men trouble. You're welcome," Aunt Glenn said, moving again.

Clarke turned her attention to finishing her meal. She had been hungry after all, even went back for one of her aunt's famous biscuits. Ten minutes later and she was leaving, waving to her aunt in her office on her way out.

***

Clarke parked outside Novak's construction office again, only this time she was here at the request of Henri Novak from when he had stopped by her house Thursday evening, and that seemed like a lifetime ago. A lot had happened in three days—or rather much had happened in the three nights since she'd been here. In the daytime, without sex between them, how would that work? Professionally, she hoped. It was the way she'd decided to proceed and she hoped he could do the same.

He was on the phone with his back turned away from the door

when she entered the office, and from the sound of his voice, he was unhappy with whomever he was talking to. He turned at the sound of the door closing. Nope, not a happy camper was he, she thought. It was déjà vu all over again. He didn't smile either—back to the angry-eyes guy—and if he was happy to see her, he kept it to himself.

She moved towards the conference table this time, taking the lead in the seating arrangement decision. She pulled out her laptop, opened it, logged in, and pulled out the folder that held the information Summer had requested on Willis Wilson when she'd suspected him of stealing. She had meant to give it to Henri on the house, as an example of her work.

"Thanks," Henri said into the phone at the end of his conversation. Another problem Willis had left behind for him to fix.

Clarke had her back to him, professionally dressed in dark blue slacks and a matching jacket—and heels, of course. He turned his phone to its "do not disturb" setting, as he tried to limit the interruptions that went on in his meetings. He prided himself on giving whomever he was engaged with at the time his complete attention.

"Good morning," he said, moving over to join her.

"Good morning," she said, watching as he took the chair opposite her.

"Okay then," she said to the man of few words. She handed him a folder. "This is the information regarding Willis Wilson that your sister requested. It's an example of my work. He wasn't a good pick-up, but Summer was in a hurry."

"So it has been explained to me by Summer and now again by you. I understand," he said.

"Would you like me go over it with you?" she asked.

"No," he said, taking the folder from her hand and placing it on the table in front of him. "So, tell me about your company." He sat back in his chair, relaxed and calm, the anger from earlier no longer visible on his face.

"Sure. Secure Investigations is the name of my company. I moved to Austin about six weeks ago. The agency I left in Dallas was a much larger operation than I want to have here. In Dallas I worked with a partner, and we spent the last five years helping to grow a one-person agency into one that employed about fifteen when I left. Our team of licensed investigators had about fifty years' experience combined. We were one of the premier, most reliable firms in Dallas. They still are."

"I know. I checked. You left that all behind because of your divorce?"

"Yes, to start new, and it's not just the divorce. The other firm had grown a little too big for me, and there were others that wanted it large, who were happy to buy me out. Here it's just me and hopefully small again," she said, and smiled.

She was pretty, he thought again, and serious about her business. He could tell by the way she packaged her work. The portfolio was uniquely hers, the detailed professional, he thought, tuning back into the rest of her spiel.

"We perform the standard private investigative services: domestic investigation, surveillance, cheating spouses, child custody, background checks. We have an outstanding reputation in working with attorneys in custody cases, a particular interest of mine. I hope to have the same success in that area in Austin. All of the investigations are customized to meet our clients' wishes. It's whatever methods or techniques are necessary to secure information for our customers. Most of my business so far has been background checks, skip tracing, attorneys searching for people. It's how most firms start. I've done just about all there is to do, and

I'm equipped to take a wide range of cases. My hourly rate is ninety and I ask for a retainer for cases over 300 hours," she said, handing him another brochure with her card inside.

"Thank you. All I'll need are background checks of businesses and people, that sort of thing," he said.

"Once again, you don't have to do this," she said.

"Do what?"

"Business with me. I know your family's company has its own in-house human resources department. You don't need me to run background checks for you."

"That's true, but I'm asking you anyway," he said, meeting her eyes.

She stared at him for a bit, not really sure what he was thinking. She couldn't tell, which was so very different from at night, when she knew how he felt at any given moment.

"My goal is to have a new superintendent in place and in charge by the end of next week, if I'm able. I plan to interview starting today, and next week if I have to," he said.

"That's ambitious," she said, reading annoyance and I'm-done-having-that-discussion, and that was fine with her. It wasn't like she couldn't use the business.

"I'd like to pass along the first set of names to you by the end of this week. I'd like to have the results returned to me by next Monday. Is that possible?"

"Of course," she said.

"Good," he said, watching her. "I misjudged you, and once again I'd like to say I'm sorry for that." He began scanning the portfolio she'd given him earlier.

"It's okay. Apology accepted, again."

"Very thorough… is your work," he said at the end of his perusal of Willis Wilson's background check, before setting the folder aside. There was most of what he knew in her results, and a few things he hadn't known.

"I try to be," she said.

"Thanks for coming in," he said, rising from his chair.

"No problem," she said, pulling her things together. "Thanks for the meeting and for giving me business."

"You're welcome," he said, standing up, moving back to his desk. He was looking through his phone while she packed up. She cleared her throat to get his attention. She was ready to leave.

"I'll see you tonight?" she said.

"Sure," he said, his eyes changing a little bit, the first sign of any kind that he was aware of what they did at night.

"I meant at the house. Summer said you're helping us? You and your knowledge of construction are helping us."

"That's true, I am."

"How do you explain your late nights?"

"To whom?"

"Summer?"

"I don't," he said.

"She keeps bringing you up as someone for me to meet, hang out with."

"She does the same with me."

"I told her I wasn't interested in that, in you."

"I told her the same."

"Okay then, afterward if you want? It's my choice of hotels, though, this time. I'm not going to let you pay for them all," she said.

"Tonight then, and okay, your hotel choice," he said.

"Until then."

"Yep," he said, watching her leave.

That had been harder than he'd thought it would be, keeping

his mind on business with the images of her nude body floating around in his head. An inspired idea, was the two of them at night. He picked up his phone and hit the button to return the first of several missed calls.

***

Noon, and she was finally headed out to her Aunt Veda's. It had taken her forty minutes to get out here, to the small town of Yolly, known far and wide for their speed traps. She'd had to go slow, bemoaning those old and antiquated methods of funding the city coffers—tickets and speed traps. There had to be some other way for small jurisdictions to raise revenue than handing out tickets.

Yolly had started out as a farming community, or maybe even just a very large farm surrounded by smaller farms. Anyhow, after the death of the main farm's owners in 1978, the children sold half of the land, including the old homestead, to a developer who built a golf course first and then parceled out the remaining land into smaller plots for homes that flanked it.

The small farms sold out too, and the town grew itself into a small city. It was incorporated in 1988, and what was once was no longer. It was a now a nice city, with a range of neighborhoods. Expensive and stately to the north—the golf course neighborhood. The business district was at the heart and the center of the city, and to the south was the middle class. The poorer people lived out in the country, which was where her Aunt Veda lived, and where Clarke stood, outside, ringing the doorbell.

"Who is it?" Aunt Veda said from the other side of the door.

"It's me, Clarke, Sandra's daughter. Aunt Glenn sent me."

"Oh, yes, Colombo," Aunt Veda said, opening the door wearing a housecoat and a smile.

Clarke chuckled. Such an old joke was that. "Yes, ma'am," she said, scooting past her aunt.

Her aunt's home hadn't changed a bit from the many trips out here she had made with her parents. Clean and neat and spare was the inside of her aunt's home, Clarke thought, passing the living room with its sofa, chair, and coffee table holding it down. It smelled of Pine-Sol cleaning fluid and Old English furniture polish. Worn wood flooring, a single hallway that led from the front door to the back, one long wall on the left, with all the rooms on the right. There was a small table by the door that held a vase of flowers and a Bible. Jesus, with his white skin, blue eyes, long-flowing-blond-hair self, looked down upon them from his perch on the wall above the table.

"Let's go outside. It's a beautiful day and I'm feeling blessed, and Lord knows I need the blessings," Aunt Veda said, moving down the hall. Her aunt, while usually pleasant to look at, today was tired. Aunt Glenn and Clarke's grandmother had set the tone of what women in this family should be, and it was by no means tired.

Tough and built to last were the women on her mother's side of the family. Tall, as were most of the women in this family, linebacker size, square blocks of women—all but her mother, who had been the baby and the runt of the litter, a trait she'd passed on to Clarke.

She followed her aunt down the hall, headed to the backyard. They passed the kitchen, two bedrooms—her aunt's and Amber's —and the bathroom, and went out through the back door. Her aunt took the back steps slowly, before leading Clarke over to a picnic table sitting off to the left of the yard. A old majestic pecan tree was their canopy.

Aunt Veda was known for her gift with plants, and proof of it lay in the flowerbeds that surrounded her home.

"Thank you for coming," Aunt Veda said, settling herself at the table across from Clarke.

"It's no trouble," Clarke said, joining her aunt, pulling out her notebook. "How long has she been missing?" she asked, getting down to business.

"It'll be two weeks tomorrow," Veda said, meeting Clarke's eyes.

"Is this the first time she's gone missing?"

"No, she comes and goes as she pleases, stays with her friends up in Austin sometimes. She usually calls me. That's how I know something's wrong. No matter how mad she gets, she wouldn't go this long without calling me. That's what's different. That's why I'm worried so. We argued; that's why she left. I asked her who was the baby's father, and she lied. Told me it was that D'Angelo from high school, but that wasn't true. You could look at the baby and tell it wasn't true. But she wouldn't say different," Veda said, meeting her eyes again.

"How old is the baby?" Clarke asked.

"Four weeks tomorrow. He was a beautiful thing. She named him Samuel," Veda said, moving her gaze away from Clarke's and out into her yard. "She had only been home a day after the hospital and then she was off, dragging that new baby all over hell and back. What kind of way is that to raise a child?"

"So she was here a day after the baby was born?" Clarke asked, working to keep her aunt on topic.

"Yes."

"Any idea where she'd been?"

"No. With one of her girlfriends, Bria maybe. She doesn't tell me much, you know. I liked Bria, so I didn't mind her staying with her."

"Who do you think is the father? If not D'Angelo?"

"I don't know. Up until the baby was born I thought him, and she never said different. Amber was a sweet girl, but she had a mind of her own, you know?"

"Yes, ma'am, I do."

"D'Angelo lives in Pflugerville. She met him at a football game last year, her senior year of high school, and they'd been dating, if you call it that, but he's not the father, regardless of what she says."

"Have you spoken to police?"

"Yes," she said, back to looking around the yard. "Last Monday. I drove into town and filed a report. I couldn't reach her on the phone, and I could always contact her. Sometimes she could be slow to answer my call, but usually she'd answer, or call me back once she calmed down.

"She left here mad, with a suitcase and all the baby's stuff. Left walking, and that was two weeks ago. I just knew I should have heard from her by now, you know, after she cooled down, but she hasn't called. So I called, and it does nothing but go to her voice mail," she said, meeting Clarke's eyes again, tears in hers this time. "Where could she be? I've called anybody I could think of and nobody's seen her."

"Which friends?" Clarke asked, writing down everything her aunt told her, including the boyfriend's info. "Does she have a computer? Is she on Facebook, any other social media?"

"I don't know. She took everything with her," Aunt Veda said, tears running down her cheek now, unchecked. "Do you think you can find her?" Veda placed her hand over Clarke's. "She's all I have. The police, I don't think I can count on them. This is Yolly, after all. A black woman missing is nothing to get up in arms about. I know you know that."

"Yes, ma'am, I do. All I can tell you is that I will do my best, do everything in my power to find her. She's family. Could I get the cop's information from you?" Clarke said, standing up.

"Yes, it's all inside. I keep all my important business in my dresser drawer," Aunt Veda said, moving toward the house now.

"Will you show me her room?" Clarke said, following her aunt inside and over to Amber's room.

"This is it. Nothing much as you can see. She took everything," Veda said.

They were standing outside of Amber's room. It was clean, free of anything personal, Clarke thought, moving around it, from the closet, the bed, and the nightstands. It was as her aunt said; she'd left nothing behind.

"I may have to go through it again. If I need to, I'll let you know. If you can think of anything else, call me."

"I will. I appreciate you looking into this for me," Veda said, moving slow, as if everything was too much for her to bear.

A few more minutes of taking down notes and telephone numbers from the card the police officer had given Veda and Clarke was backing out of the drive. Not sure what she could do, but she'd do her best.

EIGHT

Monday

It was a single-story home in a good neighborhood. Not bad, Henri thought of the exterior view of Summer and Clarke's potential home choice. He aimed his truck toward the curb in front of it, a spot directly behind Clarke's jeep. He could see the back of her head, facing downward, a phone to her ear, and her mouth moving. She looked up and met his gaze through her rear view mirror. There was a brief meeting of eyes, heat-filled and so quick, staring at each other. When would that end, stop, or lose its appeal? He had no answers to that, and no desire to stop, either. Sexually they worked, which was all either of them wanted. Her gaze moved away, returning to whatever she'd been doing before he arrived.

Henri returned his attention to the house, checking out the homes on either side of it. The best thing about this property was its proximity to the university, and that meant inner city. He wasn't sure what the asking price for it was, but he knew it would be expensive in Austin for that reason alone. Things were so much more expensive than when he and Stephen had lived here.

He and Stephen used to have a condo not far from here. Stephen's mother had purchased it for her boy. Lots of good memories of his time spent there. Easy time. No commitments. It had been nothing beyond school and women. What he wouldn't give to go back to that time and start over and choose differently.

He could not, however much he wished for a do-over. He wouldn't get it, *so get on with it*, he told himself.

He stepped out of his car and moved down the sidewalk, shooting a glance over to Clarke's jeep once again as he walked past. She was still on the phone.

Summer's car was parked in the drive—a baby-blue convertible, a gift from their parents for finally finishing college, an event that required a major celebration. She was early for once, which was another indication that perhaps she was taking this house flipping business seriously. He couldn't remember the last time Summer had showed up anywhere on time, let alone early. She'd been late to his wedding. As she was a member of the wedding party, that hadn't gone over well with Karen, and their relationship had never recovered.

There was a truck parked alongside his sister's car. Must belong to the man standing beside her, talking. He was an older man, African American, with dark brown colored skin. He must be Clarke's uncle that Summer had mentioned. Salt and pepper hair covered his head in a small afro and he had noticeable-sized sideburns straight out of the seventies. He and Summer had their backs turned to the street, unaware, it seemed, of his and Clarke's arrival. Their faces were turned upward toward the roof. Clarke's uncle was pointing to something up on the roof, and Summer was nodding her head to whatever he was saying.

"Hello," he said when he reached them.

"Hey there," Summer said, and smiled. She and the man beside her turned to face him. "You and Clarke are both here. That's wonderful. Of course, Clarke's working." She pointed to Clarke's jeep, where she sat, talking still. "So, let me introduce you to Hamp." Summer reached for her brother's wrist, pulling him closer.

"Hamp, this is my brother, Henri. He is here to help us if we need him. He grew up in the construction business with me, although he paid more attention than I did," Summer said, chuckling, watching as the two of them shook hands. "It's commercial construction that he works in, but I thought he could still help us."

"Nice to meet you," Henri said.

"Likewise," Hamp said.

"Hamp used to be a contractor in Austin, had his own company building houses. He's not building much these days, but he still keeps up with the changes. Right, Hamp?" Summer said, smiling and meeting his gaze.

"That's the truth. The devil's a liar. Got to tell the truth always. That's what I told my niece, Clarke. Have you met my niece?" he asked.

"I have," Henri said.

"Her momma and my wife are sisters. It was her that called me, asked me if I would help the two of them, and here Hamp is. Hamp don't work for just anybody. I tried to tell them," he pointed to Summer and then Clarke, in the car, "that Hamp's not into construction, not like he used to be. Hamp liked gambling and the craps table a little too much when he was young. Got himself into trouble. Lost his business. So Hamp mostly does odd jobs, and helps out when he can. I'd told my niece, just like I told this one standing here. The devil's a liar. Got to tell the truth always," he said, with a huge smile on his face. "Hamp don't mind helping, but Hamp don't want to be in charge." His gaze was on Henri as he talked.

"Here comes my niece." He pointed to Clarke, who was getting out of her car now. "This one over there is some kind of hard-headed, like her mother and her grandmother before, slow to take no for an answer. You know what I mean. She says to me,

'Oh, Hamp, you can do this.' That's what she told me. It's family, is what Hamp thinks. What can you do? You have to help 'em if you can, that's what you have to do. That's what's Hamp gone do," Hamp said, done with his spiel, hands raised in the air to accentuate his feeling of helplessness.

"Hey, Unc," Clarke said, smiling, moving over to give him a quick hug.

"Hey, Short Short," Hamp said, looking at Henri. "That's what we call her growing up. Short Short on account of she's so short, like her momma, the runt in the family. Her momma's a runt too." Hamp smiled at his niece, clearly pleased with her, and then he smiled at Summer. Done talking, Henri guessed.

It was his sister's turn to talk, Henri thought, watching it all, not sure where this was headed, with Summer and Hamp paired up. Hopefully Clarke would be the sound one, the grounding force, remembering Stephen's description of her.

"Now that everyone's here, we can start. There is something I'd like to say before we get started. No pressure, of course, as Clarke and I have to agree to whatever house we choose. But," she said, pausing for a second, "this is my favorite house. It's also the one that has the most problems, as you will see when you get inside. "But," she said again, "it also means we can really make it special. We can make a lot of money. I just wanted to say that before we got started."

"Okay," Clarke said, and smiled.

"Oh, and one more thing. It's owned by a good friend of mine, inherited from her aunt. It needs a lot of work, as the aunt was a bit of a hoarder. Not over the top, like those shows on TV, but more than normal."

"Asking price?" Henri asked.

"Three hundred thousand," Summer said.

"Three hundred thousand?" Clarke said, choking a little.

"You good with that?" Henri asked, his gaze on Summer.

"Um, yes," Summer said.

"How many homes are we looking at in addition to this one?" Henri asked, ignoring the tentativeness of his sister's answer.

"Two. This is the first of three," she said, moving her gaze around the circle they'd formed. "Okay, so what do we think of the outside?"

"Needs work," Henri said.

"Hamp thinks the same thing. Needs some yard work for sure, the front porch leans a little to the left. Needs paint, bricks could use some cleaning, there's a few missing. But mostly Hamp's worried about the roof. It looks a little janky. What you say?" he asked, his gaze focused on Henri's.

"What about the roof?" Clarke asked.

"The roof, the roof, the roof is on fire," Summer sang, chuckling at the end. "Remember our party days, Clarke? Too much fun, huh?"

"Yep," Clarke said, chuckling too.

"It's what way?" Henri asked, looking at the roof now, ignoring the two women.

"It looks thick, like maybe there is more than one of them. You can only have two before you need to start over, and Hamp thinks there might be four. I'll grab the ladder and take a look at it." Hamp moved quickly toward his truck.

Spry, lanky, and skinny was Hamp, Henri thought, watching him shimmy up the ladder. He was peeling back shingles a few minutes later.

"Yep, it's like Hamp thought, too many roofs up here," Hamp said.

"Is that supposed to mean something?" Clarke asked, looking

at the roof still, studiously avoiding stealing glances at Henri, which was what she really wanted to do. He was compelling, at least to her, in his t-shirt and jeans.

"It's costly, that's one thing, means it has to be replaced," Henri said, standing beside her.

"I take it that's expensive to do," Clarke said, meeting Henri's gaze now.

"It can be, yes, ma'am," Hamp said, on his way down the ladder.

"Are we ready to see the inside?" Summer asked, scanning their faces. "Good. Hamp first, then me, you and then Henri." And yes, she was putting her two favorite people together.

"Sure," Clarke said, following her friend into the house with Henri behind her. This was the house Summer wanted to go with, and all Clarke could think was *Why?* standing there in the living room. Okay, the old woman hadn't been a hoarder, but she'd left lots of junk behind. Junk that smelled.

"What's that smell?" Clarke asked.

"Cats," Summer said.

"Oh," Clarke said, putting her hand to her nose. It seemed like so much work to her to get this one into shape, and unlike Summer, she was not gifted with the clairvoyant ability to see beyond its current state of wretchedness. Summer and Hamp moved on to the kitchen while Clarke hung back waiting for Henri to get closer. When she felt him at her back, she turned and leaned into him, pressing her nose into his chest.

"What are you doing?" Henri asked, bumping into her.

"You smell good," she said, inhaling. She looked up and met his gaze. "Tonight?"

"Tonight," he said, his eyes doing all sorts of things to her insides.

She turned around and started after the others. He chuckled and followed her into the next room.

Thank heavens the rest of the house was only dirty. The smell wasn't as bad once they moved beyond the bathroom and the kitchen. Three bedrooms, two baths, kitchen, living room, and dining room. Backyard big and empty, needed grass, she thought, listening as Summer, Hamp, and Henri discussed expanding the patio.

They were standing outside the front door now, done with their tour.

"You have all you need, Hamp, to give us an estimate?" Summer asked.

"Yes, ma'am, Hamp thinks so," he said.

"So what do you think?" Summer asked.

"It needs work, lots of it," Clarke said.

"It'll take more work, hell, it's almost like starting from scratch, but I believe we can do it," Summer said, clapping her hands together in glee. "Okay, it's a tour of house number two on Wednesday, and house three Friday, around the same time as this. Is that okay with everyone, the days and times, I mean?" Summer asked, glancing between Henri and Clarke.

"Yep," Clarke said.

"I think so," Henri said.

"I'll text you both the address," Summer said.

"Okay," Clarke said.

"Okay then. I'll talk to you later, Clarke, and I'll see you at home, big brother, unless you have an appointment with nameless faceless again."

Henri rolled his eyes.

"It's a sibling joke," Summer said, meeting Clarke's gaze, before she turned to Henri.

"Uncle Hamp," Clarke said, turning away. Escape was always a good plan.

***

It was her turn, and the Hilton was her choice. She entered the room, the first to arrive. She'd spent the short ride over trying to come up with a way to captivate him as he had done to her with his shower routine yesterday. She blew out a breath. Henri in the shower was something she would probably never, ever forget.

She'd nixed the fancy lingerie idea, always the choice of her husband. She wanted nothing of that life in her future. Nude on the bed was the best she could come up with. It must have been enough 'cause Henri smiled, the small one he so favored. He walked towards her, disrobing as he moved. He lost his t-shirt first, before he stopped to toe off his sneakers, and last but not least went his jeans. She loved that he'd gone commando this evening, standing at the edge of the bed now, in full salute.

She fought against the desire to reach out and touch. "I like that you like being here," she said.

"I do, and enough talking," he said, reaching for her feet, using them to flip her over onto her stomach. "I've been thinking about this... you in this way since we started. Face down, lying on the bed." It was the truth. This was his favorite sexual position above all others. Not the standing-on-your-knees doggy style—that was okay, he'd take it if he had to—but really what did it for him was this, he thought, watching her on the bed, slender like he liked.

It was something about the simplicity, the beauty of the female form, from this point of view. Something about the smooth back, slim waist, tapering up and out to the hips, and that nice smooth, round mound of ass, leading back to legs kept tightly locked together, and him, lying full-out completely covering her, moving his hips in and out. It was something about the way that looked and felt that did it for him in a way that nothing else could.

She smiled, looking at him over her shoulder. "What? This?" she said, lifting her butt in the air playfully, watching as he slipped on a condom.

"Exactly," he said, smiling, and then he was on the bed, his knees beside her hips, his legs extended outward, while his hands held his upper body away from her so that only his hips touched her ass. He slid his erection across the seam of her ass, then did it again, and moaned at how nice that felt. He continued with it for a bit, moving just his hips and his erection at the end of it up and down the seam of her ass, and when it was enough, he just as slowly slipped inside her core. She moaned and tried to open her legs to give him better access.

"No, just like this," he said into her ear. He was covering her now completely, using his elbows to take his weight. His hands were under her, a breast in each hand, softly pulling... tugging, as he slowly thrust into and out of her again and then again.

"So... good," he whispered into her ear, his head beside hers. *If it was as good as she was feeling, they should never stop* was what Clarke thought. It didn't stop or he didn't stop. She mostly just lay there, face turned to the side, feeling the smooth hard muscle that was his erection push into and out of her moist core.

It went on like that for a while: nothing but the sounds of heavy breathing, mixed in with the occasional moan from one of them when it all felt too good. The smooth, slow glide in and out, and then he was up on his arms like he was about to start in with push-ups—everything but his hips; those just kept driving softly into and out of her.

"Can... you... move for me?" he whispered, dropping his

forehead onto the space between her shoulder blades. Hell yes, she thought, although she didn't say anything, just started to move her hips, to the left, to the right. And the circle once around was his all-time favorite, if the sounds of his breathing were a clue. That, ladies and gentleman, was a winner. She moved her hips, around and around that sweet muscle that was all him, moving in and out of her body.

She looked over her shoulder and found him with the most profound expression of pleasure on his face. Wow. She twisted her hips to the right and then left again, wanting him to love this as much as she did. He moaned and lowered his arms to rest on his elbows again as she continued to move.

"Clarke..." he said, holding onto both of her breasts again, squeezing them this time, as he started to move faster, and she closed her eyes and gave in to the pleasure that was his hips in overdrive now. He kept at it until they were nothing more than hips pushing downward and ass up to meet it, moans, and sweat and racing toward a climax. She moaned along with him when they reached it. Her head lay on the bed, his on top of hers. And wow, how long before they could do *that* again, she wondered, closing her eyes and letting the pleasure of her climax flow through her body.

***

Tuesday morning

Nothing like a good night of sleep, Clarke thought, taking a sip from her double-shot vanilla latte as she made the right turn that was two streets over from the Fergusons' home, her appointment for the day. Travel day, for her and Baby Girl. Up to a camp for troubled young'uns in Oregon. Of course, this young'un had no idea she was going anywhere, tucked away sleeping in her wee little bed. Ten minutes was all it would take: the time it took Clarke to park, enter the Fergusons' home, go into her room and wake up sleepy head. No drama, just "get dressed and grab the bag your mom packed for you, and let's be on our way." She wasn't having any trouble from anybody this morning.

Nope, she was feeling too good for foolishness this morning. "Thank you, Mr. Novak," she said, thinking about last night, ready to tackle just about anything today, and it was great, this feeling of relaxed energy that coursed through her veins.

She was parking her car now, checking her rear view mirrors for the taxi that had pulled up behind. Her pal Skylar, a fellow PI from Dallas, was meeting her here to help her. They had worked as a team in Dallas, transporting the young'uns to various treatment centers. Six-three, blonde, tanned, and all hard muscle was Skylar.

Everything about her said, "Mess with me at your peril," so most didn't. She banked on it during these trips; one look at her, and most kids did what was asked of them. Occasionally more was required, but really that was rare.

Clarke checked her watch. Six fifteen and she was good. Their flight was set for nine. Plenty of time to scoop up the young'un and head to the airport. How difficult or easy the process was depended on how cooperative the kid was.

Clarke made her way to the front door. The Fergusons lived in a single-story home. Nothing extravagant, it fit in with their middle-income life. They'd had to dip into their savings to cover the portion of Baby Girl's stay at the treatment center not picked up by insurance.

Martha, mother Ferguson, opened the door before Clarke could ring the bell. Mr. Ferguson was standing beside his wife, both wearing twin expressions of worry.

"She's sleeping," Martha said as Clarke entered the house.

"Good. You okay with what we discussed? You'll need to stay here. Let me do this alone. I've done it enough times to know what works best," Clarke said. She'd been down this path enough times to know that the parents had to be committed. "It will be all okay in the end, just remember that. I'll bring her out and you can say goodbye then." They nodded.

Clarke made her way down the hall, stopping at the door marked *Stacy*, spelled out in pretty pink cursive letters on the door. She knocked, and checked the doorknob. It was unlocked.

"Come in," Clarke heard through the door. Stacy was in bed, hidden under pink bed sheets and comforter. A head with a ponytail attached to it was all that was visible.

"Good morning, Stacy," Clarke said in her take-no-prisoners voice. She had on her take-no-prisoners garb of jeans, tight to her legs, ankle-slim combat boots at her feet, a long-sleeve t-shirt tight to her skin, and a baseball cap over her hair. She was all attitude, don't-mess-with-me intimidating.

She stood beside the girl's bed, waiting until the head became completely visible. Two eyes and lots of freckles on a pretty pink face stared back at her.

"Who are you?" Stacy asked.

"Clarke Kensington. I'm here because your parents asked me. I need you to get up. Put on some clothes. We are going to camp this morning."

"What?"

"Your parents are sending you to camp. They have given me permission to deliver you to this camp."

"I don't understand. What camp?" Stacy said, pushing the covers away and sitting up in her bed.

"It's called Camp Future and it's in Oregon. They will be able to help you if you let them."

"I have to go?"

"Yes, you have to go. You are a minor. Your parents can seek help for you," Clarke said, meeting the girl's eyes. Stacy was scared. It was the thing she saw most often on kids' faces. Very few of the kids she encountered had enough experience to cover that. "So the decision that you have to make is whether you want this to be an easy process or not. Easy is the way I'd go. But we could go hard if you preferred it. If you do, though, know that it's not just me you'll have to contend with, but a friend of mine, and she is taller and meaner than I am. She's outside in case I need her. But we won't need her, will we?" Clarke asked.

"No," Stacy said.

"Good. So I need you to get dressed and then we can leave. I need you to place your cell phone on your desk next to your computer. Your mother has packed a bag for you. So after you get dressed, we can leave. Our flight leaves at nine, so we don't have to hurry, but we do have to move. Any questions?"

"No."

"Good." Clarke smiled. "It seems scary now, but it be okay. Will you trust me?" Clarke asked, meeting Stacy's eyes.

"Yes."

"Good. I'm going to stay with you while you change. I have to. Oh, and the bathroom door has to remain open so I can see you."

"Okay," Stacy said, getting up from bed. Clarke stood with her back against the door, waiting, watching as Stacy moved to the bathroom. Fortunately Stacy was cooperative and dressed quickly.

In fifteen minutes they were at the front door and she was saying goodbye to her parents. Crying, of course, and pleading, but no, she was going and Clarke was glad her parents held strong. It made things so much easier. They were out the door and into Clarke's jeep. Skylar climbed into the back with Stacy. They were good to go.

***

Tuesday. late afternoon

Henri's day was not going well. There were problems with the plumbing. The inspector had arrived and said no, they would not pass their plumbing inspection, not until another of the many of Wilson's fuck-ups was corrected. In addition to that, he'd interviewed four people today. All but one of them he would consider hiring. He'd asked them to shadow him as he moved around the site, a feet-in-first kind of thing, which is what they'd be up against were he to hire them.

He placed three resumés in the pile he'd started and had planned to give them to Clarke later on this week to be vetted. He'd hoped he'd have at least five to choose from by the end of the week and of those five, if one could be a standout that would be impossible to pass on, then that would be perfect. He hoped anyway.

It was closing in on four. He'd put in a couple more hours, grab a bite to eat, and maybe call Clarke—or not, give himself and her a break, get to bed early for a change. The door opened, pulling his attention away from his thoughts. It was his mother-in-law, standing in the middle of the doorway, looking the same as she always did. Dressed to impress, like his mother and Stephen's, socialites that took their socializing seriously, and that meant their appearances too.

"Carol? What are you doing here?" he asked. And yes, he was surprised to see her.

"I'm so sorry," she said, moving towards him with her hands and arms extended to take him into her arms. It was the way she'd always greeted him, like he was the long-lost son returning home. "I'm so sorry," she said again.

"It's okay," he said, allowing himself to be hugged. He genuinely liked his mother-in-law. She was a sweet woman. He could not have asked for a better one.

"Is this a convenient time for you? Can you talk? Have you had dinner?" she asked, pulling away, hands still holding his.

"Sure, I have a minute. I have another two hours of work ahead of me before I can leave, so I'll have to pass on dinner. We can sit here," he said, moving towards the conference table. "Would you like something to drink?"

"No, thanks," she said, looking around the office, everywhere but at him. "Do you know why I've come?"

"No," he said.

"I've come to explain and I felt like I owed you an apology."

"You didn't."

"Everything happened so fast, you left the hospital so fast, and Karen is living with us again," she said, taking a seat at the table.

"All of that is true," he said, taking the seat beside her.

"Do you think you would give Karen a second chance?" she asked.

"No," he said.

"You sound so sure."

"I am."

"She is so sorry, you know, and the baby, well, she is just so precious. That's who I'm worried about the most, that precious baby."

"I understand, however, I'm not the one to talk to. I'm not the father," he said.

"I know, and I'm terribly sorry about the way you found out. I'm most disappointed in the way Karen chose to handle all of this," she said.

"She thought I wouldn't find out, I guess. Like before?" he said, watching her eyes grow large in her face. "I thought so, yet I had no way to confirm it, not until this minute. There's no way I can go back, knowing what I know now. You can see that."

"I can see that my daughter loves *you* now, very much. She might not have in the beginning, but she does love you now. She's depressed. If it wasn't for the baby, I'm not sure she'd make it."

"If it wasn't for the baby, she wouldn't have to," he said.

"You'd be still married to her if this hadn't happened. She would be with you," she said, meeting his eyes. "I knew you had doubts. That you'd thought about leaving. Karen knows it too, knew it then, and that hurt her. That's the part I think you've played in getting the two of you here."

"This is not my fault," he said, pulling his hands away from hers. He could feel himself starting to get angry.

"It's not anyone's fault. These things happen in marriages sometimes. It gets tough, and people make mistakes," she said.

"That may be true, but I'm not going back," he said, meeting her gaze again.

"Will you talk to her at least, let her explain? She loves you now and that's what counts."

He sat back in his chair, like he wanted away from her and this. "I'm not going back."

"But will you talk to her, or listen to her? For me?" she asked, her hands reaching for his again, and there were tears shimmering in her eyes. "You're the son I've never had." She looked away. "You're, more like me than my own child is. Karen is so much like her father," she said, turning her gaze to his again. "I know what you feel. I've been where you are, having to decide to stay. understand how hard it is when the people who say they love you hurt you in this way. But you can get past it. There are other ways for this to end, beside divorce. Forgiveness is also an option. People make mistakes. I'm sure you've made mistakes, and that baby, that little precious baby, will need a father."

"The precious baby has a father," Henri said.

"He's married, and what she sees in him… saw in him, I'll never know. I never will understand her preoccupation with that man. He has an unexplainable hold over her, is all I can say," she said, angry now too.

"I'm not going back."

"I understand your anger and hurt. Talk to her, please, for me, and if you feel the same afterward then I'll understand. I'll accept your decision. Will you do that for me? Give her a chance to explain."

"Fine, I'll listen to her, but only because it's you that asked," he said.

"Thank you."

"And now I have to get back to work." He stood, ready for her to leave. Really, he was so ready to be beyond all of this.

"I understand," she said, standing now too. "Thank you for listening, for doing this one thing for me."

"You're welcome," he said, his gaze clear, calm and steely as it connected with hers.

She knew then that her meeting had been useless, that nothing would change by her coming here, just as nothing would come from him talking to her daughter, but she'd let it play out, holding on to hope.

***

The last leg of her trip couldn't come soon enough, Clarke thought. She was seated in the Southwest Airlines terminal in Dallas, waiting on her ride home, a short flight that had her landing at Austin Bergstrom at nine thirty.

It had been an uneventful trip, her favorite kind. Stacy had settled into her fate without a hitch. Clarke and Skylar had parted ways after landing.

She moved on to checking tomorrow's schedule. Easy. It was more searching for Rayford Wilson, a trip to the police station, and a trip to the boyfriend in her Amber search. She moved on to answering the many texts she'd received while she'd been on the plane. Three from Summer, a couple from other PIs, one client, and mixed in there was one from Henri.

Should she? She could really use some rest, she thought. She'd have plenty of time to rest after he was gone, maybe even as early as the end of next week. Stamina she had plenty of, and apparently would need as long as Henri was here. She responded to his text with a question mark of her own.

***

Like rabbits, they were, silently rutting rabbits. *Did rabbits do it any other way but silently*, she wondered. And damn that was nice, she thought at the last push of his hips, hard into hers, bringing her thoughts back to him.

I... want..." she said, or it was more a plea, at the end of a long-ass moan.

He was silent, moving over her, pushing into her again. They were in bed, at the hotel of his choice, a small one on the south side, tucked in between a restaurant and a coffee shop. It had been like this from the start, since they entered the room earlier. Something was driving him, and whatever it was, she was good with it.

He was on top, the covers barely covering his hips, as he pushed into her again, and then again. She moaned again, her feet planted beside his hips, knees up, giving him access, as much as she could. Anything as long as he didn't stop this relentless push into and then into her again.

She pulled his mouth down to hers. "I want," she whispered against his lips before sliding her tongue in his mouth, and that small movement triggered his climax. He pushed hard into her again, and then once more, dragging her along with him, moaning into her mouth, still on her. His body quivered with the pleasure of his release, taking with it the frustration and anger that had been delivered to him unintentionally by his mother-in-law.

She held on, her arms wrapped around his back, and her legs around his hips. No worries, he didn't want to be anywhere but here inside her.

It was a bit before their breathing returned to normal, and even then she didn't let go of him. She was not sure why she wanted to hold on, but she did, deciding not to overthink it, as he didn't seem to mind.

"You pick really nice hotels," she said.

He laughed. What a nice sound. He should laugh more often, she thought.

He rolled over onto the bed, feeling better, and he was struck for the first time that he was glad that she was here. She helped in a huge way to clear away his anger too. He was bothered still by his mother-in-law's visit, angry with himself at being talked into listening to Karen again. In no way was he interested in going back.

The break, time away from one's situation, always made one see things more clearly, gave one pause to reflect, and his let him consider his life before and after the baby. Why had he stayed so long? "The good guy can fix it" — was that the reason? Too stubborn to let go, maybe.

He was angry about it, but not as angry as he'd once been. *Thank you, Clarke Kensington*, he thought. He leaned over and kissed her on the lips.

"What was that for?" she asked.

He shrugged and pulled her close to him again, and much later, lost himself within the soft folds and flesh of her body again.

NINE

Wednesday morning

Clarke pulled into the parking in front of a cream-colored brick building that was the Yolly police station. It stood about five feet from the parking lot, with *Yolly Police* carved into the center of a stone sign, placed in a patch of grass just outside the main door.

She and her Aunt Veda were here to follow up on the initial missing person's report. Of course Aunt Veda had to come; she'd insisted, so there you go.

One thousand square feet was the size of the station's interior space, Clarke thought, moving toward the counter where a young officer, dressed in the khaki-colored shirt and pants, along with all the other paraphernalia that was part of the uniform, stood behind the counter watching them. He smiled, which Clarke returned. Aunt Veda had passed the point of smiling. Finding her baby and her baby's baby was more her mission, and that didn't allow room for much else.

A smiling policeman was so much better than the alternative, Clarke thought, when she reached the counter. Jim Hampton was the name on the officer's badge.

"Hi, my name is Clarke Kensington and this is my aunt, Veda Jones. We're here to follow up on a missing person's report she filed last week. It was, what, last Monday, right, Aunt Veda, that you stopped by?" Clarke asked.

"Yes, yes… last Monday," Aunt Veda said.

"We would like an update," Clarke said.

"What's the missing person's name?"

"Amber Jones," Clarke said.

They watched as the officer typed it into the computer. "What was her name again?" he asked, his expression blank.

"Amber Jones," Veda said this time.

"Huh," he said. A frown had replaced his blank expression for a minute, and then it cleared. "Here it is," he said after a few more minutes of typing.

"Well, have you found out anything?" Aunt Veda asked impatiently.

"It says here that her name has been inputted into the national database. The database is available to police departments all over the United States, so if someone has found an unidentified person, it's one of the first things they check. There are special circumstances where we will issue an Amber Alert, say, for instance, for an elderly person with Alzheimer's, or when a child goes missing. Those are considered special circumstances. For cases outside of those parameters, we take the information and wait and input it into the database."

"I see. That means you've done nothing?" Veda said.

"No, ma'am, that's not what that means. Submitting the information into the database is only one of the things we've done. We've checked out the local places where kids are known to run off to and hang out, but as you know, we are a small town, so those places are few. We've checked with the local hospitals. We've checked the parks department, and we've checked, notified the local sheriff's office and the county. They didn't have any information on your missing person either. We're a small town with limited resources. That's about all we can do unless you think there's a reason to suspect foul play. Is there any reason we should suspect foul play?" he said, serious now.

"That's why I filed the report. I thought something was wrong," Aunt Veda said, growing irritated.

"I understand, ma'am," he said, looking at the computer again. "The report here says that you and she had an argument before she left?"

"Yes, that's true... yes, we did, but that doesn't mean anything."

"It also says she's left home before."

"Yes, she has. This time is different!" Veda said emphatically.

"It's not against the law to go missing and you'd be surprised at the number of people who decide they want to change their lives and up and leave. And young girls are prone to fall out with their parents and leave home. All the time," he said, a little more gently, Clarke thought.

"So nobody is doing anything about it, is what you're saying?" Aunt Veda said.

"We are doing all we can, unless you can bring us something that indicates some other type of offense has occurred," Officer Jim said, politely but firmly this time. "People go missing all the time, and end up not being missing people after all. If there's anything to report, we'll call you. We have your information here."

"Thank you," Clarke said, her hand on her aunt's arm. She could feel the anger, hurt, and worry swirling around her aunt.

Clarke knew that most of what the officer said was true. Add in that the chances of a serious search were even more reduced if the person was homeless, a minority, or suffered from mental illness.

"They don't care about my child," Aunt Veda said, crying now, as they walked back to Clarke's car.

"He's just being honest, I think. People do go missing every day, but that's not to say we should lose faith. I bet she and the baby are fine, sitting somewhere, thinking she's getting back at you," Clarke said, sliding behind the wheel of her car.

"That's what I think too. I would feel it otherwise, you know," Veda said, smiling weakly but visibly. She pointed to her heart. "If something had truly happened my baby, I would feel it here, wouldn't I?"

"I think so," Clarke said, backing out of the parking lot, hoping that her aunt's belief would prove true, and everything would be fine.

"Well, you can be sure, I'm going to give her the what-for when I see her, got me all worried for nothing…" Veda said, her hand covering her mouth as she tried to hold in her tears. "That little baby… I just want to know he's safe. She could call me and tell me that."

"Yes, ma'am, she could. And I bet she will, soon," Clarke said.

"You're a good girl," Aunt Veda said, her hand reaching for one of Clarke's. "That boy didn't realize what he was letting go when he let you walk away."

"He walked away, but I hear you, and thanks."

***

It was a quick stop by the one high school that bore the city's name, after she dropped Aunt Veda at her home. It was the only high school in the city. She met with one of the vice principals and the guidance counselor in charge of that age group. Amber had graduated in May, a quiet girl who had mostly gone unnoticed. In a school of over two thousand students, that was possible.

Clarke hadn't spoken to any of Amber's teachers, preferring to try and meet with the friends, two girls, and the boyfriend first. She was headed to the warehouse district now, to meet the boyfriend, D'Angelo. She'd called him this morning, caught him as he was walking out the door, he said. He had work, but he'd see if he could take a late lunch to talk to her. So far he was co-operating, so that was good. Maybe it meant that he was not the one.

Clarke gone through her cousin's Facebook page, the only form of social media she'd participated in. Her last post was well before the baby was due and it wasn't anything consequential. *I'm having a baby* was the post, under a picture of her smiling, and that was something Clarke already knew.

She was getting close, she thought, looking at the numbers on the warehouses as she passed them. Warehouse ten should be coming up on her right, and there it was, the home for Hill Country Flooring. She made the right turn into the parking lot and slid her car into a slot in front of the door. She was reaching for her purse when her cell rang. It was Stephen. This was a surprise, she thought, wondering what he wanted as she hit the button to answer.

"Hello," she said.

"Clarke. This is Stephen. Do you have a moment?"

"I do. What's up?"

"Reye and I are having a dinner party on Sunday. There will be people present that I thought you might like to meet. I know it's late notice, and I apologize for that. I wouldn't ask if I didn't think it would be good for you. Do you think you can make it?"

"I think so," she said, flipping over to the calendar part of her phone. "Let me check my schedule." She looked over her plans for Sunday. She could move some things around, but yes, she could make it. "Yes, no problem. I can make it," she said.

"Good. I'll text over my address and again, I apologize for the short notice," he said.

"Nope, it's me that should be thanking you for all the business you've thrown my way."

"See you Sunday then. Seven," he said.

"Yep," she said, hanging up. It was a quick trip into the building then, and over to the counter where a tall African American, head shaven clean and built for heavy lifting, stood.

"May I help you?" he asked.

"I'm here to see D'Angelo Simpson for lunch, I think," she said, smiling.

"He'll be out for lunch in a few. You can talk to him then," he said.

"Thanks," she said, and found herself a seat in one of the four chairs reserved for whomever. "A few" turned out to be fifteen minutes later before a young man passed though the doorway, pulling a pack of cigarettes from his back pocket.

"You Clarke?" he asked, standing in front of her, dressed in green pants, way loose and baggy. They would be at his feet if not for the belt that was actually being used as one. Who knew belts had a purpose? His shirt, also green, matched the pants. Workman's gear, she thought. Dark skinned, with braids, the making of a small mustache on his face, and handsome.

"Yes, and you're D'Angelo," she said.

"Yeah, but you can call me D," he said, checking her out. "Look at you, the fine detective."

"I'm a private investigator, not a detective," she said and smiled.

"It's all the same, asking me questions. Come on, we have to talk outside, and I can only give you a few. I still have to eat lunch," he said, holding out the cigarette pack for her.

"Sure, and no thanks," she said to his offer of a cigarette. She followed him out the front door, down the steps and over to a ledge that separated this parking lot from the next. He slid onto the ledge, and she stood beside him, watched as he lit his cigarette.

"So Amber's missing," he said after he'd inhaled, blowing out the smoke from the side of his mouth, away from her, which she appreciated.

"Yes, and thanks for talking to me," she said.

"Whatever. Her baby's not mine," he said.

"How do you know this?"

"I was there when it was born, and he looks nothing like me. He's light, damn near white."

"What do you mean?"

"You see me, girl?" he said, chuckling. "I know you've seen Amber. Neither one of us is making no white babies. Amber's baby got himself a white daddy, anybody could see that, just like I could see. Her momma wasn't none too happy about that either." He took another puff from his cigarette, blowing it out of the side of his mouth again. "I'm out, not raising some other man's baby. She was screwing around on me, so fuck that."

"You have any idea of who she might have been dating besides you?"

"I don't know, and we weren't dating, just kicking it, you know," he said, chuckling for a few minutes. "You're one of those old-school women." He chuckled again. "You *do* know that people don't date anymore?"

"Did you ever see her with another boy? White or otherwise?"

"No."

"When was the last time you saw her?"

"At the hospital. So don't be trying to pin her disappearance on me."

"So that was when? At the hospital, that you saw her?"

He paused, took a drag from his cigarette before he said, "Shoot, girl, the beginning of August, can't remember the date. It was a Tuesday, I think.

"Was she depressed when you saw her?"

"No."

"So who are her girlfriends?" Clarke asked.

"Girl didn't have that many. In school, she mostly stuck to herself. Too stuck up, which is why she's probably into white boys, you know, like I bet you are."

"Names?" she asked, ignoring him again. She was long past the days of being affected by others' opinions of her. She wanted to match his list to her aunt Veda's list. Usually the friends the parents knew about could be completely different from the real list of friends.

"Bria and Tameka," he said, "from school. Tameka and her were sort of close before they had a fight."

"Why did they fight?"

"Over me, is what they said," he said, smiling. "What can I say, the ladies love me." He took another pull from his cigarette.

"Where can I find her friends?" she asked, and spent another ten minutes gathering as much info as she could about the locations of Amber's friends before wrapping things up.

"Call me, or stop by my house if you want to talk some more, or do something else," he said, sliding off the ledge and onto his feet, smiling in that way that for some girl child was meant to be attractive.

"I will. Thanks for talking to me. If you remember anything you think might help, give me a call, anytime, day or night," she said, handing two of her cards to him.

He nodded and walked away, back to the warehouse, and she made her way to her car.

***

Stephen entered the Novak Construction office close to noon. He found Henri seated at a desk, looking over something.

"This is a surprise," Henri said, looking up.

"I know. I've been meaning to get by here to see what you're up to, how things were going. I was on my way to lunch, thought I'd check in. You want to join me?"

"I wish. Busy today," Henri said.

"How's it going?" Stephen asked.

"Slowly getting better. Interviewing replacements is my first mission," Henri said. Actually, being the superintendent had worked in his favor, as he'd had to drag the interviewees along with him around the site, which turned out to be a useful way of taking stock of what they knew or didn't know.

"That's good then. Oh, before I forget. Reye's having a dinner party on Sunday with a few of her friends, and I thought you might be interested. It's casual."

"No, I'm good."

"Clarke working out for you then?"

"She's fine," Henri said, smiling.

"Must be serious?"

"Seriously, you're kidding, right?" Henri asked, his expression incredulous. "Hell no, are we serious. We're just kicking it. That's all I can do at this point. And just so you're not worried I'm mistreating her somehow, she feels exactly the same way. No way is it serious, for either of us. In three weeks, sooner if I'm lucky,

I'm out, and she's back to whatever she did before I arrived. Trust me, we're good with this."

"She's a nice woman, smart, professional. You could do worse."

"Right," Henri said, laughing now.

"Dinner on Sunday?" Stephen asked.

"I'll take a pass on that as well. I'm good, not into meeting anyone else right now." He looked past Stephen to the door, where another man stood. "My next appointment is here. Kevin Huang?"

"Yes," Kevin said, moving toward Henri.

"I'll see you Saturday then," Stephen said.

"Yep, for sure."

***

Wednesday evening

Summer and Clarke's second house was located north of the city, where homes tended to be somewhat cheaper and residents were decidedly middle class. Henri had done some research on the city and its suburbs on his own. Now that his sister was into the house remodeling business, he thought he'd should brush up on the residential market for Austin and its surrounding areas.

He turned his truck into the front drive, parking behind Summer's car. Hamp's truck was parked next to it in the drive. There was no sign of the jeep that belonged to Clarke.

It was a single-story brick home. The driveway led to a sidewalk that led to a good-sized porch. Not bad, although the driveway was a little bit uneven, had a couple of cracks. That wouldn't be too difficult to repair, he observed as he walked towards the front door. He hoped it wasn't anything foundational. They were asking a hundred forty thousand dollars, he found out, and homes in this neighborhood sold in the one hundred ninety thousand to two hundred thousand dollar range. Not a bad profit, just not as large as they stood to make from house number one.

You stepped into the living room upon entering, which was unusual. He didn't expect that from a newer home—in the old days, yes, but he'd expected a foyer of some type. Nope, it was this large living room, with windows, two larger ones facing the front and two facing out to the backyard. A fireplace sat in between the two back windows. The carpet, which he didn't care for personally, was in need of a good cleaning, and the ceilings were shorter than his preference. Summer stood in the middle of the room, conferring with Hamp standing beside her.

Henri wasn't sure what to make of Clarke's uncle, or the way he referred to himself in the third person whenever he talked. He seemed to know his business though, but it made for an odd trio, he thought again, consisting of Summer, who talked enough for all three of them, and Clarke, who mostly listened.

"Hey, big brother," Summer said, smiling, perky as ever.

"Hey," he said.

"Where's Clarke?" she asked.

"How would I know?" he said.

"I thought she might have been outside. She sometimes sits in her car and talks on the phone. She's forever in her car, occupational hazard, I guess," she said, watching him, with an odd look on her face.

"I guess," he said, looking around the room, and away from whatever his sister was thinking.

"It looked better in the pictures," Summer said, moving on and moving her finger around the room. "The pictures of it on the MLS—multiple listing service, the old-school way of posting houses—were old, I guess, and more than a little misleading, now that I'm here. Nothing here matches up to the pictures on the computer." Her gaze was on Hamp now.

"Hamp would have to agree with that," Hamp said, nodding his head in agreement.

Summer's cell dinged. She looked at it. "Oh, it's from Clarke. She's running late. Says to start without her." Summer looked at Henri. "So what do you think?"

"About?"

"The house, silly," she said, smiling, back to staring at him oddly.

He had no idea what she hoped to see. He'd forgotten about Summer's quirks, or maybe he thought she'd outgrown them by now. Guess not. "I don't think much. I haven't seen it yet," he said.

"This is the living room."

"Really? I wouldn't have guessed that."

"Ha, so funny. Anyway the carpet needs cleaning as you can see, but otherwise it's in pretty good shape, I think. Wish I could say the same about the rest of the house." She moved past him into the kitchen. "Follow me," she said, and waited until both of them stood beside her.

It was bare in here, missing a few things, like the sink and the cabinets, Henri thought.

"See, I told you. The pictures show a fully built kitchen. As you can see, someone has removed them, 'cause they're not here," she said.

"Hamp thinks they may have been stolen," Hamp said.

"Something happened to it, is all I know," Summer said.

"Yep," Henri said.

They spent a few minutes going over what all needed to be replaced in the kitchen, Hamp writing it all down in his note pad. It was on to the rest of the home then.

At the end twenty minutes later, they were standing out in the front yard again when Clarke's jeep pulled up to the curb. She was out and moving toward them before they could blink. She'd come from a meeting with the ex-fiancé of Sarah Greentree, feeling especially proud and happy at the good news she'd delivered to him.

"So sorry," she said, coming to a stop in front of them. She was wearing a jacket and a matching skirt. Always professional and pulled together was this one, Henri thought, taking in the picture of her in one full sweep.

"Sorry, I got stuck," she said, scanning the group with her eyes, studiously avoiding Henri's gaze. "What'd I miss?"

"Everything," Summer said, smiling. "It's okay. Would you mind giving Clarke a quick tour, brother dear? Hamp and I have things to discuss, don't we, Hamp?"

"Hamp says you're the boss."

"You mind?" Clarke asked, turning to Henri, but keeping her expression neutral.

"Nope," he said, keeping his expression neutral too.

"After you then," she said, and followed him in. He turned to her, about to say something, and stopped. She had placed her finger to her lips, before she mouthed the word "Summer," and discreetly pointed over her shoulder to one of the windows to the front yard. Henri looked past her, and yep, there was his sister staring back at him. She smiled, sheepish at being caught.

"Living room," he said, deadpan.

"Got it. Next," she said, and smiled, before following him into the kitchen, restricting her comments to house stuff.

"Kitchen," he said, watching her as she scanned the room.

"Empty. Got it," she said.

"Yep," he said, and it went that way throughout the remainder of the tour, which made for a really short tour. Put them back out front to join Hamp and Summer less than five minutes later.

"Whoo, that was quick," Summer said, looking between them.

"It was," Henri said, fighting back his laughter at his sister's expression.

"Okay then," Summer said.

Clarke smiled and looked away. She wasn't going to laugh either.

"Okay, gang. We have one more house to see on Friday, don't forget, and we'll be ready to make a decision. Is Friday still good?" Summer asked.

"It's fine with me," Clarke said.

"Me too," Henri said.

"Hamp?" Summer asked.

"Hamp's got nothing but time," he said.

"Okay then, I'll text everyone the address. See you guys later," Summer said.

"Yep," Clarke said, moving to her car. She slid behind the wheel of her jeep and looked back across the lawn, expecting to see everyone gone. Nope, for some reason they were still standing there, where she'd left them.

Summer was by the front door, talking to Hamp, looking at the paper he was using to jot his notes down. All old school was Hamp, Clarke thought of her uncle and his love of paper and pencil. Henri stood near his truck, looking down at his phone, his fingers moving over it.

Not even a second later she heard her phone's familiar ping. She smiled at what she saw, and looked back at him and caught a semblance of a smile at his mouth. *The Wesleyn?* was the text he'd sent. She moved her gaze away from his to her phone and responded. *My turn.*

Next time?

Not fair to you, paying all the time.

I don't mind.

You sure?

I am.

ASAP then was her final text. She met his gaze again. Seriously sexy. She started her car's engine and drove away, with blood humming in her veins. Who knew sex could be this good? Not her, and no way was she giving it up until she had to.

***

Clarke arrived at the hotel before him, which was fine. Something alcoholic sounded nice while she waited for him to get there. She sent him a text telling him where to find her, and went in search of the bar.

She was seated alone when he found her, a glass of something dark in front of her, and the same dark something could be found in the glass in front of the seat next to her.

"Is this for me?" he asked, sliding into the seat beside her.

"It is," she said, taking a sip from hers.

"Good week so far?" he asked.

"Yep. You?"

"The same," he said, watching as she drained the contents of her glass in one gulp.

"You ready?" she asked, rising to his feet.

"In a hurry, are we?" he asked, chuckling. "I will be in a few seconds." He disposed of the remainder of his drink too, also in one gulp.

"So now?" she said, smiling.

He laughed. "Yes, now," he said, chuckling, but rising to his feet.

***

It was as it had been many times before: them standing before each other, removing shirts, socks, shoes, until they were once again nude.

He pulled her to him and kissed her, hands moving over her body, pushing her toward the bed. He didn't stop until her legs hit the back of it, and she sat then, scooting up to the middle of the bed, her movements not that different from the first time they had done this. It was nice that sex could be normal, the same, not every night an event, or over the top. She could do simple for the rest of her life and be just fine, she thought.

"I forgot," he said, and he was walking back toward his discarded clothing. She leaned back on her elbows then, watching him move away, the back of him just as impressive as the front. He picked up his pants and pulled out a few condoms.

She smiled, and then he was back, standing at the edge of the bed, staring down at her again. His erection wasn't quite there, but it was growing. She turned onto her stomach then and crawled across the bed until she met him at the edge of it, stopping when his erection reached her mouth. She smiled and looked up. He was back to being intense, and dang she knew now it would be nothing but her A-game with this dude.

She met his erection halfway and heard his breath catch. She loved the sounds he made, the surprised catches in his breathing, the moans, the sighs that came so freely to him. Like now, the swipe of her tongue was all it took for him to release another moan. She smiled and continued.

Much later, he turned her around so she lay flat on her back looking up at him, eyes all glossy with pleasure. He leaned forward and placed his lips on hers. A soft swipe of his tongue across them, then he was pushing it through and into her mouth, where it sparred with hers for a while, softer and with less urgency this time. He deepened the kiss after she wrapped her arms around his head and pulled him in closer.

She could feel him hard against her belly, and using her arm, felt around on the bed beside her for one of the condoms he'd thrown there. She wanted him inside her and now was a good time.

She pushed him back and made short work of the condom-putting-on business. She placed her arms around his head, pulling his mouth back to hers. It wasn't too much later before he was sliding into her body. A smooth glide in. *It will be hard to lose this when I leave* was a fleeting thought, replaced by a moan, as he thrust into her body again.

Later, he'd think later, right now it was nothing but his body, moving over hers.

TEN

Thursday morning

It was back out to Yolly for Clarke this morning. She had a date
with Tameka Williams, one of Amber's two friends, and the one
she was the most interested in speaking to, given her relationship
with D'Angelo. She'd called both of Amber's friends yesterday,
and both had agreed to talk to her today. Hopefully they could
point her in a direction. She stood outside the front door of
Tameka's house and rang the doorbell.

"You must be Clarke," a young woman said, standing in the
open doorway. A very short woman—shorter than Clarke's five-
one height, maybe four-eleven—African American, slim except for
her belly, which was as huge as she was short. Seven months or
more along, if Clarke had to render a guess.

"Yes, I am. And you must be Tameka?"

"That's me," she said.

"Nice to meet you, and thanks for talking to me."

"I ain't said nothing yet."

"Right. May I come in?"

"I guess," she said, holding the door open. Clarke stepped
inside of what must be the living room. A profusion of beige—
carpet and wall. It was free of furniture, beyond the one couch and
a TV across the room from it.

"So you're looking for Amber?" Tameka asked, taking a seat on the sofa. "I don't know where she is and I don't care."

"When was the last time you saw or spoke to her?"

"Graduation. I haven't seen her since and I don't want to. D'Angelo went to see her and the baby at the hospital, but I didn't. I knew that baby wasn't his and I was right."

"I thought you were friends?"

"We used to be friends, before that bitch hit me."

"She hit you? When?" Clarke asked, keeping her voice neutral, wondering if women would ever stop being bitches to each other.

"Right after school started, or maybe it was later. I don't remember exactly. I just remember kicking her ass," she said. "You can sit down if you want."

"Thanks," Clarke said, taking a seat beside her. "What did you two argue about? The reason she hit you."

"I didn't say we argued. I said she hit me and I kicked her ass. She got mad when she found out that D'Angelo liked me. She had just found out she was pregnant and had been telling everybody it was his," Tameka said.

"Is it?"

"Hell no."

"Why were you so sure it wasn't?"

She shrugged her shoulders. "D'Angelo said it didn't matter. He could be a daddy to as many kids as he wanted. No need to trip. It still made me mad, though, 'cause I knew she was sneaking out. Going to bars and stuff to meet guys. Her mama didn't know."

"What bars?" Clarke asked, perking up.

Tameka shrugged again. "Country and western bars. I don't know. I don't like country."

"You never went with her?"

"No. Amber could keep a secret. It was one of the things I

liked about her until she made up that shit about D'Angelo being her baby daddy. I was the only one having D'Angelo's baby," she said, pointing to her belly.

"Have you seen her with any other boys?"

"No," Tameka said.

"Never?"

"No, just D'Angelo."

"She and D'Angelo had to have done something together for him to think it could be his."

Tameka shrugged. "Maybe before he and I were together, but not after," she said, irritation in her voice.

"Who are some of her other friends, beside you, that maybe I could talk to?" Clarke said, moving on.

"She couldn't keep friends really. It's just me and Bria."

"Why is that?"

She shrugged again.

"And how long have you known her?"

"Since freshman year."

"Bria too?" Clarke said.

"Me and Bria don't really hang out. Her momma..." Tameka shook her head. "Too into her business for me. I stopped hanging around her."

"Anything else you can think of that might help me find Amber?" Clarke asked.

"No."

"Well, if you do, here's my card. You can call me any time."

"So why are you doing this? And what is a private investigator? You work for the police or something?" Tameka asked, reading Clarke's business card.

"She's family, my cousin. That's why I'm searching for her

and no, I'm not with the police. I find things out on my own," Clarke said.

"Stuff like is my boyfriend cheating on me?"

"Yes, stuff like that."

"Oh," Tameka said.

"Well, thank you for taking the time to talk to me," Clarke said, standing up now.

"I guess. I hope you find her. I might not like her... but I don't want her dead or nothing," Tameka said, standing too.

"Thanks," Clarke said, moving to the front door, and when she was free of the door, she moved towards her jeep, mentally working through her and Tameka's conversation. She hoped the other friend had more to offer, especially regarding the country and western bars. Interesting.

***

Henri looked up at the sound of the door opening, surprised to see Clarke entering his office, dressed prettily in a brown jacket and slacks. He really liked the way she looked.

"Summer sent me a text a few minutes ago, wanted me here. For what I have no idea," she said, coming to a stop in front of his desk.

"Really," he said, sitting back in his chair.

"Yep, really. Your sister can be one determined individual, I've found, once she puts her mind to something," Clarke said.

"And what has she put her mind to, do you think?"

"Us, or you and me becoming an us. But you know this already."

"I do. You think she suspects?"

"No, which is why I received a text telling me to meet her here."

"You want to sit?"

"Not in those," she said, pointing to the beanbag chairs. "I'd thought you'd have gotten rid of them by now."

"I thought so too, but now it's fun watching people, as it was with you."

"You were mean," she said, smiling.

"I was angry."

"Speaking of sitting in chairs, how's the interviewing?"

"Good. And you? How's the investigating—whatever it is that you're investigating—going?" he asked, chuckling, as he had no idea what she did during the day. He knew generally, but not specifically. It was odd, he thought, to have a relationship and know next to nothing meaningful about that person's life.

She laughed. "It's good," she said, chuckling over the fact that he had no idea of her life during the day—general ideas probably, nothing specific, which she was just fine with.

The door opened and they both turned to look. Summer had arrived.

"Oh goody. Clarke, you're here. Hey, brother," Summer said.

"Hey," he said.

"I was driving to my next house. That's what I've been up to this morning, looking at houses, pre-checks. Anyway, I was driving, on my way to the next house, and I said to myself, 'Summer, I can't believe you haven't invited Clarke over to the house for dinner, you know, to officially meet my brother, your two favorite people. What is wrong with you?'" She slapped her head lightly for emphasis. "All I can say in my defense is that I've been busy, so that's why I asked Clarke to meet me here with you. Tonight I'm cooking dinner for you and Henri, my good friend and my only brother, both people I love more than anything in the world. Dinner tonight at my house, I'm inviting you," she said, arms spread open wide.

God, you had to love his sister, Henri thought, watching her and the drama that was always present. He smiled 'cause he did love her.

"I know it's late notice, but you're the only one I have to worry about," she said, pointing to Clarke. "Henri's free before ten usually. He and nameless-faceless don't get started until after that." She smiled at her brother as she said it.

"What time?" Clarke asked, not even going to look in Henri's direction or try to talk her way out of it. Summer trying to set them up would continue until all lights had been extinguished, so she should start extinguishing them, or at least the possibility of a serious romance happening between the two. Not going to happen, and the sooner Summer realized that, the better for everyone.

"Seven."

"Seven's good," Clarke said.

"I know it's yes for you," Summer said, pointing to Henri.

"It's fine with me," he said.

"Excellent," Summer said, clapping her hands. "Seven this evening it is." She smiled, clearly pleased with herself.

"Now that that's all settled, I'm out," Clarke said, moving toward the door.

"What's not to like about her?" Summer said, turning to her brother once Clarke was gone.

"Don't start," he said, pulling his laptop closer.

"I won't. Thank you for not putting up a fight about dinner tonight," she said.

"You're welcome."

***

Clarke entered Ranchero's Chicken, a fast food Mexican place, thirty minutes later. Yellow and red was the color scheme in the building and in the logo prominently displayed on one wall, a red and yellow circle with a dancing chicken in the middle of it. The chicken was either happy or resigned to his fate of being shredded or cubed for whatever Mexican dish was on the menu, Clarke couldn't decide which.

A young African American woman stood behind the counter staring out into the empty room. The lunch crowd must have come and gone, Clarke thought, moving to the counter.

"May I help you?" the young woman asked. She was pretty, smooth medium-brown skinned, with braids. Pretty smile, even white teeth, slim, and not pregnant. It was Bria, the nametag above the right breast pocket of her polo identifying her. Underneath her name was the word *Manager*.

"I'm Clarke Kensington, here to speak to you regarding my cousin Amber Jones's disappearance. Is this a good time?"

"Oh, yes. Let me get someone up here to take over for me, and I'll be with you in a second. Sit wherever you like. Would you like something to eat or drink?" she asked.

"No, thanks," Clarke said. She sat down in the second booth beyond the counter. She didn't have to wait long.

"You're young to be the manager," Clarke said, after Bria joined her.

"I guess," Bria said, smiling. "Couldn't afford college. I knew that early, so I started working here. Been working here since ninth grade. They have a work/college payment program if I stick around."

"You're not pregnant," Clarke said.

Bria laughed. "I know. I have all the time in the world is what my mother tells me, all the *dang* time," she said, chuckling. "So you wanted to talk about Amber?"

"Yes."

"We aren't that close. I mean we used to be, before the baby, but not so much after that."

"How long have you known her?" Clarke asked.

"Since middle school. Her mother liked me. She'd let her spend the night with me sometimes. We both could stay at each other's houses. Did that up until our senior year, before Christmas. She started to change, you know?"

"In what way?"

"Interested in boys, talking about wanting to get married, have a baby, sneaking around. She wanted me to cover for her, and I couldn't. My mom's too nosy for that. Amber's smart too. My mom says it's a disappointment. She wanted me to stop hanging out with her."

"Did you?"

"I didn't stop completely, no."

"I met with another friend of hers, Tameka. Do you know her?"

"I do," Bria said, crinkling up her nose.

"What?"

"Nothing. Tameka wasn't all that good of a friend. I think she was jealous of Amber having a baby. I hear she's pregnant now."

"Do you know who the father of her child is?"

"No. She was secretive about it. Wouldn't tell me no matter how many times I asked."

"But it wasn't D'Angelo's?"

"No, I don't think so. It felt like it was what she wanted everyone to believe, but she never told me it was his."

"But she did date him?"

"I guess you can call it that. For a while, she'd sneak over to his house. Then Tameka came along and put a stop to that."

"So you two drifted apart after Christmas, you said?"

"Yep. She only called when she needed a favor, after that. I had a car and she didn't. She wanted rides out to the country. I've driven her there so whoever he is, he must live in the country."

"He? You think it's a man she went to the country to see?"

"I do."

"Why?"

"I don't know. It was the way she acted, I guess. She was all excited, putting on makeup, that type of thing."

"So where in the country?"

"Near Avondale," Bria said.

"Really?" Clarke said, considering. Avondale wasn't that far away from Yolly. Maybe forty minutes from Yolly, she thought. "Would you pick her up from her home and take her?"

"No, I'd take her over after school."

"When was the last time you dropped her off?"

"In the summer, before the baby came."

"Nothing after the baby was born? Did you talk to her at least?"

"No."

"Do you think you could take me to it, show me where it was that you dropped her off?"

"I guess. I could try. You think something's happened to her for real?"

"I don't know. Her mother is worried about her and her new grandbaby, so I'm trying to help," Clarke said.

"I have to be at work here at noon. I could show you in the morning."

"That'd be great. Give me your address and I'll pick you up."

"Do you mind if I meet you here? It's a ways to my house

from here. I don't live in Yolly anymore. We moved, me and my mom did, after graduation. She hated living in Yolly."

"Small towns, huh?"

"That's what she said," Bria said, smiling.

"Sure. I can pick you up here," Clarke said, sliding her business card across the table to Bria. "Call me if you remember anything else. I'll let you get back to work, and I'll see you in the morning."

She was back in her car, driving away. And no, she wasn't going to tell her mother or Veda anything just yet. Maybe she was with the new boyfriend, baby daddy, and alive. Clarke certainly hoped so.

***

He was the last to arrive, Henri thought, pulling in behind Clarke's jeep, which was parked out on the street. Summer was apparently used to living alone, as today—most days really—her car sat near the middle of what should be a two-car driveway. Not all the way in the middle, just enough into the next space to make it difficult to park beside her. He usually wound up parking on the street most nights, as he was doing now.

He grabbed his bag and made his way up the drive, his gaze landing on Clarke. He could see her through the large bay window as he walked past. She was stirring something in a pot on the stove, staring out into space, and he wondered about her thoughts.

She was cute, he thought again, at least the part he could see. The top half was the only part visible: a white shirt, cut low, fitting, and he could see the outline of her breasts. He was very fond of her breasts. Tall, which meant she wore heels—and what he wouldn't give to have his sister somewhere else and Clarke all to himself. There was something about sex with this one, and he didn't try to explain it away.

He used his key and entered the house, inhaling the nice smells of dinner—of what he couldn't make out. He dropped his keys on the table beside the door and walked to the kitchen. He found Clarke staring in the direction of the door, as if she were waiting for him, standing behind the island so he couldn't see the lower half of her body.

"Hey," she said.

"Hey," he said, stopping at the end of the island, not sure how to say, "Are you in the mood for a quickie?" He met her gaze, allowing some of his desire for her to show in his. Her breath caught, so maybe he'd said it just fine.

"I have a few resumés for you for Friday. Stop by the office tomorrow if you have time, you can pick them up," he said.

"I will. Which of them do you like?"

"Kevin Huang is my first choice; the rest are okay."

"Experienced?"

"Enough. I like how he handled himself today."

"That's good."

"Where's Summer?" he asked.

"Searching the pantry for a specific bottle of wine to complement dinner," Clarke said, smiling. And yes, she wanted what he wanted.

"Hey there," Summer said, back from her time in the pantry, where she'd been doing nothing but eavesdropping. "I can't find what I'm looking for here, so I'm going to make a run to this one little store, not far from here. Yes, we *have* to have it," she said, to Clarke's look of inquiry. "Where are you parked?" Summer turned her gaze to her brother.

"Behind Clarke, on the street," he said, keeping his eyes focused on his sister.

"Good," she said, moving around him to pick up her keys off the counter. "I'll be back in a second. Think you can be nice to my friend and business partner while I'm gone?" She stared back at him.

"I'm off upstairs to take a shower, so she'll be alone until you get back."

"I didn't mean that," she said.

"No, it's good. I need a shower," he said, moving away from counter and out of the kitchen before she could say anything else.

She and Clarke stood there listening as his footsteps hit the stairs until they could hear him moving around above them. Clarke returned her gaze to the pot before her, hoping the look of indifference was working.

"Okay, then, keep stirring and I'll be back," Summer said, eyeing Clarke now. They could hear the shower start up.

"Will do," Clarke said, and gave her friend a small salute. She continued to stand at the stove, stirring her pot of spaghetti sauce, watching Summer through the bay window get into her car and back out of the drive.

Clarke stood staring at the empty drive, listening to the sounds of the shower running above her, imagining Henri in it. Should she or shouldn't she? She liked Henri in showers. She should, she decided. She waited another couple of minutes, enough time for Summer to double back and find her absent from the kitchen. She looked down at her watch. Good, ten minutes, just to be sure, but enough time for him and her to do the do.

She turned down the flame under the pan before moving closer to the bay window. It was all clear, the drive and the street. She turned then, kicked her shoes off and headed for the stairs.

Hell yeah, maybe he would be quick. She hoped so, 'cause for some reason, she wanted what she wanted, and she'd take quick if she could get it.

Up the stairs and fast, and then she was standing outside his door, having used the sounds of the shower as her guide to which room was his. She reached for the doorknob, and before she could touch it, the door swung open and he was standing there, a towel wrapped around his waist, the only thing covering his body. "I heard your feet on the stairs," he said, smiling.

She laughed. "I wondered," she said, smiling and closing the door behind her.

"Leave it open... so we can hear."

"Right," she said. "Can you do quick?"

"Not if you waste time talking," he said, pulling her closer. He was down on his knees in front of her before she could think, lifting her skirt. It was a skirt she wore, pastel and flowery and short. Today, for what he had planned, short was good. Next came her underwear and the removal of it.

He placed his hands on her hips, leaned forward, and placed his mouth at the spot at the junction of her thighs. She about came unglued as the first swipe of his tongue moved against her. She moved her hands to his shoulders to hold herself still as he stroked and then swiped his way to her first climax, moaning all the way. He chuckled when he was done, and stood.

"More, right?" he asked, not that he waited for her reply. "Wrap your legs around me," he said, lifting her and spreading her legs wide. Her hands were opening the towel, pulling his erection free.

"Condom," he said, before walking them over to the bed where his wallet lay. He continued to hold her as she picked it up, finding a condom behind his credit cards. She leaned away from his chest and rolled it over him. He backed away from the bed, didn't stop moving backwards until he hit the wall behind him. He was pushing up into her then, pushing her hips down to meet him.

Her arms went around his neck, and he leaned back into the wall and moaned. He settled his mouth on hers while her hands wrapped around his neck. He started to move her with a vengeance, up and down, again and then again.

He moaned and it was nothing but fast after that, in a hurry to finish. He held her ass in the palms of his hands, using it to slide her hips up and down the length of his erection. Up and down, and nothing but panting and moans filled the air, and before long, he was coming, bringing her along with him.

"Wait," she said, after they were done, breathing heavily still. "I need a few more seconds please," and he gave her that, and only that. He lifted her then, setting her on legs that were a little weak, feeling like rubber, while everything else felt like relaxed and easy.

"You good?" he asked.

"You don't know how good," she said, kissing his mouth.

He pulled away, not about to get caught up again. Summer would be here any minute, he thought, and he still had a shower to take. "I know. I can't explain it either," he said, gazing into her eyes.

She saw desire in them, just that quick, and took a certain amount of solace in the fact that he was feeling the same craving for this that she was.

"I'll be down in a minute," he said, moving toward the bathroom now.

"Right," she said, slowly coming to herself, remembering that Summer would be back anytime now. She straightened up her clothes and got back behind the stove, quietly stirring the spaghetti sauce and dreaming of hips that moved just so, and of how lucky was she to be here, doing this with him, getting some of her groove back.

***

Friday morning

Clarke looked over at Bria, now sitting in the passenger seat of her jeep, trying to remember the route that she'd taken with Amber. Clarke had picked her up from the parking lot of Ranchero's Chicken forty minutes ago. She had been driving since then.

"This is the last road, I think," Bria said.

"Take your time."

"Yes, ma'am."

Clarke made the left turn onto Cr 243, the last road in the series of roads that they'd travelled this afternoon. This was definitely the country, Clarke thought, looking at all the long stretches of fenced-in land on both sides of the road.

"There should be a dip in the road coming up. I'd let Amber out on the other side of that dip."

"She never said where she was going or who she was going to meet?" Clarke asked.

"Nope," Bria said, looking intently out of the front window. "There it is," she said, and yes, they were approaching a dip in the road, to accommodate the dry creek bed that ran though this patch of land. The sign on the side read, *Turn around don't drown,* which meant the dry bed could become a running and dangerous stream in a heavy rain storm, as was the Texas way.

"I let her out here, and she'd wouldn't move from that spot until I turned the car around, headed back in the opposite direction," Bria said, staring out the window, like Amber would pop up any minute. "She would just stand there, off to the side, waiting until I left." She turned to Clarke. "One time, I thought I'd trick her, you know, wait for ten minutes and double back. She was standing right where I'd dropped her off. She even had the nerve to smile at me. All was missing was her saying *Gotcha*."

Clarke had to drive up a ways in order to pull over to the side of the road—not very easy out here. There was a good foot between the road and a ditch, which was not deep but was wide; another reliever for rain runoff.

"I'll be back in a minute," Clarke said. She was out and walking off down the road before Bria could blink, headed to the area where Bria had dropped Amber. She stood in the spot and looked around. She didn't think she could live out here. It was too quiet... too rural for her taste. It wasn't the area of rolling hills and large lawns with beautiful homes attached. This was its poorer neighbor. This was the same large land plots but covered in junk in various stages of decay.

She looked to her left, and then to her right. Property was fenced off on both sides of the street, more than a little depressing, she thought at the number of mobile homes in the lot across the street. Not that she had anything against mobile homes, except she liked them to be new if she had to have one.

Lots of land, and trees surrounding a bunch of mobile homes was how she summed up the area. So many trees, she noticed, preventing her from seeing inside a few of the lots. The owners probably preferred it that way. She needed a closer look and that would have to happen on another day. She walked back over to her jeep.

"See anything?" Bria asked.

"Not much. I'll have to come back when I have more time," Clarke said, behind the wheel now. She turned around at the first corner, drove slowly down the road again. She slowed down more when she reached the creek, trying to see beyond the trees. Nope, she couldn't.

She'd run a property search after lunch, see if anything out of the ordinary popped up, and come back another day when she had time to park and maybe even walk around a bit. Right now she would take Bria back to work. She was meeting Summer for lunch. She had time to run by Henri's, pick up his list per his instructions last night before she and he... and now was not the time to be daydreaming, she reminded herself.

ELEVEN

Friday morning, late

The end of the first week—sixty grueling hours—had been interesting and survivable, Henri thought, sitting in the construction office, catching his first break of the morning. This time last week he had been having Karen served; the beginning of the end of his life as he'd known it. This week had been mostly interviewing and finding his way through the mess left behind by Willis Wilson.

Fortunately he was making progress, not that he'd expected anything different. He was really good at his job, in almost all aspects of it. Two interviews this morning, and he had two more scheduled for this afternoon. Those were the last of them, the result of his family's human resources department and connections to headhunters whose reach extended to most large Texas towns.

He heard heels hitting the metal of his steps outside, and he smiled. It was either Ms. Kensington or his sister, and since Clarke was the only one that had promised to stop by, he thought it most likely was her. He turned towards the door to wait, relaxing into his chair, and what was this he was feeling? Excitement. It could be that; hard not to be, given their sexual compatibility. It lingered in his mind often these days. He thought of last evening and her opening the door to his room. Yeah, he liked what they did together.

The door opened before he could explore that thought further, and it wasn't Clarke who had arrived. It was Karen, his soon-to-be ex. She walked in, and out walked his excitement. He was both surprised and not to see her here. Surprised because she'd stopped calling, and he'd thought she had given up, but no, she had not. He could see the error of thinking that now, with crystal clear clarity.

"Hi," she said tentatively, standing just inside the door, wearing a black silky dress, with matching black sandals on her feet. All to highlight her figure, which it did, of course. How hardened he had become to her, he thought. Her shoes weren't anywhere near the tall heel height that Ms. Kensington seemed to prefer, but then Clarke didn't have Karen's height or her legs— long, shapely legs that seemed to go on forever. Those were one of the first things he'd noticed about her. She was beautiful still, slim always; she worked on it with a vengeance that rivaled any world-class athlete.

"Thank you for giving us a chance to talk," she said.

"I was expecting a phone call."

"I thought it would be better to talk in person."

"How's the baby? Where's the baby?" Henri asked.

"Good, beautiful, with my mother," she said, tears falling from her eyes, just that quick. "I'm so sorry."

"It is what it is," he said, and it was silent for a few, as they looked each other over. "So what can I do for you?" he asked.

"Hear me out?"

"It's what your mother asked of me."

"Yes," she said, moving toward the desk now. She didn't stop until she stood by the side of it. She leaned over then, her hands landing on the arms of the chair he sat in. She bent at the waist, moving her face toward his. *And what the hell was this?* he wondered, watching her move in closer and closer to his face.

He sat still, an observer curious to see what she'd do next. She placed her lips on his. He didn't move, didn't close his eyes, just sat watching as she turned her head to the side. For better access maybe, he thought, but he didn't open his mouth to her kiss, so no access was what she received. He continued to watch as her eyes closed and her tongue worked to wiggle itself into the seam of his mouth.

To put up a fight or move away would indicate that she affected him in some way. She didn't and he wanted her to know that, so that's what sitting there unmoving meant to him. Unfortunately, the door opened and in walked Ms. Kensington. Of course it did. That's how the timing of things worked in his romantic life these day, starting with his marriage to Karen. Beyond the great nights of sex with Ms. Kensington, his love life was for shit.

"Oh, excuse me," Clarke said, eyes round in shock, staring into his now, as he turned his head toward her, leaving Karen kissing the empty space where his lips had been a few minutes ago.

Karen stood where she was for a second, a few inches from his mouth, surprised, yes, but recovering quickly. She turned her head seeking the source of their interruption and found Clarke. Karen smiled.

"I'm sorry," Karen said, standing upright then. "I haven't seen my husband in a while, so I apologize for the PDA." She moved toward Clarke now, with her hand outstretched. Karen had grown up being the woman with the world on her string, an old attitude she fell back into effortlessly. Being a lawyer didn't hurt her confidence either, Henri thought, watching her cross the room, headed towards Clarke.

"Hello," Clarke said.

"You work with my husband?" Karen asked.

"She's a private investigator, a friend of Summer, and yes,

she works for me," Henri said, staring into Clarke's eyes. Not that it mattered; Clarke couldn't read him, had no clue to what he was feeling or thinking at the moment.

"Clarke, this is Karen Novak. Karen, meet Clarke Kensington," he said, his gaze still on Clarke's. Yeah, she was both surprised and shocked, he thought, had the same look in her eyes that she did during one of their late-night get-togethers when he'd tried something new, something unexpected but pleasurable. Her eyes always did that grow-big-in-her-face thing, usually followed by some type of moan.

"Hi, nice to meet you," Clarke said, shocked still, but playing it off as best as one could given the circumstances. "I didn't mean to interrupt. I had a lunch date with Summer nearby, and I thought I could run in to pick up those resumés from you." She moved toward his desk with her hand outstretched.

"Sure," he said, picking up a folder from his desk. He placed it into her hand.

"I'll have the info to you by Monday as agreed. Call if you want to add any more names to it," she said.

"I will," he said, watching as she walked to the door.

She turned around just as she reached the door. Her gaze meeting Karen's now, she said, "It was nice to meet you."

"You too," Karen said, watching as Clarke made her exit. She was pretty, Karen thought, and dressed well; slacks-and-jacket professional, slim. She was softly shapely. African American—that was a surprise, but not as much as her height, or more her lack of it. She had not figured African American or short for Henri, but maybe it was his way of getting back at her for the choices she'd made.

She was more than a private investigator. Karen knew that on a woman's instinctive level, yes. It was also the look of surprise in

Ms. Kensington's eyes that had Karen shifting her gaze back over to her husband. Yep, they were at least sexually active; she'd seen Henri's look of sexual interest enough to recognize it. Karen moved back to his desk, in spite of what she thought, and bent down again, to finish what she'd come here to do, which was to bring her husband back home where he belonged.

Since crying and pleading hadn't worked, she was left playing the only card she held, and that was Henri's desire for her. It was interesting to see that look in his eye for someone else. Maybe it hadn't been a good idea to keep him away during the pregnancy. Sexually she hadn't been interested, at least not with him.

"So where were we?" she asked, a little emboldened by his lack of reaction to Clarke. They were sexually involved but she apparently didn't mean enough to him, not to warrant speaking up. Henri had let her walk out the door minus an explanation, and that was heartening, Karen thought. Yes, she was pulling at straws, but she needed something to hold on to.

"You were leaving," Henri said, meeting her eyes. She moved in to kiss him again, and he moved then, pushing his chair away from his desk, out of her reach. He stood. "Your mother asked me to listen to you. It's the *only* reason you're still here. So start talking. What do you want?"

"To work this out?" she said.

"No," he said, without anger. "It's been a short time since I left, but it's really been a while, if we're being honest. The baby was just potential glue to try and keep us together and that was too much responsibility to place on a kid. I should have known that."

"One lapse, and you are ready to throw our marriage and all the work we put into it away. It wasn't as bad as you say it was. I loved you. I still love you. Maybe you're the one that didn't love me."

"It wasn't just one lapse," he said.

"What do you mean?"

"You know what I mean," he said, meeting her gaze, and yeah, he'd thought correctly.

"I don't know what you think you know. It's you and that woman who are together."

"What?" he asked, in that way of his that told her she had uncovered a truth.

So when did it start? Before the baby? Was it the reason he had chosen Austin of all places, she wondered. She smiled, feeling hopeful that she had hit upon something that could be useful in bending Henri to her will, and if not, she could always use it in her divorce negotiations. "You and Clarke. I know what I know too. I can see. Maybe you want out for different reasons, like Ms. Kensington? You and her. I can see things too."

"Goodbye. For the last time," Henri said, not even going to respond. He walked toward the door instead, meeting her gaze, hoping she could see the determination he felt. "I'm done."

He held the door open for a bit, as it took her a minute before she did anything beyond stare at him with tears in her eyes. Eventually she moved toward him, stopping in front of him.

"Fine," she said, and it was her turn to be angry. She turned on her heel and marched out the door.

And what a relief, he thought, letting the door close behind her.

***

Sharkey's was, of course, crowded. Because of the food, yes, but with women, lots of them, like Summer, eager to try to ensnare the owner. Nice guy, and although not overly attractive, there was something about the man that brought women there in droves.

He was not Clarke's type. Nobody had been, before her nights with Henri, at least. She hadn't been interested enough to break her self-imposed no-men policy. She still wasn't. Okay, maybe a little, but that was only for one dude—and he was tied up with his wife, as she found out today—and even then it had only been sexually, nothing near serious or romantic.

She actually thought she was going to be sick, after she entered his office. She felt shock and surprise, yes, but also the feeling of being played, participating in something without having all the facts, like the fact that he was still engaged with his wife. She felt ill at seeing them together, lips locked and all.

Oh, but you can bet that this was the end of that. She didn't do threesomes. It was one thing to be two consenting adults, desirous to share in the late-night call of the booty, and another thing to be a side-piece, which made Karen the main bitch, and hell no was she falling into that realm of living.

Well, she was done. He and his married ass could stay married for all she cared, she thought, her anger growing. She fought back the desire to glare at the woman who stood in her way, blocking the front of the restaurant. "Excuse me," Clarke said, moving around her, headed to the table near the right side where Summer currently sat, looking over the menu.

"Sorry I'm late," Clarke said, taking the seat across from her friend.

"You're not late, and what's wrong?"

"Nothing."

"It is not nothing. It's Henri, isn't it? And you two were doing so well," Summer said.

"What?" Clarke asked. She thought she had done a good job of keeping her late-night activities from her friend.

"Didn't you just leave him at the office? You said you were going to stop by and pick up something, and now you're here, angry. Gosh, you and he were finally cordial to each other. I thought you were finally getting past the first time you met. The other night, at dinner, you two were getting along so well."

"Oh. This is something else, nothing to do with your brother. It's a client," Clarke said.

"You're sure?"

"*Yes.*" She made a face. "How's our boy Sharkey?" she asked, changing the subject.

"The same; not interested. Or not interested in me or me alone," Summer said.

The waitress arrived, took their orders, and moved on quickly. It was busy here always, reflected in the no dilly-dallying efficiency that was the wait staff.

"So what's my brother up to?"

"What do you mean?"

"Ah… again. You just left his office. What else could I mean?" Summer asked, eyeing her strangely.

"He's fine. He had company. I interrupted him kissing his wife," Clarke said.

"What? Are you sure?" Summer said. Her expression changed from happy to pinched and downcast in seconds.

"Am I sure he was kissing her, or am I sure she was his wife?"

"Both, I guess."

"He introduced us, so yes, it was Karen. She is who he is married to?"

"Yes, Karen is his soon-to-be ex."

"It didn't look like soon-to-be to me. She was leaning over his desk, her lips locked on his."

"What was he doing?"

"Watching her," Clarke said, realizing that he had been, in fact, staring at his wife as she kissed him. Not sure what that meant, if anything, or if it changed anything. It didn't, she decided quickly.

"I'm sure there's a reasonable explanation."

"It's not my business what your brother does. Reasonable explanation or not."

"I never thought it was. Are you sure you're okay?"

"I am," Clarke said, taking her frustrations down a notch. She did not need Summer involved in the two of them. Well, there wasn't going to be a two of them any more in any capacity beyond work. "It's Amber that has me bothered."

"Can't find anything?"

"Nope," she said, but she started into telling of all she'd done so far to locate her cousin, and it moved her mind away from Henri and on to what it should be on—her work. She and Summer moved on then to discussing what Summer had done today, the places she gone: looking at flooring and plumbing, house-related things. It was enough to keep Clarke's mind off of Henri, and after forty-five minutes they were leaving.

"Don't forget tonight. We're taking a look at the last house."

"I won't," Clarke said, moving over to her car, trampling down the thought of Henri and what seeing him this evening would be like. Nope. She moved her thoughts back to work, where, come hell or high water, they would remain.

***

Friday evening

Summer and Clarke's third and final house was much newer than their first or second. It was another single-story. House number three could use some exterior paint, but otherwise it looked to be in good condition. Yard was nice, well maintained. Asking price was one hundred fifty thousand, a tidy fifty-thousand-dollar potential profit, as the homes in this neighborhood sold for about two hundred thousand and change. This one had a rectangular porch, two feet by four, and windows to the left and right, a few feet from the front door. Not as much of an update would be required of this one, at least on the outside, Henri thought, parking by the curb in front of it, checking it out as he did so.

It was located in a well-established neighborhood in Round Rock, a small city at the north edge of Austin. Out of the three choices, house number one was his favorite.

He was the third person here, scanning the cars for Clarke's black jeep, which wasn't here yet. Hamp's truck and Summer's car were parked beside each other in the drive. He made his way to the front door.

Clean, he thought, his first impression of the interior after crossing the threshold. The living room was the first room he encountered, moving past the foyer. There was a half-wall to the left, with a kitchen and a breakfast area behind it. Summer and Hamp stood in the middle of the living room.

"All that's missing is Clarke," Summer said, meeting his gaze.

"Okay," he said, choosing not to read anything into his sister's pronouncement beyond a statement of fact.

"I like it. It's nice. Not as much of a challenge as the first one, which is still my favorite," Summer said.

"Sorry I'm late," Clarke said, walking past him and coming to a stop beside Summer. And yeah, she looked good, dressed in jeans that fit her slender limbs perfectly, tucked into short boots. A t-shirt rounded out her ensemble. It was the first time he'd seen her this casually dressed.

"Hey, Summer, Uncle Hamp," she said, smiling and moving her gaze between them. It fell away a bit when she reached him. "Oh, hi, Henri," she tacked on at the end. A little like an after-thought, he mused.

"Hi," he said. Yes, she'd been bothered by his wife's appearance. That's how he'd interpreted her greeting, followed by a quick glance she'd just given him.

"Okay, the asking price is one hundred fifty thousand. Homes in this area sell for about two hundred thousand. You guys ready to start?" Summer said, all tour-guide ready.

"Hamp's always ready," Hamp said, smiling at Summer.

"I love the floors," Summer said, in full-out appraisal mode now, gazing down at the nice hardwood floors which were wide planked and a deep rich chocolate color. "I stopped by this one store yesterday, or maybe it was Monday, and I fell in love with this one color. Too expensive, I know, you don't even have to ask the price, but so beautiful," Summer said, chattering away.

In good shape, Henri thought. "Nice," he said. "If the rest of the house is like this, you don't have to do much to it."

"The asking price is a little high, I thought before I arrived, but I can see the reason for it. Lots of upgrades here," Summer said, moving toward the kitchen.

On and on it went, the kitchen first and then the rest of the house, a stream of steady chatter from Summer to mostly Hamp, and sometimes Henri. Hamp took notes as they went about the business of checking out the house, and less than an hour later they arrived at the backyard.

As with the rest of the house, it had been taken care of well. The square-shaped yard was mostly grass, with a small, bean-shaped swimming pool in the middle of it. A little further past the pool was something that might have been a grill at one time but was now a bent piece of metal. Hamp and Summer examined it more closely while Clarke, who had followed them out, stood by the front part of the pool. Henri was last to enter the backyard. He walked over to her.

"Nice selling point," he said, looking down into the empty swimming pool. This was the first time they'd been alone. She was avoiding him, and it went beyond making sure Summer didn't suspect anything.

"Yep," Clarke said, looking down into the pool.

"So later?" he asked.

"I've got a thing, so no," she said, continuing to stare at the empty pool, before lifting her gaze to his.

"No problem," he said, and it wasn't—or it wouldn't be. "I sent you an email this afternoon. Two additional names that require background checks. Kevin Huang is still my first choice," he added.

"I'll have it back to you as promised on Monday," she said.

He looked up then, catching Summer staring at them, her gaze assessing. Plenty going on in that head of hers, he thought. She was moving toward them, leaving Hamp behind. He was checking out the fence now.

"Okay, you two. What do you think?" she said, stopping in front of them.

"It's a nice home. I like it," Clarke said.

"Do you like it better than the others?"

"It's less work than the others."

"Is that a yes or no?"

"It's an I-don't-care. You're picking for us, remember?"

"What do you think, dear brother?"

"It's not my decision," he said.

"We know this. Tell us what you think anyway. You've been silent during all of it," Summer said, moving closer to Clarke. "Clarke and I would like to hear your opinion. You've had experience with this type of thing; that's why I wanted you here. So don't play coy. What do you think? Which house do you like of the three? Which house should we choose?"

Henri looked over at Clarke, who was back to staring into the pool.

"Fine. I think you should get all the bids back from Hamp before you decide anything. I think you should ask yourself what kind of company you want to be, what type of clientele you wish to attract. What would you like to be known for? Upscale? Or are you focused on the middle-income buyer? Are you interested in homes that don't require much work? The profit may be smaller, but you can flip them faster.

"All three houses are very different from each other. House number one and this one are very different from number two. Number two is much more upscale in a great neighborhood; an up and coming one, so I've read. It would cost money to purchase, and more money to turn into a high-end home. That's why you need to know who you are before you start; it affects all of your decisions," he said, glancing between the two of them.

Okay, she was impressed, a little, Clarke thought, listening to Henri talk. Handsome and smart and fine, standing there, slightly wet from the heat outside. Yummy any day of the week, in and out of bed, and it was for sure a no to the bed part going forward. How sad was that for her. The one man that sex had finally been fun with was now off-limits. She listened as he continued to talk, listing, without any notes, the pros and cons of all three houses.

"Oh," Summer squealed at the end of his spiel.

Summer squealed more than a woman her age should, Clarke thought, and it must be nice to have that amount of enthusiasm for life. Life had to have been kind to her if she could still squeal.

"That's why I wanted you here," Summer said, smiling at her brother, before moving her gaze to Clarke. "Isn't he great?" she asked.

"Yep. I have to go," Clarke said.

"She has a thing," Henri said, meeting surprised gazes from both Clarke and Summer.

"He's right. I do have a thing. You and I will catch up later. We can discuss what comes next then?" Clarke said.

"Tomorrow morning, if not before," Summer said.

"Yep," Clarke said, moving away to say goodbye to Hamp.

She waved to them both, or it could have been only Summer she'd waved to, Henri thought of the clearly irritated woman.

"What did you two argue about?" Summer asked, her gaze piercing.

"What would we have to argue about?" he said.

"I don't know, that's the reason for the question. She's bothered about something. She seemed angry about something. I thought you might have said something to her when she stopped by today at lunch. Maybe it's her work. She's having trouble finding her cousin. That's probably it."

"Her cousin is missing?" Henri asked.

"Yes, two weeks and no one's seen her. Clarke's been looking for her, along with all the other things she has to do. That would bother me," Summer said.

"Me too," he said, considering. Again he was reminded of

how little they knew about each other's lives. They'd wanted it that way.

"I'll see you at home, or do you have to meet nameless-faceless tonight?" Summer asked.

"Home, and you're not as funny as you think you are," he said.

"Whatever," she said, before walking back over to join Hamp.

Bothered about something. His sister's words were in his head. It was what he kind of figured. Clarke was bothered by what she had seen earlier, him with Karen. Not sure why she hadn't said something if it bothered her so much. She was, after all, an adult. *So be one, and speak up,* he thought. He'd had enough of no-talking, carrying-a-grudge-woman-thy-name-is-Karen to last him a lifetime. So if that was Clarke's way of settling disputes, then that was fine too, and that was good to know. This could be a good stopping point if she wanted to stop. It was fun, great while it lasted, enough to last him a while, as the idea of a one-night stand held very little appeal at this time. Not after the ease and connection he'd felt with Clarke. He been lucky to find it so quickly, and doubted he would be so lucky every time.

"Hello," Summer said, standing in front of him, waving her hand in front of his face. "You're a thousand miles away. Time to go. Hamp's done, has all he needs. I wouldn't waste my time thinking about Karen, if that's what has you preoccupied. I heard you saw her today."

"Clarke told you this?"

"Yes."

"She also said she saw the two of you kissing. That can't be true, can it?"

"It's true, but it didn't mean anything, it was just Karen being Karen."

"That's what I thought, but Clarke doesn't know Karen like

we do. It doesn't matter as long as you're not going back to her. Tell me that you're not going back to her."

"I'm not going back."

"Good," Summer said.

***

Saturday

Tia's Tacos was where Clarke and Summer sat, early the following morning. They both had breakfast tacos between them. It was coffee for Clarke and some kind of green gunk for Summer.

"So what's the week looking like?" Clarke asked.

"We have to pick one of the houses. If we select house number one, which I think we will, I'll have to start negotiations, which should be easy. Maybe even get into cleaning it before we close, if she'll allow it. Or not," Summer said, watching her friend pick at her taco. "Enough about boring houses. You okay?"

"Yep," Clarke said, taking a sip of her coffee.

"Any luck on finding your Amber?"

"Nope, and that's the reason I'm bummed," Clarke said, and spent a few minutes bringing Summer up to date on the interviews she'd conducted and the trip out to the country.

"Something will come up, you mark my words. You should talk to my brother about it. Maybe it will help take his mind off his troubles. I'd much prefer him to spend his time with you than nameless-faceless. He was home last night, looking all sad, and, well, I just thought helping you might take his mind off of his problems."

"I don't think so," Clarke said.

"Okay, forget I suggested it. You work better alone anyway. I know this," Summer said, smiling, before turning the conversation to other things.

***

Saturday morning

Henri entered the gym for a quick run before basketball. He was surprisingly still out of sorts at how things with Clarke had turned out. Miffed that she hadn't called and asked for an explanation for what she thought she'd seen between him and Karen. Yeah, yeah, he knew she had a reason to assume the worst, but still, she couldn't ask? He spotted Stephen standing near the door alone again, same as last Saturday, same early too.

"You always early?"

"Yes, scouting usually, but I was hoping that you would show early too. I've got problems at home," Stephen said.

"Really?"

"Yeah. It's the dinner thing Reye's planned for Sunday."

"The one I said I wasn't attending?"

"Yes, well, two of the men I invited bailed on me this morning, which leaves me hanging, empty-handed. Reye's been looking forward to this thing, and so far it's just women and no men. I don't have the heart to call it off, pregnant woman and all. Not without trying to see if I can pull in a few favors. I thought you might have pity on me, and stop by, help your boy out. You could even bring Clarke along at this point, to ensure that you're not bothered with anyone else."

"Doesn't that defeat the purpose?"

"At this point, I'll take what I can get..." Stephen said, palms up and open.

"Clarke and I have parted ways, it seems," Henri said, glad to have somebody to vent that to, 'cause for some reason he was allowing it to bother him.

"Oh, really, and so soon? What happened?" Stephen asked.

Henri shrugged. "Karen stopped by—well, her mother stopped by Tuesday and asked me to talk to her daughter as a favor, and I agreed. I thought she meant a call, but Karen being Karen shows up in person, kisses me, and thinks that's all I need to move back in. And because my love life's for shit, guess who walks in?"

"Clarke."

"Yep, Clarke."

"Oh."

"Yeah, oh," Henri said.

"So did you explain?"

"Nope."

"Why not?"

"Don't know. I saw her afterward, and she was whatever about it all, about us getting together, so I guess it became whatever to me too."

"It's a misunderstanding. You should just talk to her."

"Nope."

"Okay, I can see your point, and I can also see hers. You can too, right, if you think about it. If your positions were reversed, would seeing her with her husband together in that way go over well with you? Wouldn't you want an explanation?"

"We were just having sex," Henri said. And yes, he would probably want her to say something, but he wasn't afraid of asking if it bothered him enough. And not speaking meant it had bothered her.

"It's bothering you, so it must be more, at least a little bit. Put yourself in her shoes," Stephen said, watching his words find a home in his friend. "You know I like Clarke, I've said it enough, but whatever, there's more where she came from, right?" Stephen smiled. "Maybe the more where she came from will be at my house on Sunday, and now you're free... I wouldn't ask if I didn't need you. Plus you owe me."

"Owe you what?"

"How many times have I hooked you up?"

"You mean like years ago, before either one of us were married?"

"Yep."

"The statute of limitations is way over and done on that period of my life," Henri said.

"A debt is a debt is a debt. You know I wouldn't ask you if I wasn't desperate. Basically, all you have to do is show up and eat."

"That's not all I'd have to do. I'd have to make small talk and I don't want to talk, small or otherwise. That was the beauty of being with Clarke, who was perfect, by the way, for what I wanted: energetic, eager, nice ass, slim-legged, small breasts, just like I like them to be. And most importantly, not interested in talking either."

"But it's gone, right? Clarke's gone?" Stephen said, watching Henri. If he could smile at what he thought Henri was beginning to feel for Clarke, he would. "I'll take that as a yes for tomorrow at seven," he said instead. "Don't be late. You could even bring dessert or fresh flowers for my wife or something." Stephen chuckled at the end.

"Fine. If I'm not as happy as you want, or as cordial, you only have yourself to blame," Henri said, smiling before peeling away, headed toward the others on the court warming up.

Stephen stood and watched his buddy Henri fall in with everyone else. He smiled, again internally, of course, as he started into his warm-up, pleased with the outcome, thinking how cool it was when a plan came together.

***

Clarke sat at the back end of the bar, nursing her drink of Coke on the rocks. She didn't mix drinking with work. She was watching Rayford Wilson drink, talk, and bet his way through the evening. More proof that he was not the family-man real estate mogul he pretended to be.

A racing form lay on the bar space in front of her, part of her cover along with the baseball cap pulled low on her head and the earbuds that ran to her phone. All needed camouflage for people watching. Not that Rayford had any idea she was here for him. He was totally absorbed in his gambling, a habit of his that had started long ago.

Ten years, and her client hadn't heard from her father. He'd been busy, and this was the business that he'd craved, his drug of choice, and the explanation probably for why he'd needed to leave town, to leave his daughter behind.

He, along with two like-minded friends, had been here since it opened, which in the winter months was five thirty. She'd spent most of the afternoon tailing Mr. Wilson from his home in Waco to this lovely establishment. Friday and Saturday evening was Thoroughbred racing day, or rather evening.

Today was her first time at the tracks. This one was on the outskirts of San Antonio—a straight shot down Interstate 35.

Clarke took another sip of her drink, watching Rayford order another round of whatever they were drinking for the table, while flirting with the waitress. *What a douche*, she thought, followed by *Sirena was better off not knowing about this dad that wasn't much of one.* Better off forgetting about him totally, but most people needed to know, and she understood that desire sometimes. Other times, not so much.

Take her, running into Henri and his wife. What could he say that would explain him kissing his wife? So why ask, why set oneself up to hear a lie? Not that he'd even bothered to offer one.

She turned her mind to her niece and where to go next in her search, now that she'd gone through Amber's list of friends. Back to her high school, or maybe back to the country for another look.

Finally, Rayford was leaving, which meant she could leave too. Now, if he was going home for the night, that would make it even better. She could go home too.

She was tired. A week of Henri at night and work during the day, and she could fall into bed and sleep for a day or two. Much better to think of all the rest she could expect now, instead of what she was forfeiting.

He was that good, they were that good together, and who knew it could be that good. She certainly hadn't. All she had known was her spouse. She married him out of high school. She'd been one dude away from being a virgin when he'd swooped in and introduced her to more than she'd bargained for. It had been for nothing; she hadn't even gotten the kid that would have made it at least a little bit worthwhile.

Well, it was water under the bridge, and she would have to let it go at some point, that anger and all that hurt. She sighed and prepared to leave.

***

Summer entered her home, surprised to find her big brother home and seated on her couch for the second night in a row. Two beer bottles sat next to his feet, and sounds of some type of game could be heard from the TV. She stood in the doorway and stared.

"What?" he asked.

"I was just wondering if this was my house. What happened to nameless-faceless? Tonight? Last night? Don't tell me, she's tired? Couldn't keep up?"

He didn't respond.

"Can't blame her, that's got to be a lot of nonstop sex, and we're not robots, you know," she said, dropping her purse and keys on the table near the door. "Not answering is one way to go, the safest way, I guess." She plopped down on the couch beside him, reaching for a beer. "I'm going to take a shower, and then we are going to watch a movie, your pick."

"What I'm watching now is fine."

"Not if you want my company. I can't sit through anything sports. Yuck. You do realize that this is my house and you're my guest?"

"Which is why I should do the selecting," he said, smiling. "How's the house hunting?" It was the perfect question. Summer took the reins and off she went, talking up a storm. Perfect, he thought as he tuned her out, irritated still, and thinking about calling Clarke to talk, the first time he was interested in doing so.

TWELVE

Sunday evening

Henri sat in his truck, searching for all the other cars he expected to be here, to accompany the many women he expected to be here along with him… all the women Stephen had said would be present tonight. So far, there was nothing. His was the only vehicle parked outside of Reye and Stephen's home.

Maybe he was early, he thought, or maybe all the women were just one woman, Clarke Kensington, as it was her jeep in his rear view mirror, pulling in behind him. He laughed and shook his head at being caught flatfooted again, recognizing this for the set-up that it was.

He didn't understand Stephen's dogged determination to put them together. Why go to such lengths? What did his friend see that he couldn't?

He looked in his rear view mirror again. Clarke was getting out of her car now, looking good enough to devour on the spot, dressed casual—or her version of casual, which always included heels, which tonight went along well with her spray-on pants and the pretty blouse that floated softly around her hips.

She was moving toward the front of her car, stepping onto the curb as he walked over to meet her. She smelled good too, wearing the same fragrance that floated around him when he was holding her close, late at night, driving toward his climax.

"Ms. Kensington," he said in greeting.

"Mr. Novak," she said. Still cool was the tone in her voice.

"This is a surprise."

"It is? Your buddy's matchmaking again, is what I think this is."

"Reye invited a bunch of friends, and his bailed. I'm helping him out of a tight spot is what he told me, so yeah, I'm leaning toward that conclusion, too," he said.

"We could leave," she said.

"Or we could stay, make the best of it, unless you're too whatever it is that you are to stick around."

"I have a reason to be whatever I am."

"Do you?" he asked, staring at her, those blue eyes of his back to icy, like the first day they'd met, which meant he was angry. And what did he have to be angry about, she'd like to know.

"I'm not going to argue with you," she said, moving away from him, headed to the Stuarts' front door. Hell no was she leaving now.

"Of course not, 'cause that would involve talking to me—getting your questions answered, but you'd rather make assumptions and seethe silently," he said, following along behind her, eyes glued to her ass. He'd missed that too.

She reached the door first, threw him a glare over her shoulder, and rang the doorbell. "It's impolite to stare," she said, catching his eyes on her butt.

"Is that what I was doing?" he said.

They both smiled when Reye answered, looking very pregnant.

It had been ages since he'd seen her, Henri thought. She was as pretty and as open as he remembered. "Mrs. Stuart," he said, a smile in his voice and on his face.

"Hey you," she said, smiling back at him, opening her arms

wide in greeting before pulling him in for a hug. "I'm glad you're here, and you've brought wine. We love wine in this house. Such a sweetheart, you always were." She turned her attention to the other woman who stood in the doorway. *Pretty and short* was Reye's first thought. "And you must be *the Clarke* I've heard so much about, and look. You brought wine too."

"The Clarke, huh? Sounds ominous. Good things, I hope," Clarke said.

"Of course. Come in," Reye said, standing aside so they could enter.

"What a lovely home you have," Clarke said, looking around at the space.

"Thanks. It will be on the market soon if you're interested. Stephen and I are leaving it behind, moving up to Dallas. Stephen's folks live there. He and his father, who's also an attorney, will finally partner up," Reye said, closing the door behind them.

"I heard. Congratulations on your new addition. It will be great having you back in my neck of the woods," Henri said.

"That could be trouble," Reye said, smiling. "Sorry," she said, meeting his gaze.

"Thanks," Henri said, pleased that she kept it small. He was so not into talking about his divorce.

"Hey," Stephen said, entering the room. He was casual in shorts, t-shirt, and sandals. "Hey, Clarke," he said to her, smiling. "Glad you were able to make it. There's bad news, though." He moved his gaze between the two of them.

"What bad news is this?" Henri asked.

"Every person we invited called to cancel at the last minute. Every last one of them," Stephen said, not even trying to keep a straight face. "So it'll just be you and Clarke tonight." He smiled wickedly. "And yes, I know what you're thinking, and there's some truth to it. Really, it's all true. This is a set-up. Want to know why I've gone to the trouble?" he asked, his gaze primarily on Henri.

"Why?" Reye asked, smiling, clearly in on this too.

"You two don't know each other, not really, and I thought, let me help them get to know each other. Let's give you two a chance to *talk*."

Henri smiled, a full one, shaking his head.

"Clarke, you don't mind, do you? Henri's a good guy. I'm sure you know next to nothing about him. He can be that way sometimes. He can be tight-lipped, particularly when he's hurt. I've known him most of my life, so I know these things. Can't see what's good for him when he gets like that, and because he helped me once—or tried to help me see the way of things—I feel compelled to return the favor."

Clarke had no idea what he was talking about, moving her gaze between the two of them.

"So yes, I wanted you here, just the two of you. I thought you might be able to help see him through his divorce. He *is* getting divorced, by the way, and it was way past time. He's traveling a similar path as you. Thought you two might have a lot in common." He was smiling at her.

Clarke sought out Reye's gaze. She smiled back, shook her head too, but her gaze said that yes, she was on board with whatever her husband had planned.

"So what about drinks? What would you like to drink?" Stephen removed the wine bottles from his wife's hands. "Not bad," he said, eyeing their choices, then staring at Henri until they both started to chuckle.

***

Clarke had taken the seat closest to the door, the one beside Henri. Casual in jeans and a shirt, soft it appeared to be, blue to match his eyes. Clarke liked the Stuarts' home—cozy and colorful. Light green, light blue, and yellow paint covered different walls in the living room, matching the colorful rugs that lay over the hardwood floors. All of it was very different from the white that was the kitchen where they were seated now.

They seem happy, this couple, Clarke thought, sitting across from Reye and Stephen at the kitchen table, and it wasn't lost on her that she and Henri looked like a couple too, at least by outside appearances. Two mixed-race couples, although she and Henri weren't a couple in the same sense. In any sense, really.

She'd forgotten to set her phone to silent, and it was going off now, playing that Patti Griffin tune, "I Smell a Rat," catching everyone unawares, including herself. Surprise gave way to chuckles from everyone but Henri.

It was her Aunt Veda calling. "Excuse me. I have to take this," she said, heading to the door leading into the living room.

"Hey, Auntie, can I call you back? I'm at dinner with friends," Clarke said.

"I'm sorry, baby, to interrupt you. I called the police station today. Been calling them every day since Monday, not that it will get them to moving, but I want them to know that she has some-body that's watching... somebody that cares about her and wants her home," Veda said, her voice breaking at the end, needing to say this, Clarke's dinner or not. It was tears and crying into the phone for a while.

"I'm sorry," Clarke said, staring into the wall in front of her, unseeing. Really it was all she could say to all the tears.

"I didn't call you to cry, really, and I'll let you get back to your dinner. I wanted you to know that I found something, a picture," Veda said eventually.

"You did? Of Amber?"

"Yes, and some boy—a white one. What in God's name was she doing with a white man? I don't understand. I've been searching in her room, her things, you know, just like you told me to. It was pushed way under the mattress. I guess she forgot, anyway. It's a picture of the two of them standing outside some country bar —and what was she doing out there with some white man? Do you think he's the baby's daddy?"

"I don't know."

"It makes sense, the baby's coloring and all, which is why we argued so, and she was lying to me all the while," Aunt Veda said, and sighed. Clarke heard the weight of the world in that sigh.

"Do you think you can use it?" Aunt Veda asked.

"Yes, ma'am, I do. Can I come by in the morning? Unless you would rather I come tonight. It would be late, and I don't want you have to wait up for me."

"Of course. It'll keep. Go on and enjoy your dinner. It'll keep until morning."

"Try not to worry," Clarke said.

"Too late for that. A mother starts worrying as soon as her child makes that first cry and it never ceases. Good night, baby."

"G'night," Clarke said. She ran her hand through her hair and released her version of a world-weary sigh.

"Everything okay?" Stephen asked when Clarke emerged from the living room.

"A case I'm working on," Clarke said, settling back in her chair.

"That sounds so cool. So, you're a private eye," Reye said, her gaze on Clarke's.

"I don't know about the eye part or the cool part. It's work to me."

"What kind of cases do you handle?"

"It's been a mixed bag here, since I'm new to the area, but in Dallas, it was a mix of about fifty percent what-is-my-spouse-up-to —infidelity—and the other fifty percent was a mixture of family court cases, personal searches, finding missing loved ones, and 'you've come into some money, and I need to find you to give it to you.'"

"Clarke is considered one of the best for fathers seeking custody of their children," Stephen said.

"I developed a reputation for it. It's not only fathers seeking custody, but I'll admit I have a soft spot for them, for those that genuinely want to be a part of their kids' lives."

"Why fathers?"

She shrugged. "I had a friend once who loved his kids but divorced his wife, and she wanted to keep him from them as a way to get back at him. I helped him, and he ended up with joint custody. He told someone and they told someone and so on and so on, and I started to get more of those types of cases."

"You didn't mind?" Reye asked.

"Nope. Kids need both parents equally, I think."

"So half of your cases deal with infidelity?"

"Unfortunately, yes, they do."

"What was the worse infidelity case you've ever had to investigate?" Reye asked.

"My own," she said, and smiled. It was a spur-of-the-moment decision to tell all, so he—and he was Henri—would have a better understanding of why seeing him with his wife bothered her so. "It's the reason I'm not as trusting as I used to be," she said, meeting Henri's eyes. He stared back, not that she could read him. She couldn't whatsoever.

"Really?" Stephen said, shooting a quick glance in Henri's direction too.

"Really," she said.

"You don't have to talk about it if you don't want to. You can tell us your next worst one," Reye said.

"No, it's okay. Let's see. A man came to see me one day, with the usual 'I suspect my wife of cheating.' He had done some searching on his own, he said, but hadn't been unable to find anything. He wanted answers, which I understand. The desire to know, regardless of the outcome, a person just wants to know. No more doubts and wondering if you're going crazy. Then you can decide—to stay, to go, whatever—so he hired me, put me on retainer, told me to take as long as I needed."

"Retainer? Like with attorneys?" Reye asked.

"Yep, we operate similarly in our payment structures. Sometimes the cases can be time-consuming, or if I have to travel outside of town, I might have to hire other PIs to fill in, like if the person in question travels to other places and I'm tied up, or they'd fit in better in whatever place."

"Didn't know you worked that way," Reye said.

"I do. Takes a while sometimes, the same as with attorneys, and I hadn't gotten to the place in my career that people didn't question my rates or my retainer fees."

"An hourly rate?" Stephen asked.

"Yep, also like attorneys. Mine is one hundred fifty an hour. I gave you a discount," Clarke said, meeting Henri's gaze. He was quiet about that admission as well—the same unreadable.

"Is that expensive?"

"It's not cheap, but some really good investigators can command upwards of two hundred fifty," she said.

"Not bad," Reye said.

"So getting back to the story," Stephen said, feeling a little discomfort in asking, but really wanting Henri to hear, to know this part of Clarke's life. His desire for that overruled any squeamishness he felt about asking her something so personal. She smiled, and his worries faded. Clarke, he could tell, was strong, and probably didn't do anything she didn't want to.

"His wife was a stay-at-home mother of two sweet little girls, too young yet for school, probably kindergarten the next year. They played out in the front yard most days, she with them. She was with them all the time, which was cool. I liked that about her. It was my first week, and so far it was every day out in the front yard with the little girls.

"Friday was the only change in her daily schedule. She had that day all to herself. It was the perfect day for her to cheat if she wanted to. She dropped the girls at a Mother's Day Out program at the local daycare. She went shopping, had her nails done, ran errands, and then she picked up the girls late afternoon. That was the first Friday I watched.

"The second Friday, week two, she dropped the girls off at the daycare and went back home. It was a nice day out, clear, and I'd been sitting there for about two hours with nothing but quiet. Not all quiet. I was starting to worry about this older lady, the street watchman, blowing my cover. I expected to see a cop pull up behind me at any minute, 'cause she kept staring out of her window at me. I had just turned away, into figuring out what I would do next, when a car turned onto the street behind me. It was my client's.

"They lived in the middle of the block, with intersecting

streets on each end. I met his eyes as he drove past to the end of the block, where he made a U-turn and parked his car. He was facing me, staring at me through his front windshield.

"I was irritated at first. Here was my worst nightmare come to life, a client that wouldn't listen or follow my instructions and let me do the job that he'd hired me to do.

"Nothing good could come from this, I thought, and between him and the little old lady staring out the window at me, I needed to do something quickly.

"I decided calling him was my best option, but before I could reach my phone, another car was turning on the street. It passed my client and rolled to a stop in front of my client's home.

"I reached for my video camera, worried that my client had planned some type of confrontation with the other party to his wife's affair. I sat and watched, and so far, my client didn't move, seemed to be content to watch.

"So I turned my attention back to the car that had parked out in front of the house. I knew that car; I had ordered special tags for its owner, my husband.

"Why was he here? was my first thought. Did I tell him? Maybe he was bringing me coffee or something, 'cause sometimes he did that, but not today. Really, it had been a while—things had changed so much between us, I hadn't told him about my latest case. It's one of the things I miss, talking to him about my work," she said, lost in thought for a minute. "Sorry." She smiled, deliberately keeping her gaze away from Henri.

"Anyway, I sat and watched. He exited from his car and walked over to my client's front door. A few minutes later, he disappeared inside. My client was getting out of his car, and what the hell, I thought. I reached for my pepper spray in case things went crazy. Firearms and infidelity don't mix, so I left my gun in the car.

"My client hadn't gone inside as I thought he'd do. Nope, he was waiting at the front door for me. He held his key in his hand, poised to unlock the front door.

"'That's my husband,' I said.

"'I know. I'm sorry,' he said.

"'You knew? You hired me and you knew already?'

"'I did,' he said.

"'We shouldn't,' I remember saying, before he placed his finger to my lips, wanting me to be quiet. I knew it was crazy, and in any other situation but that one, I would have advised my client to leave. Nothing but trouble or more hurt would come from confrontation, and knowing all of that, I wanted inside anyway. I could finally understand the desire to see for oneself.

"I followed him inside, feeling like I was some other woman, and the real me was watching from above. It was crazy, right, to be checking out this woman's house, on my way to catch my husband cheating on me with her.

"Her home was clean, I can tell you that, not at all what I expected to find, although I'm not sure what I had expected to find. Someone that couldn't keep house, I guess, or was worse than me in some way, an explanation for why he would choose her over me.

"We walked past the living room and the dining room, into the hall where the bedrooms were. They couldn't hear us; too much moaning and other kinds of sounds to hear us. It was the last door at the end of the hall and behind it was what we expected to find. His wife, my husband." Her mind was back in that moment, finding her husband's face in between her client's legs. How many times had she asked for him to do that to her? And after all the things she'd done for him, there he was, doing it to someone else.

"I looked at her, and then at my husband, and after that it was just pure craziness. She screamed, tried to get dressed, all the while crying and apologizing to her husband, while mine just stood there, looking at me calm as... He was always an arrogant bastard," she said, feeling the anger that came from reliving this. She took a breath, looked away to calm down. "He shrugged and that's when I lost it, took a flying leap across the room to try and reach him.

"Thankfully the client caught me before I could do anything, pulled me out of the room, walked me back to the front door, and out into the yard."

"He could have just told you," Reye said, reaching for Clarke's hand across the table. "Instead of all that elaborate..." She stopped, at a loss for words.

"He told me he was sorry," Clarke said, "and he was crying along with me. We were both crying. I can't tell you how long we stood there, but it was a bit before I could pull it together. Eventually I went back to my car and he went back to his.

"I remember sitting for a while, staring at the front door, waiting for my husband to leave. Thirty minutes passed before I gave up. I drove around aimlessly after that, waiting for my husband to call, to apologize... to explain. Maybe even ask for forgiveness. But he didn't. I wasn't completely surprised. We were having trouble, I knew we were shaky, but for some reason I wasn't ready to quit. Anyway, he never called. It was over. He'd wanted out, and he needed me to know it. I filed for divorce the next day."

"Where is he now?" Henri asked, meeting her eyes with something akin to sympathy in his. The unreadable part had fallen away.

"In Dallas still, as a police officer, a trainer," she said.

"Do you plan to live here permanently?" Reye asked, squeezing Clarke's hand.

"I don't know. I'm giving myself a year before I decide for sure," Clarke said.

"I'm sorry," Henri said.

"It was coming. I knew it, and in all honesty, I needed something like it to pry my hands loose from the corpse that my marriage had become. I can see that now."

"We need ice cream, or cake, or pie; something to drown our sorrows in and soothe our souls," Reye said, standing. She picked up her empty dinner plate and reached for Stephen's.

"Let me help, "Clarke said, standing too, reaching for Henri's and hers.

"Sure, I'd like that," Reye said, smiling. They disappeared into the kitchen, leaving Stephen and Henri behind.

"That was quite a story," Stephen said.

"And I thought mine was bad," Henri said.

"Yours *was* bad," Stephen said, chuckling. "Hers was just worse."

***

"I hope it's not too obvious," Reye said quietly, now that it was just the two of them alone in the kitchen. Henri and Stephen had gone to some other part of the house. Of course, this was rigged. He'd take Henri away, show him something, while Reye would try and determine the level of Clarke's interest.

"What?"

"Stephen's attempt at matchmaking," Reye said.

"It is, as it was last week at the Basement."

"Henri probably noticed too?" Reye asked.

"Hard not to," Clarke said, chuckling. "It's okay, we're adults, free to do what we want."

"Too soon, I thought, but Henri is a really good friend of Stephen's, so that's why he's pushing a little more than he normally does. Actually, he never pushes. This is his first attempt. Henri is a good guy who's been there for him. Stephen wants to help if he can."

"Got it," Clarke said, watching Reye move about her kitchen.

"How about coffee to go along with our desserts or would you like coffee as your dessert? We can do either or both," Reye said, in the midst of slicing cake. "Stephen bought himself a professional cappuccino maker. I know he'd be happy to make one for you if you want him to. What would you prefer? Espresso or cappuccino? Or maybe you don't even like coffee. Do you like coffee? I should probably ask that first."

"I do, and a cappuccino sounds nice," Clarke said.

"Good. I'll let Stephen make them since he likes—no, he loves making them."

"Stephen loves to what?" he asked, coming to stand behind his wife. He and Henri were back from somewhere. His hands went immediately around his wife's waist. Normal and everyday in the life of men who loved their women. He moved them around to her stomach, and there they stayed, softly caressing as he looked over her shoulder.

Clarke wondered if he were even aware of what he'd done, something so protective and male. Was that what wanting a baby as much as your wife looked like? She didn't know. Hers had never wanted that.

"I'd like an espresso and Clarke wants a cappuccino. Henri,

would you like anything?" Reye asked, stepping clear of her husband's arms.

"Espresso for me," he said.

"So you like being a private investigator?" Stephen asked, pulling the espresso machine forward on the counter, picking up the conversation, resuming his quest to extract as much information from Clarke as he could for Henri's sake.

"I do," she said,

"Is two percent milk okay?" Stephen asked.

"It is," she said.

"What do you like about it?" he said, wiping the part that he used to foam the milk for Clarke's drink.

"The variety. Each day is usually different," Clarke said.

"Are you working on anything interesting now that you can talk about? You're helping Rainey on a custody case?"

"Eventually. He wants me to. I'm in the early stages of searching for my cousin. She's missing."

"What do you mean, missing?" Reye asked.

"Hasn't been seen in a while. Three weeks this Tuesday, which may mean something or it may not. She and her mother, my Aunt Veda, have been known to fight a lot, so maybe that's all it is, a way to show her mother that she is a grown-up. Who knows, but she had a baby recently so my aunt's worry is in overdrive."

"So you have family here?" Henri asked. She turned to him. He'd been so quiet since they'd been here, listening to her talk.

"I do. My great aunt owns and runs a local soul food restaurant," she said, accepting her drink from Stephen.

"Impressive," she said at the flower that he'd managed to make in the foam.

"I try," he said, and smiled.

"Really? What's the name of it?" Reye asked.

"Mrs. Drake's."

"Oh, we've been there, on the east side of town. Very good soul food," Reye said.

"It is," Clarke said, smiling.

"Two espressos. Henri?" Stephen said, handing one off to Henri and the other to Reye. He and Henri seated themselves at the table again.

"Where did your cousin disappear from?" Stephen asked.

Clarke and Reye had remained standing at the counter. Even with her heels, Clarke felt out of place in the land of the tall people, as all of them were tall.

"I don't know. Not sure where she went after she left home. She doesn't have a lot of friends—two to be exact that I can determine, and a boyfriend who was supposed to be the father. It's what she told my aunt, who never believed her, and that's the reason they fought. After seeing the baby my aunt thought that the father was most likely a white guy. Not a good thing, in my aunt's opinion," Clarke said, meeting Henri's eyes.

"The police haven't found anything? Have you gone to the police?" Stephen asked.

"No and yes," Clarke said.

"So have you talked to the boyfriend?" Reye asked.

"I did. He and my aunt are in agreement. He doesn't think the baby is his either, and he hasn't seen her since the baby was born. He went to visit her at the hospital."

"And you believe him?" Henri asked.

"I don't think he's hiding anything. He has another girl pregnant and it doesn't seem to affect him in a negative way. The opposite, actually; he considers it a badge of honor to have babies. So it's hard to imagine he's done anything to harm her because of it. I can't really rule him out until I find out where she is."

"What about her girlfriends? Have you spoken to either of them?" Reye asked, clearly caught up in the details of the case.

"Yes. Neither of them has seen her since graduation. One of them used to drive her out to the country and leave her on the roadside, at Amber's request. She has no idea who Amber went to see. My cousin kept her activities on the down-low."

"So what about the police? Are they helping?" Stephen asked.

"So far no, beyond the basic. She's not the girl that people miss."

"Not blonde and blue-eyed," Reye said.

"Your words, not mine, but yeah, I wish she were a life that more people would find criminal to lose. I might have more help then. Or I might not."

"That's not bitterness talking?" Stephen asked.

"No, it's not. It's the truth of which lives garner attention and which ones don't. But even if she had the two b's in her favor, it's a lot of effort to keep up the search for a missing person. It helps if you can afford to hire an investigator, and if that investigator is ethical, 'cause not all of us are," Clarke said.

"Well, it's a good thing your cousin has you in her corner," Reye said, reaching for Clarke's hand to squeeze again. "She's probably with the father now, and their baby, the three of them off somewhere having a nice life."

"I hope so." Clarke squeezed back. "So when's the baby due?" she asked, turning the conversation to someone other than herself.

***

Henri and Clarke were outside now, at the end of dinner, heading to their cars. They were quiet, moving slowly down the sidewalk, both of them stopping when they reached his car. She turned to say goodbye, feeling less angry now that she'd gotten her story out into the open.

"*It's not what you think*," he said, coming to a stop in front of her. "The reason you responded the way you did to seeing my ex. The reason you stopped talking, and although I don't agree with the not talking to me part, I can understand better now that you've shared your history."

"What do I think?" she asked.

"That I want back with my ex? That I was kissing her. I wasn't. That I'm using you... that I'm a man that cheats, like your ex?"

"She's not your ex yet and yes, it's what happened to me all over again, except now I feel like the cheater, and it felt like you were cheating on me at the same time. And yes, I know, we aren't like that. I'm just telling you what I felt. I didn't say it was logical. I hate the way I felt when I found out, and now I'm that person causing someone else to feel the same hurt. I'm the side-piece now. That what it's called these days. I hate side-pieces... hate cheaters and I never thought I would find myself in the position of being one. So it wasn't just you I was angry with but me, for not taking better care of myself."

He laughed. "I'm not much on them either, and if you felt that way then I'm sorry. For you to be a side-piece would mean that I'm together with my wife and I'm not. We were well past the sell-by date. I knew it before the baby, or before the potential to have one came along. There was no way I was leaving my child behind, period.

"So I stayed, but really it only prolonged what was inevitable. If only I'd manned up and done something about it sooner. Anyway, in all the ways that matter, I'm gone. I don't know how else to say it. I know what it feels like to be played, to be lied to, to be cheated on, as you do. I wouldn't wish that on anyone, let alone participate in it," he said, and she could hear the truth in his words.

"Then why the anger? If you wanted gone."

"You weren't angry about yours?"

"Yes."

"Me too," he said, and yes, there was more to it, just as he was sure there was more to her story. There always was, but it wasn't necessary for her to know all of his, just as he didn't need to know all the details of hers.

"I'm the same as you then, should have manned up too," she said.

"How long have you been divorced?" Henri asked.

"A month," she said, "and you're right, I should have left sooner, except I couldn't see straight after... And anyway, my husband was man enough for the both of us, it seemed, and as painful as my finding out was, it was the only way I guess he thought to get my attention. The only way he could make me see. No, not just see it, but leave."

It was quiet for a few minutes, while they were both lost in thoughts of their pasts.

"So?" he said, meeting her gaze again, and there was a lot to be read in his eyes.

"So," she said, and there was a lot to be read in hers as well. Equal amounts hurt, need, and desire—not only the sexual kind, but the comforting kind as well, to soothe over so much of her hurt; and by the look in his eyes, he had experienced his share of hurt too.

"You want...?" he said.

"I do," she said.

"Me too," he said.

"I think it's my turn to supply the accommodations," she said, pulling out her phone.

"I think so too, but either way works."

"The Hilton then?"

"Your favorite," he said, and smiled, his same old small one. "See you in what, ten? In the lobby?"

"That works."

***

It was different this time. *He* was different this time, she thought, fifteen minutes later when she entered the hotel's atrium. She spotted him right off, sitting in a chair across from the desk, a little ways back. He was a fine man to feast upon, both with her eyes and her body by having sex with him, not in need of gadgetry to make it more. She was enough, and what a nice feeling that was, she thought. She hadn't realized how bad she needed it... this... him. A feeling of being enough for one man. She fought to clear her mind of all the hurt feelings that the retelling of her story had brought forth. He nodded when their eyes met, but he didn't move otherwise. Waiting, she guessed, until she had checked them in and picked up the key.

Less than ten minutes later they were moving to the elevators. It was different, *he was different*, she thought again. Pensive was the word for his silence, as he stared into space.

"What floor?" he asked, after they were inside.

"Twenty," she said, standing beside him, both of them leaning against the back wall of the elevator. He hit the button marked Twenty before turning to her. He took two steps and stopped in front of her. He placed one hand at her waist, and the other hand he placed on her cheek, cradling it, before he leaned in and kissed her.

A slow playing of tongues and mouths was that kiss, nothing hurried in it at all.

"I'm sorry for what you had to go through," he said when he pulled back, staring into her eyes.

"'That which doesn't kill us...'" she said, and smiled softly before she leaned in and placed her lips on his. Nothing long and lingering, just a brush of her lips across his.

He smiled, released her, and moved back to stand beside her, leaning against the back wall again.

"After you," he said when they'd reached their floor. It was the same when he allowed her to enter first after he'd unlocked and opened the door.

It was dark inside, with the only light shining through the sheer curtain that the hotel offered to limit the amount of outside light. She walked over to the window and stood looking out, admiring the street lights, the only illumination in the room.

He came up behind her and placed his hands at her waist. He held her for a while, his chin resting on the top of her head, content to stand and look out of the window for a while. *What was this?* he wondered as he turned her to face him. He kissed her then, softly, slowly, his lips moving over hers. It was a soft meeting of mouths and tongues, in no hurry to take anything further. Two souls, hurt by people they'd thought they'd loved and had thought loved them, and for the first time, for each one, they were allowing someone to see that pain.

It was different. She was different, he thought, from the time they entered the door to the time they eventually made it to the bed. She seemed slow, quiet, contemplative as he stared down into her eyes, as she lay nude on the bed, and he watched the desire for him grow in her eyes as he undressed.

Quiet and easy it remained, him sliding into her warmth on a sigh, with their mouths touching, before moving on to all the other body parts that were in reach. Small kisses running over skin, back to lips, and then onward, to other unexplored territory of chest and breasts, all while he kept up a delicious slow and steady push and pull into and out of her body. It was quiet lovemaking, accompanied by the sounds of labored breathing and quiet moans, until they came.

Quiet they remained after, holding on to each other, he still on top, letting his climax run its course, wrapped up in her arms and legs as she held him.

"No condom," she whispered into his ear later, the only wrinkle in an otherwise beautiful coming together.

"I know," he said.

"I have trouble getting pregnant, or I have had trouble... in the past," she said haltingly. "So you don't have to worry about that. I haven't slept with anyone else since my divorce."

"It's okay. I've had lots of experience, but all of it before I married. I was careful then, and since the baby... not being mine and all, I've been tested," he said, rolling over onto his back, staring up at the ceiling. "It was the first thing I did after I found out."

"I did the same after my divorce," she said.

"I fucking hate cheaters," he said.

"Me too," she said, turning to face him. She took his chin in her hand and turned his face to hers. One hurt soul stared back at her, however much he'd tried to play it off. For the first time, he'd allowed a bit of the hurt he'd felt to bubble up to the surface. It was alluring for some reason, fascinating even; the wounded man who had not come through his marriage unscathed. He was like her. She was like him, less so now, but not by much. They were the same hurt and angry.

He placed his lips on hers, pushed her onto her back, and moved his body over hers, opening her legs with one of his, sliding back into her again. It was a good thing to have each other to get lost in for a while.

THIRTEEN

Monday morning

Clarke made the left turn onto Veda's street. She was there to pick up a picture, one that would hopefully blow a hole in Amber's case. Probably not, but if it shed a little bit of light, or pointed her in a direction, she'd be a happy camper.

She hadn't shared much with Veda. Actually there wasn't much to tell, beyond Amber's penchant for this one country road. When she pulled into the drive, Clarke was not at all surprised to see Aunt Veda standing at the middle of the window, anxiously waiting for her arrival.

The front door opened, and out her aunt came, charging toward her car. Two seconds, if that, and Aunt Veda stood beside her car window, holding the picture in her hand. *Dang, who knew Aunt Veda could move that fast*, she thought, but no way would she say that. Clarke lowered her window.

"Don't bother getting out. Here it is," Veda said, handing over the picture to Clarke. It was as Veda had said. Amber stood beside a male, white, taller by four inches or so, sandy blond hair underneath a baseball cap. Both of them were smiling into the camera, with an arm wrapped around each other's waist.

Amber was not pregnant in this picture, or if she was she wasn't showing, not that Clarke could see.

They were standing outside of a bar. The sign read *Whiskey River Bar* in red neon letters behind them.

Finally something to work with, Clarke thought, a second person to find. And hopefully he'd be easier to track down than her cousin was turning out to be.

"Have you heard of that bar?" Veda asked, pointing to the sign in the picture.

"No, ma'am, but I'll find it."

"I know you will. She's probably out there somewhere holed up with him, mad with me, wherever that may be, and I've been fretting and worrying for nothing."

"You're probably right," Clarke said.

"Well, you get going. You have work to do," she said, moving away from Clarke's car and over to the garage. Her expression was one of great sadness, Clarke thought as she waved once more before backing out of her aunt's drive. Aunt Veda was still standing there when Clarke looked in her rear view mirror a few seconds later.

She pulled over in the first parking lot she came to, out of view of her aunt, for a quick Google search on the bar. She was not surprised at all at how easy the location and that sign in the picture popped up on the web.

It was located a ways out, nowhere near the road that had been Amber's drop-off point nor there in Yolly. Out of the city in another direction entirely was Giddings, Texas, the location of the bar as per its website, a forty-minute drive from here, almost diagonally, southeast from Yolly.

Leaving Austin, Giddings was due east, out Highway 59, headed up to Houston. Make a left after you passed Elgin, another small town, famous for sausage, and it was a straight shot up to Giddings. Keep going and you were in Avondale, the place of

Amber's preferred drop spot. Make a left in Avondale, head due west, and in another thirty minutes you were back in Yolly. A square, not perfect, but a square with all the towns as points.

Clarke put her jeep in drive. Hopefully in over an hour's time, she'd have more information that she had now. Her mind shifted to yesterday and dinner last night, followed by the night with Henri, and how easy had that been to fall back into. Easy, 'cause she'd only stopped because of his wife, and she no longer had doubts about his desire to divorce.

Last night had been different and interesting and now what? 'Cause it felt like something had shifted between them, or maybe it was just her. *Anyways, don't go thinking it meant more than it did,* she thought, a reminder to herself that it was still only sex between them.

***

The Whiskey River Bar was small time, and not as down on its luck as she'd imagined it would be. It was located out in the boonies, just as she'd thought. Two businesses stuck into one mid-sized building at that intersection of two country roads. A restaurant—Comida was the name written on a wooden sign above the door and the business on the right. It sold Mexican food inside and breakfast tacos around the side, according to the sign stuck on one of those big black smokers in the parking lot, cooking who-knew-what.

The Whiskey River Bar's exterior appeared newer than the restaurant, she thought, pulling in between the two businesses, squashing in between two trucks, both overflowing with stuff: wood planks in one, landscaping junk in the other.

She looked around the parking lot at the traffic moving

toward the restaurant. Not much of it headed to her bar. It was open, as the website said it would be. Clarke stood at the door, looking around the interior now. Cement floors covered by small square-shaped tables were on the left side and the bar was to the right. A pool table stood all alone in the back of the room, with only its pool sticks for company.

It was mostly empty of people. One man sat at the bar, and a couple, a man and a woman, sat at one of the tables. Clarke took a seat at the end of the bar, away from the others, furthest away from the door, waiting for the bartender to take her order. He was standing at the other end from her, pouring a glass of beer from the tap. He looked over and smiled. She smiled in return. He handed the beer off and started in her direction.

"What can I get you?" he asked a few minutes later.

"What's on tap?" she asked, and waited while he rattled off the list, before settling for the Shiner Bock. Couldn't go wrong in Texas choosing a Texas beer.

She sat for a while, drinking her beer and taking stock of the bartender. He seemed friendly enough, she thought, finishing her beer. She waved to him for another one.

"I'm looking for my cousin," she said when he was in front of her again.

"Yeah?"

"Yeah," she said, and smiled. "I'm not a cop. Clarke Kensington's my name. I'm related to her. Her mother called my mother and I sure you know how they can be when mothers get something stuck in their claws. I'm a private investigator working with my family," she said, laying on her local country girl accent. She could do country when and if she had to. It wasn't hard at all. She could do others too: the around-the-way girl, the professional woman; all were in her arsenal for digging for information.

"Her mother is worried sick about her, you know. Left with the boyfriend, won't let her see the grandbaby, and you know how new grandmothers can be" She kept smiling.

"I do at that," he said, leaning toward her on his elbows, making himself plenty comfy. Either that or it was his version of flirting. Not her type, she thought. It was the age, close to her dad's age, and she was done with older men, plus he was missing three of his front teeth on the bottom which, if it hadn't been for the age, would have put her off too. Images of someone else entered her head.

"Can I show you a picture?" she asked.

"Sure, and anything else you think I might want to see. The name's Bill, by the way. I'm the owner of this fine establishment," he said, grinning.

"Hi, Bill, nice to meet you," she said, smiling. She slid the picture across the bar to him. He didn't move to lift it or anything, just stared at it for a while.

"I've seen her here. Not in a while, like maybe last year. I don't know her name, but she did come here. A lot. Liked to dance, if I remember correctly, and why here I couldn't tell you. This ain't no hip hop club." He shrugged his shoulders.

"I know this guy, and I don't," he said, pointing to the man in the picture. "I don't know his name but he's been here with his buddy." He looked at her again, back with his toothless smile. *Be still my heart*, she thought, chuckling inside at her humor.

"Darnell is his buddy's name. He's the one I know. Darnell works as a roughneck over across the border in Louisiana."

"Do you know how I can get in touch with him?" she asked.

"I don't, but his girlfriend will. She waitresses for me, has been since she turned eighteen. She's a sweet girl. Won't leave that boy for nothing, not that there's anything wrong with that."

"Is she here now?" Clarke asked.

"No, but later this evening she will be."

"Do you have a telephone number for her?"

"I don't like to give out people's numbers unless they expressly give me permission to, you know. You can come back tonight and I'll introduce you to her."

Clarke nodded.

"So you think she might be with him?" he asked, looking at the picture again.

"I don't know. Didn't know there was a him until this morning and this picture, so I'll have to see."

"Who gives a damn about a black woman, huh?" he said, and Clarke did a double take, not sure what to say in response.

"I didn't mean that in the way you're thinking," he said, and he was serious now. "I understand. You have to do all the looking for yourself, is all I'm saying. I'm partial to the darker-skinned ladies myself. You know, the blacker the berry, the sweeter the juice. I can attest to that little bit of truth," he said, before running his tongue around his lips. "No, I meant you all have to find out information yourself, can't depend on *the man* to find it out for you."

"Most people would consider you *the man*," she said.

"Not those that know me. Anyhow, most folks don't think about hiring their own investigator, or if they do, most don't have the money. You all can be expensive, the good ones anyway, and some of you are scam artists. It's hard to know," he said, grinning. "I'll see you tonight then?" He moved his eyebrows to go along with his grin.

"Yes, you will, and thanks," she said, sliding off the stool.

***

"I need a favor," Summer said, standing in front of her brother's desk that afternoon.

"Okay…" Henri said warily. He bet it had something to do with Clarke.

"I need you to help Clarke with her investigation."

Yep, it was as he thought. She was not giving up yet on the him and Clarke combination. *Between her and Stephen…* he thought, letting that thought drop, not sure he was comfortable with where it was headed.

"She needs help?" he asked, sitting back in his chair.

"She would disagree, but yes, I think so. Well, not so much help, but company. She called me a few minutes ago, asking if I was free to go to a bar with her this evening. I told her I was tied up with something, so I can't go. She has to go this evening. It's related to her cousin's disappearance. Has she told you about her cousin yet?"

Henri smiled while he tried to figure out the best way to answer his sister.

"She has. I can so read you," she said, smiling. "That's good. So I'll move on to the main point, which is that the bar is located in Bumfuck, Egypt, and I don't think she should be going alone."

"She seems pretty competent to me. I'm sure it won't be the first time she's gone to a bar alone," he said.

"She'd agree with you. However, she's not the one asking for the favor. I am. Asking you to help her *for me*, which will be our code for you sticking close to her. I shouldn't have to list the dangers she could encounter out in the country at a bar, all by herself, and you're a man, stronger in case she needs defending. Added to that fact is that she's searching for a loved one. Has to be tough, right? Searching for a missing woman you don't know is a completely different thing from searching for a relative."

"What if she doesn't want my help?"

"You can charm your way into getting whatever you want. You've been doing it since you were a babe in your mother's arms, so that's not an excuse." Sensing capitulation, she pushed onward. "I know it's too soon after your separation for there to be anything else between the two of you, so I'm giving up on trying to push you two together. You aren't interested in her and she's not interested in you. I get it."

"She told you that?"

"Yep. It's not only you that I've been pushing. She's the same feet-dug-in as you," she said, watching him for signs, 'cause she wasn't really giving up, just choosing a different tactic. "So, back to my favor. What do you say? Oh, and it goes without saying this has to appear like you're doing it of your own volition, right?"

"I'll think about it. I don't believe she's in as much danger as you say, but if I think she wouldn't mind my help, I'll offer it. Not as a favor to you, but because I want to. Okay?"

"Fine," she said, working to hold in her smile.

His sister was so transparent, Henri thought, and no way was she done with him or Clarke and getting them together. She and Stephen. Again, what did they see?

"I'm out then," Summer said, gathering her purse, moving to the door. She smiled the entire walk to her car. She was so going to win in the end. They had no idea who they were messing with. Scatterbrained didn't mean she was without one.

***

Henri was on the phone when Clarke entered the office later on that afternoon. He watched her walk over to his desk. She stood beside it as he finished his phone conversation. She was not what he was used to, that was a fact, but it was nice all the same. She was tall today, with pencil-heeled boots on her feet, and those tight, contouring jeans. Those and the soft silky blouse showcased her slim waist and small breasts to perfection, and all he knew was that sexy was the result.

He liked what he did with her in the hotel rooms late at night, and was nowhere near ready give it up. He liked running his hands over that figure minus the clothes. He liked her mouth and the way she kissed; liked the fact that she liked to kiss, not in a hurry to move on, but taking it slow and as it came.

It wasn't the first time he realized this. He always had, but last night had felt different, like they'd turned a corner. Not for anything long-term and meaningful, like Stephen and Summer wanted for them. He'd seen the hurt in her gaze last night and realized that he was not unique in his pain, hurt or anger. They both had survived, were surviving similar situations. He liked her story, admired the brass that was required to start over one's life in another city. Ms. Kensington had lots of chutzpah, so maybe there could be room for friendship between them.

"You okay?" she asked, and had the pleasure of hearing him chuckle.

"Is there some reason I shouldn't be?" he asked.

"No reason. You seem serious and… last night…"

"Last night was…?" he said, searching for a word other than 'needy' to describe the way he'd felt last night.

"Nice," she said.

"It was, wasn't it?" he said, meeting her eyes, and yes, he was surprised at her equanimity in all situations. He was impressed again, wondering what would it take to get under her skin, to truly rattle her. "It felt a little more serious than I'd planned. I hoped I didn't scare you," he said.

"I like your serious, and I don't scare easily," she said, and she was rewarded with a chuckle. "We've both been hurt, there's no use in pretending otherwise. It's kind of nice to know you understand and that I don't have to pretend or hide that fact, you know?"

"I do. I like you too, Ms. Kensington," he said, chuckling again.

"Here are the background checks you ordered. Kevin is clean, borderline squeaky, if he's still your first choice." She laid a folder on the desk in front of him.

"He is, and thank you," he said, moving it to another spot on his desk for review later. "Tonight?"

"I have a thing. For real this time, not for fake like the other night, when I was upset with you."

"Humor me. What were you doing that night?"

She smiled, tilted her head to the side, considering him. "Let's see. Work, a glass of wine, and eventually falling asleep in front of the TV."

"I like that you're honest," he said.

"Me too," she said, smiling, enjoying this new talking thing they'd started to do.

"So what's your thing tonight, if you don't mind me asking?"

"Something to do with my cousin. The picture my aunt gave me puts her at a bar with a guy, out in the boonies. I drove out there earlier this afternoon to talk with the bartender. He recognized her and thinks one of his waitresses might be able to help. So it's back out there for me, to talk to the waitress tonight."

"You want company?"

"Who, you?"

"Yes, me," he said, fighting to keep his smile small.

"Did Summer put you up to this?" she asked, giving him a little side eye.

"Yes, she did, but that's not why I'm offering."

"Then why *are* you offering?" she said, back to considering him again.

"Playing detective sounds dangerous. It feels like the perfect distraction from my thoughts… my life, and I'm always up for distractions. So if you don't mind, I'd like to tag along with you."

"I guess. The bar is a ways out in the country and I'm not scared or anything, but it's always good to have some company, makes me less conspicuous sometimes. If you're up for it, that is, and not tied up with anything?"

"I'm not. I do have one request," he said.

"It can't be sex, 'cause I'm already giving you that."

"True," he said, chuckling. "I'm going for a different type of sustenance. Food, as in, you have to feed me."

"I can do that, I guess, while I'm feeding myself. It's not a date or anything."

"No, not like a date or anything," he said.

"Good. It's a go, then. Tonight, say around seven. Should I pick you up here? Or at Summer's?" she asked.

"Summer's," he said.

"I'll see you later then, and thanks," she said, smiling.

"You're welcome," he said, smiling too as he followed the swing of her ass in those kick-ass boots out the door. She was not at all like he'd thought—or hadn't thought. She was more than he'd thought, was maybe the more correct way to say it.

He'd felt sympathy for her, the reason he'd forgotten the part about them being just sex for a second, and keeping his feelings to himself.

He had, up until last night, thought his circumstances had

been bad, but finding your husband set up by the other woman's husband had to be worse. Last night had been about offering comfort to each other and getting lost in the moment, in the slow lovemaking.

They were alike, just as Stephen and Summer said, both fallout from broken marriages. And enough thinking about Clarke, he thought, or it would be telling in another way and it was way too soon, if at all, for that.

***

Clarke liked the way he looked, was her first thought, when she spotted him at the top of the stairs. She liked the way he dressed, the way that clothes looked on him, the way they contoured to flatter the lean muscle that was his body, or maybe it was the confidence in which he wore them. Business or casual, it didn't seem to matter with this one. Dressed this evening in jeans and t-shirt—blue, to match his eyes—baseball cap on top. Nothing spectacular, and yet it was.

"You're staring," Summer said, hitting her in the side with her elbow. Summer had answered the door, playing the hostess part of this drama.

"He's cute—and that's an observation only—so don't start up again with your plotting and planning," Clarke said.

"You're not the first, so don't be too hard on yourself was all I meant," Summer said.

"Trust me, I won't. He's nice to look at though, right?" Clarke said, chuckling. "You ready?" she asked, her attention all on him now that he was standing in front of her.

"I am," he said.

"Have a great time, you guys," Summer said, opening the door for them like they were going on a date or something.

"Goodbye, Summer," they both said, in the same don't-start-with-us tone.

"Goodbye," Summer said, not in the least bit deterred, clasping her hands tightly together behind her back to curtail her excitement at finally having gotten them together. She wasn't going to squeal either, not until they were out of earshot, 'cause the occasion surely called for it.

"We're taking your jeep?" Henri asked, closing the front door behind them. It was parked on the street and she was moving toward it.

"Yep, why wouldn't we?" she asked, looking back at him. "Mine has all the stuff I need in it."

She was sitting behind the wheel when he took his seat on the passenger side.

"So where are we going again?" Henri asked, looking around the inside of her jeep.

"Whisky River Bar."

"And where is that exactly?"

"Near Giddings, Texas. Do you know Giddings?" she asked, pulling away from the curb.

"Nope," he said, pulling his seat belt on.

"It's about an hour's ride from here, on the way to Houston."

"Really," he said, like he wasn't all that interested in her answer. "How old is this vehicle?"

"No jokes about my car. It runs, it's paid for, and I like it."

"It's clean. You can add that to your list of its attributes," he said, looking into the back seat now. "What is all of this stuff?" He indicated the many bags she had piled up back there, on the seats and the floor on both sides. He was pulling her stack of self-adhesive signs forward into his lap. "So what do you do with these? Don't tell me these are all businesses that you own. You'd be more like my sister than I thought." He began flipping through her stack. "Let's see. There a Kensington Realty, Kensington Farm and Ranch, Clarke Survey Company, a K&S Appraiser." He read them off as he moved through her stash. "I know. You use them for stakeouts, right?"

"I don't do stakeouts. You're confusing me with the police," she said.

"What do you call what you do then?" he said, returning her stash to the back seat.

"It's called surveillance," she said, watching him returning the signs to the back out of the corner of her eye. "What are you doing?" she asked, trying to keep her eyes on the road and watch him.

"Making sure you're not carrying something illegal in case we're stopped," he said, pulling one of the smaller bags to the front. "I'm curious. Is this more spy stuff?"

"It is."

"Mind if I look?"

"So now you're asking?"

"Is that a yes or a no?"

"And here I thought you were a quiet man," she said, surprised by the change in him. The quiet angry man had been seductive, but this more open side was even more attractive.

"Why would you think that?" he said, sliding the zipper open. "I thought you said you didn't do butt plugs, and what else did you say?"

"That's not what that is."

"What is it then?"

"Spy stuff."

"Let's see what your spy stuff looks like then," he said, pulling out the first thing he came across, which was a baseball cap.

"It has a Bluetooth camera built in," she offered.

"That's cool." He returned it to the bag.

"And this is?" He held up a black, square-shaped box with an antenna.

"It's a bug detector."

"So does that mean you bug people?"

"Not usually, no."

"Could you determine if I'd been bugged?"

"Yes, but what I use for that is not in that bag."

"What's this used for?" He held up something gray in color, eight inches in length, shaped like long rock.

"It's a large-screen back-up camera."

"And this?"

"A body camera?"

"I don't believe I've ever seen so many cameras," he said, and it continued like that for a while, him pulling out things and her explaining their uses.

"I'm impressed," he said at the end, having gone through not just one bag, but the others as well. "It's sexy. The thought of you knowing all this stuff, running around in your kick-ass boots, spying on people." He looked at her.

He's teasing, of course is what she thought, enjoying the interaction between them.

"It's not all sexy," she said.

"Tell me a not-so-sexy thing then."

"Depends," she said.

"Depends on what?"

She laughed. "No, it's the diaper for adults. You've heard of them?

"You wear those?" he asked, his smile wider now.

"Sometimes. See? Not so sexy, right?"

"Maybe. I might have a fetish for women who wear them. You were worried about butt plugs when you should have been worried about me and my Depends fetish."

She laughed. "I like this guy," she said, pointing to him. "Is this who you were before your divorce?" She watched his smile lose some of its wattage. He shrugged but didn't respond.

"I do have sexier toys, if you want to see them," she said, wanting the brightness of his smile to return. "Look under your seat." She waited for him to pull out her smaller bag of gear, waited until he opened it. She smiled at his wolf whistle.

"Night vision goggles, night vision binoculars. Yep, you've redeemed yourself. You're back in the sexy column again," he said, smiling, but still not as bright.

"We're almost at the bar," she said, turning onto the road the bar was on. *Time flies when you're having fun.* One of her dad's expressions, and she'd had fun on the drive there, responding to his many questions. "We're about a mile out."

"It's dark out here. I'm glad I invited me," he said.

"Me too," she said, chuckling.

"So, your cousin has been to this bar? With a man, and we're here to talk to the waitress."

"Yes, and what's this 'we'?"

"We're a team now, a detective, mystery-solving team," he said, smiling back at her, feeling lighter than he'd felt in years.

"Okay, let's slow down just a little bit with the detective mystery-solving team."

They were pulling into the parking lot of the bar now. It

wasn't that much busier than earlier, she thought, taking in number of cars. Most of the people exiting their cars were moving toward the restaurant. There was even a line at that smoker thing.

FOURTEEN

Clarke had just turned off the car when Henri grabbed her arm, preventing her from removing the key from the ignition.

"What?"

"What's our approach going to be when we get inside? You want me to play tough cop while you play the softy?" he said, smiling.

"God, you're cute," she said, voicing her thoughts aloud. "You're not to play, say, or do anything. Grab a beer and sit, either at the bar or at a table, and let me ask any questions that I need to ask. Play the role of my bodyguard if you have to have play something."

"Fine. Have all the fun, then," he said, sounding sad but smiling with it.

A minute later, they were entering the bar. It wasn't as empty as it had been earlier. A few men sat around the bar. Couples were at the tables around the room.

The table with two women seated together spotted Henri right off, and he was well aware of it. "See you later. I'll see what I can find out on my own," he said, before he winked. This Henri was something else, she thought of that smile, all devil it was. She fought back her desire to kick him and walked over to the bar instead.

"Hi, Bill," Clarke said, taking a seat on a stool toward the back end of the bar.

"You're back. Brought your boyfriend with you this time, I see," Bill said, nodding in the direction of Henri.

"He's my bodyguard."

"'Bodyguard' is what it's called these days," he said, grinning. "You want another Shiner?"

"Thanks, I would."

"I'll have Caitlyn bring it over to you in a sec. It's not that busy tonight as you can see, so take as much time as you need." He winked at her.

Clarke turned to check out Henri while she waited. The two women were sitting up straight, looking like two pigeons with all those breasts stuck out, and probably cooing too, for the potential pigeon that was Henri, now seated between them.

"Here's your Shiner," said a very pretty young woman standing beside her, her smile shy, holding a beer on a tray. "Bill said you wanted to talk to me. I'm Caitlyn."

"I did, thanks," Clarke said, removing the beer from the tray and leaving a five-dollar bill in its place. "Keep the change. I'm Clarke Kensington. It's nice to meet you, Caitlyn."

"The same," Caitlyn said.

"Did Bill tell you anything about why I'm here?"

"No, just that you were looking for someone, some girl."

"Right. It's my cousin that I'm looking for. Amber Jones is her name." Clarke slid the picture of Amber and the man towards her.

Caitlyn's smile was instantaneous and full. "Of course, I know her. Is she the one missing?" she asked, her brow furrowed in puzzlement.

"Yes. Have you seen her?"

"Not in a while. Not like before."

"Before?"

"She liked to dance, liked the music. She would come by herself, all the time, and ask people to dance," Caitlyn said, staring at the picture. "Waylen danced with her the time he was here, most of the night really."

"Waylen?" Clarke said.

"He's a friend of my boyfriend. I was off work that night on account of Darnell, that's my boyfriend, was off that weekend from his new job. We met Waylen here and he danced with your cousin. They sort of hung out that night."

"Really."

"Yes."

"And when was this?"

"Oh, shoot," she said, "Let me see." She was silent for a bit, clearly thinking, eyes rolled up in her head. "September. I remember that we were celebrating Darnell's first time being off, on account of his job being new and all. He started working the first of September, so the next weekend, we came. He got on at this oilrig outta Louisiana, comes home on the weekends now. Waylen met us here."

"So Waylen—is that the name of this guy?" Clarke asked, pointing to him in the picture again.

"Yes."

"So Waylen and she hung out that one night."

"I meant they hung out here at the bar. We left to eat next door and she didn't come with us so I don't know what she did after we left."

"You and Darnell went to eat, or did Waylen come with you?"

"Oh, yes, sorry. All three of us went. Like I said, we didn't see her after that. I only know they still saw each other because

Darnell told me. He and Waylen keep in touch. Not all the time, but every so often. He and Darnell, that's my boyfriend, they grew up together, have been best friends since forever. Darnell is a roughneck for one of the drills offshore and they go way back. I said that already, didn't I? I'm always repeating myself. Darnell says it's on account of me getting hit in the head as a child. That's not true, you know. It's Darnell being funny," she said, chuckling.

"What's his last name?" Clarke asked, working to weed through all of Caitlyn's words. She and Summer could be twins in their verbal fluency.

"Who, Waylen's or Darnell's?"

"Both."

"Darnell Henderson, that's my boyfriend, and let me see." Her eyes rolled up in the back of her head again. "I can't remember it for the life of me," she said, chuckling. "I'm such a ditz, that's what my Darnell's always telling me too, and here I am forgetting his best friend's last name." She was clearly still thinking. "He's related to that family that used to own all that land, over near Yolly?" She looked up at Clarke, pleased to have recalled that piece of information.

"The Yollys? No, that's not it. That's the name of the city. It's something else, but they used to own most of the land, and sold it to Yolly to start that town. So see, he, I mean Waylen, comes from money, although I don't think he had much growing up, don't think they gave him much of it, his parents, I mean. Or maybe it was his grandparents. Gosh, I wish I could remember. He seemed kind of sad, and my boyfriend says he's a bit of a loner."

"So his last name isn't Yolly?" Clarke asked.

"No, it's something else, the name of the family that sold most of their land to Yolly to turn it into a city," Caitlyn said again, kind of exasperated now.

"How about your boyfriend? Maybe we can call him and ask?"

"He's out, and they don't take phone calls out on the rig."

"Okay." Clarke looked around for Henri, not sure why she did, but she did. He was fine, nothing to worry about with him, sitting between two women now, and quite happily it seemed. He winked again and she fought back her smile, returned her attention to Caitlyn instead. "So does Darnell visit Waylen much? Does he know where he lives? Do you?"

"No. I've never been there, only Darnell, probably, maybe. He don't tell me everything, says I'd forget it anyway, so what's the point?" She chuckled as she said this, apparently not bothered by her boyfriend's view of her abilities.

"It's in the country is all I know, ways away from here."

"What else can you tell me about Waylen?"

Caitlyn sat there for a seconds before her eyes grew large. "Oh, how could I forget? He's a policeman in Yolly." She slapped her hand on her head softly. "See, what a ditz, huh? Waylen Jacobs, that's his last name. Everybody in Yolly knows of the Jacobses."

"Oh," Clarke said, her voice neutral, to cover her surprise at getting a name. "Is there anything else you can remember, that you think I need to know?"

"No, I don't think so, but you never know with me," Caitlyn said, laughing, apparently taking her limitations in stride.

"Well, thanks for your time. You've been very helpful. If you can think of anything, feel free to call me. Here's my card." Clarke handed one over to her. "Oh, one more thing. What's the best way to get in touch with Darnell?"

"I can give him your information. He's not into talking with people he doesn't know. He and Waylen are both that way... big into staying off the grid, if you know what I mean. Always talking about the need to watch what you put out into space for Big Brother to see. I don't know who is Big Brother is, but anyway," she said, smiling.

"I understand," Clarke said, smiling too. "Can I call you later on, or can you call me if you speak to Darnell and he wants to talk to me?"

"Sure." She took another business card.

Clarke watched her walk away and disappear through a door marked EMPLOYEES. Was this Waylen Jacobs the father? Who knew? All she learned was that her cousin was one secretive young woman.

Clarke made eye contact with Henri to let him know she was leaving.

He left too, not much later, clearing the door just as she reached the driver's side of her jeep. She looked a little dangerous, Henri thought. A little like a kick-ass private eye, a cute one, straight from one of those detective shows. Her hair, short, fell softly around her face. Full lips. Brown eyes. Yeah, he liked the look of her, and now that he was getting to know her, he liked this side of her too. Funny and serious was Clarke, tough and soft, riding around with all her tools. "You weren't going to leave me in there, were you?"

"Not unless you want me to," she said, smiling.

"Dinner time, and you promised," he said, pointing to the sign on the place next door. He was moving past her car now, not waiting for her to agree, headed toward the Mexican restaurant in question.

"You think the food's safe?"

He smiled and kept on moving. "Don't be a snob," he said over his shoulder. "Debbie and Dora told me the food here was great."

"Debbie and Dora, is it," she said, closing her car door, wiggling her eyebrows. "Has it always been that easy for you?" He'd stopped on the sidewalk and stood waiting for her to catch up to him. She knew the answer, looking at him again, with his baseball cap pulled low, blue eyes, and artfully scuffed chin hair. That wasn't even the best of him, and she got why the Debbies, Doras, and Karens gravitated toward him.

"It used to be, before I married, when I was young and free and easy," he said, smiling.

"You and Stephen?"

"Were pretty good," he said, holding the screen door to the restaurant open for her.

"It's not as bad as I thought," she said, stepping through the doorway now, with him behind her. Actually it was a lot brighter than she'd thought it would be. She had envisioned dark walls from smut or charcoal, dark lighting, and a trip to the hospital in the morning a la food poisoning. It was clean and bright. Service was in the fast food vein, in that you placed your order, were given a number, and went back to get your food when your number was called.

"What did we find out from our talk with the waitress?" Henri asked from his seat beside her. And yeah, she had expected him to sit across from her, not beside her, but okay.

"There *is* no 'we'."

"Yes, there is. Don't fight it. Now what did we learn tonight?" He smiled back at her. "Come on. You have to admit I helped you in there."

She scoffed. "How did you help?"

"By drawing all the attractive women to me, which meant the men were staring at me and you were free to talk to your waitress, free from distraction. You can thank me now."

She just stared at him, mouth agape. He reached his hand across the distance and closed it for her. She laughed. "Who knew you had a funny side to you? The man in this picture is Waylen, who works for the Yolly Police Department." She slid the picture over to him, again meeting his gaze, which had snapped over to her. "Yep, I know." She filled him in on all that Caitlyn had shared with her. "I wonder if he's the person she was going to see out in the country."

"What are you going to do next?"

"Call the Yolly police station first thing in the morning, check into this Waylen dude, see if he's on duty. If it's a yes, then I'll make a trip up to talk to him. Go back and review my property search I ran earlier, see if his name is among the list of owners. Maybe take a trip out to the country."

"What do you expect to find?"

'I don't know. A logical explanation for all of this, maybe even one with a happy ending," she said, lifting her cup of water up in a cheer. "Here's to me driving out there tomorrow, and knocking on the front door and it will all be a misunderstanding. She's living with him, happily married to the father of her kid. She left home, tired of arguing with her mother about her choices, is all this was," she said, meeting his gaze again.

"Yep," he said, and smiled, hitting his cup to hers. No point in bringing up all the other possibilities that didn't end as well. "So let's move on to our rest of the evening plans."

"We have plans?"

"Of course we do. A hotel would be a nice way to end our hard night of investigating things."

"Always, with you."

"I'm making up for lost time."

"It was that bad with you and Karen?"

He shrugged. "Things… life didn't turn out the way we'd hoped. And no more talk of exes."

"No more talk of exes," she said.

"Summer said that you two have known each other since high school."

"Yep. I met her when our drama clubs hooked up—private school reaching out to the lesser public ones. Hit it off from the start, two semi-nerds thrown together to make props for the play. We didn't keep in touch. But it feels like we have, feels like I've known her for forever—our connection was immediate and close. I called her when I moved here, and she helped me so much. I like your sister a lot."

"Must be, to go into business with her. It's mutual," he said, smiling. "You ready to go?"

"I am. To the Hilton. I think it's my time. Do you want me to drop you at Summer's before or afterward?"

"Before, and it's the Wesleyn." He stood up, pulling the containers together while she gathered up the trash.

"The man with expensive taste."

"Yep." He smiled at her again.

She smiled too, not wanting this evening to end either.

***

Tuesday morning

Rested, up early, and armed with coffee, Clarke was driving over to the Yolly police station to hopefully talk with Waylen Jacobs. He was the officer who had taken the initial missing person's report. She found that information in the notes she taken from Veda, not sure if that meant anything.

It wasn't the only thing she had found this morning. Waylen

owned property in Amber's drop-off area. She found his name in her property search list. Too coincidental to dismiss?

It felt like a windfall, this new information, given the drought of anything useful before it. So yes, she was a little stoked. Stoked at finally finding something that might help. It wasn't the only reason she felt so bright and shiny this morning. There was another reason for her increased energy levels. Henri Novak.

She felt awakened, refreshed, refueled, restored; pick one, she was any or all of them. Follow that up with a steaming hot shower and a strong cup of joe, and she was firing on all cylinders. She dressed to impress; it always helped to look her best, especially when dealing with men. So she found something nice, which today was a dark gray tailored dress, fitted and flattering, yet profes-sional. She slipped a pair of matching dark gray pumps on her feet, added a few accessories, and she was ready to tackle the world. And when was the last time she felt like that?

She couldn't remember. Out of high school, maybe. Possibly, when newly married, starting her first business in Dallas maybe, when the world had been hers for the taking.

She turned into the Yolly police station parking lot forty-five minutes later. It didn't take her long to park, grab her bag and phone, and head to the front door.

"Hi, Officer Jim," Clarke said, after she reached the desk. He was standing behind it today. A nice-looking man was he, if you went for the clean-cut and starched type.

"Well, if it isn't the private investigator. What brings you by so early this morning?" he asked.

"I wanted to speak with Waylen Jacobs," she said.

"Waylen?"

"Yes, he was the officer that spoke with my aunt... took her statement. I thought it might help me if I could talk to him. My aunt… her memory isn't what it used to be, and I thought that maybe she told him something that might help me, or had forgotten to tell him something." And yeah it was thin, but not bad for on the fly, she thought.

"If you think it would help, sure," he said, scanning the area behind him. "He was here a minute ago, let me find him for you."

"Thank you," she said, watching him move toward the back of their office, before disappearing through a door. Not even a minute and Jim was making his way back to her, a young man following him.

Officer Jacobs was exactly like his picture: young-looking, clean, and fresh-faced. His eyes darted to hers and then away, and then all over the room until they landed back at hers. Shy and surprised were the expressions she read first, and maybe a bit relieved afterward. Or maybe not.

Clarke smiled, and he returned it. Nice was always her first option with people, men in particular, followed by flirty. Both of them had worked for her more times than not. "My name is Clarke Kensington. I stopped by earlier this week with my aunt, we talked to Officer Jim over there."

Waylen shot a quick glance over his shoulder in Jim's direction before returning his gaze to her.

"You took the missing person's report my aunt filed on her daughter. It was two weeks yesterday? It was you that she spoke with?" Clarke said.

"Yes, ma'am. It was me that took your aunt's report," he said.

"The missing report was for my cousin, Amber Jones?"

"Yes, ma'am. That's true."

"Great. I wanted to make sure my aunt didn't forget any details, and also, I'd like to know if there's been any news?"

"I can check, but chances are, if we haven't called you then there's probably nothing new to tell," he said, moving over to the computer. She watched him as his fingers moved over the keyboard.

"Could you tell me what exactly my aunt said?"

"I'll give you a copy of the report, will that help?"

"Yes, that'd be great," Clarke said. "Did you know my cousin?"

"Personally, you mean?" he asked.

"Yes."

"Yes, ma'am, I did," he said.

"Were you friends?" she asked, surprised he'd be so forthcoming.

"I wouldn't call us that. I met her one night at a bar, the Whiskey River Bar. It's about thirty minutes from here in Giddings, about an hour from Austin, I guess." He looked at the computer screen as he talked. "She asked me to dance, and I did, and as I was leaving, she asked me to take a picture with her." He ducked his head, a little sheepishly.

"But did you know her before then?"

"No, ma'am. She introduced herself to me that night."

"Did you see or talk to her after you took the picture with her?"

"You mean, that night?"

"Yes, or any other night."

"No, ma'am. I don't get out much. I only went there then to meet a buddy of mine, he was celebrating his new job."

"You're a handsome dude, so I could see why she'd want to take a picture with you or talk to you," Clarke said, smiling.

"I don't know about that, ma'am," he said, ducking his head again, back to being sheepish.

"Did you know she was pregnant?"

"Nope. She was pregnant, huh? I couldn't tell. She asked me

to take a picture with her, for her mother. She said her mother didn't like her current boyfriend, so this would make her think that she had a different one. She was nice, and I felt sorry for her, you know, so I did."

"Why didn't you tell her mother you knew her?"

"I didn't want to mess it up for her if she wasn't missing. How would it help for me to say, 'your daughter was at the bar, asking men to dance with her'? What good would it have been for me to say that to your aunt? She would have just felt worse. I did put it into her file, though, so it wasn't like I was hiding it or anything."

"I spoke with Caitlyn. She said you and Amber saw each other after that night. Is that true?" she asked.

"I don't know what Caitlyn told you. I haven't seen her or Darnell in a while."

"When was the last time you saw Amber?"

"You sound like a cop," he said, smiling.

"No, I'm not, I'm a private investigator. My aunt asked me to do what I could to try and locate Amber."

"That's nice of you. It must be nice having you around to help," he said.

"I hope I can help. So when was the last time you saw her?"

"Not since that night. It says here that there isn't any information to report... about your missing cousin... about Amber," he said.

"Okay, thanks," Clarke said.

"So... is there anything else I can help you with?" he asked, darting his eyes between her and the computer.

"A copy of your report?"

"Oh, sure, sure. I'm printing it now. I'll have to go to the back to get it for you."

"No problem," Clarke said, watching as he moved away.

"Everything okay?" Jim asked, moving toward the counter where she stood.

"I think so. Waylen was just giving me a copy of the report." Waylen was making his way back to the front, paper in hand.

"Here you go, miss," he said.

"Thanks for your time, Waylen… Jim," she said.

"You're welcome," they said in unison.

Clarke smiled and left, looking back once in Jim's direction. He'd been watching her leave, his expression unreadable. She smiled and waved. He waved back. She made her way out, pondering what to do next.

***

Kevin Huang was the right man for the superintendent's job, Henri thought, watching Kevin in conversation with one of the building inspectors. He was competent and hardworking, a combination that was hard to pass up. Yes, Henri was finally pleased with something in his life working the way that it should.

Today was Kevin's first day and it was great to have someone capable at the helm, the opposite of the wreck that had been Willis Wilson. As acting super, Kevin had taken over Willis's desk, relegating Henri to use of the conference table. He didn't mind, 'cause it meant he would be soon headed back to Dallas. Two weeks was plenty enough time to make sure Kevin was up to speed. Then it was home to deal with his wife. Home to hash out their divorce settlement, or whatever.

So far it had been quiet on the soon-to-be-ex-wife front. No more calls from Karen. No more crying or pleading, or even angry. *It was still early* was his thought on the absence of drama from her.

He expected a call from her attorney with her demands any day now, Henri thought, now that she understood that there would be no going back on his part.

Whatever her demands were, as long as they were reasonable, he would probably agree to them. He wanted on his way. And speaking of the devil, or timing or whatever, his cell rang and it was his attorney calling.

"Hello," Henri said.

"Hello, son," his attorney, John, said. John Bishop was a friend of his father's, and like most of his father's friends, considered him the boy... son always.

"I heard from your wife's attorney today. We expected this, to hear from her attorney at some point, yes?" John said, getting to the point.

"Yes, sir, we did," Henri said.

"It's not good."

"Didn't expect it to be." Henri leaned back in his chair. "Let's hear it."

"She's filed a restraining order against you. That's the first thing you should know. You're not allowed to go near her."

"I hadn't planned on it," Henri said, starting to get irritated just that quick.

"She's made several accusations against you. None of them are good."

"Really. Let's hear those, too."

"She's accused you of emptying out the joint checking account. Is that true?"

"Not true. I just took my share. I left hers alone. It's not my fault her share is smaller."

"Henri," John said, in that fatherly way, all patient admonition and I-expected-better-from-you.

"I was angry," Henri said.

"She's accusing you of kicking her out of her home. Is that true?"

"It's not really *her* home. It was a gift from my parents."

"That doesn't answer the question. Did you or did you not change the locks on your home? Pack up her belongings and send them to her mother's home?"

"I did."

"A home that, before the baby was born, you two lived in together?" John asked.

"Yes, sir, we did," Henri said.

"You didn't think I needed to know this?"

"No, sir, I didn't."

"She says you've been unfaithful to her, too."

"I was never unfaithful to her," Henri said, leaning forward in his chair now.

"She wants the house, or she wants you to sell it."

"Nope, it's my fucking house, a gift to me, separate property, and I'm not selling anything. And over my dead body will she move back in."

"Take a deep breath, son. This anger is not helpful. I understand it, but it's not helpful. This is a difficult process, even when the parties are peaceful and don't contest. We know this." It was a second or two before he added, "Now, I've known you since you were a little boy. I consider your family my extended family. You're a fine young man, and I understand your anger, given the situation, but we should work to remain calm and objective."

It was quiet on Henri's end of the phone. "I'm sorry," he said eventually.

"The restraining order is only in effect for fourteen days, so the court can set a hearing for temporary orders within that time period. So, how long are you going to be in Austin?"

"Two weeks tops. I've hired someone to replace the superintendent, which was the reason for my presence here. I'd just like to make sure he's up and on his feet before I leave."

"I understand. Good. I'll see if we can set the hearing for the following week, maybe at the end of it. Can you return for the day if we need it?"

"Yes, sir," Henri said.

"She's asked to move back into the home until we settle the divorce."

"Screw that," Henri said. Loudly, apparently, as it caught Kevin's attention.

"Henri," John said. Patient and calm was his attorney.

"I'm sorry," Henri said, and blew out a breath. "I don't want her living in my house."

"It may not be up to you. Do you understand?"

"I do, yes, sir," he said, not as loud as before but nowhere near at a conversational tone.

"You knew this might be difficult. You said so yourself at the start. Karen—and these are your words—can be ugly when pushed, so I guess you must have pushed her in some way. Now more than ever, you need to remain calm. Don't call her. Don't in any way contact her. I'm your contact. It's what you're paying me for. Let me have your word on this," John said.

"You have my word," Henri said.

"Good. Take the afternoon to calm down, then I expect you to call me tomorrow, and I'd like to know everything you've done. I can't give you my best advice if I'm not privy to all the facts. I'll be in touch." John hung up.

***

Clarke left the Yolly police station with a case of Waylen on the brain and a serious desire to take a look at his place again. She was driving out there now, even though she wasn't dressed for it. A dress with pumps wasn't the best way to trek about the country-side. She could change. She kept a bag in her car for times like these, when unexpected occurrences cropped up. She'd drive past Waylen's home first and then decide if she needed to change. Plus, she was used to working in just about anything, had worked in just about everything.

What was she to make of Waylen and his answers to her questions? Answers that weren't any different from Caitlyn's or Bill's. He'd only seen her cousin that one time, he'd said. So why didn't she believe him? No idea.

If she hadn't been looking for her cousin, she'd have thought him a clean-cut, all-around American young man. He wasn't what one would call overly handsome but she could see the appeal to a young woman with little experience with males. She'd been that young woman once.

Maybe he'd told her the truth, and he had nothing to do with her cousin's disappearance. Maybe or maybe not, that's what driving out to his home was about for her: hoping to find Amber living there, with him, the father of her child. It was a long shot, a stretch, but if she didn't, then what? Back to where she began, with no clue as to where her cousin might be.

FIFTEEN

For every action, there is an equal and opposite reaction. Newton's third law. Henri knew this, had known it when he'd sought to get back at Karen. He'd wanted revenge. He'd wanted to hurt her, to make her feel some of what he felt at finding the thing he most wanted, the thing he'd worked so hard to acquire, taken from him. So yeah, nothing else had seemed acceptable to him at the time.

Anger and regret at how he'd handled his separation flooded through his system. He knew it would eventually come to light, all the things he'd done. He could understand how a few of his actions might be considered hostile. All he could say in his defense was he'd been angry and hurt—couldn't have stopped if he wanted to.

A week away had made a difference, and if he'd to do it all again, of course he would have done things differently. He hadn't, so he had to live with the consequences. It didn't make him any less angry, knowing all of that. He withdrew his phone from his pocket.

This was a first, texting to meet during the day, he noted, inputting the question mark and sending it to her nonetheless. And no, he wasn't reading anything into this need to be with her except that he wanted… release. Yeah, it was one reason, but not the only.

He could vent all of that ugliness and he didn't have to explain it or hide. He could just let it escape, out into the open, verbally or sexually or both. Plus, she'd been where he was, had experienced firsthand the anger that came from getting fucked over by someone that said they loved you. He wanted to be calm and peaceful and relaxed again, something he felt whenever he left her, and what a surprising realization that was.

He waited a few minutes, and no response. He sat back in his desk, considering other options to rid oneself of unproductive energy. A hard game of basketball, a run around the town lake, maybe. His phone pinged, and it was her.

Now?

Now.

In the middle of something. Lunch?

Lunch works.

You okay?

Karen's attorney = foul mood

She laughed, 'cause it was funny and surprising. *You sound dangerous*, she texted.

Could be.

Where?

Where are you?

In the country, forty minutes away, north.

It took him a few minutes to find a place up to his standards near her part of town, but he was successful and typed in a nearby hotel.

See you was her final text. He sat back in his chair, calmer than he'd been a few minutes ago, but still a very angry man underneath.

He pulled his laptop closer and tried to work, only to give up not much later. He snapped his laptop closed, deciding to chuck the rest of the morning. He'd head to the hotel and wait instead. *Meet me at the hotel bar* was his text to Clarke.

"Out for lunch, and I may be gone for a while. You good here?" he asked Kevin. Hell, he'd forgotten about Kevin.

"Sure, boss," Kevin said, smiling.

"Call if you need me. Emergencies only."

"No problem, boss."

Henri felt himself smiling in return. *Cocky kid*, he thought on his way out, feeling old in the face of Kevin's youth. It felt like ages since he had had that kind of optimism.

***

Google Maps put Waylen's home squarely in the middle of the street that Bria had taken her to last week. She was turning onto that road now and driving over the dip in the road. Seconds later, the same dip that coincided with the dry bed, she now knew, was the western border of Waylen's property. The bed served as a natural property line between Waylen's land and that of his neighbor.

Two pieces of land belonged to Waylen and his neighbor, five-acre parcels each, long rectangular-shaped pieces abutted to the other's, surrounded by country roads. *Thank you, Google Earth, for the ability to see into everyone's business.* She knew the layout of Waylen's property now.

Five acres out in the country, the more rural part of the state, and nice if you could get it, she thought. She was driving past the front of Waylen's property now, past the entrance to the street. A single-wide mobile home sat not quite in the middle of the land—more to the left part of it, if you had to split the acreage right down the middle.

It was fenced in with chain-link which looked to be about six feet in height. Not so easy to scale, but doable if necessary. And yes, it was locked. A big old chain with a lock at the end of it held two gates closed. She was driving past the gate now, headed toward the other end of Waylen's road, which dead-ended into another country road, forming what was called a T-intersection.

She made the left turn onto that road, looking left at the west side of his property now, continuing in her attempt to see inside. Lots of trees and foliage along this side of the fence line too, all the way around his property it seemed, and if she hadn't done the Google Earth search, she'd have no idea what it looked like beyond the trees.

She made another left at the next street, the one that would take her past another side of his property. Another gate back here, the same attached-to-a-chain-lock-gate set-up as the front gate. It was truly *nothing to see here, folks* around this side of his property, nothing but more trees and overgrown brush that limited her ability to see inside. Waylen clearly valued his privacy, she thought, driving past the land next door to his now.

Waylen's neighbor was a corporation, as far as she could tell from her research. No one lived on the property, which could come in handy if she needed a place to hang out. It had the same fencing idea as Waylen, albeit a little less tree-lined. Across the street was nothing but woods, and there were train tracks about a quarter-mile in there somewhere. Thank you, Google Earth, again.

Spooky is what she'd feel, living out here in the boonies. She made the next left, and then another left, driving towards the front of Waylen's place again. She'd made the block. She pulled up and stopped across the street from the front entrance of his home this time.

She'd placed a Kensington Farm and Ranch Realty sign on the outside of her jeep before she'd left the Yolly police station. That was her outward excuse to be here if, say, a neighbor wondered about her. Professionally attired, befitting a realtor out scouting property for her company, which is what she would tell whoever stopped to ask.

She sat in her jeep for a while, observing Waylen's property and the homes around it for signs of life. So far it was quiet. She got out of the car and crossed the street, walked straight up to the front gate, and stood there peering in. She could see a place to park —not a concrete drive, but a graveled one, located to the left of his single-wide.

Two dogs were running toward her. They'd come from behind his mobile home. They were throwing themselves at the fence now, barking up a storm. She backed up a bit, appreciative of the gate pinning dog one and dog two inside.

She stood for a bit, waiting for someone curious enough to see what the dogs were up in arms about. If that someone could be Amber, that would be super, but nope, nothing. No movement, no fluttering of curtains, no nothing.

She looked over her shoulder, across the street, for signs of life there. Nope, it was more of the same nothing. She turned right and took off walking, following the fence line. Dogs one and two tailed her, barking alongside her the entire trip down the fence line to the end. Two yards more and she would be in the center of the dry bed, which she'd learned belonged to the Waylen's neighbor.

She made the right at the fence, she and her companions, the dogs of the alert system that they were designed for. Nothing but fencing along the back side, which she knew from her drive around the place, but she'd hoped for a hole or two, a way in, but nope, no holes available to get through. It made sense, otherwise the dogs would have used them to come after her.

She walked into the dry bed then, moving toward the fence that surrounded Waylen's neighbor, wishing she'd brought along her binoculars. Lots of old junk, old automobiles, and old farm and ranch equipment lay on the ground, as best as she could tell, and there was a house, also old, barely holding itself upright. Vacant? Maybe, she'd have to see.

She made her way back to her car, then crossed the street, not to arouse the dogs again, 'cause they'd disappeared to parts unknown, and it was quiet again. All in all, this was a quiet patch of earth for things to happen on, and no one would have any idea of it.

She checked her watch. She was good on time, her mind moving to Henri's request, as she was done here. That was a first, lunch; a meeting time other than their nightly ones, she thought. And coming on the heels of last night, did it mean something more, she wondered. *Probably not* was her conclusion.

There was nothing on her schedule that required her physical presence until late afternoon. She'd have her lunch with Henri, and whatever it meant or didn't mean. Then it was back to her office, to rustle up whatever she could find on one Waylen Jacobs.

***

He was where he'd said he'd be, sitting at the end of the bar, a couple of young women quietly trying to gain his attention. He was angry, she thought. It was something in the way he sat, staring into his drink, all erect and stiff, so unlike his usual relaxed posture. Her thoughts were confirmed a few minutes later when her gaze met his. She could read the anger simmering in the eyes staring back at her.

He was dressed the same as she'd seen him almost every other time during working hours—suit and tie, and impeccable.

He looked her over, which was cool with her. His checking her out had never bothered her. She looked good, she knew, then and especially now. She was decked out in her professional best, and was glad she hadn't changed. She removed her shades.

"You okay?" she said, sliding into the seat beside him just as he was rising to his feet. "Oh okay, you're ready now." She stood too.

"I am. Shall we?" he said.

"Sure," she said, and allowed him to lead her out of the bar and over to the elevator. They stood there waiting for it to open, not a word spoken beyond the few words in the bar. She entered first and he followed. He didn't say anything then either, just leaned back into the wall and waited as the floors zoomed past.

He allowed her to exit first, followed her down the hall, a step behind, watching her hips move silently from side to side, underneath a simple yet very appealing dress, and high-heeled pumps on her feet.

He unlocked the door to room 410, allowed her to enter first. She turned to face him, sat her purse on the coffee table in front of the couch, and met his eyes.

"You know, on second thought, maybe we should do this another time. I'm not in the best mood. It didn't help, the time at the bar, thinking about my ex. I'm more than a little bit angry, and I don't want to take it out on you."

"How angry are we talking here?" she asked, removing one of her pumps.

"What?" he asked, watching as she removed the other one.

"How angry are you? Are we talking slapping-me-around kind of angry? Or if I change my mind, you won't stop kind of anger? 'Cause that would be rape and I don't care how angry you are, that won't work. Are you that kind of angry?"

"No, and I *never* would be that angry. Did that happen to you?"

"No," she said, watching him. Studying him was more of

what she was doing. "I can defend myself if I have to, and I carry a gun, so as long as you know that, we're good."

He smiled, not a huge one, but a good departure from the stoniness that had been his countenance so far.

"You'd shoot me?"

"Hell yes, and Texas is a stand-your-ground state too, just so you know," she said.

"But I'm a white guy, so it may not go like you think it will, if you shoot me that is," he said, chuckling and losing a bit more of his anger.

"I'll take my chances, but it shouldn't come to that. You're not so angry anymore."

"Maybe," he said, closing the distance between them. He lowered his lips to hers. It was all heat, this kiss, nothing holding back. Her arms went around his neck, to hold on against the onslaught that was his mouth, pressed against hers, his tongue pushing to be let inside of hers, to push hers around after it had gained entry, until hers was done running and ready to strike back, and they were lost in battle for a while.

He groaned, moved his hands to her ass before long, under her dress. He lifted her off her feet, wrapping her legs around his hips. He rubbed his erection against her then, and she moaned.

"You like that?" he whispered against her lips. He slid her skirt up clear of her hips, and then unzipped and removed his erection. Not even a second later he was smoothly sliding into her heat. She moaned again, and moaned more as he started to lift her and then lower her, up and down his erection, a steady series of ups and downs, lifting and lowering that soon was replaced with the faster method of sliding up and down and up and she neared her climax. He was with her, approaching his; she could hear it in his breathing, plus he was groaning now too, as she removed her face from his neck to touch her lips to his.

"I…" he said, pulling away from her mouth, his gaze hot and staring into hers.

"What?" she said.

He was lifting her then, removing her from his erection. "Bend your knees," he said.

"What?"

"Bend your knees," he said, holding her under her arms until she did, then lowering her to the floor. She was now on her knees in front of him. He placed her hands around his erection, using his hands to move hers up and down it. He widened his stance after she touched her lips to the tip of his erection. He moaned after she took him inside her mouth, as he held on to her shoulders and gave in to his release, his head lowered and eyes closed in painful pleasure, moaning softly as he came.

She opened her eyes and met his smiling down at her.

"I like this arrangement," she said, rising to her feet. She reached for the hem of her dress, and pulled it up over her head, before losing her bra and her string of underwear.

"You do," he said, feeling so much better, and it wasn't all about the release either. It was her, and her attitude, the strength he knew that lay within her. He was removing his tie and then his shirt, 'cause apparently they weren't finished.

"I do." She was standing in front of him now on her tiptoes. "So," she said, leaning up to kiss him, pushing her tongue into his mouth, where it stayed awhile, playing with his.

"So," he repeated after she pulled away, eyes lowered, and he was slowly preparing for round two.

"Still angry?"

"Not as much," he said.

"But enough?"

"I guess," he said, smiling now. "Why?"

"It's my turn," she said. He gave her another one of his rare smiles and finished stripping. She watched him, and when he was done, she took his hand in hers and led him to the bed. She turned him and pushed him to sit on it. *Hers to command* was the way it would be now. She pushed him until his back hit the bed before she joined him. She placed one knee on either side of his hips, then started to crawl upwards and didn't stop until her hips aligned up perfectly to his beautifully shaped lips.

"My turn," she said, looking down past her stomach to meet up with his eyes, waiting for him to say no to this, as her husband had always done before for so many reasons. He smiled and spread her legs a little bit wider so her knees rested on either side of his head.

"Of course," he said, running his tongue along her core softly, before moving his gaze to hers. All she could do was nod as his tongue started touching her again. "Can you move your hips up and then down for me? Like this." He demonstrated.

Hell yeah. She nodded. She could do whatever he wanted her to, as long as he was willing to do this one thing for her.

And so it began; the small movements of her hips up and down—not really up and down, it was more a rolling forward and back for a while as he made slow love to this one body part. He gripped her ass tighter after a bit, moving her wherever he wanted, using the sounds she made as his guide, to bring her to one climax and then on to another.

She was done, he thought, smiling at the way she'd fallen face forward onto the bed, her butt still up where he'd left it. He gave one final swipe of his tongue, chuckling at the beleaguered moan that she released. He smiled as he lined up behind her, opened her legs a little wider, and it was his turn to be on his knees.

She moaned as he entered her, one smooth hard stroke, and then again, hard, and then harder. It was a few more strokes into her wetness, the results of all that prep he'd done a few minutes ago, that had created enough juiciness to last for a lifetime, making for one heck of a smooth ride as he so easily continued to thrust his hips into hers. He moved his hands from her hips, where they'd been holding her in place, up to her head.

His hands were on either side of her now, and he leaned into her then, until his chest and stomach touched her back as he continued his thrusts into her and out of all that wetness, groaning as he did so. She fell forward, or rather his hips pushed her forward, and she lay flat, completely underneath him, not that it stopped anything. It didn't. His hips continued with their thrusts into her, as far as he could go, before he was coming again, alone this time.

He smiled, although she couldn't see it. She was done… spent, as had been his intention.

She couldn't barely bring herself to do more than that half-smile back at him, over her shoulder, at all he'd done before. *It wasn't so bad, his anger* was her last thought before she closed her eyes amid the sounds of him climaxing.

***

They were eating lunch now. Room service had come and gone, leaving behind two plates: a really sweet steak with something pretty and vegetable for him, and a burger and fries for her. She'd been starving afterward so he'd ordered room service. It was the least he could do, he'd said, and she had agreed.

He was seated on the couch wearing one of those robes that

came courtesy of fine establishments such as this one, with a plate in his lap, while she sat the floor in front of the couch using the coffee table that came standard in most hotels as her dining table. She sat with her legs folded yoga style, clothed in a carbon copy of the robe he wore.

"What was that about?" she asked, turning the screw on that little ketchup bottle that had come with her fries, before turning it over to allow the liquid to pour out.

"What?"

"All the anger you needed to get rid of, that couldn't keep until tonight. Not that I'm complaining."

"My attorney called," he said, and went quiet.

"And he said…?"

"Karen wants the house. *My house.* A gift to me from my parents."

"Nice, having your parents gift you a house, let me say that first off."

"It can be," he said, before cutting into his steak.

"So that's the reason for your anger?"

"She accused me of other things, too."

"Like?" she said.

"Like cheating… with you," he said, meeting her eyes.

"I hate fucking cheaters," she said, chuckling, sliding her knife into the ketchup bottle.

He laughed. "I know. With you walking in, she thinks there's more to us, I guess. There is, but not before I arrived here. Not that she knows that either. Who really knows with Karen? She's angry, is all. Angry that I filed for divorce, that I kicked her out, and she's having to live with her mother."

"You kicked her out?"

"I packed up her stuff and had it delivered to her mother's."

"Like, boxed up some of her things and sent them to her mother's?" she asked, looking up at him now that the ketchup was pouring onto her plate.

"As in boxed up *all* of her things and had the movers deliver it all to her mother's."

"Oh. Before or after she came home from the hospital?"

"Before," he said, watching her open the top to the pepper shaker now, pouring it freely into the pool of ketchup she'd poured onto the side of her plate. Henri watched, mid-bite, fascinated for some reason.

"I'd say that constitutes kicking her out. A little harsh, don't you think?"

"No, I don't think. What she did was harsh. She's the one that lied and cheated," he said, meeting her eyes, a little bit of his anger flaring back to life. "Let's talk about something else. I find myself getting angry again, and all that work we put into getting rid of it would be wasted."

"Right," she said, and she started in on doctoring her burger now, piling the lettuce, tomatoes, and pickles on top. "So do you like what we do here?"

"You can't tell?" he asked, chuckling.

"I was just wondering if you wanted more… if I'm enough. And that sounded serious. I don't mean in the sense of long-term, I'm only talking sexually here."

"I don't know, is this all you have to offer?" he said, smiling.

"It is."

"How did you meet your ex?" he asked.

"I thought we weren't going to talk of exes."

"My ex. I'm okay discussing yours."

"Right. I wanted to be a cop, a police officer, and he was one of the trainers at the time. Big man on campus, all hard-nosed alpha male, used to be in the service, all take-charge. Which I get, it was necessary for his job. You can imagine the type."

"I can."

"I was impressed, and naïve, and new. I found it appealing. I fell for him hard," she said, turning her gaze to his. "I thought he'd fallen for me too."

"What makes you think he didn't?"

"I don't know. I wasn't as malleable after a while, not like when I was younger. I think that was the me he really fell for, if he fell at all, and maybe if I could have remained that way, maybe things would have turned out differently for us. It was what I began to suspect as I grew up a bit and started to form my own opinions. Some were radically different from his, when my wants and needs started to change. Maybe, I don't know. I sensed disappointment from him after a while."

"How long were you married?"

"Eight years."

"You were young?"

"Twenty-one. You?"

"Twenty-six," he said, meeting her eyes. "You're right, enough talk of exes. How was today? Did you get up to Yolly, meet Waylen?"

"Yes."

"How was it?"

"Officer Jim was manning the desk when I arrived, called Waylen up to see me."

"Officer Jim?" Henri asked, taking a sip of his water.

"He's another police officer. I met him when my aunt and I went to follow up on the initial report. Waylen was the one that took the report from my aunt. I found his card, he'd given it to my aunt," she said, finally dipping her fry into her ketchup and black pepper mix.

"So were you able to talk to him? How did Waylen respond to you?"

"Yes, and he was fine," she said. She finished chewing before adding, "He said he knew her, and yes, he took a picture with her, but that was it. Oh, and he danced with her, once. He hasn't seen her since."

"Do you believe him?"

She shrugged and took a bite of her burger.

"How was his demeanor?"

"Nice, sincere. If he's lying he's good at it," she said, after she'd chewed for a bit.

"So what do we know?" he asked, smiling, no longer angry.

And that was a good thing, she thought, meeting his smile with one of her own. "Okay, we," she said. "We know that the area where Amber was dropped off is near where Waylen lives."

"And how do we know this?"

"From our property search. I don't know if he purchased his home or the land or inherited both. I'm going to spend this afternoon doing a little checking him out, after I leave here. Then I'm going to drive back out this evening after I'm done scouring the Internet."

"You've been by there?"

"Yep, I was out there this morning after I left the station. It's where I was when you texted."

"No signs of Amber or the baby?"

"Nope. No sign of anybody but those dogs."

"Dogs?"

"Two of them. Doberman Pinscher is the breed, I think. Mean is the personality." She popped another fry into her mouth.

"You have time?"

"I think so, making time anyway. I might have to hire help, though. I'm getting more clients than I can handle."

"And that's not a good thing."

"Don't know. I didn't want big, remember," she said, and he nodded, sitting back against the couch watching her.

"When will you stop searching for your cousin?" he asked.

"When I find something conclusive either way, I guess," she said, feeling a little depressed about that too.

It was quiet for a few minutes while she ate a few more fries, finished off half of her burger. She took a sip of her water when she was done and looked over at him. She was getting to her feet now.

He watched her move toward the couch, placing his plate on the table beside hers. She pushed the table away from the sofa next.

"What are you doing?"

"A little more anger management for the road is what I think we need," she said, smiling.

"Is that so," he said, smiling now too.

"It is. I would know, having been through what you're going through, are about to go through." She settled between his knees on the floor in front of the couch.

His breath caught when she reached for his erection. After what they'd done earlier, he doubted it could move, let alone rise again. His breath caught again as her hands moved softly over him. Yeah, maybe it could.

***

Two hours later, after a quick shower, Clarke was seated behind the desk in her home office. She liked her home, appreciated that she could both work and live in it, not that she had much of a choice. Moving to Austin and putting money into two start-ups, hers and the house flipping business with Summer, had taken just about all her savings.

She had one more report to write on another case before she could return her attention to Amber, which meant Waylen. She'd caught up most of the loose ends and required to-dos from some of her other cases, so after she was done with this one report, she would be free for the evening. Free to dig up more information on Waylen, and free for another trip out to his property again. Like a dog with a bone, now that she had one to chew on, at least until she could rule him out as having anything to do with her cousin's disappearance.

The bell over her door tinkled, and in walked Summer, carrying two very large cups of coffee in her hands. A nice surprise and very much appreciated.

"It's been crazy," Summer said, kicking the front door closed behind her, handing off one of the coffees to Clarke.

"I love you," Clarke said.

"We can always use coffee," Summer said, settling her body into the chair in front of Clarke's desk.

"You're casual." Clarke pointed to Summer's attire of sweats and tennis shoes.

"I've been busy, visiting the houses again, making sure I'm fine with picking house number one. That's going to be our choice, I think. I'd like for you to look at it one more time."

"I'm good with what you decide, but I can see it again if you want," Clarke said, removing the lid from her coffee cup. Filled to the brim, with steam wafting off of it was her preference.

"How do Hamp's numbers look?"

"Good, as I expected. The house I like is the most expensive to purchase and to remodel but if we do it right, we stand to make the most. That hasn't changed."

"Your friend still okay with selling it to you?"

"Yes."

"So tomorrow, you want me to meet you at that house?" Clarke asked, pulling her calendar up to make a note.

"Yep, say about nine."

"I can do nine tomorrow," Clarke said.

"Good, then. I'll tell Henri, make sure he can make it. So…" Summer said, a mischievous grin on her face. "Speaking of seeing my brother…"

"So? What?" Clarke said. And yes, she knew what was coming.

"How's Henri?" Summer asked.

"Good, I guess. Why?"

"I mean, how was he last night, at the bar?"

"Good. He was good, stayed out of the way," Clarke said, smiling at her friend's expression, all sad and disappointed.

"So he didn't do anything?"

"Like?"

"I don't know… ask you out."

"Nope," Clarke said, chuckling. "Give up yet?"

"No, I don't think so," Summer said, smiling brightly, and the conversation moved on to bringing each other up to date on all the other happenings in their lives.

Clarke's home office had become as much of an office to Summer as it had to Clarke, so when they were done with catching up, Clarke went back to her work, and Summer opened her laptop and started into hers.

SIXTEEN

Just before dusk, Clarke returned to Waylen's home to observe him. It was the only way she could think of to rule him out as having anything to do with Amber's disappearance. She would tail him for a while, and thanks to the absent landholder next door, she'd have a place to hide while she did so.

She sat at the back door of a run-down, dilapidated old house that would be her home base. She'd parked her jeep in the front drive, covered it with a tarp, and now sat waiting for the sky to darken. She'd packed a bag, changed into black everything: leggings, t-shirt, sneakers, added on her adult diaper, 'cause it was necessary, and she was good to go. Hell no was she going to go pee in the woods, nor would she run the risk of missing seeing what, if anything, Waylen had planned. It was an occupational necessity.

She'd found a place to sit and watch Waylen's home in one of the trees in the dry bed area, one of the evergreens. She'd be upstream, upwind, or just on higher ground from Waylen's, tucked in either a yaupon holly or a live oak tree, either of the two would do.

Waylen was home, the lights were on inside, and a truck, black and shiny, was parked inside the gate, to the left of his home. A home purchased by Waylen with settlement money he'd received from his parents' death. She'd found a newspaper article detailing the car accident that had killed both of his parents. No siblings for Waylen. She and he had that in common.

The land he'd inherited had come courtesy of the grandparents, his momma's momma and daddy, the big-money tie to the town of Yolly that Caitlyn had mentioned.

Don't do this trespassing thing at home, boys and girls, she thought, putting on her night goggles before making the trek to the dry bed to select her tree for the night. In the end, she'd settled on the live oak. It looked the most comfortable.

Ten minutes later she sat looking into Waylen's yard. It was as she'd pictured it. Mobile home, with his truck next to it and his shed out back. That was the sum total of it. She leaned back into her tree, to watch and wait.

***

Wednesday morning, early

She was awakened the following morning by the sound of a car starting up. Actually it was a truck that was responsible for the noise, one of those loud-ass diesel-engine trucks. This one belonged to Waylen. He was leaving for work and she would have slept right through and missed it. Thank you again, Lord, for the loud-ass diesel-engine alarm clock.

She ran her hand over her face and checked the time. It was six o'clock in the morning. Forty-five minutes had passed since she'd fallen asleep. The last memory she had was of checking her watch. What a start to her morning, with the end of her first night, an uneventful one spent staring into the neighbor next door's yard. It wasn't completely uneventful. Waylen had gone to the shed out back once, to take out the trash before bed.

There was no sign of her cousin, out to see Waylen off to

work. He was alone, dressed in his policeman's uniform, unlocking the gate now. He went back to his truck, turned it around in the drive, and pulled it through to the other side of the gate. He stopped, got out of his truck to relock the gate. He was driving away minutes later.

She waited a bit before disembarking from her place in the tree, scanning the neighborhood with her binoculars while she waited. It was a quiet neighborhood. No kids getting off to school, or school buses passing, no neighbors leaving for work. It was a well-chosen area if your desire for privacy superseded everything else.

She pulled out behind him fifteen minutes later, craving coffee and a shower, but before all of that, a little bit more tailing of Waylen was required. She turned her jeep in the direction of Yolly and headed out.

***

Thirty minutes and some change was how long the drive took from Waylen's home in Avondale to Yolly Coffeehouse, located in the center of town, almost across from the police station.

Clarke was seated in the booth furthest from the door in this small, square-shaped box of a coffee shop situated between a store that sold all types of batteries and a computer repair place. It was all glass-fronted, and nothing out of the ordinary in coffee shop decor or theme, unless being ordinary was the goal.

She'd been staring out the window for the last three hours, watching the police station for Waylen. So far it was nothing to see or do here but drink her second cup of coffee and eat her breakfast taco. Where was Waylen going, she wondered, watching him walk toward his truck. She closed her pretending-to-work laptop with a snap and was out the door, headed to her jeep, a minute behind Waylen.

***

It was ten o'clock in the morning, and Waylen was back at home. After leaving the police station and making one quick stop at the grocery store, it had been a straight shot to his house, with her following.

It had taken him a while to get inside his home, of course. He had to stop, unlock the gates, pull in his truck, and then relock the gates. The dogs gave him less trouble than they'd given her. They were all happy to see him. Jumping up and down with tails wagging was his welcome home, and no sign of her cousin coming out to greet him coming home for whatever this was.

Clarke made the block, stopping at his neighbor's home again, making sure it was clear before she quickly jogged over to the dry bed again. She was up the tree a few minutes later, watching Waylen's home again. Fifteen minutes tops and he was out, heading to the back shed, a trash bag in his hand again. It was back inside his home, where he stayed for about five minutes, and then he was letting the dogs out and locking up the front door. The dogs were only inside when he was home, is what she'd determined so far.

It was back over to his truck, for the unlocking-the-gate-driving-through-relocking-the-gate dance. The dogs stood by, obediently watching the Waylen's ritual. Two minutes more and he was pulling away.

Another ten and Clarke was on the ground and moving back over to her jeep, hoping the rest of her day wasn't this up-and-down, back-and-forth trip to Yolly.

***

Summer stood outside the office of Novak Construction after lunch. She was in the neighborhood pricing cabinets and other home-related stuff, when she decided to stop by and remind Henri of tonight's home tour and of course to question him about Clarke. She found him standing just outside the office door, talking on the phone, clearly irritated with whomever he was speaking with.

She stood there for a second, thinking he might be at the end of his call, and she could have a quick chat and be on her way. No, he'd be here for a bit, she thought, looking around the site, feigning interest in her surroundings, as she listened to him talk. She'd been overhearing his conversations since she was little girl and could pretend indifference with the best of them while she soaked in almost every word of what he said. It was his attorney that he was on the phone with, and they were discussing something about a court date for some type of restraining order.

She left him then, headed inside to wait. She was surprised to find a new face sitting behind the office desk. He looked up when she entered, his face a mask that she couldn't read. He must be the new superintendent Henri had hired. She walked over to introduce herself.

"Hello. You're the new superintendent?" Summer said, extending her hand to him. He was not what she'd expected. Of Asian descent and tall. Did those two things even go together in the same sentence, she wondered. If not, then he was the exception, as he was both tall and Asian—and cute, she thought, adding the last descriptor while checking out the nameplate on what used to be her desk and then her brother's. *Kevin Huang*, it read.

"Yep, and you are?" he asked, all attitude, as if she were interrupting him.

"Summer Novak," she said.

"The old superintendent, the one that screwed things up here," he said, and smiled as he said it, leaving her unsure of his meaning.

"Excuse me?"

"Nope, there are no excuses for incompetence," he said, and this smile was not as big as his first one.

"You must not know who I am," she said, and that sounded so odd coming out of her mouth. She was not the person who pulled rank.

"The entrepreneurial daughter," he said, and his smile had all but disappeared.

"What?" she said, truly dumbfounded now.

"Is there something I can help you with?" Kevin asked, sitting up straight in his chair, pinning her in place with a look of hostility.

"Do I know you?" she asked, really confused now.

"That's a good question. Why don't you think about it for a while and get back to me?" he said, pulling his computer in front of his face, effectively shutting her out.

Okay, that felt more than a little like a diss, Summer thought. She stood there, looking at the top of his head; black hair, straight and cut military short. He looked up again, eyes almond-shaped, cheekbones defined. Okay, he was easy on the eyes, but there was some major hostility in his gaze. *What the hell?* she thought.

"What's up?" Henri asked from behind her. He had returned and she hadn't even noticed, so surprised was she by this Kevin person's behavior.

"I, uh…" she said, reluctantly moving her gaze away from the new dude to her brother. "Uh… we are seeing house number one again this evening."

"I know, you told me already. You didn't have to stop for that," Henri said, and she could hear the irritation in his voice.

"I also wanted to say hello to the new superintendent, maybe even offer my assistance if he needed it."

"You're fine, right, Kevin?" Henri said, moving toward the conference table. "Kevin, this is my little sister, Summer Novak. Summer, meet Kevin."

"The flipper of houses," Kevin said, smiling all cocky-like now, the anger gone. He ran his gaze over her like she was some new meal.

"So tonight, the house, and then I'll have to make a decision," Summer said, turning her gaze to Henri again.

"Again, for the third time," Henri said, typing something on his laptop.

"Well, okay, I can see that you all are busy, so I'm leaving. See you later," she said, flustered still, enough that she had forgotten all about bringing up Clarke. *Who was this Kevin person?* she wondered. Someone she should remember, but for the life of her, she couldn't.

"Sure," Henri said, distracted by his most recent conversation with his attorney. He was needed in Dallas, Tuesday next week, for his first hearing. Allowing his anger to run roughshod over his decisions had not been a good idea. He usually avoided allowing anger to influence his decisions. Believe it or not, this was unusual behavior for him.

The hurt he'd felt at what she'd done had overridden his common sense, at least that was what he told himself. Which was true, just not the complete truth. Then there was another source of anger that had nothing at all to do with Karen, and was something he still wasn't ready to face. He sighed and checked his phone for a text from a short female investigator. He could use a call from her about now, and when had that started? Since his trip to the bar, or maybe even before, since that dinner with Stephen and Reye. That was officially the time he'd started to open up, he thought. Whatever, he just knew that he liked her opinions, as he was getting to know her. He was starting to consider her a friend, with many benefits.

He stood and headed outside. A whim and the urge to talk to her had him calling her.

"Hello," she said, and it sounded a little tentative to his ears. He laughed. "Henri?" she asked.

"Yes," he said.

"This is a surprise."

"I know."

"Is everything okay? Did something happen to Summer?" she asked, to his continued silence.

"No, she's fine. She just left here. No, I have to be in Dallas next week, for a hearing with Karen," he said.

"Oh." He could hear the understanding he'd needed to hear in that one word.

"Yeah, oh," he said.

"You know this won't last forever. It will end, you know that too. It'll hurt though, no way around that."

"Yep," he said, silent for a bit.

"I'm at Waylen's, spent the night last night sitting in a tree," she said, telling him all she'd done in her attempts to learn more about Waylen, how she'd fallen asleep and almost missed him. "I know, I must sound like a crazy person, don't I? Don't you think? I mean, really. I'm the one that should be arrested for following him up to Yolly and back. Tell me to stop, right. I mean, I have nothing to go on besides this hunch, and what if it's wrong, a waste of my time? On a wild goose chase, making Waylen out to be some bad dude, just because he likes his trash separated." She chuckled, but was putting her fears out there, right alongside his.

He laughed. "How long do you think you'll need to follow him?"

"I don't know."

"Well, it can't last forever, right," he said, chuckling. "It will come to an end, right? It has to, and what could be wrong with you searching for your cousin? That's what you're doing, trusting your instincts and pursuing them, right?"

"Right," she said, and waited a second before she spoke. "Thank you for that."

"You're welcome. See you tonight?"

"At the house you mean?"

"There too," he said. She laughed.

"You will. It'll have to be quick, as I've got the tree waiting for me at the end of the night, more watching of Waylen to do."

"I'll see what I can do," he said, smiling. She could hear it in his voice.

"Bye."

"Yep," he said, hanging up. And yes to the part about her becoming a friend with many benefits, he thought again.

***

What a long day this had turned out to be, Clarke thought, following Waylen home from work now, on her fourth and—she hoped —final drive back to his house. He was going through his routine now—that's what she was calling it, all the steps it took for him to enter and exit his kingdom. And what the need for it was she'd like to know.

It was the same routine all three times he'd come home. Mid-morning, lunch, then mid-afternoon—that was his third trip, and now at the end of the day. She just about killed herself parking next door and running over to the tree to watch him do nothing more than walk over to the gate to relock it. Yeah, she'd missed the first part of the routine. He was unlocking the front door now.

She sat in her tree and watched, 'cause if he was moving according to plan, a trip to the shed out back to take out the trash was next. Yep, almost to the minute, Waylen was walking over to the shed, his bag of trash in his hand. What human being created so much trash? Another thing she'd like to know.

What a boring life we lead, she thought, watching him and the dogs return to his house from the shed. He went inside and a few minutes later he was back out, dragging one of those rubberized trashcans out to the front gate, before going back inside for two trash bags, the black industrial kind. He threw them into the trashcan. He unlocked the gate and pulled the trashcan through to the other side, and of course he relocked the gate when he was done. Waylen was not a drop-by-without-calling type of guy, no getting inside his home without an invite.

She sat back into the tree, pondering her next move. She wanted Waylen's trash, the two bags he'd just placed outside on the curb. She was going to take them, she decided, she just had to figure out how to do it. She knew she needed the cover of darkness, which thankfully was readily available, or would be soon. All she had to do was wait.

She checked her watch. It was closing in on seven p.m. It didn't really get dark until about eight thirty, which was fine. She didn't have to be anywhere until nine when she'd have to meet Henri and Summer at the house to check it out again. Not sure why, but okay, she couldn't not go. Summer had reminded her three times today.

She should have enough time to do both. She could retrieve Waylen's trash and make it to the house. She'd be cutting it close but it could work. She pulled out her phone and sent a text to Summer. *Might be late, start without me.* Just in case. She sent one to Henri as well.

About to steal me some trash, she texted and laughed at whatever this was growing between them. No complaints, she'd take it *and* the sex with Henri any day of the week.

She put her phone away and went back to watching Waylen's home, thinking through her trash-stealing plan, biding her time until it was dark enough.

***

Eight thirty-five on the dot, and dark enough finally, Clarke thought. She was back sitting in her jeep, parked near the dry bed, watching Waylen's trash, waiting to complete the second part of her two-part plan. The plan she'd hatched in the tree as she waited for darkness.

Part one was complete. It had consisted of scouring the neighborhood for two black industrial-sized trash bags to replace the two she planned to take from Waylen.

No way did she want him coming back for his trash, only to find them missing. So she'd driven around the neighborhood until she found two bags sitting unsuspecting on the curb of a neighbor. They were now in the back of her jeep, waiting along with her.

This is crazy, she said to herself more than once, along with *Why am I going to such lengths for a hunch?*

She started up her jeep anyway and drove closer to Waylen's, thankful for the trees growing around his property. No one could see in, and hopefully he couldn't see out. She hopped out of her jeep, quickly grabbing the two bags from her jeep. It was a quick trip over to the Waylen's trashcan, and one easy switch later, she was back in her car, carefully speeding away. She sent a text to Summer and one to Henri that she was on her way.

Finally, hurry. Henri is still here was Summer's response. She rolled her eyes and laughed at her friend's relentless push, releasing some of the tension she'd felt since she made her decision to go after Waylen's refuse.

***

"Hey," Clarke said from the front doorway, meeting Henri's gaze. He was alone.

"Hi," he said, and smiled. And what the hell, she thought at his smile. It wasn't his usual small one he so often gave. This one was friendly and not at all guarded. He was something to look at, always caught her by surprise. He was dressed in jeans and a t-shirt, with sneakers on his feet.

"Where's Summer?" she said, moving closer to him.

She was dressed in all black. Black athletic gear, high-top black tennis shoes, black sprayed-on legging, and an equally sprayed-on t-shirt and he really like the way she looked.

"In the kitchen with Hamp," he said.

"What?" she said, looking at him oddly.

"Nothing. Is this our surveillance wear?" he said, pointing to her clothing.

"Yep."

"How was the trash stealing?"

"Great," she said.

Excited, he could tell. He'd seen those large eyes, the labored breathing, and flushed face somewhere else. She was cute, with her eyes shining brightly over something as crazy as finding some-one's trash.

"You're stealing trash now?" Summer asked, coming in from the other room. "Whose trash?"

"Waylen's."

"Oh, that's good, I guess," Summer said, looking between Clarke and Henri.

"You were careful?" he asked.

"I was, and I have two trash bags to go through. It should give me a better idea of what's going on inside," Clarke said in a bit of a rush, her gaze and attention totally on him, which did not go unnoticed by Summer.

"One can hope," Henri said, smiling again.

"Hey, Hamp," Clarke said, waving at her uncle, who had just entered the room. "I'd hug you, but I probably smell." He smiled.

"The sweet smell of success is what you smell like. It means you've been working and Hamp thinks that's always good."

"So we're going with this house?" Clarke asked, looking around it again. It looked the same as it had the last time she was here.

"Yes. You want to see it again?" Summer asked.

"No, I've trash to go through," Clarke said, and smiled. "And I trust you."

"What do you think?" Summer asked, turning her gaze and her attention to her brother.

"It's not my call," Henri said.

"Hamp, what do you think?" Summer asked.

"Hamp's just the numbers man. Hamp don't make decision about things that aren't his to decide, but if Hamp were to give his opinion, then Hamp's partial to this house. It's a challenge for sho, but Hamp likes challenges."

"Okay, fine. I'll talk with my friend again, and if she still agrees, then this is the one." Summer said, smiling.

Great, Clarke thought, watching her friend. "I still have to go."

"I know, you have your trash to go through," Summer said.

"Yep," Clarke said.

"You want some help?" Henri asked.

"Sure. If you don't mind," Clarke said.

"Oh, thank you, brother, for helping out my dear friend. Such a nice guy, right?" Summer said, all wide-eyed innocence.

"Where?" Henri said, ignoring his sister.

"My house. You remember how to get there?"

"I do," he said.

"See you then," she said, moving toward the front door.

"Yep," he said, following her out, leaving a smiling Summer behind them.

***

"You take this bag, and I'll take that one," Clarke said. They were standing inside the garage of her home. She'd taped together four large trash bags to the floor to create a four-by-four square work-space.

"Here, you'll wear these, and thank you again for helping me." She handed over a pair of disposable gloves to him. They were small but it was all she had.

"No problem. We private eyes have to stick together, plus you pay well, in the way I like to be paid," he said, chuckling at the eye roll she gave him. "What are we looking for?" he asked, removing the twist tie from his bags.

"Anything that puts Amber or the baby with him," she said, dumping her bag onto the square. "Yuck," she said at the smell.

"This is crazy." She was squatting now, papers in her hand.

"Committed is what this is, and there's nothing wrong with that," he said, dumping his bag to add to hers.

"Waylen didn't believe in home cooking," she said, moving empty take-out containers over to one side.

"He liked his beer too," Henri said, squatting now, stacking the bottles on another corner of the workspace.

"Mail, and it's all addressed to him," Clarke said, holding up a few pieces before placing them in another corner to sort through later.

It was quiet as they worked, both concentrating and into this, Clarke thought, glancing up at Henri later, appreciative of the company.

She sat back on her heels when they were done. "You find anything?" She looked over their cache of pill bottles, food scraps, take-out containers, mix of beer bottles and cans, and mail, most of it junk.

"Nothing of importance. Shaving stuff, bathroom stuff, that's about it," he said. "A waste this was, huh?"

"Maybe. I wonder what he is storing in the shed then, if this is his trash."

"His what?"

"His shed. He has one out back," she said, and told him of Waylen's mid-morning, afternoon, and evening trips to it. "I would like to see what's inside. Maybe something in there will offer up a clue, allow me to cross him off the list." She stared at him, as intense as he'd ever seen her.

"Is it locked?"

"Yes, but I can pick it."

"I should be surprised but I'm not," he said, still squatting, looking at their trash pile. "It's a long shot?"

"I don't think so."

"How do you propose we get in there?" he asked.

"You and this 'we'," she said, smiling, pulling the sides of their trash bag mat together, starting to clean up the mess they'd made.

He smiled, reaching for the other end of the mat, helping her with the clean-up too. "I'm in now. Going to the bar and now going through Waylen's trash puts me in, so it's a we." He smiled. "So, back to my question. How do we get in?"

"It has to be at night, when the dogs are inside with him. I can climb the fence, I think." She reached for a new empty trash bag to put all the trash in.

"That sounds dangerous. Maybe you should just talk with that officer—what was his name again?"

"Jim."

"Tell Officer Jim what you think," he said, putting the last of the trash into a second bag.

"I will, but I need something like proof first. All I have is a hunch. Can't be accusing Mr. Police Officer on a hunch. You can, maybe, but not me. I have to have an overwhelming preponderance of evidence before they'll listen to this little black girl accusing somebody. Which is why I need into the shed.

"It could be anything out in that shed. Maybe he grows marijuana or makes hooch to sell to the locals, and I'm busting it up or something. Maybe that's the reason for the dogs and the locked gates. It could be. I've not seen anyone remotely resembling my cousin or a kid, it's just me with a hunch that won't go away."

He laughed. "Did you just say 'hooch'?" She laughed. "When do you want to go?"

"I don't know. Give me tonight, maybe another day or two to

watch. Plus I need to figure out his work schedule. I need him to be at home, need the dogs to be inside with him. I'm going back out tonight."

"You want company?" he said, making knots into the top of the trash bags before setting them off to the side of her garage.

"No, one person in a tree is enough."

"You leaving now?"

"No. Shower first, clean clothes, food, and then I'll head out," she said, opening the door that led from the garage to the inside of her home.

"You have time for anything else?"

"Absolutely. The shower and you, two birds with one stone." She smiled and held her hand out to him.

"I like you, Ms. Kensington," he said, accepting it, allowing her to pull him inside with her.

"I like you too, Mr. Novak.

SEVENTEEN

Thursday

She was awake this morning, able to watch Waylen exit his home again, dressed for work. She watched him head over to the shed again, trash bag in hand, before it was back inside for another fifteen minutes, and then outside again, over to his truck. Yep, the same song and dance with unlocking and relocking the gate before he was turning onto the road, headed to Yolly. She was sure she needed a look at his shed. Nothing else he did was suspicious. She'd have her answer either way.

She waited as she always did before dropping to the ground. It was over to the city again but this time she had something else to do, another way of keeping track of Waylen that didn't involve following him. Illegal for sure, but necessary, she thought.

***

Henri looked up at the sound of the door, surprised to see Clarke enter the office. "This is a surprise," he said, turning in his chair to face her. He didn't move, but kept his seat and watched her, dressed in what he called her stake-out gear of all-black athletic wear. It was such a kick seeing her this way. "I thought you'd be out tailing Waylen still."

"I am following him," she said.

"How?"

"If I tell you, I'll have to kill you," she said. He laughed.

"You're serious."

"I am," she said, moving toward him. "This is your desk now?"

"Yep. Kevin has taken over the other one, which is how it should be, since he's the new superintendent," he said.

"Summer summoned me, that's why I'm here. Sent me a text a few minutes ago, said she'd be here in five, wants to tell me the pick *again*, says it's official. You know your sister, all drama and theatrics." She stood beside him. "Don't let me interrupt you."

"You're not interrupting anything. Kevin had an errand to run so you have a few minutes, I guess, before Summer arrives. And you aren't going to tell me, really?" he asked, reaching for her hand, pulling her to stand between his legs.

The gesture surprised her.

"So how did it go… last night with Waylen?"

She smiled slowly, letting it spread over her face. "Good. I put a GPS tracking device on his truck this morning while he was inside at work. That's how I'm able to follow him without having to follow him." She pulled out her phone to show him the app that went with the GPS device. "I can't sleep every night out in a tree, right?"

"Not when there are more comfortable places to sleep," he said, smiling, pulling her closer still. He released her hand and moved his to her legs, softly caressing, like he needed to touch her. Okay, she was good with that.

"You can do that now?"

"Do what?" she said, forcing her mind to the conversation and away from his hands holding onto her legs.

"Track him with GPS?"

"No. I can't. It's illegal. Not in any way is what I'm doing legal, unless maybe it's your kid or something. No, it's cutting corners, but again, that tree is getting old, and I'm not hiring others to sit for me, not for this. Not when I don't have anything other than a feeling to go on."

"I'm not complaining. I don't want you in trees either," he said, leaning forward, resting his head on her stomach.

"If Summer wasn't on her way…" she said, looking at the back of his head, lying softly on her, bringing thoughts of last night into her brain. "I believe you do your best work in showers." She ran her hand through his hair.

"You like that, huh?" he said, looking up at her now.

"I do," she said, and leaned down to touch her lips to his for a quick kiss. "You still up for going with me? Tomorrow night, to see what's in the shed?" She looked down into his eyes.

"Up for what now?"

"To Waylen's home, to look into his shed."

"Sticking with that plan, are we?"

"Of course I am. However, if *you're* afraid or worried, and want to drop the *we* part of our team, then I can go it alone. I've done it before."

"I'm sure you have, and no, I'm fine. The offer still stands." He placed his head into her stomach again while his hands moved up to her ass. "What time?"

"From what I can tell, Waylen shuts it down by ten thirty, so maybe about ten, while the TV's on. I'll need all the cover I can get. Oh, and you should probably wear dark clothing, preferably something black?"

"Right."

"What?" she asked at his smile.

"Nothing. It's been fun getting to know you, Ms. Kensington," he said, removing his hands from her person and settling back into this chair, pulling back before he did something else that was not appropriate to do in work spaces, and because Summer was on the way.

"You too. Should I pick you up here or at Summer's?"

"I'll pick you up. My truck's black, to go along with our black outfits," he said, chuckling.

"Ha ha, very funny. You'll do what I say."

"Within reason," he said, smiling at the look she gave him. "You're entertaining if nothing else, Clarke. I thought sex with you would be the thing that makes going through the divorce easier, and it is, but it's also the rest of you, too."

"Thank you. I think there was a compliment in there some-where," she said, chuckling now.

"Don't get me killed."

"I won't."

"Oh, aren't you two a picture," Summer said, coming through the door with her arms spread wide, a huge smile on her face. Her gaze moved over to the desk where Kevin should be. She let go of her breath at finding his chair empty. She had not wanted to see him again.

Henri shot a quick glance at Clarke, who was moving away from him now.

"We have ourselves a winner, and I don't mean the two of you. I mean the house. I spoke to my girlfriend this morning, and she accepted my offer. All we have to do is close. In a month, which gives Hamp and me time to organize everything. We'll be off and running the first day," Summer said, squealing in pleasure again.

Henri smiled in spite of it all, at the joy that seemed to sur-round his sister, happy that she was happy. "It's a lot of work, so don't forget that part."

"I know. I know." Summer went back to squealing.

"Is that what you wanted me here for?" Clarke asked.

"Yes. It's wonderful news, right?"

"It is, and now that that's settled, I'm out," Clarke said.

Summer and Henri watched her leave. Well, Henri did, while Summer watched him. "I'm so glad that you and Clarke are getting along," she said.

"Yep," he said, thinking about all the ways they got along these days. Clarke's face and her body entered his mind again. Actually, it had been there off and on since their first night, even when it was just sex. It was still just sex, but there was a friendship growing between them too. He was learning about her and she about him, not that he thought anything would come of it beyond friendship.

"What are you thinking about so seriously, dear brother?" Summer asked, moving toward him, standing at the door of the office.

"Nothing," he said.

"You and Clarke," Summer said, meeting his gaze. "What's up?"

"Nothing's up."

"What were you and Clarke talking about so seriously when I arrived?"

"Waylen, we were discussing Waylen."

"Waylen, huh?" she said, eyeing him as if she didn't believe him. "I know what I know."

"Whatever that means," he said, moving his attention back to his work.

"It's sex. Sex is what's up with you and Clarke," Summer said, eyeing him for signs of the truth of her statement.

"Excuse me?"

She smiled. She was so right. "Sex is up with you and Clarke." A split-second was all it took to read him.

"Really, that's what you think's going on?"

"I know it is. You always were an easy read. The same as when you were a teenager, sneaking some girl out of the house. You have that same look about you."

"And what look is that?" He laughed, surprised by her comment. "You know what," he said before she could reply, "I don't want to know." He shook his head. "You're right. It's just sex between us, so don't get carried away, thinking it's more."

"Yep, sure, it's just sex. I got it," she said, and winked. "I understand the need for it. It's good sex, though, and maybe even friendship. You like her."

"I do."

"That's a start. I think it's more, could be more, but let's go with your opinion for now. You're less angry than when you arrived, so I'm happy for whatever it is that makes you happy."

"Thanks, and that's the end of me discussing my private life with you."

"Fine, keep your little secrets that aren't really secrets," she said, making a fluttering gesture with her hands to accentuate her point.

"I will," he said, chuckling at her again. His little sister, who had grown up but in so many ways was the same as when they were little and he wouldn't let her tag along with him and Stephen.

***

Summer exited the door five minutes later before she let loose her smile. She wanted to squeal so badly after she'd entered the office earlier to find her brother sitting in his chair, staring up at her friend with something more than interest in his eyes. And there was Clarke standing in between his legs like she'd been there before. *Yes! Yes! Yes!* She refrained from shouting.

Clarke was the nameless-faceless. "Yes!" Summer shouted aloud this time, couldn't stop herself. They must have started right after he'd arrived here, she thought, trying to figure out the when. The first Saturday night? And a big wow to her brother's and Clarke's duplicity. Clarke hadn't said a word, and it had Summer mentally riffling through her brain for other signs that she might have missed.

She did squeal then, now that she was no longer near the office and there was no way Henri could hear her. She threw her purse into her car and squealed again. Could life get any better? Yeah, if she could find a man for herself, that would do. Although finding one for her friend was a good substitute, especially if it was her brother. She squealed again, turned up the volume on her radio, and did a little dance in place; mostly it was swinging her arms around her head.

She put her car in gear and started to back out. The horn from a big-assed truck blew, scaring her to death. Ugh, that Kevin. And what was his problem, she thought, reluctantly thanking him for blowing his horn. Otherwise there would have been a double fatality, as he'd kept her from hitting his big monster of a red truck as it was pulling in. And yeah, she knew what his problem was. She had finally recalled where they had met. Not one of her finer moments, but she'd been young, right along with him.

She lowered her window to apologize, but the scowl on his face had her hitting the button to close her window again. Hell no was she apologizing, standing up for herself as she thought Clarke would do. Screw him.

She drove away, checking in the mirror once more before she

turned out of the parking lot. He was out of his truck, walking towards the office, but not before he met her eyes again. Cute but angry, she thought, as she made a right turn out of the parking lot.

***

Friday night

"He lives there," Clarke said, pointing to Waylen's home as she and Henri drove past. "The lights are on and his truck's parked outside, so he's home."

They were headed to the T-intersection now, about to make the left turn that would put them on the road that ran behind Waylen's property. "It's all fenced in and hard to see into, but I feel comfortable with my knowledge of it. I've walked it, watched it, studied it so much that I could probably cover it with my eyes closed.

"There's a back entrance, just like the front, all on lockdown too, with the chain and the lock. I'm not going in through it. The shed's closer to the dry creek than the gate, so that's where I'll go in."

"You sure we should be doing this?" Henri asked, scanning the property as much as he could while driving.

"I am," she said, searching the road for signs of anything out of the ordinary. "Hey, do you need your headlights?" she asked, worried that they might be seen.

"Only if you want me to see where I'm going."

"Let's pull over here and park. It's between the shed and the dry creek," she said, staring into the darkness that was the night out here. She'd decided against parking at the neighbor's next door. Too much distance to travel, plus she had Henri who wasn't used to doing this. Not that she was either, hadn't done much breaking and entering before tonight. Still, she felt that she was the more experienced of the two.

The full moon was on display tonight. A good sign or a bad one, she'd yet to settle on its meaning. "It's a good hundred-yard dash back from Waylen's if I need to make a run for you," she said as she adjusted her night goggles, which were on the top of her head.

Henri wasn't going with her. He was going to remain behind with his truck, parked near the dry bed, while she was going to climb the fence from the dry bed and make her way to the shed. She'd decided and told him. It was safer for her without a novice tangling things up was the way she'd viewed it, but didn't say so.

"This is crazy," Henri said, staring into the night.

"Yes, it is, but I'm doing it anyway. It's against the law, which is why I'm doing it alone. Let's hope I don't get caught," she said, getting out of his truck. To say she was surprised to see him standing beside his door would be an understatement.

"Where are you going?" she asked softly.

"With you."

"You can't. You're to stay here and wait. I know you heard me," she whispered, and this was another time she wished she was taller, the reason she loved her heels so.

"I heard you," he said, keeping his voice low too.

"That's not an answer."

"Do you want to argue or do what you came to do?"

"Please stay here."

"No."

"I knew I was going to regret bringing you," she whispered. "I'll be fine. Someone needs to remain near the truck in case I need to leave fast. Plus I know what I'm looking for and you don't." She met his eyes. "So will you stay here?"

"No."

"Ugh!" she said in frustration. She blew out a breath. "Only to the fence then. You can't come in with me or I won't go. It's either alone or we go back."

"Fine."

"Promise me?"

"I promise."

"Ugh!" she said, handing him a flashlight now that he was coming with her. She only had one set of night vision goggles. She was moving away from him. He fell in behind her, and they moved quickly and quietly down the road, stopping when they reached the dry creek bed and the fence.

He was silent, watching as she climbed over it. She stood on the other side as if waiting for whatever, the dogs. Nothing but crickets and sounds of other small animals, not dogs, thank you, Jesus. She started toward the shed, and it wasn't long before he couldn't see her. Hell no was he going to wait in the truck. It was enough that he wasn't going in. He smiled, not sure why, but he was amused for some reason.

***

Oh god, it stinks in here, Clarke thought after she'd entered the shed, relieved at how easy it had been to get inside. She panned her flashlight around, moving over nothing but trash bags. Which one to pick? The shed was just that, a shed, a four by four room with dirt for flooring. Four basic walls without shelving, nothing but trash bags piled high, to her knees high. They smelled awful.

Should she open one or just take a few, leave, and check them when they were back at her home? First she was going to kill Henri... Take a bag, don't open one, in case this turned into something that required the police, and she didn't want any tampering-with-evidence charges if they found out she been here.

She reached for a few bags and started tying them together, thinking that they'd be easier to carry that way. She stopped, mid-tie, listening. That sounded a little like dogs barking. Or maybe not. It could just be her imagination and fear causing the amplification of every sound.

Uh oh, she thought. *The dogs were out.* For sure that was them she heard. "Hurry, Clarke," she whispered, to keep her mind on task and her fears at bay. She threw the bags she had tied together around her neck, like they used to do in the old days to carry water. So much easier to run with. She hoped so anyway. She turned off her light and opened the door.

Calm and cool, she thought. *All you have to do is get to the fence, you're good, don't panic, take your time*, she told herself over and over, moving toward the fence to her right. She scanned the fence line as she quickly made her way to it, and like in some scene out of a movie, she saw the light from Henri's flashlight. A beacon, her beacon. She was glad he'd refused to stay behind at the truck.

The dogs were gaining ground, their barking had grown louder, and by the sounds of it, they were close, not that she'd look back. She was too busy full-out running now, the light of Henri's flashlight her beacon still. She hoped she wouldn't fall like those white women did in the movies, and at the most inopportune times, too.

Run, run, run, run ran on a loop in her head. She was at the gate now, and the expression on Henri's face told her all she needed to know.

"Hurry," he said, with his eyes glued to a point past her. "Throw the bags over," and she did quickly, one over the fence, and then the other. She was scaling the fence next, reached the top just as the dogs arrived, barking and throwing themselves on the gate.

"They're heavy," she said in warning, as Henri lifted the bags —with ease, wouldn't you know. *Boom*, the blast of a shotgun. That was what startled her. The unexpectedness of it had her jumping into Henri's arms, which was not a good move on her part as the force of her body, along with the weight of the bags, pushed them all to the ground.

"Fuck," Henri said as the flashlight skidded away. *Boom* again, over the noise of the dogs. She and Henri scrambled to their feet, made a mutual quick decision to leave the flashlight behind as they took off, running full-out toward Henri's truck. Henri was out in front, carrying a bag in each of his hands, with Clarke hard on his heels.

He reached the truck first and threw the trash bags into the back. He'd swung the driver's side door open just as she reached him. She latched onto his outstretched hand, holding on tightly, 'cause he was pulling her along. He lifted her off her feet. She was surprised that her arm was still attached to her shoulder, so hard had Henri pulled. He threw her into the front seat and was coming in fast behind her. She scrambled over to the passenger side to get out of the way. Not even a second later, Henri was turning the key in the ignition, starting up his truck.

"Fuck, that was close," he said, thankful that he'd left the keys in the ignition, hoping he wouldn't regret it later, hoping no one other than him would find it and get behind the wheel, leaving him and Clarke with no way out. It could have gone either way. The dogs were running up the road now. The lights of his truck highlighted two black dogs, barking like wild beasts, and Waylen walking up the road behind, shotgun pointed at them.

"Waylen must have unlocked the back gate, come through it," Clarke said, staring at the dogs and Waylen moving toward them.

"Fuck," Henri said again, putting his truck into reverse. He hit the gas pedal hard, moving them backward as fast as he could. He hit the brakes equally hard a few seconds later, turning the wheel as they went sliding out into the middle of the intersection. He held his arm out to keep Clarke from going into the dashboard, then put his truck into drive, and he and Clarke were moving down the road and away. "Fuck, Clarke, that was close," Henri said again, his adrenaline all over the place at seeing Clarke running full-out towards him, those bags around her neck, eyes big as saucers, and the dogs closing in on her heels.

He started laughing and looked over at her, pushed up against the door still, holding onto the handle above the door. "I can't believe that just happened," he said, looking at her again. She was smiling too.

"Is this your life?" he asked.

"No, not at all," she said, sitting up in the seat, her adrenaline running crazy through her veins too as she buckled herself in. He did the same.

"Your eyes were huge and damn, you're fast, girl," he said, laughing, looking in the mirror and no, there was no one behind him following them. He continued on but slowed down a bit, didn't want to get stopped for speeding.

"Turn in here," Clarke said, pointing to a side road.

"Where's here?" he asked, quickly glancing at her.

"A place I scoped out earlier in case we needed a place to hide. I scoped out a few, but this one is the first one we've come across."

"You sure?"

"I am," she said, watching as he followed her instructions and turned onto a small dirt road, barely visible unless you were looking for it. High grass on either side of it obscured them from the street.

"Make another right here," she said, and watched as he pulled into another drive, a short one, blocked off by a fence.

"Where are we?"

"Safe. Now turn off your lights. We're going to sit for a while, in case he thinks to follow," she said, but that wasn't the only reason.

"This is crazy," he said, chuckling. "I can't believe I just did that."

"I know," she said. Her hands were at his waist now, feeling around for the zipper to his jeans.

"Fuck, it's dark out here. Hey, what are you doing?" He looked down at her hands.

"What do you think? There is something about doing this kind of work that gets me going, energized, and since I'm no longer married, there's nowhere to put all that energy, you know what I mean?" She looked into his eyes. "You want to, don't you?" She lowered the zipper and slid her hand inside. She smiled at his sharp intake of breath.

"What do you think?" He was grinning now.

"Come on then." Her hands back in her own lap, she kicked off her sneakers and wrestled out of her leggings and underwear.

"In the back?" Not waiting for his answer, she crawled over the front seat. "Hurry up," she said, landing in the back.

"Yep," he said, and he was following, laughing at how crazy this was.

"Ouch," she said, as he landed on her breast. "Ouch," she said again, pushing him off. She was lying on her back.

"Turn around, put your knees in the seat and face the back

window," he said, leaning away to avoid her feet as they swung around. He laughed, watching as she scooted over, giving him the back view of her ass.

"Right," he said, looking down at her, chuckling at being here after all that had happened, but moving behind her. It was tight in the space and dark, but he could think of no other place that he'd rather be than here now, with that lovely ass of hers waiting for him to do what he wanted to it. He placed one hand on the top of the back seat near her head, and the other hand moved to her core, where it softly played for a bit before moving upward to her hip.

"So good," she said, her face turned sideways, laying against the back seat, meeting his gaze.

"You like that, huh?" he said, smiling.

"Don't go easy on me," she said over her shoulder.

"No problem," he said, settling himself behind her, moving his erection to the entrance of her vagina. His face was at her neck now, breathing short from all the maneuvering they'd had to do to get here. She pushed back when he was settled in for good, and rolled her hips, up and down his erection. She smiled at his intake of air.

"Remember, you asked for this," he said from just over her left ear.

"Yep," she said, and that quickly gave way to a moan as he slid into her. *Feels so good*, she thought, may have even said it aloud.

"You ready?" he whispered into her ear.

"Yes," she said on a pant.

He pulled his hips back and thrust into her, hard this time. He leaned forward, completely covering her back, his head near hers, moving his hands under her shirt, under her bra to take a breast in his hand. He liked to hold them or kiss them while he fucked her, and right now, holding them tightly as he thrust into her again seemed to fit his mood. All that adrenaline was flowing strongly and he wanted release, and he didn't want it easy or soft or smooth, either.

He pulled his hips back and thrust into her hard again, and then again. Damn that felt good, her here with him, doing them. He pulled his hips back again, thrust hard into her again. She asked for it, and he wanted to give it to her. And in again, and then again, and then he just let himself go after that, following the demands of whatever this was raging in his veins, and apparently in hers as she moaned and encouraged him... *Henri... please... harder* was what she said, and very encouraging those sounds were, urging him along to take, to touch, to fuck, and thrust in, and in hard again, and again, harder, a rhythm. That was just fine, judging by the sounds of her moaning against the back seat. He thought that was what she was doing, but really he was too far gone to worry, just hoped she wanted what she'd asked for.

Fuck. Again, he thrust into her, squeezing her nipples, just 'cause he could, plus he liked the way she moaned when he did it, and again, and again. "Clarke..." he might have said, or maybe that was her, and he thrust into her again, adjusted his knees in the seat beside her and thrust into her again, hard. She moaned, and he did it again, and then again. She was with him, pushing her hips back, up and back to meet the force of his, told him so.

How long before they were both racing toward one hell of a climax? Not long if the sounds coming from both of them were any indication. "Fuck" was his last word before he closed his eyes. *Damn she felt good* was his last thought as his end came, sweeter than he'd expected, and he closed his eyes and leaned into her to take it all in. He moaned and let it come.

They remained that way for a while afterward, him at her

back still, her face in the seat still. She turned to the side and met his gaze staring back at her.

"Any time you need me to help you with anything remotely like this, call me, please," he said, pulling away, falling into the seat beside her, laughing and trying to breathe normally again. He looked over at her again, and she hadn't moved. "You okay?" he asked, concerned a little.

"I am. Thanks for coming with me. Thanks for everything," she said. She leaned over and touched her lips to his, then pulled back and looked into his eyes. Something had changed with her. He'd seen that look before, too many times before he'd gotten married, to not recognize it when he saw it. It meant she was falling for him.

"You're welcome," he said, letting her look pass without comment.

"Napkins or a towel?" she asked. She watched as he dug up a few and they spent a few minutes putting their clothes to rights. Ten minutes later and they were pulling onto the larger highway that led to Interstate 35 which would take them back to Austin.

***

Henri stood watching Clarke as she pulled out the first piece of trash from one of the two bags she'd managed to take from Waylen's. They were in the backyard of her home, later. She wanted privacy and fresh air this time. She was different, quiet at the gravity of what they had uncovered... pulled from the bags.

She covered her nose at the smell. A baby's diaper, a small one for a newborn, was the first thing she'd removed. It was not the last. There were more from both bags, along with wipes and empty formula cans, the kind that you give a baby for food, especially if the mother wasn't around.

"He has a baby living with him," Henri said.

"It would seem so. His son, Amber's son."

"Looks like it," Henri said.

"That's why he's home so much during the day. He's coming to check on him," she said, staring out into the back yard. "Then where's my cousin?" She sort of screamed it, the full import of what they'd found and had not found hitting her. She walked away, stood staring into the night.

"Don't know," Henri said, quietly coming up behind her, placing his hands on her shoulders. "It's probably not good."

She leaned back against the wall of his chest and sighed. "Fuck," she said, tears starting to form as she processed that fact. "Now what do we do?" she asked, not for him to answer, he didn't think. She was talking more to herself, he thought.

"Go to the police, tell Officer... What did you say his name was?"

"Jim," she said.

"Talk with Officer Jim, tell him what you know."

"Maybe Amber decided to leave him with his baby. Took off, tired of being a mother."

"You know her. Is that something you'd think she do?"

"No."

"Talk to Jim, don't think past that."

"Okay," she said, turning to face him. She yawned, the day's events catching up to her.

"Come on, let me help you clean up. You need sleep," he said.

"Did I say thank you already?" She put her arms around his neck.

"You did, more than you needed to. It's been nice hanging out with you, again," he said, his hands going to her waist.

She yawned again. "Me too."

"Another week, and you will have your nights to yourself again," he said, needing to remind her that he was going back to Dallas after this was over. He still had a divorce to get through, but she'd been a huge help, as a diversion and as a friend.

It didn't take long to clean up and trash the trash, as it wasn't good for anything else, couldn't be used as evidence. She stood by her front door and waved once more as he pulled away. She would hate to see him leave, 'cause somewhere along the way, it had changed from good-sex-late-night-booty-calling to wanting him to stay.

EIGHTEEN

Saturday

"Ouch," Henri said, as the basketball hit his head and bounced off. He and Stephen were done with the morning's basketball game and headed to their cars.

"Hello," Stephen said, chuckling into the quiet.

"What?" Henri said, turning his gaze to his friend. He'd been lost in his head, replaying the final shot he'd missed and the ribbing from his teammates that had followed. Two weeks almost to the day since he'd arrived in Austin, and he was in such a different head-space than he'd been when he arrived, relaxed and carefree in a way he hadn't been in a while. His thoughts turned immediately to last night with Clarke, and all the many other times they'd spent together, along with aiding her in her search for her cousin. Both were responsible for his improved disposition.

"Hello," Stephen said again, full-out laughing now.

"Sorry, preoccupied."

"Really? I hadn't noticed," Stephen said, chuckling. "How is she?"

"Clarke?" Henri said. He brought Stephen up to date with all that had transpired since the dinner at his home.

"Henri the private investigator?"

"I'm probably more trouble than I'm worth, but I find that I'm interested in the outcome."

"It's more than that, right. You like her."

"I do, but again, not in the way you want."

"I want to see you happy and I never thought Karen was the one for you. However, you didn't ask my opinion. Now Clarke, I like for you. I think she's more of what you're looking for, more of what you need."

"All that, huh?" Henri said, smiling. "What is it about her that you like so much?"

"I don't know. It's a feeling more than anything. She's solid, works hard, is kind. You could do worse."

"I could, you're right. I agree. We're friends now, and that's far from where we started, but I'm home in a week."

"True."

"I'm tired of talking about me. How's the house-selling business? When do you and Reye plan to make the move?"

"Soon. She's up to Dallas next week, going house hunting with my mother."

"That can't be good."

"Surprisingly, they have grown to be quite close. They like each other and who would have thought that possible."

"See, all those worries for nothing," Henri said, smiling.

"Yep."

"One more Saturday of basketball."

"One more," Stephen said, smiling, watching as his friend headed to his truck. He was disappointed, but things weren't over until they were. Things had a strange way of working themselves out, so he wasn't giving up hope yet.

***

Clarke checked her phone for the umpteenth time that morning.

The tracker she'd attached to Waylen's car was still showing up at Waylen's home. She'd been worried that perhaps they'd spooked him, frightened him enough to leave. So far he'd stayed put.

She hoped she didn't regret this decision to call Officer Jim. He was the only alternative in her mind. Nowhere else to go but to the locals. It was a choice with a serious downside if, say, Officer Jim cared more for his fellow officers than the people he'd sworn to protect. She had to go somewhere... tell someone. There was too much information, too much at stake for her to keep it to herself. She dialed the number to the police station and waited.

"Jim Hampton here," he said.

"Hello, Officer. This is Clarke Kensington. The woman that is searching for my cousin Amber Jones."

"The investigator, sure. I remember. Hello, Ms. Kensington. What can I do for you?"

"I need to talk. I've found some information regarding my cousin and her disappearance that may involve an officer in your department. I thought you might be open to listening to me."

"Which officer?"

"I'd rather we talk in person."

"Waylen?"

"What makes you think it's him?"

"You're not the only person that knows how to conduct investigations," he said.

"Oh..." she said, surprised.

"I remembered something about that young woman. I can't put my finger on what, so I started looking into her on my own. Meeting you would be helpful to me too," he said.

"Oh, okay. That's great. Where would you like to meet?"

"Are you familiar with Yolly's Coffee and Yogurt Shop, located in downtown Yolly?"

"Yes," she said.

"Good. I usually take lunch at noon. Waylen's off on the weekends, so I could meet you there. Will that work for you?"

"Twelve it is, then. Thank you."

"You're welcome. See you then," he said, disconnecting.

***

Clarke was seated in the booth furthest from the door, staring out the window of Yolly's coffee house, when she spotted Jim crossing the street. He came through the front door a few minutes later. He smiled when he spotted her.

A nice-looking man was Officer Jim, she thought, watching as one of the waitresses walked over to greet him. He took his workout and keeping his body in shape seriously, she thought, checking out his physique as he stood waiting to be seated. Medium build, dark brown hair underneath his police cap, all of which coordinated nicely with his neatly trimmed mustache. He and the waitress spoke for a bit before they both looked her way. The woman smiled and walked away, headed to the counter and then behind it, while he made his way to Clarke.

"Good morning, Ms. Kensington," he said, sliding his muscular frame into the chair across from her.

"Please call me Clarke."

"Only if you call me Jim," he said.

"Okay. Thanks for meeting me," she said.

"My pleasure," he said, moving his gaze to the waitress he'd spoken to earlier. She was standing beside the table with a cup of coffee in her hand. She placed it on the table in front of him.

"Can I get you anything more?" she asked, addressing Clarke now.

"No, thank you," Clarke said.

"So, what's this about Waylen?" he asked, after the waitress walked away.

"I show you mine first?"

"That's it exactly," he said, and smiled, and took a sip from his coffee.

She told him everything, all she'd found, everything that had led her to Waylen's home, followed by what she had found out last night from inside his shed.

"None of that I can use. You know this."

"I do."

"You and I have been on similar paths in our investigations. Or it's more like I've been following you. I've talked to the suspected boyfriend and the two girlfriends. The difference is I knew who lived out in the area where your cousin was being dropped off. I didn't have the picture of him and your cousin together. That would have helped considerably."

"So what's next?"

"To talk to him, eventually, see if we have enough evidence for a search warrant. I'm not sure if I want to bring him in for questioning or just wait and talk to him when he comes in to work on Monday. In the meantime, I'll follow up on the woman at the bar, and make sure I reach the same conclusions that you did," he said.

"Okay."

"How is your aunt holding up?"

"I've not told her anything, but I think I'm going to have to talk to her soon," Clarke said.

"No more trespassing," he said, his voice firm.

"I know," she said, smiling.

"Why aren't you working for some police department?"

"I tried. It's not for me. I like my freedom too much."

"I understand."

"I'll call you if I find out anything more and you'll do the same?" she asked.

"I will," he said, and watched as she slid out of the booth and went out the front door.

"Gotcha self a new girlfriend?" the waitress asked. She held a coffee pot in her hand.

"Not enough time in my day as it is," he said, smiling. *But if I did, she wouldn't be a bad idea*, he thought but didn't say.

***

Early Sunday morning

"What time is it?" Henri asked, sitting up in the bed at his favorite hotel later on that night, or was it morning. It was morning, two-thirty in the morning to be exact, checking the clock on the nightstand. He was some kind of tired, between work and Clarke. Clarke was sitting on the side of the bed, bent over staring at her iPhone.

"Sorry, I didn't mean to wake you. I'm going back out to Waylen's home again."

"Is that your tracker?" Henri asked, pointing to her iPhone.

"Yep," she said.

"So he's moved, he's not at home anymore?"

"No, the tracker puts him at home still."

"So what's the problem?"

"A feeling," she said, eyeing him as she put her phone down and reached for a sneaker. She was partially dressed, in her jeans and bra only.

"That?" he said, running his hands up his face and upward through his hair.

"That I need to go out there again and check. That something's up," she said, tying her right sneaker.

He set his feet onto the floor and stood, stretching his arms up and over his head. Yeah, she was watching him. Didn't know when she'd really get her fill of watching him move about, with or without clothing.

"I'll come with you," he said.

"What? No. You have work, and I'm okay going alone. I feel bad enough as it is for keeping you up."

"Tomorrow's Sunday, and what, I can't be a detective anymore? No more team, just use me and push me aside?" he said, moving toward the bathroom.

She tied her other sneaker. It took her a second, and then she was moving to the bathroom, picking up her shirt from the floor on the way. She paused mid-step, waited until the toilet flushed before she moved to the door that he hadn't bothered to close. *Somebody's getting really comfortable here*, she thought.

"Do I have time for a shower?" he asked.

"Not really, no," she said, standing in the doorway, staring at him—admiringly, he thought, smiling internally. He liked the way she looked at him most times, all hungry gaze. An equal hunger could be usually found in his eyes. She was holding her shirt in her hand as she met his gaze in the mirror.

"Really. You've done enough and I don't mind," she said, staring again at his nudeness and the fineness that was this man, so early in the morning.

"Give me five," he said, turning on the water in the sink. He rinsed his face before meeting her eyes in the mirror again. "Coffee. I need coffee." He winked at her now. "By the time I'm done, you should be finished getting us some. I'll meet you downstairs. I can drop my truck off at Summer's and you can follow me, drop me back there when we're done."

"You've got this all figured out," she said, smiling, not even going to answer the question of why she was allowing it.

"Yep," he said, and winked again. He'd added a smile to go along with it.

"Okay… I guess," she said, surprisingly appreciative for the company.

***

"He's not here," Henri said. They were driving past Waylen's mobile home an hour later. The gate was locked but there was no sign of Waylen's truck in his front yard.

"I can see that. However, the tracker puts him here. Crap, he must have found it somehow and removed it. Left it behind," she said.

Henri was looking past her, trying along with her to see inside, through the vegetation. She made another left at the T-intersection, and then another one, turning onto the road that led behind Waylen's property. Memories of last night flashed through his head, how close they'd come to getting shot. It seemed even more crazy today.

"Clearly he's not here and I bet he's gone for good. It's what I would do, given what's happened, and if I found a tracker on my car. If I were hiding something, that is, which he is. We scared him off. Damn," she said. She pulled over to the side of the street across from the back gate and stopped the car.

"Tell me we aren't going in again."

"*We* didn't go in the last time. I wonder if he left the dogs behind," she said, opening her car door.

"Yep, they're here," Henri said, standing beside her. He'd followed her over, watching as the two dogs came charging to the gate. "Why not give the Yolly police a little time, see what they come up with? I know you're worried, but maybe you could let it go for a while. Go home and get some rest. You're starting to look tired."

"I am tired," she said, turning away from the dogs and the fence to face him. "You mind if we watch a while?"

"I don't mind as long as we stay on this side of the fence."

**

Two hours passed of nothing. The dogs would meander away for a while, and then come back. They were good watchdogs, she'd give Waylen that. Henri yawned, waking up from his two-hour nap. He'd resisted at first, really fought the good fight, but eventually succumbed, head falling over to the side, where it lay against the window. He was cute when he slept.

"I've been asleep the whole time," he said, more statement than question.

"Do you think Waylen would have left his kid behind?" Clarke asked.

"I don't think so."

"Maybe I should go in and check, just to be sure."

"Dogs?"

"But can we, in good conscience, sit out here and not check?" she asked. She was leaning over the steering wheel now, her night vision goggles over her eyes. "I would hate to think he's in there all alone, no mother and no father... no anybody looking out for him." It had been on her mind since they'd found Waylen gone. It was all she could think about.

"Hey, I bet he's with his father. He has to be. Why would Waylen stop by so many times during the day, three times, you said? To take care of his son. He wouldn't do that unless he cared. So I doubt he'd leave him behind."

"I guess you're right," she said, turning her gaze back toward Waylen's home. "I would hate for him to be in there alone. Babies..." She stopped. Whatever she was going to say, she kept to herself. "We'd better head back. I've kept you out here way past your bedtime. You're not used to my crazy hours."

"I'm okay. Apparently I can sleep anywhere, as I've just demonstrated," he said, chuckling, hoping humor would lighten the mood.

"Thanks for everything. For coming out here, helping me talk through all of it, going through dirty diapers and all sorts of trash. I appreciate the company and the help," she said, reaching for his hand.

"You're welcome, and it's been good for me too. Nothing takes your mind off your issues like being shot at."

"There is that," she said, chuckling as she started up her jeep.

***

Sunday morning

She'd made a last-minute decision to return to Waylen's house. There was no way she could not check to see if the baby was inside. She just couldn't not and live with herself. So while Henri had slept beside her, she'd come up with a plan to get inside Waylen's property and have a look-see. She dropped Henri at Summer's and headed to a 24-hour HEB grocery store. All she needed were two steaks and a couple of diphenhydramine tablets, a.k.a. Benadryl, one tablet for every forty pounds of dog. Of course she had some back at her house, a tool of her trade.

After leaving the store it was home to cut up the steaks and stuff them with the tablets, then she'd head back out to Waylen's. It was six before she was able to get back there. She had driven around the neighborhood for a while, making sure it was quiet, looking for Waylen and maybe the police, 'cause she was creeped out by it all. Plus it never hurt to check and then recheck. She eventually parked next door, covered her jeep with a tarp, and made her way over to the dry bed.

The dogs were quick. They came charging before she reached the fence. She threw the meat over the top of the fence and watched as they gobbled it up. They must have been hungry. She decided to leave the rest of the meat behind, the part she hadn't doctored, so they wouldn't starve out here now that Waylen was gone. It took a good hour before they gave up. Sleep overtook them, and down they eventually went. She looked around one more time before she climbed up and over the fence. Inside, she stood for a moment, just to make sure the dogs were asleep, and then she took off, keeping low, moving toward the driveway first.

She found the GPS she'd placed on Waylen's truck lying near the end of his gravel drive. Of course, she picked it up and put in into her pocket, moving over to the house. She stood at the front door, glad today to be short as she played with the lock on the door. A couple of minutes and she was inside. It was musty-smelling, quiet, and surprisingly clean.

She landed in the kitchen. There wasn't a baby in here, or in the living room to the left. She moved quickly down the hall to the bedroom. Again, no baby, no signs of anything belonging to him. She checked out the closet. It was full of clothes, but no baby. Last but not least was the bathroom. She sighed in relief. There was no baby here either. It was as Henri had told her. The baby was with his father, who knew where.

It was a quick trip back the way she'd come. The dogs were asleep still as she passed them, went up and over the fence, and back over to her jeep, and her nerves were all over the place.

She pulled over to the side of the road not far from Waylen's, feeling needy and strange and worried still. She reached for her phone, wanting to talk to Henri. Not Summer or her mother or her dad... him. And yeah, she knew what that meant.

"Hey," he said into the phone. And was this another first, a phone call instead of a text? he thought.

"I woke you," she said.

"It's okay, what's up?"

"Nothing. I went back out to Waylen's. I found the GPS, but not the baby."

"You went in again," he said, not really surprised. She'd seemed worried about the baby.

"Yes."

"How? The dogs?" he asked, and chuckled after she told him.

"I hope he's okay, wherever he is," she said. And why did she feel like crying all of a sudden? She knew. It was the thought of the baby, and what would happen to him.

"You okay?" he asked. She sounded a little strange.

She swiped at her eyes, tired, worried, and more tired. "I am tired is all."

"Go home then. Get some sleep. Try not to worry. If something happens you'll need to be at your best and that means sleep. You'll have an answer soon enough."

"You think so?"

"I do," he said.

"You're right. I am tired. I'm hanging up now, going home to get some rest."

"Good. I'll check in later."

"I'd like that," she said. She pulled away from the curb and headed home, hoping that everything would work out for the better but realizing that it probably wouldn't.

***

Monday morning

Clarke had just taken a seat behind her desk when her cell rang. She felt better; not one hundred percent better, but better. She'd taken Henri's advice and spent the rest of day in, alone. She answered her cell and it was Officer Jim. "Good morning," she said.

"I wish I could say the same. We are on our way out to Waylen's with a search warrant. He didn't show up for work this morning," he said.

"You must have found something then?" And no, she wasn't going to share all she'd done Sunday night, just as she kept what had happened with her and Henri Friday night to herself.

"We did. We found Darnell. Waylen and Amber were a couple," Jim said.

"I see. I'd like to meet you out there," she said.

"I wouldn't expect anything less. I don't have to tell you that we are there in an official capacity, so you'll be limited in where you can go. But I'll do my best to keep you informed as we go along."

"Thank you. I'm on my way."

***

Clarke stood by the car, outside of the back gate of Waylen's property, watching as the police officers moved about. Four hours into this little operation and still no sign of Waylen. They'd put the required all-points bulletin out on his truck, but who knew if he was still driving that truck. She would have traded cars by now, were she the one evading the law. He'd left because of her breaking in, and maybe if she'd left things alone... She wasn't sure how she felt about it all now. Taking the law in one's hands was never good, but necessary? Jim had surprised her, that's for sure. She hadn't expected his help.

They'd had to cut off the locks to get onto the property. The police had brought along Animal Control to take care of dog one and dog two, who were back in fighting form. Up until then it had been a quiet morning of removing trash bag after trash bag from the shed, which were mostly filled with baby paraphernalia, lots of proof of Waylen's and the baby's existence. Toward the bottom of the trash pile, they'd found bags filled with clothes belonging to a female and a purse with Amber's state-issued identification inside. Yeah, things weren't looking good.

Jim and his fellow officers must have found something. They were in swarm mode now, she thought, watching them converge on one area behind the shed. It was a rectangular patch of dirt, like a shallow grave, not too recently dug, but recent enough to mean something. Her heart sank. Actually, it had sunk after the first hour of the police checking out Waylen's home. They'd found blood in the front room, and lots of it.

She pulled out her cell and dialed her mom's number, fighting back tears at what this all meant, hoping that Waylen and the baby would survive this. Hell, screw Waylen, she was only holding out hope for the baby.

"Hey, Mom," she said.

"Hey, baby," her mother said, and there was nothing more comforting than those two words said the way only her mother could say them. Years of *Hey baby*'s at the end of a hard day, or at the end of a good one; it didn't matter, it was the same. Those two words had been a little more emotion-packed through her divorce, but it was all the same sense of *home... I'm here for you always.* That's what those two little words meant to her. They had gotten her through so much.

"Hey," she said, taking in a breath of air, fighting back tears. "I… think… you and Daddy should get down here, as soon as you can."

"They've found Amber?" her mom said.

"Yes, I think so."

"Alive?"

"No."

"Oh, baby, I'm so sorry. What about the baby?"

"No word yet," Clarke said.

"I'll find your daddy, and we'll be on our way. Have you spoken to Glenn or Veda?"

"No, not yet. It will be a while before they have official proof of what's here, so I think we should wait."

"That makes sense."

"Call me when you get into town," Clarke said.

"I will, and you take care of yourself, baby."

"I will," Clarke said. She disconnected and continued to watch the officers.

***

There wasn't a good way to tell someone that the person they loved most in the world was dead, Clarke thought. One look at

Sandra's face and Veda knew. Clarke was there, along with Aunt Glenn and her parents. Officer Jim had just left, the official deliverer of the city's bad news, looking like he would rather be anywhere else. She certainly understood. "Find my grandbaby… please" had been Aunt Veda's plea to him. Crying, loud and long, had been Veda's response.

He would do his best, he'd said. They were searching, and he would notify them as soon as anything happened. To the larger question of why, only Waylen had the answer, and they hoped to find him to get it.

Clarke was outside now, taking advantage of Veda's beautiful backyard. She'd needed air, and the sounds of Aunt Veda were hard to hear for her. The loss of a child was hard to take.

Clarke heard the screen door open. It was her mother, standing at the top of the steps.

"Hey, baby. I wondered where you were."

"I needed air," Clarke said.

"I understand." Sandra moved to her daughter to wrap her arms around her. "They'll find him," she said, aware of her daughter's fears.

"You can't know that."

"I can hope. I can pray," Sandra said.

"He's so little," Clarke said.

"God looks after the young."

"Not always."

"It'll be okay."

"Really, Mom? How will it be okay?" Clarke asked, suddenly angry. She swiped at her eyes. "I've got to go."

"Where?"

"I don't know. I can't be here. You understand."

"I can ride with you. I don't mind."

"I'm good. I'm not that girl anymore, so you don't have to worry."

"That was a tough time. It would be hard for anybody."

"I know. I just have to feel this, and get past it, and I will. I won't do anything crazy, don't worry," Clarke said, tears starting to fall faster. "I'm okay, Mom. I just need a break."

"There's nothing that says he will turn out like…"

"I can't, Mom," she said, and tried to smile. "I'll see you later."

"Whatever you think," Sandra said, watching her child do what she'd done before, during another time of great loss: retreat into herself, shut all others out.

"Where's Clarke?" her father said, standing at the door.

"Gone, said she needed air."

"It has to be tough for her, with the baby and all."

"I know," she said, turning to face him, standing at the door still. "How's Veda?"

"As well as we can expect. It's hard losing a child, no matter how old. It's tough," he said, watching his wife. "She'll be alright eventually. She just needs time," and he was speaking of his daughter then.

"I know. I just want her to be happy and I'm not sure she will ever be that again."

"Give her time," he said.

***

What was she doing here? Clarke asked herself, parked outside of Summer's home. It was late; one in the morning late. She had gone home, tried to work, to take her mind off of everything, but had driven around for a while before she'd ended up here. She wanted, no, needed a distraction from all of her thoughts, all the past being dredged up, along with her where-was-the-baby-was-he-safe worries. She hoped he was okay, and just like that her tears fell. She reached for her phone, moving to the text app where she input-ted her question marks.

Where are you?

Your house, outside.

Meet me at the front door.

He was a sight for sore eyes: ruffled, sleepy and sexy, minus everything but shorts. She walked into his arms, and if he thought it strange he didn't say, just pulled her in close and held her. She was crying. He didn't say anything about her tears, either. They made it upstairs to his room eventually.

"Sleep," he said to her, lying by his side now.

"You sure?"

"I am," he said, and pulled her into his side, one arm holding her close.

She didn't fall asleep immediately, just lay there for a while, listening as he slept, safely tucked just under his arm, into his chest, smelling the familiar scent of him. She closed her eyes and eventually drifted off to sleep.

***

Tuesday morning

He was gone when she awoke. She hadn't heard him leave. Dead to the world, she'd slept. She felt better, not completely rested, but better. One more week and he would be headed back to Dallas, and her overflowing river of sex would stop, not to mention the other things about him she'd miss.

She reached for her phone to call her parents. There were so many texts from them, all with increasing worry as the night had progressed. And then they'd stopped. She had also received a text from Henri. He was in Dallas for the day, but would be back by the end of it.

She hit the button on her phone to call her mom.

"Hey, Mom," she said.

"Hey, baby," Sandra said.

"So... I'm over at a friend's house, Summer's. I know I should have called last night, sorry, didn't plan to stay all night but I fell asleep," she said, not sure what else to say.

"I understand. You were tired. Your friend called. He probably got tired of hearing your phone ring, but I was worried. Anyway, Henri, I believe he said his name was, said you were asleep and okay. A nice young man?"

"He is," Clarke said, hoping that would suffice on the information tip.

"Your dad and I are leaving in an hour, thought we might see you before we left."

"Sure, I'm on my way," Clarke said, standing up, throwing on her clothes as she spoke.

"Oh, good, baby, I'll tell your dad. See you soon."

"Yes. Soon," she said, and hung up. She found Summer sitting on the couch in the living room, watching TV with a coffee cup in her hand. There was another one on the table in front of her.

"You okay?" Summer asked, her gaze filled with sadness, moving toward her friend, more like sister. "Henri told me everything before he left. He must have been worried, 'cause he's not the sharing type, at least not with me. I'm so sorry." She pulled Clarke into her arms.

They stood there for a second, holding on to each other. "I know they'll find him."

"You think?" Clarke said, and no, she was not going to start crying again.

"I do," Summer said, releasing her friend. "I'm sorry."

"Me too, and I have to go. Sandra's worried, wants to see me."

"Of course. Take this with you. You know we can't function without it," Summer said, placing the cup of coffee in Clarke's hand.

"Love you," Clarke said.

"I know. Love you too. Now, take care of yourself and call if you need me or Henri," she said, winking and smiling at the end.

Clarke smiled and shook her head at her friend. She was through the front door, trying to remember what her day was supposed to look like. It and her world had been knocked a little off kilter by all of this.

There were also thoughts of Henri and what a good guy he'd turned out to be, at how far they come in such a short time. She made her way to her car, offering up another prayer that things would all end well, for everyone, including herself.

***

Tuesday evening

She was with Henri when the call came—not actually *with* him, in that sense, but about to be. They were downstairs in the lobby, eating dinner in the restaurant, which was another first.

"I think you should get here," Jim said. "Here" was in a park, a local one surrounding Balcones Lake, home to a big bass fishing competition. One of the park rangers had found Waylen's truck. It was parked in an area on the west side of the lake, known for its spectacular sunsets.

The truck had been running when they found it. The heat was

turned on to keep Waylen and his son, sitting beside him in his baby carrier, warm while the hose that ran from the exhaust pipe to the window had put them to sleep permanently. He'd left a note. *I'm sorry. I didn't mean to hurt her. I loved her. Me and Samuel are on our way to see her again.*

Henri drove them over. Jim allowed her close enough to see the baby. She knew she couldn't touch him but she wanted to, desperately. Wanted to pick him up, lying there so peacefully, wrapped in a blanket, a hat on his head to keep him warm, and all those memories of her loss—losses—came flooding back.

"I'm sorry," Jim said.

She nodded and walked back to Henri, who hadn't been allowed to get close. She walked into his arms again, same as last night, along with the same crying. She didn't look up, didn't want to see his reaction; she just wanted to be held. He walked her away from the crowd, to his truck, parked a ways down the road. She clung to him still, arms wrapped around his waist, continuing to cry. He walked her around to the passenger side and opened the door.

"I'm sorry," she said.

"It's okay. It's tragic. It's hard. I get it," he said. He'd been affected by the news too, glad that he hadn't seen the baby.

"I don't usually cry so much," she said, in between taking in air and trying to smile. "I had a little boy once, a perfect little baby boy." She looked away, taking in a breath of air before she faced him again. "It took me forever to get him. Three times I was pregnant, three times I miscarried. He, my ex, wanted to stop trying, he wasn't really sold on the idea of children to begin with. But we continued on. I continued on, dragging him along. He owed me for all the crazy sex stuff I had to put up with, right? It wasn't only the sex, we really didn't belong together, too different. I can see that now. By then my marriage was a trade-off. He got the sex he wanted, and I'd get a baby. It's no wonder it didn't work. So we tried again, and the fourth time worked. We passed the first trimester, then the second, and I was cautiously optimistic.

"If I was careful before, I was even more so then—excited, crazy worried, but careful, did everything I could to make sure I didn't mess it up. Thirty-seven weeks, and everything and we were doing fine. Went for my checkup, and I kind of thought maybe something was up with Junior. He wasn't kicking as much, but it was more than that, I found. He had quietly died," she said, meeting his gaze.

He was flummoxed by her words. Of all the things he thought she'd say.

'I'm sorry," he said, pulling her into his arms again.

"Seeing Amber's baby just brought it all back; the divorce, the reason for the divorce, but mostly I just miss my son. I would've been a great mother," she said, giving him a fake smile, but no longer crying.

"Life just sucks sometimes," he said, and smiled. Who knew she'd been hiding all that inside? He leaned in and placed his lips to hers softly. "I'm sorry for your loss," he said after he pulled back.

"Me too."

NINETEEN

Wednesday

Henri sat across from her in a chair on the other side of her room, watching her sleep. It had eluded him for the last two hours as all sorts of thoughts ran through his head, caused by her admission.

He checked the clock on the nightstand beside her bed. It was five thirty and he was waiting for her to wake up. He wanted to take her somewhere. It had been formulating in his brain since last night after all that she'd shared with him.

He looked up. She was staring at him, unsure probably at how he'd taken all she'd told him last night, maybe even regretting that she had told him anything. "Good morning," he said into the silence.

"Is it?" she asked, her eyes puffy. She bet she looked a mess, she thought, not sure why he was sitting there, staring at her.

"It is. I'd like to take you somewhere, show you something. It will take up most of the day, this thing I want to show you," he said.

"Okay…" she said, surprised. However, the idea of getting away held an appeal.

"It will take us awhile to get there, so I thought we could leave now, and you could sleep in the car on the way."

"Okay…" she said, sitting up in bed. "Time for me to shower?"

"Yes," he said, watching her stand. He smiled. She was cute, and really this… being with her had been so what he'd needed. He had no idea how much until now. Life was crazy, stranger than fiction, he thought, and smiled again.

***

"Dallas," she said, recognizing the skyline from the front window of his truck.

"Yep," he said, smiling at her. She had slept the entire trip, curled up in a ball in the seat beside him.

"Okay," she said, no clue to what he wanted to show her here, but going with the flow. "I thought I would miss this place more than I do, at least a little bit, but nope. Not at all."

"I thought the same," he said, exiting the main highway onto a shorter one that would lead them to another major one. Dallas was huge compared to Austin, and no, she wouldn't choose to live here again if she didn't have to.

"I'm not sure I can have kids. I haven't produced any yet and believe me I've tried," he said.

"Excuse me?" she said, turning to face him.

"You heard me. That's the first time I've been able to say that without anger," he said, and blew out a breath. "I was married for three years. Karen and I weren't a love marriage. Or it was, but not in the same way as Reye and Stephen's, or maybe as you thought going into yours. I met her in high school, and we hung out off and on all through college, though b-school for me and law school for her. Kept in touch. She wanted marriage and I wasn't sure. Or I was sure, that it was probably not going to be her. Nothing was wrong. I mean, she was nice, but I didn't get any huge feeling of love, not like I thought I would. However, after she told me she was pregnant, I married her.

"It was my thing to want to raise kids, have a family, with

both parents. It was what I knew, the way I was raised. I liked my family, and although it seems like the world is moving away from this, I wanted a family of my own. Anyway, she miscarried, after we were married," he said. He was taking another exit off the highway and they were in central Dallas now, close to one of its major colleges.

"We got along okay for a while afterward, like I told you. She was a big-time lawyer at one of the city's major law firms, and I was starting to work for my dad, learning the ropes, that type of thing. Our life wasn't spectacular, just regular, you know. We were going to try and make it work," he said, glancing at Clarke quickly and back to eyes on the road.

"We both wanted kids, so we started into the process of trying to have one. We jumped in, feet first and all in. And we tried, and tried, and nothing. And all the baby making business was beginning to be anything but fun, and a year later, it was nothing.

"Well, she started to get concerned. I never considered that it could be me, but she had, because unbeknownst to me, the pregnancy on which our marriage was based was a lie. That baby wasn't mine either. The same dude both times, as it turned out. I didn't learn that until after I left. Now that dude could give her babies, and I think that's who she really loves. How else to explain it? At any rate, it was all about the fertility doctors, and finding out that it was me that was the problem. It's been me all along, who knew, never entered my mind. But yep, it was me, the man that can't produce kids."

"I'm sorry," she said.

"Me too," he said, smiling. Or trying to, she thought of his efforts. Who really knew what went on behind the masks of people, 'cause no way would that have been what she'd thought his story would be, continuing to listen as he shared his tale, not that different from hers.

"So it was a series of tests and a series of shots and one surgery to help, that so far had not, and another year of trying, and one day I'd just had enough, and told her so. 'Maybe we should take this as a sign,' I said, and no, 'cause guess what, we were finally pregnant." He turned into a neighborhood, a very nice and expensive one. Old and established, and she knew it well. Quaint little houses filled with women who stayed home and raised kids mostly, was what she thought of it.

"And things eased up a bit between us. We were happier, we stopped arguing, focused on the baby and pulling for something that might make our marriage work, and I'd like to think she was trying too," he said, and some of his old anger had crept in. That was where his bitterness lay with her, with the fact that she'd play-ed him, lied to him, not once but twice, and she hadn't lost any sleep over it.

He was quiet. He met her eyes and smiled. "Sorry, got lost in my head." He was pulling into the driveway of a home that looked as she expected his home would look. Old-school cottage-styled and immaculately kept. The kind of houses she'd seen often in movies where everything was perfect, at least from the outside.

"Come on," he said, pulling into the garage. They entered into what looked like a mudroom, moved through it and the laundry room next, followed by the kitchen. It was up the stairs to the second floor, where they stopped outside the second door on the right. He entered first.

"What happened?" she said, scanning the room, trying to take it all in. Destruction was the most accurate word for what she saw.

"Me," he said, scanning it again, remembering. Seemed like forever since he was here. "My anger. Not usually a problem, didn't know I could be so angry until my divorce." He met her gaze. Yeah, he probably was angry, but all she saw was hurt, a feeling she was well acquainted with.

"I remember that day like it was yesterday. I'd dropped her off at the entrance and then went to park the car," he said, leaning against the wall. "The contractions were coming five minutes apart, and I didn't want to miss a thing. I parked in the emergency lot and entered the hospital on a run. I knew the way, our parenting classes were held there, so I had it all mapped out.

"A child, my child, was arriving today. Lots of sperm-in-a-cup action and surgery, and it was worth it. I was happy we'd stuck it out, worked through our problems. It all seemed worth it that morning.

"Anyway, it was me, by her side in my gown, breathing right along with her as she pushed, and pushed, and not even a few seconds passed and I heard my child, or what I thought was my child, cry for the first time. A child I'd helped create, the one I'd been talking to all this time, through Karen's belly.

"'She's precious,' the nurse said, bringing her around to the new parents to take their first look, the umbilical card still attached.

"She was, I thought, but she wasn't mine. I said that aloud, didn't know I had until I met Karen's gaze. Too brown to be mine, not in that way, but you know what I mean. She was too brown to be the result of us. And Karen's expression confirmed it. I don't remember much after that, just stood there, staring at a very lovely child and wishing it were mine, wishing I could pretend that it was. But I couldn't. All I could see was the lie behind it.

"She asked her mom to give us a minute, said she didn't know for sure, she thought it might be mine, and why tell me before she knew.

"'When?' I asked her.

"She shrugged her shoulders. 'Does it really matter?' she said.

"'Were you even going to tell me?' I asked her.

"'Not if I didn't have to,' she said.

"I left then," he said, before going quiet, thinking back through the whole of it, Clarke thought.

"I drove here on autopilot. I don't remember a thing except picking up the bat, and well, you can see the result," he said, meeting her eyes. "More than the divorce, this is what hurt the most. The loss of my child, one I'd so looked forward to." She didn't say a word, just met his gaze.

"So I know what it feels like to want what you can't have. You are not alone," he said.

She nodded, running her gaze around the room. It was a pretty shade of green, not sage, more the sharp green of rye winter grass. The furniture was bashed to bits, but even with that, she could tell that it had once been a very lovely room. "It was a pretty room," she said.

"Green, a neutral color, nothing gender-restricting for our daughter."

"This is *the* bat, huh?" she said. It was leaning against the back wall. She lifted it while he walked over to a trunk. It was filled with balls of all types: pink and blue balls, footballs, soccer balls, and of course baseballs.

"You had the sports thing covered," she said, chuckling

"Yep," he said, chuckling too.

He removed the bat from her hand. "This was my favorite when I played high school ball," he said, holding the bat in his hand. "A Louisville Slugger, for my daughter, the next Mo'ne Davis, to grow into." He smiled, and she could see the hurt he so tried to hide beneath the anger. "It felt good in my hands that day, a sufficient weight with which to destroy, which was what I had in mind. Hit the crib first, then the dresser." He pointed to each item with his bat as he talked. "It didn't take long, five minutes, not even, to destroy what I'd spent the last three years trying to build."

"I'm sorry," she said, moving to him. She placed her arms around his waist.

"Me too. What a waste huh, the marriage, and all of this. I fucking hate cheaters," he said.

"I know. Life sucks sometimes."

"Yes, it does," he said, smiling his old small smile, letting the bat fall to the floor, pulling her in closer to him.

"But we're still here, still standing, ready to maybe even try it again with right person," she said.

"Yes, we are."

"Are the other rooms bashed in too?" she asked, chuckling.

"No, just this one," he said, chuckling too.

"Show me."

They spent a few hours walking through his home, she listening as he talked mostly, the first time he'd talked about himself this much, ever.

They left and it was her turn to show him her old Dallas haunts. They drove by the home of the woman who her husband had cheated with. Cheating screws up... destroys so much, she thought, looking at the FOR SALE sign in the yard. It was on to the cemetery to visit her son afterward. Henri was quiet, mostly letting her talk and cry, as she had allowed him. It was what they needed... to release that part of their lives, and telling it, getting it out into the open, had helped them do that.

***

It was dark inside her room, later on that night. They were back in Austin, at her home, in her bed.

"I want," she whispered into his ear.

"Me too," he said, before pulling her underneath him. He settled his hips in between her legs and slid his erection into her, one smooth slow glide in. She moaned. He reached for her hands, pulling them together above her head, to be held by his much larger one as he pushed his hips into her again, and then again.

He lowered his head to her right breast, taking it into his mouth, then moved over to the left one. She moaned again and wrapped her legs around his, pushed against his hand to free her arms, so she could wrap them around his head.

She held on to him as he moved within her, slowly. It was only this and now and him, she thought, losing herself to the feel of him, moving above her, his fingers caressing her skin, anywhere he could touch, as his mouth softly mated with hers. There was a lot to be said for the old missionary style of sex, the touching of bodies and limbs, the rhythm of two people in moving in tune with each other, holding each other, loving each other.

It was him, his breathing, the sounds that he made, to go along with the thrust of his hips, that propelled her toward her climax, and then it was nothing but holding on tightly to each other as the pleasure of what they felt coursed through their veins.

"I'm so sorry for your loss," he whispered to her, afterward.

"And I'm sorry for yours," she said, before touching her mouth to his again.

***

Friday

Henri sat in the office of his attorney. He was in Dallas again, discussing his new goal in life—to be free of his wife, and the sooner the better. The need for revenge, along with the need to punish Karen by making this process difficult, had vanished right along with his anger. He wanted to be free.

He'd driven up early yesterday, cleaned up the nursery, hauled away all the brokenness that had been the nursery, and set up this meeting. He was willing to do whatever, even sell the house, if necessary.

"You're sure about this?" his attorney said, eyeing him warily.

"I am," he said.

"Okay, then. This is all I need from you. I'll of course keep you informed."

"Thank you," Henri said, standing now. "I'll be in Austin for the remainder of the week, and then I'm back to Dallas for good."

"I'm sure your father will be pleased."

"That makes two of us," Henri said.

"Take care," the attorney said.

"I will," Henri said, and yes, he was ready to return home. His time in Austin had been perfect, and had given him the desire to live again. He still had his issues to get through—those hadn't gone away—but he'd lost the feeling of heaviness that he'd lived with since he'd walked out of that hospital.

***

Saturday

It was just the two of them, Henri and Stephen, once more walking to their cars after a serious game of basketball.

"I'm leaving for good Sunday," Henri said. They were at Stephen's car.

"Oh, yeah? What does Clarke think about that?" Stephen said.

Henri laughed at the tenacity of his friend on this one issue. "She's fine with it, I think."

"It's not over yet?"

"We're friends, good friends. We'll always be that."

"You like her," Stephen said.

"I do," Henri said.

"But not long term."

"Too soon, still, to know."

"You thought about it?"

"I have."

"I'm sorry to hear about her cousin," Stephen said. He and Reye had caught it on the news.

"I know, me too."

"She's holding up?"

"Yep," Henri said, chuckling. "I hope I don't regret saying this to you, but you were right. She is a lovely woman, and it's been nice getting to know her. She did help me."

"I told you," Stephen said.

"I knew that was coming too," Henri said, chuckling. "So when are you moving to Dallas?"

"In a month or so, if all goes well. We have a contract on our home here. So, soon."

"Joining your father finally. You excited?"

"Yes."

"Reye doesn't mind leaving her mom?"

"She can come up whenever, and I'm sure she will. We'll make it work."

"Let me know when you get to Dallas for good," Henri said.

"Of course," Stephen said, smiling as he slid behind the wheel of his car. Hell no, was this the end, he thought. He'd give them six months tops, pleased to have played a part in Henri's happiness.

Henri continued on to his car, thinking though his friend's words before moving on to thoughts of Clarke. He liked her. There was no doubt in his mind about that. Could they be more? Did he want more with her? Was she a rebound thing, one that he could forget easily?

None of those questions did he have answers to. What he needed was time. Time for his divorce to be finalized. Time to do nothing. Time to assess if what he'd started to feel for Clarke was real.

His future was his to command, once again, and he meant to command it, a little more seriously this time. The next time he married, if he married, would be closer to what Stephen and Reye were lucky enough to find, or he wouldn't do it at all. Of that he was certain.

***

Clarke sat in her home, later on that night, staring out at the backyard, mostly debating if she should send a text to Henri. She was reluctant to, 'cause she'd taken up most of his days, weeks. She reached for her phone just as it pinged, and the old familiar question mark was there.

She smiled. *Yes,* she texted.

Her cell was ringing now.

"How are you?"

"Okay."

"The Wesleyn?" he said.

"I don't mind here, if you want to save money, not that you have to worry about that."

"It's okay. I'm leaving tomorrow."

"Back to Dallas for good."

"Yep. I thought it would be nice to spend a little of what's left of this weekend with you," he said.

"I like that idea."

"Good." He chuckled. "So pack something for tomorrow. Not sure where we'll end up, but more casual than not."

"You sure?"

"I am."

"In ten then?"

"In ten."

***

Sunday

What a way to end whatever this was, Clarke thought the following morning, having slept most of the night. She looked over at Henri, who was sleeping and tired. He was leaving, and yeah, she was sad, for all manner of reasons. She was also happy that he'd shown up in her life, given her something back that she'd lost. Faith. Faith in herself was what he'd helped her to find again. Faith that all would be well, that she would be well, and maybe even married someday. For the first time in a long time, she felt like that was possible.

"What?" he said. He was awake, had caught her staring at him.

"Nothing. Are you hungry?" she asked.

"For food?"

"Yes, food," she said, chuckling. "I know a place."

"Not right away," he said, pulling her down to kiss.

***

Sunday evening

Breakfast turned into lunch, which they'd also skipped. They decided to order in. Afterward, it was back to doing the same thing they'd done since they'd checked in last night. It was a shower late afternoon, before they were done.

"So, it's back to Big D finally," she said, standing just outside of the hotel's front door. The valet had delivered his car. She had parked her own car in the garage across the street when she had arrived there yesterday.

"I am," he said, standing inside the driver's side of his car, saying goodbye to one tired woman. He could see the toll all of this had taken: late nights and case solving and last night, this morning, and this afternoon. And no, he wasn't going to even try to explain what had driven either of them since they'd checked in here yesterday.

"Thanks for everything," she said.

"You're welcome."

She waved once more as he pulled away. He checked his rear view mirror but she must have gone back inside. He turned his car in the direction of the freeway and headed for home.

***

Friday

Somewhere along the line, rainy days must have had a serious talk with funerals, Clarke thought, looking out of the front window of her Aunt Veda's home. Made some kind of secret pact that they would show up together, every chance they could. People died every day, and some of those funerals were held on sunny days, but today, the day of the funeral for Amber and her son, it had been raining off and on for most of the morning.

Clarke stood at the front window of her Aunt Veda's home, on the lookout for the limousines that would transport the family to and from the funeral. Surprised did not began to describe her feelings at seeing this truck, black in color, drive past. She continued to follow it as it pulled over to the curb and Henri stepped out.

"Surprise, surprise," Summer said, meeting her brother's gaze.

"Did you know he would be here?" Clarke asked, her eyes never leaving him. She had missed him. A week and she had turned into some kind of fiend, and it wasn't just sex, although she'd missed that too. It was all of him; the talking, the nice guy he turned out to be. She fallen in love and no, he had no idea, and he wouldn't if she had anything to say about it. She hadn't talked to him since they said goodbye Sunday.

"He called this morning wanting the details, the address of the church. I told him that you'd most likely be here first, and he could follow us if he wanted to. He didn't tell me what his specific plans were, so I didn't have anything to tell you," Summer said.

They were both staring in Henri's direction as he walked toward them, dressed in a black suit, white shirt, and dark tie. Impeccable as always was the case with this one, Clarke thought admiringly.

"How much time until the arrival of the casket?" Summer asked.

"Fifteen."

"Let's go outside and meet him," Summer said, pushing Clarke to get her moving.

He was in front of the house when he spotted Clarke standing at the door beside his sister. She was pretty, less tired than the last time he'd seen her, he thought as he moved closer. No more circles under her eyes. She wore black, a different dress from the one that had so captured his attention that night at the Basement.

This one was buttoned down the front, more professional, where the other had been all sex. She was covered in black tights and pumps that made her taller. Her hair was the same as always, short and softly framing the same pretty face he saw most often in his thoughts and dreams at night, and the times in between.

"Hey," he said when he reached her. He leaned forward and placed his lips squarely on hers, softly, quickly, as if he had every right to.

"Hey. Thank you for coming," she said, and smiled.

He had missed that smile, more than he had expected to, and he knew at that moment that he was just marking time. That a future that didn't include her was not going to work for him, that he'd fallen in love again, or maybe for the first time. "Of course, I'd be here," he said.

"It's really good to see you," she said. And why had her eyes started to water? She had no explanation except that he was here, and she was touched by his thoughtfulness.

He pulled her into his arms then, and held her as more of her tears fell.

"You're fine," he whispered into her ear. He was cool and calm, and it had been helpful and comforting when she'd been searching for Amber, and it was the same soothing now.

"I know. I don't know what it is about you that makes me cry," she said, chuckling as she pulled away. She placed her hands over her eyes to try and stem the flow of her tears.

He handed her a handkerchief and watched as she wiped her eyes with it.

She blew out a big breath. "Come in, and I'll introduce you around," she said, reaching for his hand.

***

"He appears to be a nice young man," Sandra said, standing beside Clarke. They were waiting by the front door along with the rest of the family. The transportation had arrived. Henri and Summer had headed to his truck to follow along behind, but not before she'd introduced him to her parents. *Might as well take the bull by the horns and get that out of the way* had been her thinking. It would be nothing but stares if she hadn't.

"He is," Clarke said.

"So that's Summer's brother?" Sandra asked, although it was more confirmation than anything.

"Yes."

"How did you two meet?"

"He came down here to help her with their family's construction business. They were having problems, and I ran a few background checks for him."

"What construction company?"

"Novak Construction."

"Oh. *The* Novak Construction company? They're huge in Dallas. I've seen their name everywhere."

"Yep, that's the one."

"And this is just friendship."

"Yes," Clarke said.

"So he lives in Dallas now?"

"Yes, ma'am."

"So his coming back to the funeral was for you?"

"He's a friend, Mom. He helped me a lot with the search for Amber. Not so much helped as kept me company."

"He's the one that I spoke to that night, when you needed to get away."

"Yes," she said.

"I see. I'm surprised he's still single. He can't have a problem finding women, not with his money and looks."

"He's in the middle of his divorce," she said.

"Oh, that's too bad," Sandra said, although it sounded anything but regretful. "Children?"

"Nope. It's nothing, Mom. He's a friend. We helped each other out for a time, and now that time is over," Clarke said.

"I understand. I do in no way wish to pressure you. I was curious. He's the first man you've been friends with or gotten close to since… well, you know."

"Well, now you know. Any other questions?"

"No," Sandra said, and smiled. "You seem happier," she added, sizing up the calm that was her daughter today, in the midst of her hurt. There was a different type of energy, not like before. She seemed less weary.

"I agree with your mother. You do seem happier," her father said. He'd stood by listening until now.

"I'm okay. Finding some peace with it all, I guess, is what you see," Clarke said.

"I'm glad then, and if this Henri was helpful in getting you to this place, then he has my gratitude," Sandra said, squeezing Clarke's hand.

"As long as you keep your gratitude to yourself, and don't go trying to match-make."

"Of course not," Sandra said, offended. "I've learned a thing or two."

"Good. Love you, Mom, but no more having a say in the next man I pick, if I pick."

"And that's as it should be," Sandra said.

"What? Look at you, growing up," Clarke said, and smiled. Her dad winked his eye, smiling too.

"One is never too old to learn. You know how much I love you, baby."

"I know," Clarke said, leaning into her mom, using her head, laying it on her shoulder, a practice she'd started when she became a teenager and felt like she was too old to hug. It was a joke, a running one, her head the only thing touching her mother's shoulder, and Sandra would laugh and pull her in closer.

It had stopped after all that with her babies, or lack of them, as Clarke had retreated into herself. Sandra had missed it tremendously. She was glad they had started it up again.

***

Interesting the way her daughter sort of folded herself into that young man's arms at the funeral, and now at the gravesite, Sandra thought. Of course, she'd watched the two of them today. Hard to miss the way he just sort of showed up whenever her daughter seemed to need a shoulder to lay her head on. A nice couple they would make, should they wish to, she thought, sitting at the table. They were back at the church for the repast.

Substantial, he must be, to be here today to support those he cared about. Super important it was to have shoulders to sink into or to stand beside you as you weathered whatever came your way, 'cause if you lived long enough, you would have plenty storms to get through. It was one of the telltale signs of a keeper, not that she was seeking signs, but if she were… well.

There was more than friendship going on with those two, despite what her daughter had said earlier. She had so many questions to ask her daughter, with no way to ask them, she thought.

Cautiously, slyly, or not at all, she decided in the end. Take this morning and let it rest.

She was much too happy that Clarke had returned to the land of wanting men again to muck anything up. This one was white, which was another surprise. She hadn't seen that coming, not that it mattered. Not if she wanted a shot at grandbabies, and she did. Wanted so many, she'd have to add on to the house to accommodate them all. She wouldn't give up on that idea until she had to. Adoption was always a way—so many children were in need of a home. She was hopeful again that she'd get that chance too, for the first time in a long while. Clarke was finally moving on, seeking happiness for herself, and wasn't that nice.

Sandra glanced over at her husband, sitting beside her, watching Clarke and Henri disappear though the door leading out to the parking lot. She knew him well enough to see concern, worry, and love. *Parents.* She squeezed his hand and smiled, hoping it was reassuring enough. He smiled back, so maybe it was.

***

"So it's goodbye again," Clarke said, standing outside the church beside Henri's truck, impressed that he'd stayed this long. She'd expected the funeral service and then *I'm out*. But nope, he had remained by her side, throughout the gravesite and back to the church, enduring his share of stares and curious glances.

"Yes, it is." He moved closer to her and pulled her in for a hug, letting go of his desire to kiss her and all the other things he wanted to do.

"Thank you again for coming. It means more than I can say that you did."

"You're welcome," he said, before he leaned in again and kissed her this time.

She stood waiting until he started his car and pulled away before she turned and headed back to the church.

TWENTY

Friday, one month later, almost to the day

Clarke had finally gotten around to working the custody case brought to her by Rainey, which was the reason she sat in her car now. She was here to watch and document the activities of Franklin Forrester's wife with the pool boy. Such a cliché they were turning out to be, on her third day on the assignment. Franklin had given her excellent access from which to take excellent shots of the two of them together, which she had. She was done for the day, packing up her gear, leaving the wife and the pool boy behind in the backyard, probably on round number three or four of some extremely acrobatic sex. She missed sex, and just like that her thoughts moved over to Henri. She missed sex with Henri.

It was over to the house after this, to check in on Summer and Hamp and whoever else they'd hired to work this week. They'd closed on the house two weeks ago and it had been full speed ahead since. She'd looked at more flooring, studied the pros and cons of more appliances, and participated in enough other stuff related to house remodeling to last her a lifetime. She had started to enjoy it, though.

Her cell phone dinged. She picked it up and about had a heart attack at what was there. A question mark. And yeah, it was from him. She was surprised, as she hadn't called and neither had he.

She'd been quiet on the subject of Henri to Summer—to anybody really, but she still missed him. She smiled.

When?

Lunch?

Hell yeah, she said, aloud as well as via text, laughing, 'cause there was no use pretending she didn't want to see him. *Where?*

The Wesleyn?

Of course, that's your pick. In 10? she texted.

Thumbs-up was the emoji he sent, and although she resisted it for a second, she smiled.

***

Clarke picked up the key from the front desk. How easy was it to fall back into this, whatever this was. She knocked once, not sure why, before unlocking the door. She found him seated on the couch, a drink on the table before him, some type of dark liquid, one fourth of the way up the glass that held it. He was casual in jeans and a t-shirt that hugged his chest. God, she missed hugging it too. He smiled, all casual and so appealing.

"This is a surprise," she said, standing at the door still.

"A good one?"

"Yes."

"I'm celebrating my divorce. I thought you might like to help me celebrate. It's final today," he said.

"Congratulations."

"It's not the only reason I'm here."

"It's not?"

"Nope. I missed you."

"I missed you too," she said, smiling.

"Life's been good?" he asked.

"It's been fine, but can we talk later? Let's do something else first," she said, smiling.

"Yes," he said, chuckling. "Come here?"

"You don't even have to ask," she said, reaching for the bottom of her shirt. She was casual in black today. Must be a surveillance day, he thought, watching her disrobe. Her leggings were next, and then shoes. In record time, he thought, watching her walk to him. All that was left were two remaining pieces of undergarments, a soft pink, pretty against her skin.

He leaned forward and rested his head against her stomach, his hands at her waist. He held her for a bit, not in any hurry, even though it been a month since the last time he'd been with her, with anyone.

He moved his hands down her hips, taking with them her panties, all the way down to the floor, before bringing his hands back to the top of her thighs. He leaned back on the couch, bringing her with him, until her knees were on the couch beside him, and his face near her core. She wrapped her arms around his head, moaning at the first swipe of his tongue. His hands went to her ass, and he pulled her closer, chuckling at first at the sounds she made as he brought her to her first climax, continuing on to her second, and a minute or two later, her third.

He wanted her pliable and wet, something he'd dreamed of her being often while he was in Dallas. He stood up then, walking her backwards toward the bed. Waited for her to scoot up to the middle before he joined her, stood for a second, poised above her, before he entered her. He was past ready, feeling all kinds of pleasure at being inside. Seemed like forever since he'd been here, and yeah, he was home.

He tucked his head into her neck, which was all he had the strength for, placed his hands over the breasts he had missed too, and began to move. Slowly, not in any hurry, and it would be a while before he was ready to leave the confines of this. In and out, slow thrust of hips, eyes closed in pleasure, lost in sensation, with her holding him tightly in her arms.

In and in, and inward slowly again until he couldn't hold back any longer, and he was moving toward his climax, could feel it just at the base of his erection, edging its way upward. He moaned, increasing the speed of his thrusts, squeezing her breasts, and he was there and damn, how he'd missed this... missed her.

***

Saturday morning, early

"What the hell?" Henri said, turning his head to the side to better follow Clarke's mad dash to the bathroom. What time was it? he wondered, running his hand over his face, searching for his phone. He found it. Six thirty. He'd slept like the dead or how he imagined the dead slept. And what was that? Sounded a whole lot like Clarke being sick in the bathroom... sounds of retching. *What the hell?*

He sat up, nude still, as it was the way he slept most nights. Last night, Clarke hadn't seemed to take offense to it, using him as a space heater. "You're warm" had been her only comment as she moved in just under his arm, her cold ass to his hips, and he had smiled and pulled her closer.

He stood up and walked to the door, found her sitting on the side of the tub with her head bent over the top of the toilet.

"You okay?" he asked from the doorway. And as if she was answering his questions without words, she threw up again. He grabbed a washcloth and ran it under the water, wringing it out when he was done soaking it. He flushed the toilet before he squatted down beside her.

"I'm pregnant," she said, and watched his face register shock. Actually, it had done all sorts of things before it settled on shock. It would have been funny if she'd been in the mood to laugh. The shock soon gave way to a huge smile, like the sun coming out from behind a cloud after the rain had stopped.

"No fucking way," he said, smiling still.

"I know, right. Surprise," she said, smiling weakly.

He moved the hair from away from her brow. "How long?"

"Six weeks or so," she said.

"Been to the doctor?"

"Yep, 'cause of all the trouble I've had, and I wanted to make sure."

"No, I understand," he said, but she could tell he was still working through her announcement. "Good thing I returned, huh?"

"You sure it's yours?" she asked, watching for signs of worry. Given all he'd been through it was a legitimate question.

"I am. I don't have any doubts about you," he said, back to smiling.

"That's good," she said, using the washcloth he'd given her to wash her face.

"I'm going to be a father," he said, his smile huge on his face still.

"You're happy?" she said, peeking over the top of the wash-cloth.

"Hell yeah, I'm happy, and you already know the reason. You aren't?"

"I'm not unhappy. Apprehensive. You get that, right?"

"I do. You'll be fine. We'll be fine. I can feel it. This was meant to be, we were meant to be, tell me you can see that, right? I was meant to love you and you me," he said, placing a kiss on her brow before taking the washcloth from her hand. He was up and running it under the water again. She looked tired and sick, and he smiled again, handed her the washcloth, and squatted beside her again.

"So it's love now. You love me?"

"Like you do me," he said, with such conviction.

She laughed. "This is crazy."

"It is, but it's also… I don't know, great."

"It was. It is," she said.

"You *were* going to tell me, weren't you?" he asked, pushing the hair away from her eyes, holding it on the top of her head, clear of the washcloth.

"Eventually, 'cause you know my history."

"I do," he said, standing up, reaching for her hand to help her up. "It is crazy, that we're here, the two of us, with all of the problems we've had, the marriages that didn't work. You with your problems conceiving, and me with mine, trying to get some-one to conceive. We were meant to be here. A do over is what this is, what we are, and anytime you want to say you love me would be good."

She laughed. "I do," she said, at the sink, going through her travel case for her toothbrush.

"You do what?" he asked, watching her remove the top from the toothpaste and squeeze it on her brush.

"I love you."

"Good. You have any thoughts about marriage to me?" he asked, watching as she started into brushing her teeth. He had to wait until she was done.

"I have one condition if we're discussing marriage between us," she said, after she was done rinsing her mouth.

"I am, and what is the condition?"

"Not until after the baby is born. I need you to agree to that," she said, reading the refusal on his face. "I need time to make sure, will need to make sure. Will you do that for me?"

"I will," he said, releasing his desire to push. They were meant to be here, and this was meant to happen. He felt the truth of his thoughts. How else to explain her getting pregnant, given the odds? He could wait, if that's what she needed. It would work for them, as it had done up until this point.

"Okay, in the hospital room. That's as long as I'm going to wait," he said.

"Agreed," she said turning to face him. He met her coming toward him.

"I thought something was different about you," he said, his hands on her breasts now, softly squeezing them. "I thought they felt fuller, and that was in no way a complaint." He took the nipples in between the pads of his fingers, to softly squeeze as he kissed her again. She moaned and he chuckled against her lips.

"You sure?" she asked, gazing into his eyes.

"Never been surer. The fifth time's the charm," he said, smiling, as he set his lips to hers.

EPILOGUE

Seven months later

He'd been here before, Henri thought, rushing into a hospital. It was déjà vu all over again, except it wasn't. He hadn't talked her into marriage yet, not until the baby came. Or didn't, is what she said, and surprisingly she'd stuck to her demand. He was a patient man, or he'd learned he could be. He'd moved to Austin, first in with Summer and then with Clarke. He was also heading up the expansion into the Austin market for Novak Construction.

It would be house hunting for them both soon. There wasn't enough room in her work-home space for the three of them, and the many more that would follow, either biologically or via adoption. It really didn't matter to him as long as she was by his side.

He was inside the main door now, headed to the baby wing. He'd been here before too, taken all the classes right alongside her as he'd done with the first wife. But things were different; she was different and in all the ways that worked for him. *Thank you for all what came before, for the opportunity to do it all over* was his silent prayer upwards, a chance to get it right this time.

He stood at the door, watching as the woman he loved met his gaze, her face all pain-filled but smiling. He'd already called the parents, both sets. They were on their way.

She reached out her hand and he went to her, grimacing at the strength in the grip of this woman. It was all go from there, and ten minutes later, one Nigel Warren Novak was born, peeing on the doctor and making his presence known. What a welcome! Life was so good.

***

A year later

Clarke was gritting her teeth, wondering how long did it take to park a truck. Where was Henri? She hated contractions, not without his hand to hold, to see her through as he had done the first time with Nigel, a year old now, with a second sister on the way. They'd fostered almost immediately, a much older child, and were in the process of adopting her—Sloan Novak.

Henri was standing in the doorway, smiling at her now, and how lucky was she, to have this do over, this chance to get it right. A lot had happened since the last time she was here. They had been married, in a small ceremony with close friends and family. Not at the hospital, but almost immediately after. They'd also found a home in an older neighborhood, one of her and his sister's redoes. Work was good for them both, although Clarke's had tapered off and she was moving on to working with Summer full time. It was better for the babies and his schedule, and she was okay leaving the investigation business behind.

She reached for his hand, squeezing it as another contraction started up. He smiled and went to her. Life was so good.

THE END

About the Author

RUTHIE ROBINSON resides in Austin, TX with her family. She holds a bachelor's degree in economics from Clark College and a master's degree in economics from the University of Texas in Austin (Hook 'em horns!). She worked for more than a decade in the banking industry before turning her love of stories into a second career.

She may be contacted at her website—
www.ruthierobinson.com.

OCT   2016

CPSIA information can be obtained at www.ICGtesting.com
Printed in the USA
LVOW08s2019250816

501857LV00003BA/389/P